The Silent Sleep
of the Dying

Also by Keith McCarthy

A Feast of Carrion

The Silent Sleep
of the Dying

Keith McCarthy

CARROLL & GRAF PUBLISHERS
New York

Carroll & Graf Publishers
An imprint of Avalon Publishing Group, Inc.
245 W. 17th Street
NY 10011
www.carrollandgraf.com

First Carroll & Graf edition 2004

First published in the UK by Constable,
an imprint of Constable & Robinson Ltd 2004

ISBN 0-7867-1454-9

Printed and bound in the EU

Part One

The old man moved with increasing frailty around the large house, feeling the cold more deeply, the damp more painfully. The draughts that accompanied him to bed each night were becoming harsher in their whispering viciousness, less willing to give him mercy. Soon, he knew, he would have to move his bedroom down to the ground floor, as if he were a cripple, but at least then he would not have to negotiate the rickety second flight where the bulb had blown and he could not replace it. Twice in the past month he had fallen there, lucky not to have died and thereby solved his problem.

He sat at the bench and scribbled on printouts, just as he often did, just as he planned to do until he had what he wanted, until he had found the cure. That he was close, he was certain; but close was failure, and failure was death.

All those months ago, when he had finally dared to repeat the test, expose the lie, he had wondered long and hard what to do. To tell? To hide? To work? He thought then that the answer had been easy. It was in his nature to tackle the problem, throw his time and money into a final project, one to repair the damage. That he had chosen not to tell the others was his only source of discomfort. Had he done right to keep quiet? Should he have brought them into the circle of worry and dread that the truth would form? It was, he acknowledged, actually an intellectual conceit of his to suppose that he, and he alone, could solve the problem; that it was better for their peace and contentment that they should be kept ignorant.

He guessed that he didn't have too much time left to him. His ankles were tending to swell, his breathing to complain unless he propped himself on pillows. Once, he had lost consciousness, a

1

staccato, irregular pulse beating in his ears; his last thoughts as the world greyed had been that he was dying, but he had once again been spared.

He should have gone to a doctor – there was one, but only one – knew that it was merely cowardice that stopped him. If his heart stopped, he would not then have to face death by a far more vicious, far more painful killer; that he would be spared what the other five would probably have to endure.

So he ignored the signs and symptoms of his heart disease, and strove to try to put right the wrong that had been done.

Part Two

She had lived with no one and was not sociable, two factors which contributed to a solitary end. Had she not been in work, she might have been alone in her death for many more days, allowing entropy to seep into her tissues, dissolve them into vapours and fluids, and thus reclaim her being into the uniformity of the universe. As it was, she had probably been dead for a day before Robin Turner, her supervisor in the laboratory, thought to telephone her, ostensibly because she was due to present her research findings at a seminar. Since she was supposedly ill in bed with influenza, the fact that there was no answer left him irritated – even if she were ill, she ought to have contacted him to let him know what was going on – although he could admit only to himself that such irritation was by far the main driver for his interest. When he telephoned again at eight the next morning and still received no answer, he began to experience genuine concern, although again he told no one else of this. She ought to have told him when he could expect her back. He asked the other post-doctoral students in the laboratory whether any of them had seen her since she had gone home early, complaining of a temperature, but none had. Few even knew where she lived, an unusual finding since the doctoral and post-doctoral students tended to live lives of great social complexity and not a little alcohol. The one person whom he had hoped would have information of use to him was Susan Warthin, her closest associate and apparently similarly allergic to male company, but she, too, was off sick, also stricken by that year's particular variant of influenza virus. He decided to ring her to see if she knew anything of her friend's condition.

3

The call was short and difficult. Susan Warthin was still feeling distinctly unwell and Turner hid his concern under a brisk and somewhat businesslike manner. No, she had not been in contact with her best friend since she had gone home sick. She was sure she must be quite ill not to have contacted Turner. When he asked her for the address, Susan Warthin denied having it.

Frustrated, Turner then went to the Personnel Department for the address but was once more refused this nugget of information, the idiot girl who answered the phone hiding behind some regulation about privacy.

After this, Turner sat in his office and wondered why he was now so worried, as if each reverse were a portent of oncoming doom. Yet why? Why was he so fearful?

She was sick, that was all. Just the flu.

But the past whispered to him and, try as he might, he could not silence it.

Susan Warthin still hadn't fully recovered as she sat on top of the bus the following morning.

You must be bloody mad, was the refrain which bounced soggily around her skull. Her chest felt as if she had been breathing in kettle descaler, her head seemed to be filled with a viscous fluid not unrelated to slurry and her limb muscles would not stop twitching. Every movement of the bus seemed to do peculiar things to her balance and subsequently to her stomach; that she had not eaten for four days did not preclude sinusoidal waves of nausea from sweeping all other sensations away in their ferocious assault upon her. Also the bus was intensely cold and extremely noisy.

Mad or not, Turner's phone call to her had started this insane adventure. When her phone call had, like his, been unanswered, she had begun to worry. Three further calls, the last at midnight, had served to increase her anxiety to the level at which it could not be ignored. Turner's concern had proved infectious, then, even though he had attempted to douse in the camouflage of dry, professorial indifference.

Indifference that might have fooled her, had she not been privy to the truth.

It's history, Susan. Something that happened and then ended. Now, that he's married, I'm going to leave, find another post. I don't even want him to know where I'm living.

4

The words of this injunction came back to her through a blanket of misery.

She stepped achingly from the bus outside a run-down public house. It was beginning to rain and she hadn't thought to bring an umbrella; hadn't really thought at all. She felt so miserable she reckoned a few spots of rain wouldn't make matters worse, but when the sky began to pour water in a serious and determined manner she changed her mind. Dry misery was better than the wet kind after all.

The street was long and monotonous, strewn with rubbish and unfriendly. The hulk of the Hospital and Medical School loomed over it, an orange-red, square-edged edifice that had forsaken character for bulk. The few people she met looked as though only the apathy of dampness prevented them from knifing her. As she passed one house a dog, evidently large from the amplitude of the sound and the vigour of the scratching, took exception to her presence and began to bark ferociously from behind the front door. Several houses were boarded up.

She knew the area only vaguely, having been to the house on very few occasions, each one pervaded by a feeling of black foreboding. If the world were going to end, in places such as this there would be only relief.

Why did you decide to live here?

She began to cough and had to stop, knowing that it was going to hurt. Unfortunately she was entirely correct and it was a further five minutes before she felt able to carry on.

At last she found the house and walked up to the front door. It was, as were most of the other houses in the street, a terraced house divided into two maisonettes. The evening was dark, cold and unpleasant, but there was sufficient light to see that the area was not salubrious. Some of the neighbours appeared to be under the impression that the small, walled-off area in front of each house was not a garden but a kind of personal refuse dump, kindly provided by the council in lieu of dustbins. Others had apparently decided that it was the ideal place to store animal hutches; what was in them could not be discerned and she did not investigate closely. The number of satellite dishes visible up and down the street was astronomical.

The ground floor was in darkness but there were lights on upstairs. She passed through the gap in the wall where once had hung a garden gate and was almost immediately standing in front of the door. There were two doorbells, one above the other. The light was poor and she had trouble reading the faint names scrawled in biro under each button. Hers was the bottom flat and presumably the bottom bell. She pushed the button and the cheap bell chimed within the darkness behind the door. There was no response.

The downstairs curtains were drawn in the front room, and that gave her a feeling of trepidation. The burning pain in her chest was still curiously vicious, the rain by now seeping down her neck and into her shoes.

After three minutes she repeated the action with no greater success. Then she tried the top flat but again without response. She looked through the glass of the front-room window but the curtains were thick and dark and drawn completely across.

There was an alley of sorts, she knew. It was narrow and would be extremely muddy in this weather, but it might enable her to gain access to the back of the house.

She trudged off further up the street until she came to a side road. She turned down this and walked the length of the house on her left; at its rear was a small garage, the door of which was tastefully decorated with a brightly-coloured representation of a breast, under which she was informed that "Kelly is a fucking tart." Beyond this was the entrance to the alley.

It was overgrown and dotted with dustbins, many of which were overturned. She expected to see rats but they were too quick for her. Branches of sooted trees blocked the path in many places, cascading yet more moisture on to her. The fences on either side were rotting and bowed. A pool of vomit stank.

The only way she could be sure that she had reached the right house was by counting back from the corner. In her state she just had to hope that she had not miscounted; the thought of what would happen to her if she were caught in the wrong garden was truly terrifying.

The garden gate was closed and for a moment she thought it was bolted. She pushed against it, putting her fingers on cobwebs and lichen. It didn't give at first but the second push caused it to move slightly, grating on the ground. A further push and it was just open enough for her to squeeze through.

The garden was overgrown but the vegetation was not thick enough to hide completely the garbage thrown around. There was glass everywhere and she had to pick her passage carefully to avoid what appeared to be excrement; in a place such as this she suspected it might be human.

At last she managed to traverse the twenty metres or so to the back of the house.

The curtains here were not drawn but it was dark in there and the windows were dirty. It took her a long while to make out anything at all. Then she began to discern a desk and the fireplace. Next she made out the bed and she saw that it was not made up, that the sheets and the blankets were hanging half off it, the pillows at an angle.

The first thing she saw on the floor was a glass tumbler on its side.

The second thing she saw on the floor was a head.

Frank Cowper hated cases like this. In truth he hated all cases of unexpected death, since he was a Coroner's Officer and all such cases fell under his jurisdiction, but deaths like this were the worst.

Murders – straight forward stabbings, shootings, bludgeonings – he could cope with because they were, like acts of God and income tax, inescapable; there *would* be lots of paperwork and they *would* have to pay for a forensic pathologist to come and perform the autopsy. There was no point in becoming distressed at their occurrence; one merely had to hold on until they had passed.

And some unexpected deaths he could, with a craft learned over many years in the job, subvert. The general practitioner might be persuaded to write a death certificate based on his knowledge of the patient, despite the fact that he had not seen him in his surgery for months or even years. Hospital doctors could occasionally be convinced of his towering medical knowledge and, like an accomplished illusionist, he could then lead them to certificate deaths even though they had never really been sure what the patient had actually been suffering with; this only worked with junior hospital doctors but they were usually the ones who were given the job of ringing him up. Rarely, but most pleasurably, these doctors could be persuaded to ask for a hospital autopsy – for which the Coroner's Office would not have to pay – thus allowing the correct cause of death to be found without undue expenditure on his part; unfortunately the hospital pathologists were mostly wise to this ploy and would often bounce them back to him.

Then there were the majority of deaths, ones in which there was no obvious homicide but in which no one could be persuaded to put their signatures to a cause of death. Mostly sudden collapses in the elderly but a fair admix of suicides, accidents both on and off the road, deaths possibly related to industrial diseases, and deaths in prison or on railway property. Like it or not, in such cases the fee for a Coroner's autopsy had to be paid. Of course then there was the further pain of the post-mortem result coming back as "unnatural," a word which caused him yet more angst since this would result in the expense and work of an inquest.

All these left only a very small minority of deaths, but they were always tricky; this was one such.

An unmarked police car drew up on the opposite side of the road, parking behind an untaxed, rusting van. Cowper got out of his car and went to join the man and woman who had just arrived. The man, Lambert, he knew but the woman was a stranger. She was, Cowper noted, really rather attractive, with blonde hair and a nice figure that Cowper would rather have liked to see more of. Like Lambert she had the weariness of a senior police officer, although Cowper was astute enough to notice that there was a hint of friction between them. His appearance before them did not lighten their mood.

"Frank," said Lambert by way of greeting. He was well built and tall, but he was very slightly paunched, just starting to get out of shape. He pulled his shoulders back and then suddenly forward as if stiff, then looked at the houses up and down the street. His face spoke of loathing. He was balding though his hair was strikingly black; only a fool would have made too much of this. When Cowper had been in the police force, Lambert had been one of his juniors; it had been a perfect position to view Cowper's loathsomeness and incompetence, but always in silence.

The woman, Beverley Wharton, ignored Cowper altogether. She had heard too much to feign any emotion whatsoever.

In desperation, Cowper turned to their driver, a rather effeminate young man with a grin on his face, and was relieved to receive a smile in return.

"Bit of an odd one, this," said Cowper, apparently happy that the introductions were formally complete. He laughed, because he always laughed and not because there was anything amusing. The fact that neither Lambert nor Wharton said anything at all to this was as eloquent as a fifteen-minute diatribe on Cowper's incompetence, laziness, venality and enormous, jocular stupidity.

A uniformed constable stood just inside the doorway out of the gusts of drizzle. There were no inquisitive onlookers, chattering and gawping, to keep away from the scene, testimony to the apathetic state of most of those who lived in the surrounding houses. He looked exceedingly bored.

"I didn't go in because I didn't want to disturb anything."

Cowper's words were an itch, nothing more.

The two of them moved inside, Cowper following and still grinning.

They saw the flashes of the camera light bouncing faintly in the decayed hall. That the temperature was no greater in the house than outside was because the front door had been kept open, but no amount of heating could have warmed its atmosphere; certainly not now, but probably not ever.

Within the flat, a young constable stood with a notebook in his hand for no obvious reason, his fair hair tinged with red. He straightened slightly as the party entered. The Scenes of Crime Officer, a fat man with a long-dead tailor, looked up only briefly before continuing with his artful depiction of the body.

Lambert looked around him. He saw that the room they were in, the back room, contained a bed, a bedside table, a wardrobe and a curtained-off kitchen area. It appeared neat and tidy but relatively poorly decorated. He glanced through to the front room, which was separated by louvre doors, and saw that there were a sofa, an easy chair and a dining table with three, ill-matched chairs within it; all of the furniture had almost certainly come from a second-hand warehouse. A small, black-and-white portable television was the only concession to luxury. The thick, dirty-looking curtains were drawn across the bay window in which was a heavy wooden dining table. On this were piles of papers, notebooks and a coffee mug. He nodded to Wharton who moved to the table and began to look through the papers.

He looked down at the sheeted shape on the floor, almost a caricature, a theatrical corpse, though this one finding it easy to take no breath. A brief assessment and then he bent down to pluck the sheet away.

"I think I should warn you . . ."

The SOCO's voice was normally so overweighed with world-weary cynicism that the novel note of edginess lent it a curious, unexpected tone, and one that was therefore shocking. Lambert paused at once, his head jerking up to look at the fat photographer and, although he said nothing, there was a quizzical look on his face. When he turned back to the body, there was noticeably more caution about the act.

Wharton's gasp from across the room was part of a general, sharp increase in tension, as they were all drawn into the terrible thing that had befallen the girl; no one was looking elsewhere – even those not newly arrived, who had seen it before, were drawn into its horror again.

"Fucking hell." Lambert, who had seen faces blown apart by shotgun blasts, a young woman slashed through the eyes from temple to chin, an elderly man doused in burning oil, seemed to allow the imprecation to slip past his lips unheard, as if the awfulness of what he had uncovered numbed him.

And there he remained for long minutes, frozen into his contemplation of whatever had been done to this girl. When at last he spoke again, it was from a place of deep emotion.

"Name?" His eyes didn't move from the body, the question asked of the room in general.

The uniformed constable moved as if suddenly awoken. He looked down at the notebook, found it was still there and said, "Millicent Sweet. She's twenty-two. Works at the hospital."

"Who found her?"

"A Miss Susan Warthin. She's a friend of the deceased."

Lambert might not have heard for he didn't react and, abhorrent of this vacuum in the exchange, the constable added more information. "She received a phone call from Professor Turner, their supervisor. The deceased had gone home early from work on the fifth, complaining of flu. He hadn't heard any more from her and, when he'd telephoned, there had been no reply. Worried, he'd then contacted Susan Warthin, who was also off work with flu."

Still Lambert made no response. The fat man clicked and flashed away from every angle, while the corpse, unregarding, remained at the centre of it all. Wharton had finished looking through the papers on the table and was drawing back the curtains carefully. She began to examine the windows behind. These were thick with grimed debris, the paintwork ragged and splintered.

Cowper gave a laugh before saying, "You can see why the doctor was worried." Another laugh.

Lambert asked, "Where is she now?"

"She's been taken back to the station. We didn't think it was a good idea to have her hang around here. She was screaming and crying."

A short nod, economical of movement, was Lambert's first concession to approval. It persuaded the constable to continue. "She made her way round the back when there was no answer from the doorbell. She looked in through the window and could only see her head. She almost had a nervous breakdown on the spot."

Cowper's snort of laughter was a lonely thing in the cold of the room.

"Who lives upstairs?"

Again the nervous glance down at the notebook before replying. "A medical student, Melvyn Pick."

Lambert moved to door out into the hall. While he was looking at the wood of the frame he asked, "Have you spoken to him?"

"He's out."

Presumably learning doctoring. The doorframe was freshly splintered, the pristine wood contrasting with the dirty painted surface around. It looked as though someone had put primer on the wood but never quite got around to the undercoat. From the door itself hung a chain at the end of which was a small piece of the frame.

"Did you do this?"

Lambert's question was not asked in an accusatory manner, but the constable could only manage a guilty nod.

Wharton had finished her investigations. "Scientific stuff on the table. Nothing personal."

"What about the windows?"

"Haven't been opened for years. Haven't been cleaned for as long, either. Nothing to suggest anybody got in that way."

The fat man finished his picture taking. He knelt down on the tatty carpet to open the metal case in which he carried his camera. When it was safely stowed and the case shut he stood and said only, "I'll be off then."

He was ignored by everybody except Cowper who said, "Right-oh. Thanks for coming," and laughed.

Lambert turned back to the body, crouching down beside it. There was no smell but that which his mind told him was there.

She wore a cotton nightie over which was a towelling dressing gown. The dressing gown was open and the nightie had ridden up slightly, exposing no more than her knees. What remained of her face pointed to the ceiling, stretched out and half in the front room, half in the back. Very, very gingerly, he reached out and gently touched her on the arm. He pulled back almost at once and, although he did not show it, he felt deep, deep nausea. Cowper said, "The doctor wondered if it might be an acid. Didn't think it was fire."

Standing up, expelling air and wiping his fingers on his handkerchief, Lambert observed, "There's no sign of fire or acid anywhere around here, and her clothes aren't marked." Then he asked, "Who was the doctor?"

"Dr Caplan."

Cowper's information made Lambert momentarily close his eyes and sigh; there was a small smile on his face for the first time that morning, but there was precious little of amusement in it. Wharton, too, reacted, similarly unimpressed, it appeared.

"Was he drunk?" enquired Lambert.

Cowper laughed before he realized that jocularity was missing from the question. "Oh, no," he hastened to reassure.

"She was found. . . when?"

The constable read dutifully from his notes. "I broke in at nine fifty-six, sir."

Two and a half hours ago.

"And did Caplan grace us with his wisdom as regards an approximate time of death?"

It was Cowper who supplied his answer. "No more than six hours, possibly as few as three."

Lambert wandered over to the dining table, picking up papers at random in an uninterested manner. He looked around the room before saying to Wharton, "Have you found her handbag?"

Wharton produced it immediately from down by the bed. She opened it and picked out the keys. She did not use gloves.

Lambert seemed to come to a decision.

"Right. So the scenario is this, is it? Millicent Sweet lets someone in; she has to let them in because no one has broken in. This person overpowers her by means as yet undetermined and then takes her out of here to some other place. There, if we are to believe Dr Caplan, he undresses her and either sets fire to her or covers her in some sort of acid. . ."

"Or alkali," put in the constable, eager to show off his forensic knowledge.

"Presumably he then neutralizes said acid in alkali. . ."

"Or, if it was an alkali, in acid," the constable reminded him, apparently retaining a large part of the chemistry he had learned in early secondary school. Wharton allowed a small smile to stretch the corners of her mouth as Lambert glared at him.

". . .and returns the girl to the flat. He dresses her either in the clothes in which he found her, or possibly some fresh ones, and lays her here on the floor. To complete the act he exits the flat, the final flourish being that he passes through the front door and leaves the chain up."

He looked enquiringly of Cowper who giggled. "I know," he said. "I thought it was absurd, but after the doctor said that we thought we'd better let you guys have a look round."

Lambert looked down at the girl again. "That's not acid, or fire." He broke off to glare at the constable, daring him to shine brightly with his chemistry knowledge. Then he resumed, "In fact, it's no means of death that I've ever seen before." He let out a long, long breath before turning to Cowper. "Suicide? Disease?" Another, more nervous giggle from Cowper before he suggested, "Spontaneous human combustion?"

Lambert missed the joke. He asked, "Who's going to do the post-mortem?"

This was delicate. Handled the wrong way, Cowper could cost the Coroner nearly a thousand pounds. "Well, I know the circumstances are odd, but if you're happy that it isn't murder, I should think we could just opt for an ordinary autopsy. No need to call in the forensic boys."

He tried not to let the last mutate into a question. There was a pause, perhaps the malicious might suggest that it was longer than it need have been, before Lambert agreed.

He walked out into the hall followed by Wharton. From behind them the Constable asked, "What about talking to the neighbours, sir?'

Lambert almost smiled. "I'm not sure it would be wise to disturb them from their reading, Son." To Cowper "When's it being done?"

"Tomorrow, if that's all right."

Lambert nodded condescending permission. "I might drop in and have a look-see."

"Of course, of course." Cowper laughed and now didn't mind that the world did not laugh with him. "Thanks for coming."

They climbed back into their car.

"See you, Frank."

"Bye."

They drove away and Frank thought that it had all gone rather well.

In the front passenger seat, his eyes closed and his head resting against the headrest, Lambert enquired of no one in particular, "Why is that guy such a stupid cunt?"

It was Wharton who voiced what he had been thinking. "Even if it was natural, I wouldn't want to die like that."

Susan Warthin returned to her flat after giving her statement, taken there by police car. She was still feeling deeply shocked and severely weakened by the effects of influenza. The police-woman who escorted her made unilateral conversation whilst in the back of the car but Susan's mind was stuck in the scene of Millicent's death and her answers were connected neither with the present nor with comprehension.

"My husband's got the flu as well. It's dreadful, isn't it? He's been laid up in bed for four days now and it doesn't look as though he'll be getting up for another four."

"Mmm."

"There's a real epidemic this year, isn't there?"

"Mmm." Susan wanted to close her eyes but that only left a blankness into which the horror of what she had seen seeped like black oil. She kept her head low and tried to concentrate on how physically awful she felt.

"We're really stretched at the station. Still, plenty of overtime for those of us who are still on our feet."

The policewoman's face, its plainness not helped by a lack of make-up, betrayed a moment's concern at the lack of reaction. "Are you sure you're all right?" she asked and from somewhere Susan found the strength to nod.

"It must have been a terrible shock for you," she continued "Finding her like that."

Susan was feeling sick. Her stomach felt as if it were distended to bursting point by thick, creamy mucus and her eyes were sore; her throat felt corroded and her head was pulsing to a pain-filled beat. She forced her eyelids to rasp down over her eyes and tried not to see the picture of Millie dead on the floor.

"Have you got a GP we can contact?"

She didn't actually hear the question and so didn't answer. Instead she said suddenly, "She was terrified of dying."

The policewoman thought, *Aren't we all?* but said only, "Was she?"

"Cancer. She was terrified of dying from cancer."

"Oh, yes, so am I." If Susan were just saying things to stop thinking, her companion was just saying them because she had never started. There was a pause and then Susan said, "She was caught up in some sort of fire once. She only just escaped with her life."

And then she realized what she had just said. Into her head came the sight of Millicent's excoriated face, looking exactly as if it had been blasted with a blowtorch, melted, and then congealed into tuberose distortions. It would not shift. She began to cry. The policewoman put her arm around her shoulders as her head went down. Her whole body began to shake with her sobs that gradually changed into a hacking cough interspersed with sore wheezing.

"What happened to her?" she asked at last and it was a terrified, agony-filled plea to God. "Her face was . . . horrible."

"I don't know, love."

"I thought at first that she was burned, but what were those things on her face?"

They were nearly back at Susan's flat.

The policewoman hadn't seen the body and felt rather glad about it. "The post-mortem will tell us."

15

The driver stopped the car and turned to Susan. "There we are."

Susan was helped by the policewoman through the hall to her front door. "Do you want me to stay?"

Susan shook her head. She was feeling faint, as if her leg muscles were dissolving. She just wanted to go to bed.

"Is there anyone who can look after you?"

But again this was met with refusal. She just wanted to be left alone. As she was going out of the flat, though, Susan asked suddenly, "She wasn't murdered, was she?" Somehow the thought that another human being could have done that. . .

"Oh, no. We're perfectly satisfied it was natural causes." This confidence was surprising and somewhat inaccurate, but Susan wasn't to know that. Having closed the door, Susan noticed the day's post. Most of them looked like bills and the effort of bending to pick them up made her feel on the point of vomiting. She had to shut her eyes and lean against the doorframe, putting the post on the table to her right and at once forgetting about it. Then, almost blindly, she made her way back to her bed.

Thus it was that she missed the flashing of her answerphone telling her that someone had called whilst she was out.

Hartmann was home by seven. This was too early despite the fact that he had been travelling for ninety minutes, that he had crawled along miles of dual carriageway, that he had been cut up three times by Neanderthals with large and over-expensive cars, that he hated work and he hated driving, and that he was desperate to relieve himself.

Eight, nine, ten would have been too early.

"Mark? Is that you?"

The fatuous question floated down from the landing as he shut the front door.

No.

He took off his coat and hung it in the hall wardrobe as Annette descended the stairs. She was wearing smart clothes and make-up. Even he could read the signs. Accordingly he was ready for her next question.

"You haven't forgotten, have you?"

"Of course not," he smiled. "Sorry I'm late. You know how it is. There was a ton of work, and then the traffic was bloody awful. . ."

16

"Don't swear, Mark." The rebuke came as she was looking at herself in the mirror, primping. It cut across his lies, an uncaring but vicious knife through his bluster. Then, "You'd better hurry up. Mum and Dad will be here soon."

He'd been wondering who was coming to sup with them, but the information didn't lighten his gloom. She wasn't his Mum and he most definitely was not his Dad and Hartmann, as they made plain whenever he was with them, was not their son. He said nothing and trudged upstairs while Annette exhorted him with a following, "Do get a move on, dear."

In their bedroom he undressed and then stood under the shower, slowly rubbing his expanding stomach with soap, his mind full of questions, chief amongst which was, *When did I start to hate her?*

The question of when he had stopped loving her was not relevant here, since he had now to admit he had never actually started. Infatuation had masqueraded as that purest of emotions, had fooled him into thinking that she was the one for him. Infatuation with her snub nose and with her money.

He could not stop the merest of involuntary shudders rippling the more superfluous rolls of flesh as he thought of her snub nose.

And, bastard that it was, infatuation had remained disguised just long enough to see him married and the father of a small daughter. Then, the process undoubtedly exacerbated by the arrival of a son and the subsequent tantrums, insomnia and constant smell of infant faeces, his feelings of affection for his wife gradually ebbed, drying to nothing. That would have been bad enough, but it had not stopped there. From the vacuum had germinated a rising level of dislike; dislike that had inevitably deepened, broadened and gradually darkened until he had to admit that he now hated her.

He turned off the water and stepped from the shower. He had forgotten to get out a towel and he had to walk across the vinyl flooring to get one, thus leaving wet footprints. He knew that if he failed to dry these Annette would be angry with him, perhaps even sufficiently aroused from enervation to initiate a row; he knew, too, that he wouldn't be bothering to dry them.

Did she hate him? The recurrent question was unanswerable. Certainly she no longer loved him, but it was hardly a question he could pose with ease. They rowed with increasing frequency and about matters of increasing pettiness, and in those rows she was becoming noticeably more vituperative, but they weren't yet at the point where such basic truths could be tested. Thus he was left with mere suspicion that his feelings were matched by hers, a suspicion that was worse than knowledge, that irritated and gnawed at him, that left him eroded and dissatisfied.

There were no clean socks, nor underwear. The cleaning lady was paid to do the ironing but not to put it away, and clearly Annette had not had the time again. Exasperated he found his dirty socks and pants and put them on. At least there were some clean shirts and slacks; his father-in-law always turned up in a jacket and tie but he was damned if he was going to be the victim of social coercion in his own home. Defiantly he left the neck of the shirt open and pulled on a lambswool sweater.

. . . And what if she did? What if she did hate him?

What if she left him or, more accurately, she made him leave her?

The consequences were . . .

He couldn't even form the thought. Its very existence made his mind cramp into a distortion; it stopped thought as effectively and completely as cyanide.

He began to comb his hair in lieu of further examination of his situation.

He might have fallen from love but marriage, he knew, was about a good deal more than a useless emotion. Certainly his marriage to Annette had become an insoluble complex of feelings, reliances and interdependencies . . .

No!

His arm whipped out and the comb was flung across the room, clattering against the wardrobe. A futile gesture for a futile life.

Who was he fooling? There were no interdependencies in their marriage, only dependency. He on Annette. Annette, the daughter of a High Court judge and a well-thought of young barrister in her own right; Annette who earned three times his salary even without the money from Grandpa's trust fund; Annette who owned most of their belongings and subsidized the rest of his life.

He stood still, listening to his breathing, trying to dispel the feeling of panic that arose when he thought of how much he needed her. His life would be destroyed if she chose to end matters, not just because of what she had given to him, but because of what she had not.

"Mark? I think they're here." The voice was faint for it was a large house. He heard the excited shouts of the children as their grandparents came to the door.

"Hooray," he whispered.

Siobhan was out at her creative writing class when Turner got home. The emptiness of his house was a relief to him; he didn't feel confident that he would hide his worry and he did not need the understandable inquisitiveness of a newly acquired wife.

His smile at the thought was rueful.

He moved from the wood-panelled hall into the sitting room where his cherished collection of malt whiskies was arrayed on the sideboard. He picked one, poured a large volume into a heavy, cut-glass tumbler and topped it up with water from a jug. Only after swallowing half of it did he sit down and let out a long, long sigh.

Millicent was dead.

But how? How had she died?

He had heard rumours during the day, rumours that she had been burned, possibly even murdered.

God, how he hoped they were true.

He took another long swallow, emptying the glass. At once he was up and repeating the prescription. What, he wondered, if it weren't true? What if it were what he dreaded?

On the table beside him was a wedding photo, still new enough to be more than a relic of history; Siobhan's beauty was still painful to him, still precious, his astonishment that she should have chosen him – running to fat and to seed with equal speed – still great.

His smile was far sadder than tears would have been.

He was recently enough married to find pain in the fact that he could not confide in her. He knew that he should have told her about Millie, knew also that he had never been going to. Millie had just been a fling, an infatuation, an episode in his past; Siobhan and he had never talked about previous lovers and that was what Millie was. It would only have made trouble to go into details, so that to Siobhan she was merely part of his team, no different to any of the others.

Now she was different, though.

A sudden shaft of panic spasmed his gut.

This had to be coincidence!

He had been assured that they were clear. They were all in the clear. *No spread.* That was what they had said. He had even seen the results of the tests, because he hadn't entirely trusted them, and they had been negative, just as they had said.

But again the fear recurred, voiced as a question – *What if Millicent's death were related to the accident?*

He had to find out the results of the post-mortem examination. It would be done tomorrow, he assumed. He knew Professor Bowman – godawful woman that she was – and he was confident that she would let him know. If it was as he feared, he would contact PEP and raise some hell.

In the meantime, he would repeat the tests himself. He was certainly in a perfect position to do this, and he had all the equipment he required. So why not? He finished the whisky again. Yes, that's what he would do. Find out what Millicent died from, repeat the tests on himself, then, depending on what he then knew, act accordingly.

If PEP had lied to him, they would be sorry. Very sorry indeed.

It was much later, while he was in the kitchen fetching another bottle of vintage port for his father-in-law, that Hartmann found the day's post. Annette had propped it up behind the toaster, to the left of the Aga, but it had become obscured by a tea towel.

The evening had been as excruciating as he had expected it to be. Superficial friendliness overlain with a thick, corrosive layer of disdain. Annette had married beneath her was the constantly reiterated subtext, both socially, financially and intellectually, and her parents, whilst fully understanding of their daughter's right to choose, were not about to stop reminding him of his inferiority on all levels. That on at least two of these three charges no jury, nor even a hanging judge like his father-in-law, would ever convict, was a concept he knew he could never bring them to accept. Annette was very bright but he felt it was unlikely that you could become a Senior Lecturer in Pathology if you had the intellectual ability of a pumpkin, and doctors might no longer have the standing of lesser gods but then he didn't exactly feel that the legal profession were seraphim made incarnate.

Yet the financial matter was something else, something on which even he himself would have to pronounce sentence. He earned a not unreasonable whack but it was far from megabucks and it was pitiful when compared with Annette's salary – and it was minuscule when her inherited wealth was factored in.

It wouldn't have been so bad but for the financial arrangements that he had to endure. Perhaps inevitably these were legally impregnable and detailed down to the commas; he and Annette had different incomes and they were immiscible, now and forever. Only in certain areas – all well defined and strictly circumscribed – was Annette's money allowed to be polluted by his; in all others they effectively lived separate lives. He was convinced that this arrangement had originated with her father, but her obvious compliance – at least willing if not enthusiastic – was another cause for disgruntlement.

Yet whatever the sources of his situation, the effect was that she had a luxurious life, he a relatively penurious one. The need to insert the word, "relatively" would have been little problem (he could not deny his salary was not small) but for the fact that he didn't have enough money. This was partly due to the fact that he had a taste for luxury, partly due to the need to keep up in appearance with Annette, and partly because he owed twenty-three thousand pounds in a variety of gambling debts. This last accompanied him at all times, a shade that lurked unseen but watchful over every thought, action and dream.

And the letter that he discovered that night, amongst the circulars and bills, proved to be an incarnation of that spectre. It was a letter from his turf accountant threatening court action if he did not make an immediate repayment of sixteen thousand pounds.

From the sitting room he heard his father-in-law's booming patrician laugh and he began to cry.

When they were preparing for bed, Hartmann said, "Don't forget, I'm away for the weekend." He was undressing and Annette had just gone into the en suite. From there her tired voice came back. "Are you? Where are you going? You didn't say."

He knew that he, too, was tired and that he was in a bad mood. He couldn't help this show as he replied, "Yes, I did. I told you weeks ago. It's a conference near Glasgow. Lymphomas."

"Did you put it on the calendar?"

She always asked that, but only because she always knew that he would not have done. He always forgot. It was one of his many faults.

"I don't suppose so," he said belligerently.

"Well, how am I supposed to know? I've got a professional life of my own, you know, Mark. I can't be expected to keep track of you if you don't write it all down on the calendar."

The calendar. The bloody calendar. A sort of totem pole around which he was supposed to dance his life.

"Well, I bloody forgot, didn't I?"

If he thought that was the end of it, he was once again wrong. After a pause Annette demanded, "What the hell was your problem?" Her voice was harsh, demanding.

He remembered once that he had been to see her in court. The case had been one of complex, and therefore tedious, fraud and the pomp of the law always left him scathing, but he had been impressed by the skills of the counsel. Annette in particular had seemed to him to be almost supernatural in her art; he had watched and listened in admiration as she had used all the components of classical oratory combined with quick-wittedness, bullshit and a charming smile to make her case. It had been a turning point in their developing relationship.

Where now, he wondered, were those oratorical talents? Were they tucked beneath her wig in the locker by her walnut-veneered desk in chambers?

It was then that he decided he wanted an argument and was at once delighted to realize this. Coming to the door of the en suite, he demanded, "What do you mean?"

She was rubbing some sort of lotion on her face – she never actually put soap or water on it. "You were bad enough when you came in, but after you'd fetched the port, you were completely impossible. You hardly said a word and there was one occasion when you were positively rude to Dad."

Only one? I must be slipping. He had lost count of how many times "Dad" had been subtly but quite mercilessly rude to him.

"Missed one of his jokes, did I?" he enquired, his voice slightly more bitter than he intended. Before he could stop himself he went on, "Failed to guffaw with the required amount of gusto?"

She had her back to him but he knew that with this he would score a palpable hit. From over her shoulder he saw her frozen in mid-lotion, staring into the mirror at him. "There's no need to be so nasty about Dad. He's been very good to us – to you, in particular."

He gazed at the flatness of her reflection. *Good? Good?* If by good she meant condescending much as Zeus might have come to earth for a spot of rape, or she meant making damned sure that plebeian son-in-law was caged in both socially and financially – a clear glass cage in which he was exhibited as an interesting example of a lesser thing, a social-climber, a piece of human excrement – then yes, it could be said that her father had been "good" to him.

He turned away and she said to his back, "Are you short of money again?"

She used the phrase much as she might have asked if he had a venereal disease again.

"No," he said. He tried to impart a tone of dismissiveness; *the very idea*, he wanted to suggest. She stared at him for a while, then recommenced her work with the lotion, more vigorously than ever. He found himself wishing it were vanishing cream.

It was the guilt at this last thought that drove him to sigh, to throw his trousers to the floor and to come up behind her. "I'm sorry," he said, taking her shoulders. They were cold and she was thin enough to make the contact hard. She responded by dropping her hands and putting her head on one side. "Do you like that?" he breathed in a whisper. Her reply was a murmur and a breath combined. He began to kiss her skin and she moved around so that he was kissing her neck.

He pulled away. "Tired?" he asked. She picked up a face flannel and wiped the excess lotion from her face. "Not especially."

They had just undressed when the inevitable cry came from Jake's room. "Mummy? Mummy?"

Hartmann flopped back on to the bed with an irritated groan while Annette reached for a dressing gown. Four seconds later and there it was again. "Mummy?" This time it was the cry of someone in desperate peril. "Fuck," he whispered to himself, but not quietly enough for Annette caught it and frowned at him as she went to the four-year-old. Annette had a puritanical dislike of profanity.

While he waited for her to return he tried to work out what he was going to do. Even if he admitted to his debt, Annette would refuse to advance him as much as sixteen thousand pounds; whatever money she did deign to impart to him would be accompanied by severe disapproval, possibly even an interview with his father-in-law. He had an overdraft facility of five thousand pounds and he supposed that the bank might consider upping that to six, but since he was already five and half thousand pounds in the red, the effort hardly seemed worth it.

A mental image of a shiny bright, black and beautiful soft-top roadster drifted into his head, the thought not so much unbidden as completely forbidden. He did not want to think about having to sell his new car.

Annette returned. "Jake's been sick," she announced. "Every-where." This was not a news report; this was a call to arms. She disappeared again, along with Hartmann's erection. He climbed out of bed just as Jake's elder sister, Jocasta, began to join her brother in the weeping and wailing.

Lambert made Wharton drive them to the autopsy rather than use a driver. Wharton knew what this meant, knew that this was an excuse for a little private discussion between them. She knew also that it was likely to be quite forthright on Lambert's part.

He sat in the passenger seat and stared straight ahead, erect as if in back pain or embarrassment; his mouth was set into its perpetual disapproval, his eyebrows lowered and his brow wrinkled. The silence, Wharton had learned, was a usual thing. She changed down a gear and was aware that her skirt had ridden up slightly over her left knee, exposing much of her leg. Most men that she had known would by now have been making covert glances at it, but not Lambert. If he saw it, he saw it in a different way to most of the men that surrounded her.

She almost missed the start of the conversation. They had just stopped at some lights and the ratchet of the handbrake almost stifled his comment. "I want you to be certain that I know all about you."

His eyes were still looking ahead, ostensibly at a dog that was crouched in a defaecatory position beside a lamp-post. The owner was glaring around, daring anyone and everyone to point out the sign by his head promising a five-hundred-pound fine for such canine habits.

Wharton glanced quickly across then back at the lights. She said, "Sir?"

Lambert turned to look at her profile. If he saw beauty in it, he masked the discovery well. "I said that I know all about you, Inspector."

The lights had changed. She had the car in third before she replied. "I'm afraid I don't know what you mean, sir."

"Really, now. Don't you?"

She kept looking in the mirror because there was an idiot behind them who wanted to overtake. Perhaps that was why she didn't respond.

He went on. "I was told that you're a tart, Inspector. I was told that you've slept your way up the tree and out of trouble on more than one occasion."

She kept her face passive. The idiot behind had turned off but now she had to negotiate her way into the right-hand lane and there were two artics who wanted to hold hands and she could fuck off. "And you believe that, do you?"

He had had enough of her profile and was now back to straight-ahead. "I believe you were something of an embarrassment at your last posting. Something about the Exner case. Our superiors wanted you somewhere else and unfortunately I was that somewhere."

At last she managed to break her way between the two friendly truckers at the cost of a few unheard profanities and some flashing of lights. "There's nothing in the official reports to suggest that my conduct in the case was in any way negligent or corrupt," she pointed out.

Lambert seemed to find that amusing. "And we all believe the official reports, don't we, Inspector?"

They had to wait to turn right, which was giving the trucker behind some sort of apoplexy, and she took the opportunity to look directly at Lambert, although he was still staring outside. "I heard you were a cold-hearted bastard, but I was willing to give you the benefit of the doubt, *sir*."

There was silence in the car until she saw the chance and shot suddenly across the oncoming traffic. It was only when they were safely in the side road that he replied. "You heard right, Inspector. I am a cold-hearted bastard."

In the three weeks that she had been working with him, she had seen no evidence to call him a liar. There had been not one sign of a thaw in the frozen, harsh facade with which she had been first greeted. She had spent several off-duty hours asking questions of her new colleagues, from whom she had learned only that Lambert was in a stable, unmarried relationship, but nothing more. He was remote and cold with everyone – superiors, equals and subordinates – although it had been hinted that especially cryogenic conditions had been presented to Wharton; why that should be so, her informants either could not or would not say.

She had taken the implication and kept herself very much to herself in her first three weeks.

And now this. At least she was being supplied with a few answers to her questions.

"Not everything that's said about me is correct."

His uninterest was a weight around his words. "Really? So what's the truth and what's the lie?"

They were driving along the perimeter of the hospital, heading for the back entrance to the mortuary. She thought about denying the rumours of her promiscuousness, but she saw that there was no point. He would believe what he wanted to believe. She decided that if there was a way into his approval it would not be a path of words. She said only, "I'm a bloody good copper, for a start."

She turned left into the discreet, screened area that was used by the undertakers' cars. She stopped under the metallic canopy over the doors to the mortuary. As he got out, Lambert said only, "Prove it, Inspector."

Hartmann could have done without being on the rota for Coroner's autopsies but he certainly couldn't do without the money it brought. He sat in his office, having arrived in the department some twenty minutes earlier, still in his coat, still with the scarf draped around his neck, still wishing a thousand wishes that could never come true. The night had been awful, constantly broken by the cries of his children, the smell of vomit and the thoughts of his financial predicament. It seemed to him as he sat in his drear office that morning, tired and depressed into morose introspection, that he had escaped none of these by coming to work. The traffic had been awful, the weather had been uncompromising and the pollution had seeped into his stomach like poison.

He closed his eyes, hoping for peace, perhaps even perpetual peace, allowing his head to tilt back and his mouth to hang open. The office was cold, even though the fan heater was busy vibrating itself into orgasmic glory, and even with his coat on he still shivered at irregular intervals, partly from cold and partly, he suspected from self-indulgent self-pity.

Why did he keep spending so much money?

The monthly question, usually provoked by his credit-card bills but made even more urgent by the rather nasty letter from his turf accountant, was asked again and passed into time unanswered. "Turf Accountant" – that was a joke; like calling a bin man a "refuse operative". It was a nice name for a nasty, offensive job.

Where did all the money actually go?

This question, asked with greater frequency, was as ever unaddressed and doomed to slip away from him. No matter how often or hard he perused his bank statements, there was no solution. Perhaps there *was* no solution; it was an irrational number like pi. He wasn't, he considered, profligate, although he was forced to admit that he could never be described as thrifty. He preferred to think of himself as "generous," although this preference did not extend to probing to whom he was generous.

He felt ill, he decided. He stood and went to the mirror above the wash basin by the door. He looked at himself for signs of sickness; perhaps he had the children's bug – certainly there had been ample exposure to potentially infected material during the night. He saw a man who was slightly above average in height, with pale brown hair, blue eyes set in a long face, a nose he considered aquiline (though a departing female acquaintance of long ago had once called him "Beaky") and a mouth which, although not unpleasant, hid teeth which were irregular and ill-met, albeit fairly white. His physique was slightly flabby, but clothing, he thought, hid that quite well; he would worry about the flab when the opportunity arose. Not that it often did, Annette frequently seeming to have some reason for not indulging in marital games.

He did, he thought, look pale. Drawn around the eyes, with largish bags. He felt sick, too; might even vomit now he came to consider. . .

He sighed. He couldn't afford to be sick, not with Coroner's work to be done and therefore extra cash to be made.

The phone rang too loudly, interrupting his descent from hope into reality.

"Yes?"

"Doctor Hartmann?"

The voice was familiar. He couldn't think who it was but the sound of it raised no pleasure.

"Speaking."

"Frank Cowper here."

Which explained why he could locate no joyful associations. Before he could say anything, Cowper was talking again. "I thought I ought to have a word with you about one of the cases you've got today."

Beware the Coroner's Officer who wants to talk to you about an autopsy.

He didn't know anything about the cases yet but he wasn't going to let Cowper know that. "Which one?" he asked.

"It's the girl, Millicent Sweet."

"What about her?"

Cowper hesitated. Although the police had not formally demanded a forensic post mortem, if he did not handle this conversation adroitly, he would alarm Hartmann. If Hartmann refused to perform the autopsy and insisted that it was sufficiently odd for it to be performed by a Home Office pathologist, all his good work so far would be for naught.

"She was found alone in her flat. The police have done a thorough inspection and there are no suspicious signs; nothing to suggest anyone else was there. . ."

Hartmann was not so forlorn that he failed to miss the air of overprotestation that permeated the words.

". . .but it appears as though she's been seriously burned."

Fire deaths always caused problems; it was all too convenient to die by a means that destroyed evidence as well. Hartmann was already thinking about not doing the post-mortem even before Cowper had finished.

"Oh."

"The odd thing is, her clothes weren't burned and the flat was entirely okay as well."

"Oh," This time a semitone lower.

Cowper laughed. Then he said, "You see what I mean, don't you? There's no question that there was any foul play, but it's all a bit, well, odd." And he laughed again.

Hartmann immediately did not like the sound of all this. Cowper was a tricksy bastard who would attempt, as he had in the past, to fool him and others into performing autopsies, which ought to have been left to the forensic guys. The most famous example was the man found in a bath with fifty-three stab wounds to his body and two hammer blows to the head; the information from Cowper had, somewhat disingenuously, failed to mention these wounds and had concluded with the statement that there were "no suspicious circumstances."

But there was always another hand.

It was only eighty pounds, but it was eighty pounds that he would quite like to possess. "Was the house secure?"

Cowper assured him that it was.

"Was there a fire in the room?"

This time Cowper had to think hard before answering. "Yes, but she wasn't anywhere near it."

"Was it on?"

"No."

The confidence with which this was pronounced was impressive; Cowper didn't bother trying to remember after the negative had come from his mouth. Hartmann hesitated, but not for long. "I'll tell you what, Frank. I'll have a look at it. If it looks squeaky clean, I'll carry on, but anything funny and I'll come running for the forensic boys."

This was not entirely what Cowper had wanted but he was realistic enough to know that there had been little chance of anything better. "Okay, Doc."

He tried to make this sound cheerful but, strangely, it seemed to Hartmann to be merely resigned.

Hartmann took off his coat and tried not only to look not tired, but also happy and ready for work. The skin of his face felt cold and taut and his eyes didn't seem to fit properly in their sockets. Another blossom of nausea rose from his stomach and made him pause with his hand on the door handle of his room. When the discomfort had passed he walked out into the drab corridor.

The department had been built by someone who had clearly possessed no intention of working there; perhaps there really did exist an architect's department in which half the rooms had no natural light, all of the walls were unplastered (possibly the chocolate brown paint on the breeze blocks was an attempt at disguise), and all of the corridors were straight and met at right-angles, but Hartmann had his doubts. Any newcomers or visitors invariably spent considerable, uncountable time wandering aimlessly through Stygian light down corridors which all looked identical. There was an air of the asylum here, an impression not altered by encountering the inhabitants.

To reach the secretaries' sanctum he had to traverse about two hundred metres of corridor enlivened by only the occasional tatty poster and empty notice board. A few scientific presentations on the walls, telling of great research triumphs, indicated when he was passing through the domain of Professor Bowman, head of department and infinitely irritating.

Amy and Cynthia sat in the secretaries' room at their desks, talking across the third desk, the one that was always empty. They didn't stop their conversation when Hartmann came in, didn't even lift their eyes to him. Amy was Nigerian, a pleasant but unintelligent woman whose sole existence seemed to revolve around the church; she was, to be fair, the one secretary who could be relied upon to concentrate on her work for longer than ten minutes at a time, although her typing of reports often resembled attempts at Jungian self-expression, so liberally sprinkled were they with words that had been misheard as various parts of male and female pudenda. Cynthia was Australian; an adjective that largely encompassed her entire personality and which rendered any further description both redundant and inadequate. Hartmann had spoken to people who'd seen her working but, as with the Aurora Borealis, he had never experienced the joy personally.

"Have you got the Coroner's requests for today's post-mortems?" he enquired of both which, of course, meant neither. His interruption of their social discourse earned him cold stares. At last Amy reluctantly mumbled, "I think they're on the desk. I typed them up last night."

She indicated the empty secretarial desk and Hartmann sat down behind it while they took up their conversation across him.

There were two. The first was a road traffic accident, another cyclist who hadn't been observing the speed limit, committing the unpardonable sin of travelling at fifteen miles an hour in a forty-mile-per-hour zone. A lorry driver had sought to go past him but had succeeded only in going over him. The second was Millicent Sweet.

Twenty-three years old. That fact, baldly stated on an official form that told of her death, was the embodiment of sadness; that she should have lived and died alone, in an uncaring and decaying back street of the city, deepened the sadness into despair.

The free text information that Cowper had supplied was, as always, brief and constructed with grammar and syntax that suggested English was his second language, learned from a deranged baboon. It ended with the mantra, "no suspicious circumstances," – a phrase which had the same power and tokenism as "touch wood" – telling him nothing that he did not already know.

"Have the boys in the mortuary picked up the copies?"

The mortuary technicians came in first thing and took copies of the coroner's requests for autopsies; they would have opened the bodies and eviscerated them by the time the pathologist arrived.

Amy nodded slowly and distractedly. Cynthia stopped talking and began to search through her desk drawer for something. It was at this moment that Patricia Bowman came in holding a box of slides.

"Ah, Mark, just the man I want."

The concept of being wanted by Patricia Bowman left him momentarily paralyzed. He generally enjoyed female companionship but in Patricia Bowman he drew a very thick, very prominent line. She might want him, but he could see no circumstances in which he might want her. Despite this he smiled in a superficially friendly way and said, "Hello, Pat."

Professor Patricia Bowman was the head of department but hers was a headship characterized by unconcern. Since she had no interest whatsoever in any form of diagnostic pathology (she appeared to consider it on a par with prostitution, albeit considerably more messy) the budget and management of the department were concentrated in the area that reflected her interests – experimental pathology. On average it was estimated that seven rats per day were escorted into the undiscovered country. The diagnostic service existed therefore on starvation rations. Even though Hartmann and the five other consultant pathologists were independent medical practitioners, because of these considerations she had considerable power over their lives. Hartmann viewed her much as he viewed sexually-transmitted diseases – nasty, irritating and best avoided – but he was sage enough to know that it would not be wise to antagonize her.

"I've just received the next round of breast EQA slides. Would you care to do them first?"

She proffered the box as Hartmann hesitated. In his mind formed the words, *What's the point?* EQA – External Quality Assurance – was an exercise designed to test his competence and he knew that he didn't have any. He took them with a brief "Thanks."

She turned to a set of pigeon holes set against the wall and took out a bundle of request cards. When slides were reported the request card was handed to Amy and Cynthia so that the report – either written on the back of the card or dictated – could be typed onto the system. When that was done, it was put into the appropriate pigeonhole so that the reporting pathologist could authorize it via the computer.

"You've got a few in here. Would you like them?"

No.

"Sure."

She handed them to him and left the room.

Hartmann returned to his room, physical sickness now hand in hand with depression. The box-like room was gloomed by the chocolate-brown paint on the bare brick walls and the poor winter light. Because Histopathology was situated on the lower ground floor of a six-storey building and his office looked out onto a square courtyard that was in effect the bottom of a deep well, the light could gain access only at an extreme angle. By the time it reached Hartmann it lost any desire to warm or to exhilarate.

He walked to the window and surveyed the courtyard. In its centre was a monstrosity that the artist had described as a water sculpture. Hartmann had few artistic sensibilities and he considered the thing that lurked some twenty metres from his window was an ugly and shapeless cackpile, but he was never sure whether his opinion was valid or not. Certainly Patricia Bowman, who had commissioned it and pushed for the £10,000 to be found from the departmental budget, appeared to have different views on its qualities.

The rain, which had been more or less constant for two days, splattered gently down on the concrete before the window while Hartmann wondered if things could get any worse.

He had thrown the box of slides that Bowman had given him on to the top of a filing cabinet. The last thing he needed was another EQA test; more pressure, more work, less certainty about life, the universe, anything. Soon he would be spending more time on doing proficiency testing and Continuing his Professional Development than in actually doing anything useful; it seemed to him that perhaps his predicament was a tableau that represented the farce of modern England.

Abruptly he turned away and sat down, feeling almost ready for tears. He knew he couldn't go on the way he was, but he knew also that the road he was travelling had never once had a turning. A recipe for despair, baked to perfection.

"Fuh-kin-ell!"

The labiodental fricative, dissected into extended syllables and shouted, bounced around the dissection room's bright, hard walls.

Hartmann smiled weakly at Denny, the origin of this colourful greeting.

"Where the fuck 'ave you been? We thought you'd probably died from overwanking in the bogs. Lenny was all ready to go in there and sacrifice everything to pull your hand out from your trousers."

Hartmann sighed, knowing from several years' experience that there was little point in trying to respond to this onslaught. Lenny and Denny – what passed for mortuary technicians in the strange subterranean world that was the Histopathology Department – had no formal power but an infinite amount of its informal counterpart. He said merely, "I had a few things to do, Denny. Sorry if I held you up."

Denny grinned.

"I opened one up. I thought I'd leave the other one for you."

Hartmann didn't like the way his lips smiled and his voice assumed a faint cruelty.

They were in the body store, a rectangular room in which there were forty-eight fridges and four freezer compartments, two mortuary registers (one for hospital deaths, the other for deaths outside the hospital), a wooden measure and a hydraulic body trolley which could be raised to any height so that bodies could be put into and taken from the higher fridges. Hartmann had just come from the male changing room, a deeply depressing chamber which contained battered lockers, sundry items of male clothing (many of which seemed to be perpetually sweat-soaked) a rather sorry collection of weight-lifting equipment, and quite an astonishing collection of pornography. There was also a shower and a small toilet but Hartmann had never had the courage to investigate that particular part of the room.

Changing consisted of trying to find somewhere to put his clothes (the floor was filthy, all the hooks were either occupied or broken and the lockers, perhaps logically, were all locked), trying to find some clean theatre "blues" (there were usually none to be seen and a visit to the laundry room then had to be made – this room resembled a set from a gruesome horror picture) and then trying to locate his wellington boots; although they had his name on, they were apparently in constant use by anyone and everyone.

Once attired, he would cross to the body store by way of a room that housed spare instruments, specimens for later histological examination and, more often than not, a registrar performing a foetal autopsy. Every time he encountered some poor unfortunate engaged on such a task, Hartmann felt sympathy welling up within him, so vivid were the ghastly memories of his time spent in paediatric pathology.

In this room were the gowns, plastic aprons and rubber gloves – assuming he was lucky and they had been re-plenished. This time his luck was in, and it was on his way through the body store to the dissection room that Denny accosted him.

Denny was tall and thin and short haired. He claimed to have been a skinhead earlier in his short life and his general demeanour supported that proud boast; certainly Hartmann had never felt the urge to contest it with him, nor to make jocular remarks about his ginger hair and freckled face. Denny regularly reminisced about fights he had won, people he had "decked", and women he shagged.

In actual fact, Hartmann rather liked Denny. He was intelligent, for all his violence, and could be pleasant company. Certainly it paid Hartmann to be companionable, because it not only meant that he was assisted rather than obstructed when doing autopsies, but also because he received a regular supply of cremation papers to sign and thus collect the fee for.

Hartmann had never met Denny's father but he assumed he was a man who considered himself to have a fantastic sense of humour. Either that or he was immensely dim, for he had thought it normal to name his two sons Denny and Lenny; bad enough in itself, but catastrophic when combined with the surname of Tennyson; Hartmann had often wondered what Alfred, Lord, made of it all from his presumably lofty vantage point.

"You've got company," Denny informed him in a voice that was not only not confidential but was positively boastful of the fact.

Hartmann showed interest but only of the polite variety. A clinician, he assumed, although Denny's demeanour made him suspicious. "Have I?"

Denny nodded but said no more on the subject. "Let me know when you want some help," was all he said. He walked out of the body store whistling and left Hartmann vaguely uncertain of why he was worried.

Walking through the wide doorway to the dissection room, the uncertainty left him. He didn't have Denny's heightened sense of what was "police" and what was "non-police," (Denny moved in a world where this was the single most important survival trait) but he could tell that the man and woman waiting side by side in the clinicians' gallery were not doctors.

The clinicians' gallery was slightly raised with respect to the rest of the large room and separated from it by thick perspex screens which came up to head level of anyone performing a dissection and waist level of anyone in the gallery. It ran for the entire length of the room. The dissection room itself held six white porcelain tables, all topped with stainless steel trays perforated with rows of slits. Over each table was a bright light and at the base of each was a water supply connected to a hose. Two of the tables were occupied, one by an elderly man who was naked and who had been eviscerated, leaving his body open and empty like a primitive, landed boat; on the other table was a white body bag, clean and bright.

Hartmann's entrance made the two visitors look up at him and move to the perspex divider. It was the man who spoke. He was losing his hair and his face was creased with fatigue; he exuded a kind of masculinity that Hartmann envied. The woman was younger and undoubtedly extremely attractive. She had, though, a cruelty around her eyes that Hartmann found unnerving. She hung slightly back, clearly the subordinate.

"Dr Hartmann?"

"Yes."

"My name's Lambert, this is DI Wharton. I believe Mr Cowper told you we might be here."

Experiencing irritation and concern in equal measure, Hartmann shook his head. "He didn't mention anything."

Lambert sighed and Wharton smiled a smile of contempt.

"I see. Well, the fact is we're ever so slightly intrigued by the death of this girl, Sweet. We can't find any evidence to suggest that there's anything to worry about but the suggestion has been made that she died from burns. The circumstances in which she was found would argue against that, however."

"You're sure, are you? You're positive that there are no suspicious circumstances?"

Hartmannn's plea for reassurance was understandable. He would be chewed up, swallowed and then excreted by the forensic pathologists if he undertook a post-mortem on somebody who, it subsequently emerged, had been the victim of a crime. It had happened to him once before and he did not want to repeat the experience.

Lambert shook his head and, although his superior couldn't see her, Wharton did likewise. "None at all," he said. What did it matter to him? The door from the department opened and one of the Registrars, Belinda Miller, came in.

"Mind if I watch?"

Belinda was short and slightly overweight with short black hair and a mobile, boyish face. She was the brightest of the registrars and Hartmann got on well with her. According to the registrars' rota it was her week for autopsies but juniors were not permitted to do Coronial cases and there were no hospital post-mortems that day. Hartmann smiled and consented, slightly relieved to have an ally in the room.

Hartmann glanced at the body in the bag. He had been hesitating but knew in his soul that he was at least going to have a look at it, if only because he was curious. He nodded minimally to Lambert and then turned away. He would have preferred to have done the autopsy on the cyclist first – road traffic accidents were easy money, the autopsy merely a catalogue of superficial, bony and soft tissue injuries – but he thought it would be unwise to antagonize his guests.

"Denny!"

The shout echoed indistinctly around the room and produced no immediate response. He began to unzip the body bag, knowing that Denny had heard and that he would take his time. No amount of screaming, calling or pleading would alter that. Anyway, his first sight of the girl immediately struck Denny from his mind.

Hartmann was used to Death and he was used to the varied marks that Death left. He knew that some people would emerge from their inevitable encounter with Death apparently unscathed in body, some even (those who chose to leave this life with the aid of the internal combustion engine and a long length of hosepipe) looking in ruddier health than ever they did in life. Many would disgrace themselves, soiled in vomit, blood or even faeces and a few would be disfigured by abrasions, lacerations, even amputations.

But this girl. . .

He heard Belinda whistle softly and when he looked up at Lambert there was a small smile of little amusement. Lambert raised his eyebrows. *See what I mean?*

Denny came in, followed by Lenny. "Wotcha want, boss?"

"Can you give me a hand getting her out of the body bag?"

Denny signalled to Lenny and they both came over. Hartmann was effectively pushed aside as they both quickly and fairly efficiently rolled the body first one way and then the other so that the unzipped body bag could be taken away.

Lenny asked, "Do you want her undressed?"

Lenny was two years older than his brother and considerably less bright. He wore glasses which he presumably thought were okay but which were square, thick-rimmed and black; they eliminated any chance that people might think he was intelligent and any chance that he would ever have much sexual success. His love life seemed to consist of keeping the ugly one occupied with numbing conversation while Denny rogered the attractive one in the next room. Occasionally Denny would give him a cast-off but even then, as far as Hartmann could work out, Lenny's usual line of attack was to soak the girl in alcohol before launching himself upon her unconscious body.

"Please."

The word "undressing" was accurate only in that it referred to the removal of clothes. It consisted in this context of opening the dressing gown and then taking a pair of scissors and slitting the clothing up the front. Hartmann could imagine that under other circumstances this was their idea of foreplay.

The nightie, rather prim and proper, fell away and revealed the extent of what Death had chosen to inflict on this particular human.

Her entire skin seemed to have been burned off her, leaving the raw, redness of the underlying soft tissues and these seemed to glow with warm, bloodied pain even in the harsh light of the dissection room. There was not a square centimetre of her body that was not thus affected, even the soles of her feet, her scalp and, Hartmann saw as the boys tilted her to pull out the nightie and dressing gown, her back.

He moved closer as they stepped back. He glanced up at them but they were passive, Lenny because he was stupid, Denny because it wouldn't have been manly to show any emotion at the sight of a corpse, no matter how bizarre.

There were skin scales present, he now saw. He put out a gloved hand to touch her abdomen and rubbed the surface gently. A few small flakes came away. Then he noticed small, irregular lumps, darker than the background, scattered about her body, clustered in the groins and the axillae.

Suddenly relieved he looked again at Lambert.

"I don't think this was caused by burning of any kind."

Lambert said only, "Oh?" Behind him Wharton looked disappointed. Belinda had moved forward in order to see better. Her face bore a look of concentration and interest. She had a way of puckering her lips when she was thinking that had often struck Hartmann as oddly attractive. Lambert's question interrupted his musings on Belinda.

"What is it, then?"

"It's some sort of skin disease. Psoriasis, maybe."

Lambert frowned as he sifted through his vast medical knowledge.

"Can you die of that?"

Which was Hartmann's problem. "Not usually," he admitted, "But then you don't usually get it as severely as this."

He turned back to the corpse and asked Denny for a knife. This was produced and he made the first incision, starting at the neck, just in front of the larynx. He drew the knife down over the sternum, onto the abdomen, curved gently around the umbilicus and then down to the pubic hair.

"Could you get me a pot for histology, please?"

Both Denny and Lenny went off, although only Lenny returned, in his hand a small white plastic pot that was half-filled with formalin, the preservative that was routinely used. Hartmann had cut off a thin strip of skin from the edge of the incision and he dropped this into the pot. He could hear Denny whistling in the body store. Then there was a long, loud ring. Denny moved across the doorway between the dissection room and the body store in response to this. There was the sound of voices and various clanging noises followed by a car door being shut.

"I think you can carry on the evisceration now, Lenny."

Lenny grunted, displaying a lack of enthusiasm for this request but nonetheless taking the proffered knife from Hartmann. He might have been stupid but he was undoubtedly quicker and surer at removal of the organs than Hartmann. Two undertakers, dressed in dark clothes, appeared in the body store. They didn't look into the dissection room. Any impression of reverence that the dark clothing might have given was dispelled by the open shirt necks, the ties at half-mast and the coarse laughter that surrounded their discussion with Denny.

Lenny began to strip the skin off the ribs on the left side so that the breasts hung away like sandbags. As he did this he pulled away the edge of the abdominal wall to expose the left lobe of the liver and the stomach. Hartmann said suddenly, "Hang on, Lenny."

Lenny looked up, the welcoming light of intelligence singularly missing from his eyes.

"Look." Hartmann gestured down at the abdomen. Lenny grunted and stood back.

"What is it?" Lambert's question came from behind Hartmann.

Hartmann had taken the knife and was exposing more of the abdomen. He stripped the skin off the right side of the chest in a mirror image of what Lenny had done, careful not to let the blade slip through the skin and form a "button-hole". This was a crime, as it required Denny or Lenny to suture it and thus work harder; should any of the junior pathologists do such a thing, Denny's usual punishment was to insert a hose down the back of their trousers and turn the water on. Hartmann didn't think Denny would do that to a consultant, but he didn't want to test the proposition.

After a few minutes the entirety of the abdominal contents was displayed.

"Fuck me," was Lenny's invitation, not for the first time unfulfilled.

"What is it?" Lambert was clearly not used to being ignored. Hartmann turned to him and found not only had Wharton come forward but also Belinda had moved within touching distance of the police officers.

"She's got cancer."

Lambert's face complemented the disappointed tone with which he said, "Oh."

"Judging from the extent of the disease, I don't think there's any doubt that's what killed her."

Hartmann, at least, was happy; there was nothing that warmed the cockles of his heart more than finding a cause of death. The constabulary, however, were less than delighted. Clearly they considered that they had been wasting their time. They would probably have left without any further acknowledgement of Hartmann had he not called to their departing backs, "Do you want a copy of the report?"

Lambert looked back and said, "No thanks, doctor. That won't be necessary." It was left to Wharton to say, "Thanks for your time."

They walked out, leaving the world to Belinda and to Hartmann. She moved closer, into the police-shaped gap that had been left by Lambert and Wharton. Her mouth was puckered again. "It's a bit odd, isn't it?" she mused, staring at the girl.

Hartmann had been swept along by the relief that it wasn't a suspicious death, that he would get his eighty pounds and that he wouldn't get bollocked by a forensic pathologist. Her tone caused him to look again. "What do you mean?"

She was hesitant. It didn't do to point out to consultants that they might have missed something. "I was wondering if the skin might not be mycosis fungoides," she explained.

Lymphoma affecting the skin. He was forced to admit that it might be.

Then she said, "But the tumour in her abdomen isn't lymphoma, is it?" And while he was considering this, she continued, "In fact, it's odd-looking altogether. I mean, I've never seen a tumour that filled the abdominal cavity like that. Have you?"

"Oh, yes," he pronounced after a short hesitation that betrayed his lie. "Occasionally." He dredged his false memories. "Ovarian can, sometimes."

He glanced at her, hoping to see confidence in his experience rather than mockery of his falsehood, but she was still staring at the opened corpse and this lack of reaction undermined his hopes. "Two tumours?"

Which was odd, he knew, but odd things happen. "Well, perhaps she really does have psoriasis. Just an incidental finding, and the thing that killed her was the ovarian cancer."

Belinda leaned right over and indicated the nearer shoulder of the corpse with her right hand. "But those growths on her skin. They must be tumour-stage mycosis."

He looked at what she indicated – red, ulcerated nodules, angry and lethal. They might, he thought, be the end stage of skin lymphoma, when it stopped being a rash and became a proper lump-forming cancer, but he wasn't sure. He said only, "Mmm."

"Has she got anything in her past medical history? I mean, you can't develop a huge abdominal tumour like that overnight. Surely she was seeing somebody for it, whatever it is."

He hadn't thought to investigate that – after all, it had been given to him as a possible fire death – and he had therefore to confess that he didn't know. At once she was at the nearby computer terminal, typing in the details that she took from the top of the Coroner's PM request form.

"That's very peculiar," she said after a while.

"What is?"

"There's a record of her because she's on the Medical School staff – you know, Hepatitis status, that kind of thing – but there's nothing about cancer."

Lenny was tired of being ignored. "Shall I carry on or not?"

"Please, Lenny."

Belinda left the terminal and came back to look. The undertakers were leaving, complete with extra passenger. She asked, "Do you mind if I get changed and come round and look. This is a fascinating case."

Hartmann didn't want fascinating, he wanted easy and quick. He also wanted to be left alone to his own incompetence, not constantly made to feel a prat by a registrar. Yet what could he say? It was a teaching hospital, after all. "Of course."

He turned to inspect the body a little more closely, afraid lest he should miss something, as Lenny began to progress the dissection. The whole of the liver was replaced by tumour; dead and dying grey-white tissue splash-painted with areas of haemorrhage and, in the liver particularly, small green patches. The wall of the stomach was covered with nodules of tumour, most about a centimetre in diameter, although one was significantly larger and measured nearly ten centimetres. Similarly the omentum – the sheet of fat which hangs from the lower border of the stomach – had been infiltrated so that it was thickened, stiff and solid. Beneath this, the coils of intestine also showed nodular tumours.

He knew that it wasn't ovarian and as soon as Belinda got there, she opined similarly. "That greenish staining looks like bile."

"Hepatocellular carcinoma?" he said quickly before she could, "Yes, that's what I was wondering." Primary cancer of the liver was the only type that produced bile.

"But there are also tumours on the intestinal wall – small intestine, too."

The small intestine – a rare site for tumours.

He nodded, as if understanding her consternation from the vantage of greater knowledge.

Lenny had been opening the chest. He took a steel tenon saw and began to cut through the ribs on the left hand side, starting at the bottom perhaps ten centimetres from the midline and working up and in so that at the clavicle the cut was adjacent to the sternum. He came round to the other side of the table and

42

repeated the process on the right hand side. Then he lifted the bottom end of the sternum and began partly to pull and partly to try to cut the sternum off the underlying tissues.

Only it wouldn't come.

It ought to have been easy, the sack around the heart and the soft tissues in the middle of the chest coming away like sticky grey candyfloss.

Lenny looked up at Hartmann who was watching him. Lenny was sufficiently well trained to know that it was Hartmann's job if something untoward occurred; this, of course, suited Lenny and it was therefore one of the few rules he obeyed.

"What's up?" asked Hartmann.

"It won't come. There's something sticking it down."

Hartmann took the knife back and, grabbing the sternum in his right hand, began to cut at the tissues under it. The knife met fibrotic, almost solid tissue. He took a firmer grip of the handle and began to saw through it. Ten minutes later, the sternum came away at least and revealed what had glued it down so firmly. Hartmann could only stare at it.

The entire chest seemed filled with friable, mottled tissue laced with areas of fresh bleeding. The bag in which the heart was hung was encased in it and the lungs on either side were lost in it. A few pockets of fluid in irregular spaces were all that was left of the space around the lungs.

Her chest had become merely a box of tumour.

He heard Belinda mutter something beside him. It was only after a few seconds that he realized what she had said.

"Bloody hell."

It took Hartmann and Belinda an hour to take out the organ mass and a further hour to dissect the organs from it. Lenny retreated, claiming that it was Hartmann's job, given the extent of the cancer, and Hartmann couldn't really argue. Denny dropped by, taking a break from whatever mysterious tasks occupied his time and earned his wages, to whistle, much as he would have whistled at a mate with a penis of impressive size.

"Poor bitch," he offered but empathy was again absent from his voice.

The organs were now neatly arrayed on the dissection board, and on Hartmann's face was arrayed a look of deep bewilderment. Belinda stood beside him, trying to make some sense of it all.

Every single organ had some form of tumorous involvement. True, some had more than others, so that the lungs were effectively completely effaced as were the liver, ovaries and thyroid, while the kidneys, intestines, heart and uterus still retained their overall structure albeit liberally dotted with cancer. The brain was also affected, Hartmann's neat slices revealing a large mass of dead and dying tumour in the left hemisphere that measured eight centimetres across, another, smaller one in the right and two in the cerebellum.

One by one he had sliced into the organs and one by one had revealed a greater or less degree of malignancy. When he had opened the intestines – all ten metres of them – he had expected to find only surface involvement by tumour, spread from outside, but he had instead found the lining of both the large and small intestines carpeted with polypoid growths large and small. Nestling amongst which were no less than six cancers, two in the small intestine and four in the large.

The stomach contained three tumours and the lumen of the gullet was obliterated by a solid mass of cancerous tissue; these lesions rested on a curious, velvety-red surface which was quite unlike the usual appearance. Hartmann suspected that it represented some form of "field change", that all of the stomach and oesophageal lining was turning malignant.

Even the larynx contained scattered nodules that were almost certainly cancerous. The spleen, normally weighing between one and two hundred grams, was huge and clocked in at nearly two kilograms; its cut surface was speckled with white spots, some nearly a centimetre in diameter.

Hartmann had gone back to the body cavity and began to feel the dead, firm muscles and bones. It had not been long before he had felt a firm lump in the musculature of the right calf and, uncaring of the danger of a hosepipe down his trousers, he had incised the skin to reveal yet another tumour. In a similar fashion he had found two more muscle tumours and then gone to find that the right femur, right humerus, left side of the pelvis and left shoulder blade were all focally expanded; he had chipped away the surface bone to reveal yet more tumours.

The bone marrow, exposed by stripping off the front of the spinal column was pale grey and softly fluctuant; Hartmann could find no surprise within himself when he discovered this. He looked in the mouth and found extensive ulceration and Hartmann knew that its cause wasn't ill-fitting denturework.

"This is impossible." Belinda's remark was understandable but neither helpful nor, by definition, accurate. Hartmann had been afraid that she would show him up for a fool, but it was clear that this case was showing them both the limits of their wisdom. He knew that he was hopelessly lost but he had enough experience and enough innate wisdom to try to adopt a reasonable coping strategy.

First, run through the facts in your mind. Lay them out before you try to connect them. "Look," he said to Belinda. "Let's just start at the beginning. She was a girl in her early twenties. It's improbable but not impossible that she might develop cancer at that age, but the range of tumours she's likely to develop is limited. I wouldn't be surprised to see a thyroid tumour, or even some types of gynaecological malignancy. Other possibilities include lymphoma or leukaemia which may well affect this age group, bone cancers and a variety of soft tissue tumours."

"And brain tumours."

"And brain tumours. And, it would appear from macroscopic examination, we actually may well have those tumour types here."

"But she should have only one of them."

"And that's the problem. She hasn't just got one of them, or two of them. She's got all of them and more; tumours she shouldn't have developed for another fifty years – lung carcinoma, colorectal carcinoma, what looks like a liposarcoma."

Belinda was frowning intensely. "You don't suppose," she said tentatively, "that it's just one of them that's spread all over the place?" she asked.

There was a pause while Hartmann thought again about that possibility but, if he wasn't the best pathologist in the Royal College, he was good enough to know that wasn't the reason. He indicated the lining of the intestine; it was covered in a carpet of red growths like tropical sea anenomes. "Look at those adenomatous polyps. They're premalignant, suggesting she has a primary colonic carcinoma. Yet if you look in the breasts, both of them contain not only invasive tumours but also evidence of cancers that are still in-situ, yet to spread."

"Suggesting that the breast cancers are also primaries."

"Exactly. And then there's the spleen. I suppose it could be carcinoma from somewhere, but if I didn't know better, I'd say that has the classical look of lymphoma, wouldn't you?"

She was forced to admit that it did. "And there are about a dozen other findings that indicate multiple primaries," she added.

"Exactly."

"So . . ?"

There, so quickly, was the rub.

It was really only to say something, anything, so that he wouldn't look stupid that he remarked, "This must be an inherited syndrome."

To his great relief, Belinda didn't dismiss this with a contemptuous snort, but actually took it seriously. "Of course!" Disillusionment set in immediately afterwards, for she then enquired, "But which one?"

Which one indeed. There were numerous inherited syndromes, usually caused by a single gene mutation, that resulted in families dying of cancers in their early years, often dying of a variety of cancers, but Hartmann could not think of one that resulted in fifteen or twenty tumours occurring simultaneously in a single individual.

"I don't know," he admitted.

"The odd thing is," Belinda was off again, musing into areas that were beyond Hartmann, "she's not known at the hospital. Surely if she had cancer – only one cancer, let alone so many – she would have found her way into the hospital system."

"Perhaps she didn't want to know."

Belinda clearly found this unlikely. The very old, afraid or just uncaring were the ones who kept their fungating tumours hidden under layers of clothing, not young people; certainly not young people working in the Medical School.

He knew that he wasn't going to get anywhere solving this without time, thought and a good few textbooks. It was already nearly eleven o'clock and he still had another autopsy to perform as well as some paperwork to clear up before he left for Glasgow. Deciding that he had made enough of a prat of himself, he said,

"Whatever's going on, I think the thing to do is to take some samples for histology."

Which meant that he would have to give the Coroner's Office a presumed cause of death as opposed to a definite one (they hated that); the relatives would have to be informed of the samples he took for microscopy and much paperwork would have to be completed.

Denny came in. As it was nearly time for lunch, not even a Royal Command from Genghis Khan would have made him do any work in the dissection room in the afternoon. "Haven't you fuckin' finished with that one yet?"

Hartmann smiled at him.

"Nearly, Denny. Nearly."

"Well don't forget you've still got cocky to do," he pointed, gesturing at the unfortunate cyclist who was slowly desiccating behind them. "If I'm still clearing up in here this afternoon there'll be fuckin' hell to pay."

The implication was menacing and not lost on Hartmann. He said sweetly to his subordinate, "Don't worry, Denny. I'll be finished soon."

When Denny had again wandered away Hartmann began cutting a small piece of tissue from each organ. Each was about five millimetres thick and two by one centimetres in area. These he dropped, about twenty in all, into the pot of formalin.

Belinda asked, "What about freezing some tissue? It might be worth doing some genetics."

Again she had proved to be ahead of him. He nodded and she said at once, "I'll do that."

He was undecided between trying to appear in charge and trying to appear anal-retentive. He decided on the latter and asked, "Why?"

"You know I've been doing some research in Professor Bowman's laboratory? On the cell biology of adrenal tumours?"

One of Patricia's interests. Belinda had been enlisted, as all registrars were.

"I could probably do some of the analysis. . ." She paused, uncertain. "If that's all right. . ."

He said only, "Let's see what the microscopy shows first, shall we?"

This was clearly a rebuff. He caught her fleeting look of

discomfort and said, "We ought to proceed in steps, don't you think? We'll take the samples but before we do any fancy molecular biology, I'd like to have a chat with Medical Genetics. See what they think, okay?"

She nodded and went in search of sterile pots to label for the various specimens. She came back with them piled in her arms. They spent the next fifteen minutes taking further samples and then labelling the pots. Having done that, Hartmann began to pile all the organs into a silver bowl.

"I probably ought to be going now," said Belinda.

Hartmann had turned his attention to the cyclist. He was feeling and bending each limb in turn. He didn't look up as he said, "Fine."

She began to strip off her gown, moving towards the body store, while he tried to reassert his self-confidence. He had picked up a clipboard on which were cartoons of a human body, front and back, and was noting down the external injuries. He had just started on the dissection of the organs when Belinda tentatively came back to the viewing balcony to speak to him over the perspex screen.

"Would it be all right if I were to come and see you when you're going to look at the tissues down the microscope?"

Hartmann hid his concern that here was another chance to play the jerk. "Of course. It'll be a couple of days. I'll let you know when the stuff's ready."

Denny and Lenny came in some ten minutes later. They had considerable fun in telling Hartmann exactly what they thought Belinda needed to make her a happier human being.

Belinda had been entrusted with the samples. She had taken the ones in formalin through to the cut-up room so that the laboratory technicians could put them into cassettes for processing over the weekend; the slides made from these would then be ready by Monday afternoon for Hartmann to examine. She was now taking the fresh samples to the molecular biology lab to put them into the freezer.

Hartmann had told her not to start the analysis straight away but she suspected he didn't know how long it took. The tissue had to be digested with enzymes, the nucleic acids extracted and stored before any tests could be run, and that would take several days; the analysis itself might take a further week.

Surely it would be better to start matters at once. She wasn't, she rationalized, disobeying Hartmann, since her action would not technically be starting the analysis, merely preparing the tissue. And it would save valuable time when, as she was sure it would, the analysis became necessary.

Thus decided, she didn't put the samples directly into the freezer. As per the protocol, she split the tissue pieces into two with a sterile scalpel on sterile petri dishes; half of each sample she froze (this was done to provide spare tissue in case something went wrong), the rest she put into plastic disposable test tubes. Then she poured onto them a solution of protease. The rack of test tubes she then put into a waterbath set to body temperature.

In truth, Hartmann wasn't particularly interested in non-Hodgkin's lymphomas but at least it was a weekend away, and away, moreover, at the luxurious Pretender Hotel on the southern edge of Loch Lomond, all paid for, bar the drinks. Three days of relative freedom; freedom from responsibility, freedom from Annette, freedom from Jake and Jocasta, freedom from debt. He planned to enjoy himself.

On the Friday afternoon, he flew up to Glasgow Airport then took a taxi to the hotel. It was every bit as splendid as he had hoped, the hotel a converted castle set in pinewoods that sloped down to the loch's edge. There was a gymnasium, a swimming pool, a sauna and an eighteen-hole golf course. There was also an air of opulence that he found at once relaxing. He decided that perhaps life wasn't too bad.

He was checked into a room that managed to avoid the sterile conformity of most modern luxury hotels, then showered, changed and wandered down to the reception buffet. The procedure over the next few hours was exactly as it always was on such occasions. When he registered, he picked up the obligatory wallet (filled with a list of delegates, a plastic name-tag, a bound collection of abstracts, a pen and a pad of lined writing paper) and headed for the nearest wine waiter. Red wine in hand he turned to look around at the assembled company. Perhaps thirty of the expected sixty were there and he recognized no one. He was neither surprised nor disappointed by this since he was a newcomer to the subspecialty. He found a rather comfortable chair in a bay window that looked down through the woods towards the loch then he took the programme and the delegate list from the wallet. *New Advances in the Understanding of the non-Hodgkin's Lymphomas.* The programme of speakers was, he had to admit, impressive; the problem was that he wasn't particularly interested. He was only there because he had been forced to take over reporting haematological malignancies and, since his knowledge of this area of pathology was less than complete, he had thought it wise to undertake some rapid cramming on the subject. He had chosen this conference as much because of the location as the educational content, but he had to admit that it was a fairly high-powered line-up.

He went in search of more wine and decided to raid the food table. The room was filling up but he was again unsurprised to note that there was still no familiar face in the room. When his plate was full he returned to his station and scanned the delegate list. He recognized none of the names.

It wasn't that he was pathologically unsociable, but this weekend he rather fancied freedom; there were certain lectures coming up in the next two days that he had already marked down as too indigestible for human consumption and during those he planned to partake of the various hotel facilities without having to explain himself to some over-attentive colleague. Anonymity was his desire that weekend.

The food was the usual curious buffet mixture of sandwiches, sausage rolls, samosas, chicken sati and quiche – around the world in eighteen dishes – which he ate without enthusiasm, then packed the documentation back into the wallet. The inevitable selection of gateaux was arrayed on the table but he decided against them, opting instead in favour of some more wine and he accordingly obtained a full glass.

The room was now quite crowded, most of his fellow delegates appearing to know each other. He had to move across the room by constantly edging around people and avoiding elbows and glasses and the occasional flipped backhand. It was like ten thousand other medical or scientific conferences.

At the back of the room were some double doors that he guessed led into the main conference room. Arranged along either side of these were sales stalls, another unchanging component of such occasions. The things they sold were usually related to the subject of the conference and in this case they were telling him of new treatments for lymphoma. On either side of the stalls there stood the representatives, people who, in Hartmann's opinion, had the hardest of all jobs, having to sell to doctors. Normally his contact with such a tribe lasted only until he confessed that he was a pathologist, whereupon their smiles remained while the expectant, welcoming light in their eyes went walkies. You can't sell drugs to a pathologist.

It was no different this time. His brief perusal of their displays was followed by a bright conversation that became rapidly desultory when they found he wasn't in any sort of position to prescribe several tens of thousands of chemotherapeutics. He could only offer them interest and that was not enough. They allowed him to take the cheap pens and sticky paper pads, but the real prizes – the desk lamps, the laser pointers and the elegant clocks – remained under the table. He left the room, went to the bar for a final malt whisky, then went to his bed.

He slept quite well, considering it was a hotel. The bed was comfortable and the sheets smelled wonderfully fresh. He had, he mused as he showered, stayed in considerably worse establishments than this.

He enjoyed the full Scottish breakfast and then, newspaper tucked into the wallet, he took his place at the back of the conference hall, ten minutes before the scheduled start. He was relieved to find that the chairs were fairly plush (his buttocks had painful, ache-filled memories of many long lectures) and that the projection screen was large.

The day passed uneventfully. The lectures varied from incomprehensible to dull but he was able to extract some sense of self-justification for his presence, actually making the odd note. The lunch was another buffet but he expected no more; at least the coffee was drinkable. By the time the afternoon break came he felt that he had learned enough to merit skipping the last two talks – and headed for the bar. He bought himself a large gin and tonic and ensconced himself on one of the large, olive green sofas dotted around the open plan lounge. He took two long draughts and then closed his eyes and relaxed, feeling happy with the world.

"May I join you?"

The voice startled him. On opening his eyes they revealed a rather attractive young woman. He looked around. He must have dropped off for the bar was now busy with conference delegates and the lounge had filled up considerably. He smiled at the woman and said, "Of course, of course."

She sat down opposite him and he thought that she looked vaguely familiar but he couldn't place her. She had long black hair, dark blue eyes and full lips and he guessed that she was perhaps thirty years old. She also had a figure to die for. Hartmann felt irrationally flattered that she had chosen to sit with him.

She took from her handbag a gold lighter and a packet of cigarettes. "You don't mind, do you?" He shook his head at once, noting her voice had a trace of Essex in it. "Help yourself, if you want," she offered, indicating the cigarettes and lighter that she had put on the table between them.

"Thanks, but I don't smoke."

By now she had lit up and she was drawing in the smoke as if it gave her something that oxygen never could. With a sigh she leaned back and let the smoke stream out from her lungs, an expanding column from the round of her lips, heading for the ceiling. "You would if you had my job," she remarked.

"Bad day?" he asked. She laughed.

"They're all bad."

She had no drink and his glass was nearly empty. He offered to get her a drink and she smiled and said, "Bacardi and Coke, please."

It was while he was paying for the drinks that he placed her. She was a rep on one of the stands at the back of the conference. Her partner was a tall, muscular-looking blond chap who had struck Hartmann as being really rather moody. When he gave her the Bacardi, he said, "You're one of the reps, aren't you?"

She had finished her cigarette and was starting a second. She took the drink with thanks and sipped it, leaving a red mark at the glass's rim before she nodded. "That's right. Wiskott-Aldrich. King bastard company of the world."

"That good, eh?"

She smiled and he decided that it was a nice smile. She

drained her drink with another long swallow and said, "Absolutely. Who'd be a rep? Would you?"

He admitted that no, he would not. But would she like another Bacardi? She protested that it was her turn, but he was not to be denied. By the time he returned she had shed her jacket and he could not help but notice how pneumatic she was.

Proffering a thin, manicured hand she said, "I'm Claire, Claire Verner," to which he said, "Mark Hartmann."

And it was about this time that he later remembered thinking how wonderfully easy and natural all this seemed.

She wanted to talk and he was happy to listen. Around them the lounge became full and noisy but it seemed to Hartmann that theirs was an isolated spot, away from the rest of humanity. She told him how long the hours were, how poorly she was paid (before commission) and how sick she was of hotels. She had changed companies six times in the past eight years and she had decided she was reaching the end of her patience with selling, but she didn't know what else she might do.

He asked her occasional questions, noticing that she was becoming slightly drunk and that she was leaning more and more towards him, drawing him into intimacy. He, too, was becoming drunk, but that didn't bother him in the least. At the back of his mind he began to wonder where this might lead. . .

It seemed that she was single and that she had a boyfriend called Jerry whom she hadn't seen now for five weeks, both because of her job and because he was European Sales Manager for a computer software house and therefore hardly ever in the country. She didn't ask about his personal life and he didn't tell her.

He did ask about her companion, the blond, surly man and she said, "Alan?" Then she laughed. "Alan's no help to a girl. He's as gay as they come. You'd be far more likely to get off with him than I ever would." And they both laughed.

It was eleven o'clock and after they had both consumed a pleasantly large amount of alcohol that she said quite suddenly, "Shall we go to bed?"

He looked at her, unable to believe what he had just heard, unable to believe that he had not misheard and unable to believe that his vague, fantastical wishes had just so spectacularly come true. For the first and only time that night, he also felt a single brief spasm of guilt, but then it had gone, and lust rushed in to fill the space.

After he ushered her into his room, he was suddenly taken by panic at how to proceed next. He needn't have worried, however, for no sooner had he closed the door than she embraced him and planted her lips upon his. Even before this had ended he could feel her hand moving down around his crotch, the heel of her palm rubbing up and down, up and down.

She pulled away. "Come on," she said, and she took him by the hand and pulled him towards the bed. She began to strip with astonishing speed and was naked before he had finished unbuttoning his shirt. The sight of her made him stop for a moment.

She was gorgeous, he decided. She was his dream partner, with breasts that he had known in his fantasies a thousand times. Her legs were long, her waist narrow and, something that he found almost uncontainably arousing, she was shaved. Her eyes were bright as she waited for him to finish undressing, her tongue moving between her lips.

He at last got his shirt off and began to remove his shoes, overbalancing and falling back to sit on the bed. She moved around and knelt before him. He thought he would explode at the sight. She helped him off with his shoes, then his socks. They stood together, hand in hand as if they were dancing a courtship ritual, and before he could do anything himself she had taken down his trousers and his underwear. They fell on to the bed, she on top of him, her breasts bouncing and squashing into him. Kissing again she grabbed his prick and began to rub and squeeze it. He put his hand over first one breast, then the other. The nipples were large and hard and rubbery. He took one of them in his mouth while his hand massaged the other. She moaned encouragingly.

And all the time there was a small voice whispering, *I cannot believe this.*

She took his hand and brought it down to the smoothness and the wetness between her legs. He found time to groan lustfully before resuming duties on her breast. She opened her legs and his fingers found their way inside.

"Kiss me," she said and he took his mouth from her nipple to find her face.

54

"No," she explained and pushed his head down her torso. He shifted position and did as he was told, so that his tongue moved down over her belly and onto her vulva. She tasted slightly of cinnamon, he thought. He began to gyrate his head so that his chin rubbed her clitoris and she, in turn, moved so that her head came between his legs and took his prick in her mouth.

He woke with a start and at once his head was full of the most intense guilt he had ever known. Images of the night rushed through, confused, jumbled and yet vivid, carrying emotional weight that crushed him. Memories of sexual acts that even now caused him to tumesce, tinged with the recalled passion and pleasure he had experienced only served now to deepen his remorse.

How could he have done this thing? He had betrayed Annette, betrayed his children, endangered the safety of his comfortable life. God, if she ever found out. . .

He was alone. Claire must have sneaked out not long ago, for he remembered that they had been busy quite late into the night. Busy in ways he had only ever dreamed of before.

The bed was a mess, most of the duvet hanging off the end, the undersheet rucked and twisted. *Rucked by your fucking.* The thought sounded in his head and there was mockery in his conscience. He lay back and tried to stop panicking. There was no point in getting totally screwed up about it; it had happened and he had enjoyed it. The important thing now was to ensure that it became an enclosed, sealed event. He was in a different place and soon he would be in a different time; this would become the past and it need never live again.

At last he felt able to get up and face the day. It was already nearly nine, so he was going to be late for the day's programme, but he saw no point in rushing. A shower, a shave and a good breakfast. He would creep in at the back, spend the rest of the day absorbing academic knowledge as if nothing had happened, then drive home to Annette and the kids.

Yes, he felt that he could cope with that.

On his way down, he suddenly remembered Claire but this time not as a sexual partner but as someone who was going to be in the same room as him for much of the day. What would she say? Would she feel ashamed of what they had done? Perhaps she ought to. . .

He picked up a Sunday newspaper from reception, then walked into the dining room. As it was Sunday it was still quite full despite the relative lateness of the hour, although he was relieved to see that Claire was absent, presumably working. He chose a table in the corner, his back to the room and, having selected some cereal and ordered coffee, he started to read the paper.

It wasn't long before he was joined.

Alan. The name badge supplied a surname – *Rosenthal.*

"May I?"

Unfortunately he had already sat down with his bowl of figs and his glass of apple juice. He concentrated on his food while Hartmann stole worried glances at him, trying to assess the implications. Why should he choose to sit with Hartmann, now of all times? They hadn't spoken a single word to each other before now. . . before last night.

Yet his face was neutral. He seemed to be taking no interest at all in Hartmann. He was eating his figs and occasionally glancing up, over Hartmann's shoulder, at the other breakfasters. He had exceedingly pale eyes so that the pupils were accentuated, set in a face that was broad and deeply lined. He looked muscular under the expensive suit and he was over six feet tall. He looked, in short, as if he could look after himself and quite easily look after Hartmann, should Hartmann have trodden on private ground. Claire had said that he was homosexual, so perhaps this was a coincidence. True, he didn't look homosexual, but then it wasn't obligatory to mince and wear pink and yellow. Perhaps (and here Hartmann was undecided between alarm and relief) he was making a play for Hartmann.

After a while Rosenthal said, "One should always start breakfast with fruit." Then he continued with his meal. The tone had been conversational.

Hartmann began to relax. The waiter came and Rosenthal ordered tea and bacon and eggs. Then, his figs consigned to the food chain, he leaned back and looked directly into Hartmann's eyes. For perhaps the first two seconds, Hartmann assumed that this was a brief glance, of no more significance than catching someone's eye in a crowd on the station, but it continued. It continued until Hartmann, awash in a rising gush of embarrassment, confusion and fear, was about to ask what was going on.

And then, "Claire is a remarkable girl, isn't she?"

Hartmann understood. At least the uncertainty was gone. Rosenthal had discovered what had transpired and didn't like it. . . although his tone had not been particularly angry. Admiring would have been a more apposite description.

Before he could reply, Rosenthal went on, "I have had her several times myself, and I would suggest that she is the best fuck money can buy."

Hartmann unwound his mouth to protest at this outrageous denigration, then stopped as the implications of the words found their way into his understanding.

"Of course," the voice of sweetness and reason continued (as if discussing a vintage port or a Grand Cru), "she is not cheap. But she is undoubtedly good value for money."

A prostitute? He was saying that she was a prostitute?

His bewilderment lasted little time as he realized what was going on. Bullshit. A kind of petty revenge for Claire finding Hartmann attractive. This brought some pleasure which, alas, was also to prove ethereal and brief. He was just about to argue when Rosenthal fished in his inside breast pocket and produced a photograph. He looked at it, smiled appreciatively, turned it around and placed it face up on the table, just on Hartmann's side. It showed, in remarkable detail and clarity, Claire braced against the wall at an angle, her breasts hanging low, while Hartmann held on to her hips and thrust himself into her from behind. He felt his eyes widen involuntarily and his mouth desiccate as he looked down at it and then up at Rosenthal.

A smile met his gaze. "It is so refreshing and rare to meet a girl who is not only willing to have anal sex, but actually enjoys it. Would you not agree?"

He had in his hand more photographs and these he now dealt out before Hartmann's terrified, silent stare. Hartmann in Claire's mouth, Hartmann in Claire's vagina, Hartmann in Claire's. . .

All of them unmistakably containing Hartmann and unmistakably not containing Mrs Hartmann. Then, as if to prove that this was not some camera trickery, some magical illusion produced by jiggery-pokery (Hartmann was in no state to

57

appreciate a pun), from inside his newspaper he produced a videocassette.

Hartmann could only stare mutely at it, then at Rosenthal, then back down at the video, now resting on the photographs like a paperweight. The waiter came with their breakfasts and Hartmann had to rush to take the small pile of artefacts before they should be spotted. Then, when they were alone again and Hartmann was looking at Rosenthal with a mute question, he was told airily, "Take them. There are plenty more."

"What do you want?" The enquiry came slowly and with a croak, as if his vocal cords were cracked by drought. He held on to his mementoes, comically unsure of what to do with them. Rosenthal was tucking into his bacon and eggs with some gusto.

"Me?" Rosenthal seemed surprised by the question. Then, appearing to consider, he suggested, "How about twenty-five thousand?"

Hartmann was beyond shock and beyond despair. He was looking now into complete destruction and all that was left within him was hysteria. "Twenty-five thousand?" he asked incredulously. "Twenty-five thousand? I haven't even got twenty-five hundred. You've caught the wrong man if that's what you want."

Rosenthal was already shaking his head. He put down his knife and fork and was wiping his mouth delicately on the tartan napkin. "You don't understand. I give you twenty-five thousand." He emphasized the pronouns with appropriate gestures with his knife.

Hartmann was by now incapable of being astonished. His world had, in the last twelve hours, been inverted, upended and then shaken loose from its fixings. He was drifting into areas of the map that he hadn't even known existed. "What?"

Rosenthal looked up from his yolk. "Is that not enough? We could perhaps stretch it to thirty thousand. . ."

"But I don't understand," protested Hartmann. "Why are you offering me money?"

Rosenthal nodded, implying that at last Hartmann was shaping up. "Because we want you to do something."

Illegal, obviously, and when Hartmann voiced this Rosenthal waved his knife again, this time dismissively. "Let us say, merely 'unethical.'"

And Hartmann, as if he had a choice, decided to display some morality for the first time that weekend. "But I can't."

Rosenthal had by now completed his repast, although Hartmann's lay unheeded upon the chinaware. He expressed some surprise at this assertion, as if he had been bitten by a teddy bear. Then a look of weariness stole over him and with a languid smile he asked, "Oh no? Let me see. . ." He frowned as if searching his memory. "Bookmaker's debts of sixteen thousand. Credit card bills of seven thousand. Repayments on the car of five hundred and six pounds per month."

He waited as if there was something that Hartmann might care to say about all this. When he was greeted by silence, he continued. "And there is the other side to all this, of course." He looked from the pathologist to the video and photographs, still in Hartmann's hand, then back to the pathologist. "Mr Justice Brown-Sequard, your wife, your mother. . ."

Hartmann's face felt suddenly cold and stiff at the thought.

Rosenthal went on, "By the way, they are not, of course, the only copies. Indeed that tape is extensively edited – your whole performance was recorded."

Hartmann knew, as he had known secretly all along, that he was going to do exactly as he was commanded. He had no option. He felt crushed and humiliated and, the inevitable corollary, he felt impotent anger that he had been manipulated so easily and thereby made so willingly the fool.

"How do I know you won't send them anyway?"

Rosenthal's face showed tiredness at this. "You overestimate your importance if you think that we are interested in destroying you, Dr Hartmann. We want your cooperation in one matter and one matter only. It would not suit us to take it further."

It took him a little while to find the words but find them he did.

"What would you like me to do?"

Part Three

Eisenmenger had just returned from a long walk when his past found him at last. The weather was gusty, seeming both bright and dull, cold and yet warming; the optimism of spring fitfully leavening the dull depression of winter. His back and legs ached and he was sweating abominably but he was at the same time savouring the feeling of accomplishment. He sat on a bench (placed in honour of *Rosemary Egger, widow of this parish, who died in 1998, aged 93. From her daughter, Mavis*) on the small, triangular green and contemplated the view. Before him was the hill ("tump" as the locals called it) and the ploughed field that surrounded it, muddy and puddled with too much recent rain, while a small copse to its right hid the schoolhouse where he was living, and to the left the lane wound through more fields and copses down to Castleberrow House.

It was a beautiful scene, with no more intrusion from the modern world than a distant rumble of traffic from the main road and occasional forays from training flights of the RAF.

So why couldn't he connect with it? Why was he able to know but not feel that it was beautiful?

He knew that it wasn't familiarity; he had only been staying in the tiny, two-bedroomed house with its grimy windows and damp stains for two months. He knew also that it wasn't in his nature to find such a scene unmoving, for he remembered appreciating other such views, other such pockets of peculiarly English loveliness. Remembered them but could not empathize with them.

He heard the car before he saw it. The wind blew and the wild daffodils bent before it and the smell of the garlic grass came to him. He was getting cold just sitting there and the idea of idleness was still sufficiently novel for him to have to fight to suppress the urge to get up and just be active. In the early days it had been the restlessness that had been the worse thing to deal with. *Do something* his mind kept saying, *Do something*, else you might fall back into the past.

And fall back he had done many, many times. Back to Marie, thence back to Tamsin. Too much had happened to people he had known, for reasons that he couldn't entirely separate from emotion.

His lips smiled. Euphemism; for *emotion* read *guilt*. He had learned that the mind was very good at avoiding awkardnesses. He had learned much about his mind in his attempts to control it, bring it back to him. Much but not yet enough.

The car appeared, slowing then parking in front of the schoolhouse. It was yellow and adorned with a taxi sign. He could only just make out the figure who sat in the back of the car looking out uncertainly at the house, but it was one he knew well. Again he had to suppress memories, associations.

Helena.

The desire to get up and go to her was strong but not strong enough. The stench of muck as it was spread in the field behind him drifted around the bench. The small war memorial in the middle of the green didn't seem to mind so Eisenmenger thought it was probably okay. The tractor's roar became louder; Eisenmenger was by now used to the modernization and thus destruction of the rural myth. He tried to ignore Helena; he knew that sooner or later he would talk to her, but he saw no reason to hurry the encounter.

His palms were itching as they often did and he had to fight the urge to scratch them. He recalled his mother telling him that itchy palms meant that money was coming to him. It was a deep and untainted memory, and thus a pleasurable one.

Helena had got out of the taxi and was still looking at the School House, examining its shoddy outside, half covered with ivy, half with dilapidation. Even from this distance he could see that she was wondering if he could possibly be living in such a dwelling. Surely a consultant pathologist, foremost member of the professional middle classes, should reside in a more salubrious place?

She had presumably told the taxi driver to wait.

The smile returned to his lips but this time there was more than muscular contraction to it.

Why had she come?

That was the question, but a tricky one to handle without treading on mined territory. He had last seen her nine months before when he was still in hospital, the burns still hurting almost as deeply as the emotional wounds. It had been an awkward meeting, but all their meetings, ever since they had first met, seemed to have been awkward. The talk had been small, so desultory as to be turgid, so artificial as to be tasteless. What was it about Helena that had inspired in him such mute desire, such impotent craving? He was aware that she too had tragedies in her past – her parents murdered, her stepbrother accused, convicted and subsequently taking his life – and he was aware also that these events had sculpted a carapace around her, but for the moment he could think only of himself. In the pecking order of those assaulted by life, he reckoned that he outranked her.

The distant figure had rung the doorbell twice. She had stepped back from the house to look up at the two small windows on the first floor. With no response she now turned back to the car, looked up and saw him on the bench. She dismissed the taxi driver with payment and, as it drove off, she began to walk up the curving lane towards him.

She looked good, he decided. He now realized how much he had missed her and that he really liked her very much indeed. Her hair was even shorter, he noticed, and he thought perhaps that she had lost some weight, although not as much as he had.

"There you are!" she called from five metres away. "I thought I'd missed you."

He smiled a greeting but stayed sitting. "Ten minutes earlier and you would have done."

She sat on the bench beside him, perhaps half a metre away but angled towards him so that her knees almost touched his, a pose of concern. *She wants something,* he decided and then, *So what else is new?*

He tried to ignore the tinge of sadness that these thoughts brought.

"You're looking well."

Now that was a lie since he had lost four stone and found to replace them a pallor that he feared the sun would never hide, but he admired the brazenness of the falsehood's delivery. Part of a lawyer's training, he supposed. "So are you, Helena." And he meant it. And he found himself hoping that she heard that he meant it.

"How do you feel?"

What did she want – the truth or the platitude? He reflected that only when asked by a doctor was that particular question answered honestly. He shrugged and that, it seemed, was enough.

"I had trouble finding you. This place is miles from any-where."

From the field behind the breeze blew muck fumes around them and Helena wrinkled her nose. Eisenmenger looked at her out of the corner of his eye. He knew the farmer vaguely – a large corpulent man who was perpetually short of breath and short of money in the way that only the wealthy have – and had grown used to the less romantic aspects of modern agriculture, but clearly Helena still had more roseate notions, despite the two squashed rabbits, now surrounded by crows, that were clearly visible on the road before them.

She said then, "I didn't tell you, but I went to the funeral."

Not that there was much to bury.

"Did you? I didn't."

He knew that he was making it difficult for her, but she had always made it difficult for him. She pressed on through this solid wall of cold indifference. "Nobody blamed you, John."

Why was she trying so hard? Love?

He didn't think so.

He said tiredly, "My problem was never other people's view."

"No, but. . ." she faltered, finishing lamely, "you know. . ."

He did know. Marie's suicide – her spectacular, tortured suicide – had inevitably raised questions about his part in the affair. Just as it was always assumed that a police investigation implied guilt, so Marie's action was automatically linked to his supposed culpability. Even though she had been clearly dis-turbed in the days leading up to the tragedy, the question that recurred in his mind and therefore presumably in everybody else's was, what had happened to make her disturbed? It was that unknown that had played on him in the months since. He didn't know and because he didn't know he wondered where he might fit in. It was only fair that others who had known her might also wonder what part her former lover might have played in the tragedy.

"How are your hands?"

Her question brought him back to the present and for that at least he was grateful. He shrugged. "Not too bad. Getting there."

There were no contractures, a fact for which he was so grateful to God he had sometimes wept, but much of the feeling had gone from the palms, although not from the fingertips. Still, he not infrequently dropped things if he wasn't paying attention. Slow improvement had come and it still continued.

There was a hesitancy about the next enquiry. "What about. . . working?"

And then he understood.

"No, Helena," he said firmly.

She wanted to go for a drink to the local pub, but it wasn't a model village where a microcosm of society was clustered about the village green and the friendly pub landlord had a paunch and five teeth missing.

"The nearest pub's five miles away."

So they had gone back to his house and there he had made coffee without too much difficulty whilst he watched her watch him through the kitchen doorway, and she talked about the relatively few things they had in common.

He brought the coffee in two bone china mugs to the small sitting room. She thanked him, picked up the coffee and cradled it in her hands although he did not think it was cold in the room.

"Are you renting?"

She asked this hopefully, implying that she could not believe that he would have bought such a hovel.

"It's mine."

"Oh."

She looked around, baffled. He wanted to tell her that the atmosphere meant something to him, that its smells and simplicity took him back to before Marie, before even Tamsin, back to his childhood. A place of safety, as simple as that. For the time being he wanted it preserved. Maybe later he would gut it and turn it into a twenty-first-century home.

He wanted to tell her but he wanted more to keep things to himself.

Instead he said, "Having sold the flat, I thought a nice little place in the country. Buying this hardly dented the proceeds."

Another pause. The questions formed on her face as she looked at the dry rot around the windows, the peeling of the paint on the door, the threadbare carpets, but not one of them chose to explain itself.

She said, "Bob's retired."

Bob Johnson. One of the few images of the past that didn't come packed with panic. Bob had always understood Eisenmenger more than most, had seemed unlike most other policemen, both in character and in outlook. Eisenmenger was more grateful to Johnson than he had ever dared to admit. When Tamsin had died in his arms it had been Bob who had been there with him.

"How's his wife?"

"She seems fine. She left hospital about five months ago. They moved and now Bob's working with his brother-in-law."

"What was wrong with her? I never found out."

"She had some sort of nervous breakdown. . ."

Helena's face matched her silence as the words took on their own significances and echoes. He could almost laugh at her embarrassment, enjoying this thing of poise caused to stumble, but the pause lengthened and therefore became intolerable. "And you?" he asked. "What are you doing?"

"Oh, still the same. A bit more criminal work, I'm glad to say."

"And what about a boyfriend?"

Had he mean that to sound so crass? Or had he meant to imply it didn't matter in the least to him whether or not she was seeing someone else?

Helena seemed for a moment to freeze, then withdraw, then make an effort and come back towards him. She wore a smile that was shy and ghostly, gone with a glimpse. "Not at the moment."

He was trying to analyse why he had asked the question and in doing so he allowed his subconscious another sneaky chance at the controls. "Look, Helena..."

She was at once turned towards him.

". . .I know that I should have tried to contact you. . ."

She raised two thin eyebrows. Her lips were a dusky red, her eyes green. "Your choice." There was a tonal shrug in the phrase.

"I'd just like to say that. . ."

Her expression was full of innocent interest and he suddenly realized that she was teasing him again. On her face was the expression of someone who knew precisely what was to be said and knew precisely how much pain there was in saying it. The first time he had ever spoken to her she had begun to tease him and it had made him at once delighted and frustrated. Once again he found himself both cursing her and wanting her. Once again he found himself manipulated and pleased. Once again he ducked out.

". . .that I'm grateful to you for coming."

She was drinking her coffee but over the brim of the mug her eyes were grave as they appraised him. "I should be going," she announced as she placed the empty mug on the table. "I must ring for a taxi."

Yet now she had come, for whatever reason, he didn't want her to go. He had found that he didn't need to hide from all the memories, that some of them were good ones and worth holding. The ones about Helena, for a start.

"What about dinner?" he asked. "We could go into Melbury. There are some good restaurants there and it's only four miles away."

She was looking at her watch. "It'll take me three hours to get back," she said doubtfully.

"You could stay here. . ." And then because he didn't want to scare her he added, "There's a spare room made up."

But whether it was the relative meanness of the accommodation, or whether it was something else entirely, she was shaking her head. He had only one more weapon to use.

"We could talk about this job you want me to do."

He took her to the Chequers, a seventeenth-century inn that was all oak beams, walls that were out of true, and unexpected steps and low doorways. It had enough charm and period atmosphere to satisfy the most demanding tourist, as well as a small bistro in the conservatory at the back that Eisenmenger had discovered was really quite passable.

They sat at a small table next to an ancient, woodworm-riven pillar and he ate a Thai chicken dish while Helena satisfied herself with braised quail. The lighting was subdued, of course but he didn't mind. He had forgotten how enchanting she could look and how enchanted he could be. Although their relationship had never got beyond work, his regret only fuelled his romanticism as he covertly watched her every move.

After the meal they moved from their table to a small lounge for coffee having declined a sweet. They sat in overstuffed armchairs that had cigarette burns in the fabric, and the low table before them was ringed with stains. "So what is it that you want me to do? Another right to wrong?" He had feared that his desire to see her stay had overstretched him, that when it came to pay the price for seeing more of her he would suddenly remember his malaise. Yet he found real curiosity within himself.

Helena leaned towards him confidentially, her perfume suddenly his. Her eyes held the light of the wall lamp behind him.

"It may be nothing, but about a week ago I was contacted by a man called Sweet. Raymond Sweet."

The coffee came. Then, "He had recently lost his daughter, Millicent, to cancer."

"How old was she?"

"Twenty-three."

"And what kind of cancer?"

"Lymphoma."

He nodded. That was reasonable. "So what did he want with a solicitor?"

"He had a complaint against the hospital; it seems that there was a mix-up over bodies and she was cremated in the place of someone else."

"And I take it he didn't want her cremated?"

"He didn't want her interred at all."

He had just taken a sip of coffee and he pulled the cup away from his mouth before murmuring, "Ah." Then he frowned. "Why not?"

"He didn't believe the autopsy report. He said that she had been killed."

He looked at her and she gazed back and he would have enjoyed matters a whole lot more if he hadn't been trying to cope with his incomprehension. "But clearly she wasn't," he pointed out.

"He insists otherwise. He's adamant."

"Is he mad?"

She sought the appropriate words. "No, he's not mad. Driven, I suppose, would be a better word to describe him."

"So who does he say killed her?"

"Pel-Ebstein Pharmaceuticals."

It seemed to Eisenmenger that things were going from the ridiculous to the ludicrous. "PEP? You mean he's saying that she died from some sort of adverse reaction to one of their drugs?"

"Not exactly." She sipped her coffee, her lips hardly seeming to do more than brush the surface of the drink. *Lucky coffee.* "Here."

She had by her side her handbag and from it she now produced a small hand-held dictation machine. She put it on the table between them and looked around as if afraid of being overheard. "I hope this isn't going to attract too much attention," she muttered, then she switched it on.

Intrigued Eisenmenger leaned forward to listen, but all he heard was a hissing, gurgling noise that he realized only after a short while was the sound of someone breathing. The sound quality was abysmal and it sounded as if it had been recorded in the rectum of a whale; then after a primordial age of strange, guttural, bubblings, ". . .*Help*. . ."

Eisenmenger was so surprised to hear anything intelligible that he glanced up at Helena. She was looking at him intently and he thought that he caught the start of tears in her eyes. The voice had been almost alien in its character, the word's meaning completely at odds with the peculiar, half-wheezed, half-gasped sound. It was as if a zombie had spoken.

There were a few more seconds of background before the voice came again. ". . .*Please, help me*. . ." There was agony in those syllables; agony in the speaking and agony in just existing. It was a monster that was talking, a monster born of pain beyond Eisenmenger's power to imagine. Just listening to those words seemed to draw him into this thing's torment.

". . . *Sue?. . . Sue?*"

The name brought humanity. Suddenly he could hear a real person and that only made it far, far worse. He thought that it could be no harder to bear, but then there was a whimper of even greater suffering, as if God had at that time briefly twisted the skewer in her eye. Then,". . . *They lied, Sue. . . It's Proteus. . .It must be Proteus . . .*"

And then there was a sigh and the breathing stopped and Eisenmenger felt peace and relief as he had never known them before.

He looked up into Helena's face and, seeing tears, felt like crying himself.

The pub's chatter went on around them; if anyone had overheard then they kept this to themselves.

On the way back to his house he tried to think, Helena beside him sunk into gloom as well as darkness. The night was clear but dark, with no moon or light pollution to hide the stars. Helena had barely touched her coffee again after listening to the tape; it had grown cold and covered with dark, fragmented skin as they had sat in the lounge and tried to soak up some comfort from their surroundings. It was as if the awful words and the pain-filled breathing had become a pall upon them. Even now he could still hear what had been said and the torment from which the words had been cast.

"Susan Warthin only discovered that message three days after she had found the body?" he asked at last.

"That's right. She'd had the flu. She only made the trip to Millicent Sweet's house because there was no answer when she telephoned. What with the effects of the bug and the shock of finding the body, she was laid up in bed for seventy-two hours."

"And we're sure that that is the voice of Millicent? It couldn't be a hoax?" Even as he asked this he was thinking, *Some hoax.*

She shook her head. "According to the phone company that call came from Millicent's number. It came through at eight twenty-two on the morning of the fourth. Just after Susan had left to go looking for her."

Some idiot in a white Porsche overtook them at speed on a blind bend. The headlights were gone from sight within a few seconds. The road was always being used as a racetrack.

"So presumably Millicent must have heard the telephone when Susan tried to contact her but couldn't get to it before she rang off. In the time it took Millicent to get to the phone and dial her number, Susan had already left."

"That's the way I read it."

He considered this, then realized that he was about to miss the turning. He swung off the main road down the long, serpentine lane that led to the hamlet where he was living. Occasionally brave moths were caught in the car's lights. "I take it she wasn't expected to die from her lymphoma quite so suddenly."

Helena was staring straight ahead through the windscreen. She said only, "She wasn't expected to die at all. When she had gone to her GP ten days before, there was no sign she had anything other than flu."

Eisenmenger glanced briefly at her profile. They passed the duckpond on their left and the car braked outside the schoolhouse. "None at all?" he asked.

She shook her head. "The GP gave her a thorough examination, concluded it was just the flu and advised her to go home to bed with regular paracetamol."

They got out of the car and he unlocked the door. The house was cold and there was the slightest smell of damp in its air. He offered her a nightcap of brandy, which she accepted. As they sat with them in the small sitting room he tried to sort things out in his head.

"So she went from no tumour to death by tumour in ten days." He considered. "Well, it's possible. Certainly there are some haematopoietic tumours that can behave extremely aggressively – acute myeloid leukaemia may and I would guess that Burkitt's lymphoma could do it – but it's still odd."

"Why?"

"Because we have to postulate that the disease process was so rapid that it literally prevented her from contacting anyone about it – her friends, her doctors, even her neighbours. No cancer should do that."

Helena was huddled forwards on the fraying fabric of the sofa. Clearly she found it cold in the room. "I guessed as much," she said. "The ironic thing was that she was terrified of cancer, and yet here she is, dying from it quite suddenly. Presumably that was why she worked in the field."

Surprised, he said, "Did she?"

Helena nodded. "At the Medical School. She was a cell biologist working with Professor Robin Turner in the Department of Cancer Genetics."

71

Why did that make him feel slightly perturbed? He couldn't dissect out the reason for the discomfort he now felt. The scar tissue on the palms of his hands began to itch again. Hands cupped around the glass of brandy, Helena asked suddenly, "Why do you have to have it so bloody cold in here? Can't you put some heat on?"

He feigned surprised, mumbled, "Is it cold? I didn't realize," then bent down before the gas fire to light it with the box of matches on the mantelshelf. He didn't bother to explain that he hated the warmth because the sweat made him aware of his scars.

When it was alight and gently hissing heat into the room he stood and she said, "That was where Pel-Ebstein come in. Before this job she worked for them."

Sitting down as far from the gas fire as he could, he asked, "How long did she work for PEP and how long ago?"

From a slim grey briefcase Helena produced a file. Consulting it she said, "She was with them eighteen months ago, having spent a year and three-quarters there."

"And how does her father reckon that they killed her?"

The warming of the room seemed to be working, for Helena's body was slightly less foetal. "He doesn't know. He's devastated and he's bewildered and he's angry. He can't put together a coherent explanation of why he's convinced that her death is connected to the work she did for PEP, but he's one hundred per cent sure that it is."

It sounded like an exaggerated grief reaction to Eisenmenger. Doctors were used to it; relatives, unable either to explain or to encompass the shock of losing someone close, were filled with rage, rage that was usually directed at the easiest target. Often it was the doctors but not infrequently someone or something else that was peripheral but conceivably involved.

Still, there were undoubtedly odd aspects to the case. . .

Helena said, "When the body was accidentally cremated, you can imagine how that seemed to him."

Feeding the paranoia; solidifying suspicion into delusional reality.

"How did that happen, precisely?"

"There's an internal hospital enquiry going on, but as far as I can determine, two bodies were mislabelled. The undertakers took what they thought was the body of Clara Fox, a road traffic accident victim. The cremation took place on Wednesday morning. It was only when Mr Sweet went to view Millicent on Wednesday afternoon that the error came to light."

Bodies in mortuaries were identified theoretically by at least two labels to prevent such cock-ups – one tied to a toe, the other to a wrist – but often that didn't happen and anyway when undertakers came to pick them up, no one had the time or the inclination to make a detailed examination of a cold, flesh-white corpse. Again it was an entirely feasible error that had been committed before, but Eisenmenger found himself wondering. . .

"I assume you have a copy of the PM report," he said with a faint smile.

Helena returned the smile as she produced some A4 sheets from her briefcase.

As he took the report he murmured, "This seems familiar," but in truth it seemed many more than twelve months since their first meeting at which she had last handed him an autopsy report. He began to read it.

Over the years Eisenmenger had read a great many such reports, had written perhaps a thousand more, and he had seen almost as many styles. Some reports were prolix to the point of boredom, others were so truncated that they were practically negligent. Those written by forensic pathologists tended to concentrate, almost to the exclusion of all else, on the external examination, paying scant attention to the internal organs. Older pathologists, especially when close to retirement, tended to write the same report for every autopsy, having neither the enthusiasm nor the wit actually to find out the real reason why the death occurred.

His first impression was that this one was unnecessarily long, for it ran to four and a half sides and most autopsies could be summarized in two. His first impression, however, was wrong. It was long because it had to be long; every organ system – cardiovascular, respiratory, gastrointestinal, genito-urinary, lymphoreticular and central nervous – had something wrong with it. In fact, every organ system was involved by malignancy.

And, as he read through it, he found himself becoming submerged by disbelief. He read it again, but still it made no sense.

Looking up he found Helena watching him intently. "What's the verdict?" she asked.

He didn't know what to say at first. He opened his mouth, closed it, shrugged and then returned to the report briefly before commenting, "This is unbelievable."

"In what way?"

"She had cancer everywhere. There wasn't an organ in the body that wasn't affected."

"Isn't that what happens in terminal cancer?"

"Cancer can spread but, if we're to believe this report, she was consumed by it."

"And all in the space of a week and a half," pointed out Helena. Eisenmenger looked at her, feeling slightly chilled by the reminder. She said, "She had non-Hodgkin's lymphoma. What is that?"

"It's the general term for a group of tumours derived from the cells of the lymphoreticular system." When Helena made a face over her glass he explained, "White blood cells."

"Ah."

"At the last count there were something like forty different types, ranging from those that are so indolent the patient usually dies of something else before the lymphoma gets them, to those that grow rapidly enough to require high dose, multi-agent chemotherapy in order to save the patient's life."

"Presumably that's the type that Millicent Sweet had."

He was frowning, back at the report. "Presumably," he said but it was a distant polysyllable. Helena waited. She had seen the look before and knew what it meant. After a few minutes he turned back to the front page of the report. "Hartmann."

"Do you know him?"

He shook his head. "Never even heard of him." But under the heading of those in attendance he spotted a name he knew – Belinda Miller. He went back to the main body of the report. "This isn't right," he decided at last.

She waited and he noticed that her eyes were large. The room was now warm and he could feel his scars, feel that because of them he was no longer entirely normal. He tried to ignore the discomfort as he went on, "Different tumours have different patterns of spread. For instance, some types of lung cancer characteristically metastasize to, amongst other places, the adrenal glands; most cancers arising within the large bowel usually go first to the liver. Lymphomas, especially if they're advanced, involve three sites primarily – the lymph glands, the liver and the spleen. This thing has gone everywhere, including both the small and large bowel, the skin and the brain."

"Can't you get lymphomas that affect those sites?"

"You can, but you shouldn't have a single type of lymphoma doing it. These results argue that it was at least three different types of lymphoma, probably five or six."

"Unlikely, then."

"Unlikely and not squaring with his microscopy report." He turned to the last page. "He sees only one type of non-Hodgkin's lymphoma."

She paused before asking, "So. . ?"

He was tired. He became tired very easily these days. "So, why are you showing me this? What do you want me to do or say?"

Leaning forward to put her glass on the table she said gently, "I came to ask your opinion, John. Not just on the report but on the whole situation – the death, the mistake over the cremation, the phonecall. You're good at seeing things, things that other people either don't see or don't want to see."

Flattery and guile. He recalled that she was good at those; certainly better at those than she was at opening up herself. Hesitantly he said, "I think that if I were paranoid, I'd see a conspiracy; a cover-up."

"And if you weren't paranoid?"

He smiled. "I'd still be wondering."

She had her elbows on her knees and her hands clutched. It brought her shoulders together and made her pose one of supplication and perhaps promise. "I need you to help me investigate this, John."

He had known that this would come and, in truth, had been quite looking forward to it, but now that they were there, his fatigue and discomfort felt too strong to be fought.

"Let me think about it, Helena. I'll sleep on it."

Annette met with her father after work in a restaurant some hundred metres from Lincoln's Inn Fields, near her chambers. It was a fairly regular arrangement and indicative of the continuing closeness between them. She was an only child and, although she had always got on well with her mother, it was to her father that she had always preferentially turned. As ever he stood when she came in, as if the past fifty years had not happened, or rather as if he was damned if he was going to acknowledge that they had.

Piers Brown-Sequard had pure, grey hair that was swept back over his head to reach almost to his collar, sharply ridged brows that sheltered dark brown eyes, and a face that was shaped by a thin but prominent nose and a long chin. There was a superadded effect of cruelty given by a scar to the left of his mouth – the result of a cycling accident when he was a teenager – which tended to distort his smile; he found the impression it conveyed useful.

They kissed and he waited while she settled herself before sitting.

"How are you, Annette?" he enquired, then at once, "And how are the children? Over that sickness thing, I trust?"

She hastened to reassure him "They're much better. Back to normal."

He nodded. "I wondered if it was the flu.'

"Just a tummy bug."

They ordered a bottle of Frascati, neither of them apparently interested in Mark Hartmann's health. The wine arrived and they ordered salads. Small talk fell from them like drops of perspiration from a champion racehorse. Then, midway through their meal, Annette said, "I'm worried about Mark, Dad."

The judge looked up at her for a second, then continued to ingest his green stuff. Still interested in the flora on his plate, he asked, "Worried? In what way?"

In truth Annette was uncomfortable with herself. She knew that her father did not much like Mark and she knew also that her father was capable of a considerable degree of callousness – callousness that in the past she had found indistinguishable from viciousness – and she did not want to give him ammunition against Mark. The hesitation produced from her father a reassurance. "Come on, Annette, out with it. I could see that there was something amiss. Perhaps I can help."

He smiled, the distortion induced by the scar, in his daughter's eyes, an integral part of the father she loved. "He's changed," she said at last.

"Changed? How?"

Annette was an advocate and used to language, but this was a situation far removed from the clinical void of her profession and she hesitated before continuing, "Well, he's suddenly got more money for one thing."

Brown-Sequard was well aware of his son-in-law's parlous fiscal state; how could he not be, considering that he had himself engineered it? "Are you sure?"

"He's betting again. That means he must have paid off the bookmakers. Also, he's traded in his car for an Audi roadster."

This information caused Brown-Sequard's silver-grey eyebrows to elevate themselves. Hartmann's previous car had been brand new but a long way from an Audi. "Anything else?"

She considered. "It's his whole attitude. He came back from his meeting in Scotland and for a day or two he was very quiet, very subdued. But now he's changed completely. Half the time he's high, the other half he's really touchy, really nasty."

Her father sighed. He had tried hard to like his daughter's choice of husband, but from their first meeting he had detected something about him that had precluded any warmth between them. He knew that he had always been a strict, almost unreasonable assessor of Annette's suitors, but by any standards Mark Hartmann seemed to him to be a poor choice. His character was weak and he was shallow; also he was prone to panic. Had Brown-Sequard been given the choice, he would not have had him for a son-in-law but no such opportunity had come his way and he had been forced to accept the reality of the situation. Accept it but ensure that it was at least bounded in one or two significant areas by certain contingencies.

Brown-Sequard had no problem with small flaws in a man – he was aware that he had some himself – but those in his son-in-law seemed to be gaping.

Gaping and growing.

He pointed out, "He's hardly likely to take kindly to me butting in."

Annette's face showed alarm. "God, no, Daddy. That's the last thing I want."

He looked at his daughter and remembered that she had once been deeply in love with Mark, but he also wondered if she would now profess to being quite so deeply besotted as once she had been. She continued, "He thinks you hate him. Anything you said would just make matters worse."

He knew that Hartmann had never understood his father-in-law's reserve towards him, seeming to believe that it was a question of social status and breeding, whereas Brown-Sequard saw only the man, saw only that Hartmann had personality flaws aplenty, flaws that signalled danger for his daughter and his grandchildren.

He put down his knife and fork, the salad unfinished. "Then what would you like me to do about it, Annette?"

"I suppose I'd like you to reassure me, tell me that it's all nothing, or something, but I know you won't do that."

"No," he agreed. "I won't."

She sat back in her chair and fingered the stem of the wine-glass. It was wet with condensation. "Do you think he's having an affair? Getting money from some woman?"

He slowly reached forward and lightly put his fingers on her hand. It never occurred to him to hide what he thought. "I don't know, but whatever it is, I think that it means trouble."

She nodded, her mouth turned down, her eyes on the abandoned meal. "What should I do, Dad?"

Her father felt a curious mix of outrage, disgust and exhilaration but on his face there was only concern. "We need proof, Annette. Then we can act."

She said nothing, which was itself an admission of consent. He tried reassurance with a smile. "Leave it to me."

Turner sat in his office and tried to remain calm. It was three days since he had initiated the tests, three days in which it had gradually borne in upon him just how potentially devastating were the results; now he found himself almost paralyzed with nerves. Certainly work was beyond him, as was politeness. He had not found it within himself to be civil to anyone that day, and that included his wife and his secretary. Only the Dean of the Medical School, telephoning with regard to some matter of overwhelming uninterest to Turner, had been spared outright rudeness, although Turner's clipped, somewhat peremptory and telegraphic replies had left the Dean with the quite accurate impression that Turner wished he would just piss off.

And the closer came the time for the truth, the more certain he became of what he would learn. Without any evidence, only untrustworthy, unscientific intuition, he was convinced that what was coming was a monster, a thing that was going to rip him apart, gouge out his heart, and then eat it.

Suddenly he shivered. Where were those bloody results?

And then there was a knock on the door.

"Yes?" he demanded, aware that his voice was loud and hopeful. The door opened and Harriet, the research assistant he had asked to do the tests, came in while behind her could be glimpsed the disgruntled, tight-lipped face of his secretary. Harriet was holding large photographic transparencies.

"I've just pulled these off the developer. They're the tests you wanted done urgently."

He snatched them from her and turned away to the light. They looked like X-rays but there were no bones to be seen on them, only short, black lines strung out in columns. Harriet was speaking. "Everything seems to be all right, except that there's some sort of artefact. It's really annoying. I can't get rid of it. It's present in all the samples, always down at the bottom at five-point-six megabases. . ."

But Turner wasn't listening. He wasn't even looking at the sheets any more. His arm had dropped and he was staring out of the window, although his eyes were seeing a million different things. Harriet continued her monologue for some seconds more before she realized that her audience had left the building.

"Professor? Professor? Are you all right?"

But this plea to the void had not even an echo to give it succour.

"Professor?" She moved towards the head of her department. It was as if he was in a fugue. Gently she touched him as she repeated her call.

Quite abruptly and with an exaggerated start he reacted. For perhaps half a second he seemed confused and then, "What the hell?"

He focused on Harriet as if her presence was an affront. Then he looked again at the X-ray films hanging from his hand by his leg. She noticed that he was gripping them so tightly that his fingers appeared a murky white through their opaque blueness. She noticed too that there were sweat marks on the film.

"Get out!" he moaned. "Please get the fuck out of here!"

She wasn't used to this from Turner and was at first puzzled, then outraged. She began to speak, to argue and protest, but the look on his face was implacable. She pinched her face into silent protest and hurried from the office.

He sneezed violently.

On the Monday evening, Rosenthal was waiting for Hartmann by the third-year noticeboard in the main entrance foyer of the Medical School. He was closely examining the rugby team lists, the crude, amateur posters that advertised discos from weeks ago, the handwritten small ads for flat-shares and the odd official notice. Hartmann only saw him at the last moment – would have tried to avoid him if he could have – and his expression told of dismay and shame. He didn't want to be reminded of what he had done, both at the hotel in Scotland and subsequently in the department.

Rosenthal had a smile on his face as he turned to Hartmann and said, "Brings it all back. The sad squalor of student life."

Hartmann didn't know how to react. In his mind Rosenthal was associated with memories and emotions that made him feel subhuman, yet the man was behaving as if they were the best of friends, as if no adultery, blackmail or professional misconduct had ever occurred.

"Shall we talk? Over here?"

Rosenthal indicated the seats on the far side of the large foyer. Hartmann didn't say anything, didn't even nod, but then he didn't need to, for Rosenthal was in complete command of this situation. He ushered Hartmann to a seat and they sat together. There were small groups of students scattered around, and passing through there was a small but steady stream of students, nurses, porters, doctors and others, but the foyer was large and there was no chance of being overheard. "Tell me what's happening," suggested Rosenthal. "There was a fuss, I hear, about the body."

Hartmann heard the words but couldn't believe them. To describe the furore that had exploded around the department as a "fuss", to encapsulate the unadulterated torrent of grief that he had known over the past few days in such a belittling way, was too much for Hartmann. He was tired and he was worried and he was sick of himself, and suddenly he wanted to make someone else feel miserable too. He grabbed Rosenthal's arm and said, "Fuss'? Do you realize what I've been through? Do you know how much shit's been flung at me? Do you? Do you?"

Rosenthal reacted only by looking down at the hand on the arm of his jacket. He regarded it for a moment, much as a cat might examine a mouse, then raised his gaze to Hartmann's face, who was immediately aware that Rosenthal's arm had no give in it. He could have been holding a prosthesis.

"Get the hand off me, will you?" Rosenthal had the accent of an officer and the manner of an easy-going friend. His words were a request but the look in his eyes suggested that it was a mandate backed by force. Hartmann, suddenly feeling as if he'd touched the Pope, released him.

And, as though it had not happened, Rosenthal suggested, "Tell me."

So Hartmann, unable to stop a little fear of the other colouring his attitude, followed orders once again. He told him of the Wednesday when he had changed the labels on Millicent Sweet's body with those of a similar young woman, as Rosenthal had instructed. He described how the first consequences of this action had reached him when he had had to go down to the post-mortem room and had first seen, then been implicated in, the discussions that were occurring between some undertakers, Professor Bowman, Lenny and Denny. The undertakers were returning a body because when Mr Raymond Sweet had gone to pay his last respects at the funeral parlour, he had been presented with a stranger.

From there it had blossomed. It soon became clear to all what had happened – that Millicent Sweet was now labelled as Clara Fox, that unaccountably there had been an almighty cock-up in the mortuary. The Dean of the Medical School got involved; the Bursar of the Medical School got involved; the Chief Executive of the Hospital got involved. When the Chair of the Trust Board rang up (a man normally so somnolent that he was rumoured to have fallen asleep in front of the Queen when she opened the new wing) it percolated through even the brains of Lenny and Denny that here was major shit.

An internal enquiry was instigated and the press got hold of it. There were even rumours that Raymond Sweet had consulted a solicitor. Hartmann was targeted because he had performed the autopsy – was it possible that the labels had become switched during the post-mortem? Purely accidental, of course.

Hartmann had known that he wasn't being suspected – inevitably Denny and Lenny were the main target of the investigators and inevitably they met this threat with intransigence and profanity – but he had known also that his soul was lost, even as he gave profligate assurances of his innocence.

The upshot of all this was that Raymond Sweet had indeed contacted a solicitor, who had written to Bowman, a serious clinical incident had been declared and an investigative team of one manager, one independent clinician and one lay member of the Trust Board had been convened. Denny and Lenny had come close to offering Hartmann physical punishment since they were convinced that he was somehow responsible, although they could not articulate why. It was a minor thing but one that, in Hartmann's mind, seemed unduly significant.

Rosenthal took no kind of note but his expression suggested he was memorizing the detail. "What was the name of the solicitor?" he enquired. Hartmann took a moment to recall it. "Flemming, I think. Helena Flemming."

"And the letter said what?"

But Hartmann hadn't seen it. Rosenthal seemed disgruntled but he didn't push it. Instead he said, "I want a copy of your report."

"My report? Why?"

Rosenthal smiled. "To make sure that you're keeping up your end of the bargain, old chap."

"I've done everything you've asked me to."

"I'm sure you have. I'm sure you have." But Hartmann understood that he would have to provide the copy.

"You swapped the samples that were taken at autopsy?"

"Yes, yes."

"And the special ones?"

For a moment Hartmann didn't know what he meant, then he understood. The fresh samples that Belinda had taken for genetic analysis. His instructions from Rosenthal had been quite explicit – he was to dispose of all evidence that might suggest that Millicent Sweet had died from multiple cancers and he was to substitute evidence that she died from something else. Hartmann had had to exchange the specimens he had taken for microscopic examination with others from a case of lymphoma, then tailor his report to reflect the new diagnosis. His only difficulty had been with Belinda, since she had not taken to his conclusions easily.

"Lymphoma?" she had said, her voice not so much carrying incredulity as being moulded from its substance. "That was lymphoma?"

Hartmann's nod had been as natural and convincing as he could make it. He did not feel that he made a great job of it. "I know. I couldn't believe it either, but here are the slides. Take them and have a look yourself."

And this she had done, returning an hour later, admitting that he seemed to be right but perplexed nonetheless. It was then that she had asked, "What about doing some molecular biology? We've got those fresh samples, don't forget. I've already extracted the genetic material."

But he had forgotten, and the shock when she said these words was almost sickening. "But you can't!" he shouted.

The vehemence of this caught Belinda by surprise. She wasn't prone to break down under difficulty or stress but the shock of being harangued by Hartmann – someone she considered to be somewhat weak and shallow – unnerved her. "But. . ."

"You had no right!"

". . .But why not?"

And this question, it seemed, was a good one, for Hartmann appeared to have to think about the reason. Then, "You know the rules. The cause of death is known. The Coroner's jurisdiction is over and we can't do any more investigations."

"But is it? I mean, you saw the body. I've never known a lymphoma do that before, have you?"

". . .Oh, yes. On occasion."

But the pause had picked out the lie and Belinda's vision was acute. "I'm sure if we explained to the Coroner, he would allow. . ."

"No!" Again the violence of his refusal was surprising. Perhaps aware that he had overstepped the mark he added more gently, "The coroner has my definitive cause of death. He won't allow further investigation without the permission of the next of kin, and I really don't have the time or the inclination to pursue it."

Belinda knew that this was odd, that this wasn't just another cancer death, and she wanted to argue but he was the Consultant and she only the Registrar. He said, "We cannot justify extracting or analysing the genetic material from this tumour. Please destroy it."

And reluctantly she had nodded.

In the foyer of the Medical School he said to Rosenthal, "Don't worry. It's all been disposed of."

Helena's journey back home was long and frustrating due to a huge points failure in Berkshire causing an hour-long delay. It was unseasonably warm and the air-conditioning in the carriage didn't seem able to cope with her temperature or her mood.

He had refused, and that was bad enough, but there was something else. Something that she now put from her mind. She had undertaken a round trip of three hundred miles only to have him say that he was sorry, but no, he wasn't able to help her. Bloody man. Why couldn't he behave normally? Why did he constantly have to make her life difficult?

The train began one of its sporadic, slow and brief crawls forward and for a few seconds her mind wandered from her anger at John Eisenmenger. He had looked ill – awful, in fact – and there was no doubt that the night's sleep had done him no good. His pallor had become more pronounced and his skin had seemed almost transparent, as if he were covered in a thin, plastic film of exhaustion. Words had been few from him, and those that he found had been for her the wrong ones.

Over a breakfast of fruit and coffee he had said, "I'm sorry, Helena."

"You're not interested in helping?"

He had smiled as if he had heard her tone and understood its purpose. "It's not that I'm uninterested. . ."

"Not interested enough, though."

He shrugged, refusing to react to her jibe. He had dropped his head at once as if afraid that she would see something in his dark-rimmed eyes. For a moment she had allowed her frustration to swell, then she had seen not intransigence but fear in his demeanour and she had understood. Marie.

She hadn't dared mention Marie by name before and in truth she didn't dare to now. She could appreciate how Marie hung over Eisenmenger like a wraith, how her terrible, terrible death had eternalized her so that perhaps he would never be free of her. Certainly as long as the scars from his burns persisted, she suspected that he would have to endure her memory.

She reached across the small wooden table and touched his hand. It was the first time that she had touched him and his head jerked up as if shocked at such forwardness. For a moment he just stared at her hand over his, then his eyes moved up to her face and she had suddenly realized how deeply she could fall in love with him.

If she ever allowed herself to.

As soon as she had seen this truth, it must have shown on her face for his expression had changed to sorrow almost at once and her hand had been lost from the touch.

She had left shortly afterwards, wondering to whom she could turn now.

Turner had always been a driven man, whipped by ambition to ever higher peaks, but always deep down he had wondered if he was being forced away from his past rather than towards his future. An occasion in his childhood when he was perhaps six rested within him like a splinter of metal, unremembered and unforgiving. He had come home from school early, dropped by a neighbour, assuming to find his mother home. She had not been there, although there was no fear of loneliness for his father had been unexpectedly present. Present and standing to attention, in the company (and body) of his sister-in-law, known to little Robin as Aunt Andrea.

His surprise was one of uncomprehending stupefaction, theirs one of comprehending fear and alarm. He had run away despite their calls that he should return, his consciousness filled with certainty that here was *sin*, here was a monumental *wrong*, yet incapable of analysing just what he had seen and why it was so wrong.

He had taken what refuge he could in the garden, in the overgrowth at the back of the shed, oblivious to the calls, first of his father, then of his mother. Only when darkness had given him smothering did he come into the house. If his father was worried about what might be said, he concealed it perfectly as he beat his son slowly, methodically and with enthusiastic grimness. His father had never actually threatened him to keep silent, but the malevolent, burning gaze had been message enough.

And now the memory was gone from Turner's gaze, gone from his conscious attitude to the world, yet from its deep, septic locus it coloured every thought, every judgement that he made. It made him a man who saw those around him as competitors to be, as the world a place to be won. Even now he was running from something, and would be forever.

He had never felt the need for drugs, but desperation, Turner was now discovering, was an opiate. Having entered his consciousness, injected by fear, it now seeped into every synapse and there switched the entire focus of his being around so that every other thought, consideration and emotion were lost, reduced, trampled. His world was now discoloured, his vision distorted, his judgement lost because of the progressive horror of his suspicions.

But he had to know more. Specifically he had to know just how Millicent had died. He strongly suspected, but that wasn't enough. He felt weakened by his ignorance and completely paralyzed by his foreboding. This loss of control was novel, and therefore frightening, and therefore exhilarating.

He had spent the rest of the day first establishing from Professor Bowman that it had been Hartmann who had done the post-mortem and then trying to contact him. This proved difficult but eventually his calls were returned.

"Professor Turner? It's Mark Hartmann. I understand you wanted to talk to me."

Turner suddenly felt his heart squeezing itself like a dying man's fist. He heard his breath harsh and unforgiving as if the devil were listening with tasty anticipation.

Steady now. Don't be too eager. "Yes. I hope it's convenient."

Hartmann had been teaching medical students. He hated teaching, hated medical students even more, and now he had too much work left to do; it was work that he hated most of all. "Of course."

"I understand that you performed the post-mortem examination on Millicent Sweet."

And now, ironically, it was Hartmann's turn to feel apprehension. It suddenly seemed to him that it was unfair that he should be rung about Millicent Sweet's autopsy when he was never rung about any other.

"That's right." He tried to make his voice one of insouciance. He almost succeeded, but Turner wasn't listening to shades in Hartmann's voice.

"She was an assistant of mine and. . ." He knew that he ought to have prepared his speech better – had actually tried in a distracted way – but the tension within his intestine had proved too much. "We're obviously very concerned about what happened."

Hartmann heard only a concerned colleague and was deaf to any other possibilities. "Of course, of course." He paused. "It's actually slightly difficult," he admitted, having decided on the cautious, officious approach, "I'm not really allowed to give out any information. It was a Coroner's case, you see. It's really up to him whether or not to release such information."

Turner hadn't expected this. His plan had been predicated on this being an informal chat between two professionals. "But surely. . ." he began. Then his fears turned his surprise to irritation and the words reflected this as he went on, "For God's sake! It's not a state secret I'm after. I just want to know how she died! Is that too much to ask?"

Actually it was and Hartmann certainly wasn't about to tell him any truth about how Millicent Sweet had ended. He had hoped to say nothing and force this inquisitor to go through the Coroner's Office (who would certainly refuse to give him any information as he wasn't a close relative), but Hartmann now heard professorial anger and the last thing he wanted was a vengeful professor loose in the Medical School. He decided the wisest course was to give Turner the official cause of death and trust that this would satisfy him.

"Well, I suppose it wouldn't hurt. . ."

Turner hastened to agree. "Of course it wouldn't."

"Actually she died of non-Hodgkin's lymphoma."

Turner had at last had an answer. He had been desperately hopeful that one of the rumours had been true, that she had been murdered, that she had taken her own life, that she had had an undiagnosed congenital heart defect. Now he learned that she had died from cancer and the narcotic within his blood at once transformed into turgid terror.

"Lymphoma? You're sure?"

"Oh, yes. Quite sure. It was a very aggressive lymphoma, quite unusual." Hartmann was completely oblivious of the effect that his prattle was having. Into the silence on the other end of the phone line he said, "It must have grown with astonishing speed. . ."

It was then that he realized that Turner had just put down the receiver.

Somewhat disconcerted, Hartmann looked down into the mouthpiece for a moment, as if within its depths he might see the Professor's image and thereby ask him why he had rung off. Alas, no such miracle occurred and he too replaced the receiver, a puzzled look turning slowly to concern.

There was something odd about the call and the reaction and he was beginning to wonder if it was connected with Rosenthal.

What the hell was going on?

Not unnaturally he had asked this question of Rosenthal whose reply had been concise and explicit. "If I ever hear you ask that question again," he had said, his smile stubbornly remaining despite the words, "or learn that you've asked it of someone else, I'll slice your dick off, then I'll stuff it down your throat. And then I'll send copies of the tape to everyone who has ever heard of you."

Hartmann hadn't asked the question again.

At least not out loud, but it reverberated inside his head time and time again. Clearly he had wandered into something potentially nasty, smelly and dangerous, for someone had gone to the trouble of setting him up for blackmail and bribery combined. Tens of thousands of pounds had been spent, and that meant whatever it was, it was big. Men like Rosenthal didn't work for the minimum wage either. Rosenthal had the look and sound of a killer and Hartmann believed every one of Rosenthal's quietly spoken threats. The man was outwardly calm and cultured, but beneath that Hartmann had glimpsed madness. What he said, he would do.

But why? What was it about Millicent Sweet's death that had to be covered up? Why should an ostensibly natural, albeit bizarre, death be such a threat to someone? The question was obvious and, when he had first asked it, apparently unanswerable, but Hartmann wasn't stupid. There was now developing a theme.

Cancer.

At their first meeting, Rosenthal had pointed out that life with thirty thousand pounds and cooperation was far preferable to life without thirty thousand pounds and widespread distribution of the videotaped evidence of his sexual shenanigans. This he had followed with instructions on what Hartmann was to do. He was to rewrite his autopsy report on the death of Millicent Sweet. He was not, Rosenthal was quite explicit, to mention his findings of multiple cancers. Nor was he to suggest in any way that her death had been unnatural (and thereby invoke an inquest). Rosenthal had suggested that she should have died because of a spontaneous subarachnoid haemorrhage and Hartmann was willing to concur with this, until he remembered Belinda.

"I can't put that," he objected, and went on to explain. A brief wash of anger had come over Rosenthal's face, then he had shrugged. "Can't be helped, I suppose," he had murmured and Hartmann had then had the feeling that Rosenthal had momentarily experienced intense, violent anger. Rosenthal had looked up at Hartmann then and asked, "What do you suggest?"

"It has to be cancer of some kind. Belinda saw enough to know that she had massive amounts of cancer."

This had not been received well. Not well at all. Rosenthal had had an aversion to that idea and he showed it. Only after long (and tactful) argument did he accept that lymphoma might be a suitable substitute.

"It's not unreasonable for a young adult to get it, and it can be exceedingly aggressive," Hartmann explained. "Also it should just about keep Belinda happy."

And eventually Rosenthal had agreed. Not happily, but admitting that there was no alternative.

But Hartmann had been struck by Rosenthal's desire to avoid the subject of *cancer*. And now Turner, her boss, had received a dose of the collywobbles when he had heard that Millicent had, officially at least, died of cancer. Hartmann wondered what his reaction would have been if he had known the truth, that she had died from perhaps twenty cancers, all at once, in every tissue of her body.

He looked out of his office window at the monstrous water sculpture, feeling unsafe. His debts were temporarily gone, and he had a newer, even better car but that, now his wishes had come to pass, was scant and hard comfort. The tapes were still there in Rosenthal's possession, and Hartmann could sense greater evils stalking him.

Whatever had led to Millicent Sweet's death was clearly something that somebody wanted kept secret, at any cost, and he, the slightly tubby but – he considered – still loveable Mark Hartmann, was enmeshed in the middle of it all. Firmly clamped in its maw.

Turner put the phone down, almost dropping it on the base set. His eyes saw that his hands were trembling, although his mind was beyond caring. Hartmann's words were loud in his head, their conversational tone strangely at odds with their significance.

. . .*It was very aggressive. . . Unusually so. . .*

Turner had known that if she had died from cancer it was going to be aggressive, and not just because she had been perfectly well a week or so before, but to hear his nightmare articulated brought the dread to leaden, crushing life.

He tried to force calm on himself. It wasn't certain that her death was significant, after all lymphomas occurred frequently in young people, so perhaps it was just a coincidence.

But the question suddenly erupted – could it be *Proteus?*

His mind had a kind of spasm. He realized that he had been preventing the word from entering his consciousness and its sudden, unbidden arrival temporarily shocked him. The word was like a daemon; it had too many bad memories attached to allow rational consideration.

…*Unusually aggressive.*

Perhaps it really was just coincidence.

But then certainty, like a spear, shot through him and he knew. *Perhaps,* be damned. This was nothing other than cause and effect.

He sat back in his chair, staring into space. Then abruptly he leaned forward and picked up from the desk the photographic films that Harriet had brought. The lines across the bottom were still there, of course, and their sight seemed to break him. Suddenly he collapsed, his head on his forearms. He didn't cry but that was only because the overwhelming fear that he now felt was like a paralysis on his emotions.

He knew then that he was going to die. Knew too that it would be in a horrible, horrible way.

But how? How was it possible?

Perhaps in an effort to overcome his terror he forced his mind to think through the events of two years before. They must have fixed the results, but it had been done subtly. Like conjurors they had invited him to inspect their every move and then – *hey presto!* – they had produced the results that he wanted to see.

Except that they had been falsified.

And he and Millicent and the others had gone on their merry way, believing that all was well, ignorant that they had lives that were disastrously foreshortened.

It must have been assumed that their deaths would be too quick to allow them to make trouble and, in Millicent's case, it had been. But not his.

Suddenly Turner found anger within his fear. He sat up and began to think. He was still well and he had proof that they had lied to him. Even if he couldn't escape his fate, he would make sure that he caused the maximum of grief for them.

Oh, yes. With nothing left to fear now that death was coming, he at once felt emboldened to take on the world. He reached for the phone again. He didn't need to look up the number, for it was one he had once known well.

He was starting to get a headache, but in his desire for revenge he thought he could put up with a minor thing like that.

Frank Cowper was worried about the Sweet case. His police instincts had never been particularly good – he had retired as a Chief Inspector after thirty-one years of polishing the brass on his uniform and making sure that whenever faeces and fan collided (as they frequently did when he was involved) he was out of the room, out of the building and preferably tucked away up the Chief Superintendent's rectum – but they hadn't totally atrophied. Nobody avoided trouble as well as he had without being able to smell the sweetness of decay before anyone else.

Hartmann's report for a start. Frank was no doctor but he'd been a Coroner's Officer for over seven years and he'd read a lot of reports, and he'd read this one with some surprise. "Slight redness to the skin," in particular. Who was Hartmann kidding? The girl had looked boiled to Frank's stupefied gaze. And the rest of the report seemed to be downplaying the findings, as if Hartmann didn't want anyone to make too much of a fuss.

Then, of course, she had been accidentally cremated. Just a clerical error, easily done. The letter from the solicitor to the Coroner, expressing concern that the mix-up over labels had occurred whilst the body was legally within his jurisdiction, had been repulsed with a reply that put the responsibility on the Medical School and nowhere else, but it had hinted at deeper things. The letter had gone on to suggest that Mr Sweet had been considering a second autopsy, that perhaps there had been a degree of deliberation in this "error".

Frank had been considering these matters for a while and now he was beginning to wonder and, having wondered, he reached for the telephone and dialled Chief Inspector Lambert. He might, he reasoned, be totally wrong to incubate concern, but equally he might not. It would not do any harm, he reasoned, to pre-empt any possible fuss. If it came to nothing, then he was merely being over-zealous; if it blossomed into something, he would look really rather good.

Unfortunately Lambert was not there and Wharton took the call. Since he did not know her, he was at first reluctant to discuss the matter but she soon made it plain that he was not to be allowed a direct line to Lambert while she was around. Some people would have taken this as a message to piss off, but Frank was made of oilier stuff.

"I appreciate how busy he is," he said, then, "it's Beverley, isn't it?"

Her response suggested that whatever her name was, he was a prick. "Just what, precisely, do you want, Mr Cowper?"

Cowper's brain never stopped calculating advantages and disadvantages, whom to cultivate and whom to cut, when to speak and when to dismiss. Wharton was still unknown, but he had a feeling that she would be a good person to nurture. Accordingly he told her about the mix-up over the bodies, without *actually* implying anything. He also slipped in his vague disquiet about the autopsy report. The overall impression was one of a man just making sure that she knew what might, or might not, be going on.

Beverley Wharton thanked him. Her manner was polite but peremptory; she, too, saw no reason to make enemies unduly, especially so early in her time in this posting. In truth, she would have dismissed the whole thing as irrelevant and a waste of her time, but for the fact that Cowper had mentioned the solicitor's name.

Helena Flemming.

A name from Beverley's past.

She decided then two things; that she would like to look a little more closely into what may be going on with the body of Millicent Sweet, and that she would forget to mention it to Lambert.

Turner had arranged the meeting for seven o'clock in a theatre bar. His problem was that Siobhan had arranged that they should attend a dinner party.

"No, you're not. You're coming with me, as arranged. To the Gilberts'. It's been arranged for weeks."

Siobhan was a determined woman, an Irish streak lending her not only obstinacy but also stridency. She had big eyes, big lips and a big bust; Turner had decided when he met her that he liked bigness. Unfortunately, it appeared that the gene coding for the physical size of such attributes also coded for the size of temper. In their relatively short marriage it had led to not infrequent episodes of explosion interspersing the more intimate moments.

"I'm sorry, Siobhan. It's important." He heard his voice sound terse. God, how he wanted to tell just how important it was. He didn't know how much time he had left. He felt sure that he was getting the flu. He had woken in the night sweating. Sneaking to the bathroom he had taken his temperature and seen the numbers sneak up and up, eventually stopping at just over thirty-eight Celsius. The sight had left him weak, almost unable to move.

"Really important," he repeated.

"What do you mean? Why is it important? Who are you meeting?" Her voice was suspicious.

He didn't want to deceive her. He loved her, loved the intimacy that they shared, loved being married to her. He had come to marriage late and considered himself blessed to have found someone like her in his middle age. "I can't say. It's confidential."

This paradigm of lameness temporarily discomforted her. "Confidential?" she said at last. "What does that mean?"

And he had been forced to shrug his shoulders, seeing anger flaring in her eyes and afraid that it would soon scald him. Yet she had seen something in this gesture and in his whole demeanour that checked her anger and turned it to concern. "Robin? What's wrong?"

"Nothing."

She put her hands on his shoulders, one of their private displays of love. "Please, Robin," she insisted, putting her head beside his. "I can see that there's a problem."

He smiled, an effect that was spoiled to destruction by his jittery behaviour and the wateriness of his eyes. "There isn't. It's just a meeting with. . ." the pause was brief but destructive of sincerity ". . .a potential sponsor. May be able to donate upwards of a million."

She knew it was a lie but fear stopped her from denouncing him. "What's his name?"

"I don't know," he said and, aware that it sounded pathetic, he continued. "It's Pel-Ebstein."

She frowned. "Didn't you used to work for them?"

He nodded. "Yes. That's how I've made the contact."

She knew that there was a lie somewhere in his words but her suspicions were tempered by the fear she could see within his words. He continued, "It shouldn't take too long, Siobhan. I'll join you at the Gilberts' a bit late, that's all."

She had reluctantly agreed, as he kissed her cheek and hugged her.

Feeling lousy, a discomfort growing in his chest, an ache in his limbs, Turner ordered a large gin and tonic, then sat at a table near the door of the theatre bar. The drink was gone quickly, another also proving transient. A third lasted longer, taking him past the appointed hour. It was only the fourth that produced company for Professor Turner.

The man that sat down opposite him was familiar, but he had by now consumed enough ethanol to be significantly slowed in his reactions.

"You." This vowel served as a greeting.

Rosenthal smiled. "Me," he agreed. He was dressed in a black leather jacket, the buckle hanging down to the ground. He wore leather gloves that he did not take off.

Belligerently, Turner pointed out, "I wanted to talk to Starling. Not you."

"You got me." Having disposed of that issue, he asked, "What's the problem?"

Turner found himself propelled by gin-soaked fear of what he suspected. He leaned across the table to put his face close to Rosenthal's. "Proteus, that's what."

Rosenthal could scent dread and trouble, and began to calculate likelihoods, but nothing of this reached his face. "You're shouting, Robin."

"Don't you call me Robin! To you, I'm Professor Turner."

Rosenthal's voice was monotonic, his face passive. "I'd forgotten that you'd been elevated."

Turner sneered. "Don't forget it. It's Professor now."

Rosenthal pointed out gently, "Perhaps you shouldn't forget who facilitated the chair."

Turner was too inebriated for a moment to react. "Perhaps you shouldn't forget what I know."

"Meaning?"

Turner coughed, finding that it hurt. The room was warm, but then it was full of people and the night was mild. Perhaps it meant nothing. . .

"Get me another drink," he ordered. Rosenthal nodded once, a look on his face that was inscrutable. When he brought back the drink, he said, "You're upset."

Turner looked at him in owlish disbelief. "Upset?" he demanded. "Upset? You can bloody bet I'm upset!"

"You're shouting again."

Turner had downed the drink in the time that it took for the four syllables to hit the air. He hissed at Rosenthal, "You think I'm shouting now? You wait 'till I've finished."

Turner's words were only confirmation of what Rosenthal had suspected ever since Turner's histrionic, voracious call. He could have abbreviated the conversation at any time, cut into the heart of Turner's bluster to ask what he was after, but he was keen to find out as much as he could about the circumstances of Turner's suspicions.

"Perhaps you could actually tell me what this is all about."

Turner looked as though he would have quite liked another bolus of ethanol, but he at last consented to divulge the source of his agitation. "You lied to me."

"About what?"

Turner reacted badly. His voice rose high and loud. "Don't, Rosenthal. Don't. If you want to play stupid games, I'm quite willing to oblige. Would you like me to start shouting here and now? Words like, "Proteus," perhaps? How about "Pel-Ebstein Pharmaceuticals," followed by "The death of Millicent Sweet?"

Rosenthal smiled, his hands raised in supplication. "Okay, okay. I get the message."

"No!" Turner contradicted. "I got the message. You lied to me. You told me the tests were negative."

Rosenthal judged it wiser to concede the point. "And you've discovered otherwise."

"Too bloody right I have! And suddenly I wonder how and why Millie died."

"Your conclusion?"

Turner's anger flared again. He leaned forward and poked his finger into Rosenthal's shoulder while a snarl distorted what he was saying. "My conclusion is that Proteus killed Millie, and that maybe I'm next. Maybe this cold, this flu or whatever it is, might just be the last sniffle I ever get."

Even while he was speaking and emphasizing the points with jabs he was aware that he was prodding something that didn't give, that Rosenthal's face was passive like a waiting lion's, and that his words were not threatening, certainly not to Rosenthal who had seen the worst of humanity's depravities. He was not a naturally aggressive man.

"What would like me to do about this situation?"

"Situation? Situation?" The volume was increasing again. "You call this a 'situation'?" There was an indistinct slur to the word, no matter how often he repeated it.

Rosenthal shrugged. In retrospect it was an error. Turner took it badly. His voice rose even higher. "Listen, you bastard! I want money. I want lots and lots of money. I want more money than I've ever thought it possible to own." He was attracting attention. Rosenthal ignored the glances of the increasingly numerous crowd. "And if you don't, I'll do a bit more shouting. To the papers, to the television, to whomever else would like to know."

Rosenthal made a decision then. He said quietly but earnestly, "Okay, okay." He looked around. "You've made your point. We obviously need to talk, but not here."

Turner stared at him. "You're just trying to put me off!"

"Not at all. It's clear that you have a grievance against us. . ."

Turner laughed. "Oh, that's good. A grievance. This is a *situation* and I have a *grievance*." Suddenly he lurched forward. "Did you take lessons in understatement?"

Rosenthal said only, "Would you like another drink?" He

didn't actually wait for an answer. Turner asked as the glass was put in front of him, "Why?"

"I beg your pardon?"

"Why? Why did you do it? You should have told me." Rosenthal noticed again that Turner seemed to be taking a somewhat self-centred line on things.

"It wasn't my decision." Not the truth, certainly, but Rosenthal considered the truth to be a parallel universe rarely intercepting his own. "I'm sorry."

Turner's expression didn't exactly convey acceptance of this proffering, but he didn't react quite as violently as he might have. Rosenthal went on, "You clearly have not only a moral right to some form of compensation…" Turner nodded fiercely, "But also the means to enforce compensation."

"That's the least of what I'm owed. What we're all owed."

Rosenthal was smiling; Turner had calmed down. He could sense success. "Very well. But we can't negotiate here."

Turner was now distinctly drunk, "Where, then?"

Rosenthal stood. With a smile he suggested, "Somewhere private. Why don't I take you to Mr Starling? He's the one with the authority to give you what you want."

If Turner was suspicious, he failed to show it. As he stood, he was swaying noticeably. Rosenthal said, "I'd better drive."

"What about my car?"

"You can pick it up when we've finished." He walked out and Turner followed.

He led him out on to the street where his car was parked. Turner got in and Rosenthal drove off. He cut across the city, eventually ending up outside a multi-storey car park near the Medical School. He turned in with out pausing, driving straight to the top floor. Turner was dozing and it was only when the car stopped that he awoke and realized where he was.

"What's going on?"

"I've arranged for Mr Starling to meet us here."

Turner accepted this. They got out of the car and began to walk towards an impressive Mercedes in the far corner. It was dark and so impossible to see whether or not it was occupied. They were nearly at the car, walking side by side, before Turner's befuddlement cleared enough for him to realize that this was all slightly odd.

He paused in his stride, then turned to Rosenthal. "What's Starling doing up here, in a car park?"

The answer he received was not the one he expected. Without saying anything, Rosenthal grabbed the cloth of his jacket sleeve from behind – careful not to take flesh in his grip – first the left then the right. Before Turner knew what was happening he was being propelled forward, towards the edge of the car park. When they reached the metal fencing at the edge, Rosenthal released one hand, bent down, gripped Turner's ankle and upended him with insolent ease.

He turned away from the scream.

Eisenmenger had sat looking at the letter for a long time before finally deciding to open it. He hadn't even moved it from the dirty, ever-damp carpet behind the front door, as if merely touching it would shift it from potential to concrete, from irrelevance to stinging account. He had heard it at once, although he was out at the back by the bird table, as if the slight sound of stiff paper falling to the floor was so odd, so sinister that significance had amplified the sound and struck alarms in his mind. He had not received mail in all his time at the schoolhouse, other than the unsolicited dross that every house, whether half-derelict or half-completed, had to endure. The very existence of the letter was profound. No one wrote because no one knew that he was there; no one except Helena, and Helena would not write without good reason.

And there was only one good reason. He knew what it was, at least in a vague way, knew that opening the envelope would prove decisive and would release a power over him, power that his seclusion for the past months had partially nullified.

He made himself a cup of tea while it lay on the mat, not looking towards it but aware of its presence, as if it were a rat that had crept in and he were trying to fool it into a sense of security before killing it with a sudden lunge. During this time he kept asking himself why he was so afraid, so suddenly emotional – it was only a letter, and possibly not even from Helena – but the answer that came, and kept returning, was not one that he felt comfortable with.

Because he loved her.

He had loved her since perhaps the first day he had met her, back when he was still with Marie, back when he had been able to pretend that was not in some way damaged. And this admission could not be allowed because it meant guilt; guilt that Marie's death had not been the meaningless act of a self-pitying and self-deluded woman, but an inevitable consequence, at best of his own selfishness, at worst of his deliberate but unconscious decision to cast her off in favour of Helena.

Yet all this was not the worst of it, for the letter that lay there stark and angular, was also a reminder that he was afraid of loving her. He did not even have the relief of her indifference, for she seemed to find him not only attractive but also useful; useful to find out who had murdered Nikki Exner and now apparently useful to find out if Millicent Sweet's death was straightforward.

And so he delayed picking up the envelope, while he sat in the small sitting room and drank his tea and tried to tell himself that he had the choice not to open it, while a voice that was surely his own sighed words of pity at this fallacy. Yet still he thought to escape or at least temper his fate. He told himself that he had to weigh options before committing an irrevocable act. He had to control his fate, not submit to it.

Abruptly he stood up and almost without consciousness he strode across to the envelope, picked it up and tore it open. It felt at once both like folly and like redemption, like both the bleakest and the brightest of futures.

Inside was a handwritten note and that made him happy because it was not typed; with it was a newspaper clipping reporting the death of Professor Robin Turner who had fallen from the top of a multi-storey car park. No one was yet sure if it had been accident or suicide, although the police were apparently satisfied that there were no suspicious circumstances. Helena's note said;

John,

Millicent Sweet worked in Robin Turner's laboratory. I haven't officially seen the autopsy report but I understand that he had cancer, too. I have spoken with his wife – he had

had a check-up three weeks before and he was told he was one hundred per cent fit.

Helena.

Not much of a billet doux but he found himself gripping the paper as if it were a proposal of marriage. Once again he felt warmth that she had written, cold that she had not written enough, despair that she had written of the wrong things. He looked again at the note. So Turner had cancer, too. Did that matter? A medical had missed it – so what? Helena clearly had seen significance, but Turner was presumably of an age when cancer could not be considered surprising, and it was entirely possible the tumour had been small and occult. Or perhaps he had lied to his wife, perhaps he had been told that he had cancer and the short step off the multi-storey car park had seemed the easiest way to face the future. There were many explanations of this particular concatenation of circumstances.

Yet Millicent had had cancer and now she was dead; same too for her boss, although he had died in a fall. Something, nothing and somewhere in between. Was it enough to make him leave his exile?

The tea was cold, as was the room, and with the cold came the smell of damp. Suddenly everything was revolting to him and a feeling of disgust arose within his soul; disgust at his self-pity, disgust at his surroundings, disgust that he should again feel want for anything at all, let alone Helena. He told himself that Helena was using him, as she had used him once before, yet that made no difference and this realization only added to his self-loathing.

He stood up, knocking the coffee table so that it jerked up as if rearing at his carelessness. For a second he wanted to screw the note up and fling it across the room but he found that he couldn't. Couldn't even do that, so weak was he.

In total despair he picked up the mug and flung that instead, so that it cracked apart against the far wall, the tea forming jagged, black-flecked streaks that wove drunkenly away from the point of impact.

Even purgatory was not to be his.

Part Four

Eisenmenger had expected Raymond Sweet to be small, perhaps decimated and therefore crushed by grief. He couldn't decide where this impression originated, wondering if it was something that Helena had said, although in truth he could not pinpoint any precise words she had used to suggest it.

The reality was different. Millicent Sweet's father was large; large and composed, but composed into incandescence, defined by his anger and his disbelief that Millicent was dead. Eisenmenger could see that those three words had corroded him, eaten into him like a parasitic grub, and now all that remained was the anger, girded by determination.

He worked as a building labourer, the weather having blasted him, cursed him and then kissed him with its burning lips, the work having left him strong and hard and quiet. His wife had died five years before -"Blood poisoning," he said, "following a dog bite" – and, although he gave forth no more details, it was clear that he had seen Millicent's death as the second half of a terrible, terrible bane, a misfortune beyond all others. In this light, the subsequent loss of Millicent's body was only another strike against him in what had become his personal battle with a malignant fate.

Perhaps, Eisenmenger wondered, he was right. Certainly it had given him an overwhelming presence, an aura of quiet dignity.

Raymond Sweet was frowning and staring at his knees. "Millie was terrified," he murmured. "Scared shitless."

Eisenmenger glanced at Helena before asking Sweet, "How do you know she was so scared, Mr Sweet? I mean, what did she say to you?"

Sweet continued to stare downwards at the leather patches on his olive green cords. "It was when she got sick. She kept saying that she was afraid she was going to die."

"When she got sick?" Eisenmenger enquired. "But I thought that she died in her flat. You mean she died at home?" He looked at Helena but before she could explain, Raymond Sweet was talking, as though his mind was softly stroking tender memories.

"No. Millie died in her flat. I never saw her after she left me the last time – about five months ago."

"Then what do you mean. . ?"

"She rang me. The day before. . ." He paused. When the pause started it could have been to remember, but as it continued, it became clear he recalled things only too well. Eventually he whispered, through a sniff, "Millie rang me to tell me that she was unwell. It was then that she said she thought she was going to die."

Eisenmenger thought at once, *This is a waste of time. She got the flu. Felt awful and said the kind of thing anyone might say.*

Sweet was openly crying now. Eisenmenger felt exposed to something secret, felt as if he were blaspheming by bearing such witness. "But that was probably just an expression, Mr Sweet." Eisenmenger tried to be gentle. "Just something she said because she felt so awful with the flu."

"No. It wasn't like that."

"How can you be sure? It's the kind of thing anyone might have said, if they felt really under the weather."

But their client was adamant. "She meant it. Millie knew she was going to die."

"From cancer?"

A nod, but nothing more. Eisenmenger looked to Helena for help but she was looking at her client, staring at him as if trying to see some overlooked speck of truth in his face. She asked, "Why do you blame Pel-Ebstein, Mr Sweet?"

"She worked there."

His voice was so full of certainty it was nearly bursting.

"But what else?" persisted Helena. "There must have been something to make you think that they were responsible for her death."

He found it difficult to articulate why. In his mind it was a fact, incontrovertible and therefore unrequiring of substantiation, that her early death was linked to her time at Pel-Ebstein. Eventually, as if he had spent the intervening moments leafing through a dusty archive, he said, "She was terrified after the fire, when she came home. She said that she was going to die."

"When was this, Mr Sweet?" asked Helena.

"'Bout two years ago."

"What was her job at Pel-Ebstein?"

"Research." This with more than a sheen of pride. He even sat up a little straighter.

Eisenmenger said at once, "Do you know what type of research?"

But Millie's father didn't. Research was research was research.

"Did Millie mention the term 'Proteus'?"

Not that he could recall.

"Do you know whom she worked for? Who her boss was?" Eisenmenger persisted.

No.

Eisenmenger subsided and Helena, when she had finished writing, asked, "Do you know which laboratory she worked in?" PEP had facilities up and down the country and throughout the world.

"She worked on an island. In Scotland."

But he had either never been told or he had forgotten the name.

"What did she tell you about the fire?"

Nothing of substance. It had been a large fire, destroying a substantial part of the facility, but beyond that. . .

"Was she burned?"

"No."

Eisenmenger looked up at that. "Why was she sent home then?"

Raymond Sweet, he noticed, was sweating, as if he were trying to hide something, but they both knew that his distress grew from grief, from the memories they were coaxing back into sad existence. "Because they closed the laboratory."

Helena expected Eisenmenger to pursue the matter, but he had sunk back into reverie. "It must have been a bad fire," she remarked, at which Sweet merely shrugged. Helena had the feeling that they had found all the diamonds that were to be dug from this mine. "But it was from that time that she became convinced she was going to die?"

"That's right. As soon as she came home, she said she was afraid she was going to die. I asked her why, but she wouldn't tell me any more."

"What did she do about it? Did she consult a doctor about this? Have tests?"

"She didn't need to. PEP did 'em."

Eisenmenger jerked his head up at that. "Really?" he asked.

"Oh, yes. That was what reassured her. She said the tests were negative."

Helena looked up from her notes. "But you don't believe that now."

Raymond Sweet snorted. "At the time we both thought that was end of it. But now I know different. They lied."

He began to cry again, his head down, shaking slowly from side to side. "They lied," he whispered.

They had no more questions that mattered, but he still had a surprise for them. Just as Helena was ushering him out, he asked, "Do you think that I should try to get into contact with Carlos? Warn him?"

"Carlos? Who's he?"

"Friend of Millie's. He worked at the laboratory as well."

After Raymond Sweet had gone, Helena got more coffee. While she was gone, Eisenmenger looked out of the window, onto the courtyard three stories below. Her address had improved, he mused. When first they had met her office had been on the high street of a decaying suburb, but now the postal code numbers were lower, the distance to the seat of government considerably reduced. The air was calm and patrician and far removed from all that was depraved, deprived or just despairing. It felt to Eisenmenger as if Helena had homed here.

The office, too, was considerably plusher, considerably more ordered, as if Helena herself, having come to a place of sanctuary, were now more relaxed, more confident. The furniture was new, the clutter was gone and there was less dust; much less dust. Even the potted plants looked happier and more inclined to survive.

Helena returned. As she put down the coffees she remarked, "Well."

"That's one of the reasons I gave up clinical medicine.

104

Irritation with patients. It doesn't matter how closely you question them, how carefully you build the picture, they nearly always hold back some vital piece of information. It's as if they just want to play games."

"Clients are the same, as you've just seen. Sometimes it's wilful, but usually it's just humanity's endless ability to exasperate."

She poured cream into the cups and proffered one to him. "The question now is whether he'll be able to find a surname and an address."

"Even if he doesn't, we've got enough to be going on with, for now."

"So you'll help?"

He smiled. "Let's just say I'm intrigued enough to look into what happened."

The smile she returned, one of relief and (he dared to think) genuine pleasure, was broad. "Good," she said. "I'll write at once to the Medical School about your enquiry. Let them know you're coming and in what capacity."

"Fine."

She then said, "I've also written to Pel-Ebstein."

Surprised, he looked up. "Really? To what end?"

"To ask them for details on Millicent's employment with them."

"You really think it's connected to her death?"

She shrugged. "The client does. That's really all that matters. He'll expect me at least to have asked."

Eisenmenger allowed a small smile out for an airing. "I guarantee you'll get nowhere. Even without commercial confidentiality, they'll clam up if they so much as suspect that you're trying to demonstrate some form of liability."

"Maybe." She sounded surprisingly positive. Suspicious, he asked, "Do you know something I don't?"

From the file she produced a letter, which she gave to Eisenmenger. "The reply came this morning. They want a meeting."

He looked at her for a moment. The sweetness of her smile was as good as a scoreboard proclaiming her small victory.

The letter was from Benjamin Starling, the Head of Biological Research at Pel-Ebstein, inviting her to attend his office on the seventeenth.

"Sometimes the direct approach works," she remarked.

He sighed, accepting defeat graciously. "You win."

"I'll need you there. Can you come?"

As if he had sixteen other commitments that day. She went out to copy the letter for him and when she returned he asked, "How's Raymond Sweet paying for this? The fees, I mean. He doesn't look as if he's got more than ten pounds to his name, and he certainly doesn't have the brains to earn much."

"Mrs Sweet was considerably brighter than her husband, I think. At least she had the sense to arrange life cover for the pair of them. Her death left him quite well off."

"And obviously she passed the IQ onto their daughter."

"Apparently."

They sat and finished their coffees. The silence changed imperceptibly but surprisingly rapidly into one that was faintly embarrassing, as if they both had things to say, and both had reasons for saying them. At last Helena asked, "How are the dreams? Are you still having them?"

He shrugged. "Now and again." True but misleading. Three times a night and worsening, Marie would come and burn before him. Before – before Marie had turned fire into hell and life into ashes – it had been another victim who had haunted him. Little Tamsin, burned beyond life by her mad mother, had died in his arms and had somehow come to represent something to him, something significant but elusive of analysis. Marie's self-deluded sacrifice had wiped Tamsin from his sleep, erasing her but leaving her own scratched scar. Tamsin had somehow been comforting – innocence destroyed – but Marie's shade was negative through and through, sapping something from him.

Why was she returning so frequently now? Was it because he was edging back into life, into pathology and crime, or was it (as he feared) because he was reminded now of how beautiful Helena was, and how much he wanted her.

Eisenmenger said, "I really think, if you agree, that. . ."

She looked at him over her cup and it was as if she knew what he would say. Her eyes were large. He couldn't see her mouth. There was a pause and he was just about to ask her out to dinner when she said, "Formalize the agreement? You're quite right. At least this time we're both going to get paid."

106

And the moment passed.

Helena was not one of life's shoppers. To her it was not a pleasure but a distressing need, like having one's hair cut, or urinating. It got in the way, it took her from other matters; it brought her out of the world she had created into the one she had chosen to abhor. It was not that she disliked food – she loved to eat well – merely that shopping exposed her, displayed her (or so she felt) before those whom she did not know and therefore did not trust. It was because of this that she tended to hurry when shopping, and this hurry extended to her exit from both the supermarket and the car park.

Thus it was that she ran someone down.

It was, even the victim admitted, a low-impact collision, but nevertheless it sounded distressingly solid to Helena in her car, and it produced a sound that was half-cry and half-imprecation from outside. Helena stopped reversing at once and swore under her breath. She got quickly out of her seat and rushed to the rear of the car, very afraid at what she would see.

She had recently been involved in successful litigation in which her client had sued for damages in just such an incident; he had suffered a fractured hip as a woman had backed out of a parking space of a gymnasium. Not unnaturally she feared that here was some form of cosmic vengeance. In fact, the scene that met her somewhat fearful eyes was not as bad as it might have been. The victim was just rising, apparently suffering no permanent injury; he did not even seem particularly put out.

"Are you all right?" she asked anxiously. "I'm terribly sorry. . ."

She shut up, partly because of the legal training, partly because he was holding up his hand and grinning. "Not at all," he said, "My fault entirely. Should have been paying more attention."

He brushed from his trousers some gravel and dust but then straightened quickly with a sudden intake of breath and a grimace.

"Are you all right?" she asked.

"Just a twinge," he reassured her. He had, she decided, an attractive face. He smiled. "No harm done, I'm sure."

She could – should – have turned away then, except she didn't. It was an important decision, although she didn't yet know it. Instead she said, "Look, how about a drink? It's the least I can do."

He hesitated, then grinned. "Why not?"

Eisenmenger was renting a mews house. It was hideously expensive and not much less damp than his previous abode, but it had been all he could find on a short timescale. His savings, although not small, were not large enough to sustain this sort of outlay for long, and soon he would have to ask Helena for an advance on his fee or live on the streets.

God, he was tired.

Marie again. In life she had been clinging, hysterical, vindictive, and death had brought no respite for those she had loved. She came to him in his sleep, continuing the possession of him that had become her obsession wreathed now in flames, silent except for the crackle of fire and the sizzling hiss of burning fat, and he would awake and fight a guilt that he knew should not be his. Eventually he knew that he would have to resort to tablets, but he clung on to normalcy – at least his version of normalcy – as long as he could.

He had returned from the meeting with Raymond Sweet and, bottle of wine on the table before him, he now lay on the sofa, his eyes staring upwards to the over-ornate mouldings on the ceiling. Proteus. He knew it mainly as a bacterium. He also vaguely recollected something about a genetic disorder and something about Greek mythology.

He sat up abruptly, then got to his feet and went to the table by the window, where the sunlight was forming a distorted rectangle, a trapezoid of illumination, crossed by the ugly bars that help both to ensure his protection and to ensure that he felt imprisoned by the nefariousness of others. He put on the table a laptop computer, plugged it in and connected it to the phone socket. When it was powered up his first act was to search an on-line encyclopaedia for references to Proteus.

He found thirty-one.

Proteus– a gram-negative bacterium, the most important clinical aspect of which was that it could cause septicaemic shock that was frequently fatal.

Proteus – one of the Two Gentlemen of Verona.

Proteus – one of the minor moons of Neptune.

Proteus – the genetic disorder from which John Carey Merrick, the "Elephant Man," suffered.

Proteus– in Greek mythology, a god who had knowledge of all things, but who was reluctant to divulge what he knew. He could assume any shape and as such was considered to be made of the basic substance of the universe.

Proteus – a cave-dwelling salamander.

They went on, increasing in obscurity as they decreased in any possible relevance. He looked at the list, saw nothing that gave him stunning enlightenment.

He left the encyclopaedia and went on to the official Pel-Ebstein website. It was superbly done and told him everything they wanted him to know, little that he wanted to find out. His only revelation was in the breadth of their reach. He had assumed that they were merely a large pharmaceutical company, but a name once again proved misleading. They claimed interests in everything from food production to alternative energy research. They even owned a bank.

He then started trawling through all the other references to Pel-Ebstein; there were four hundred and fifty-eight. Some of them were unrelated, but the majority of them were openly hostile, mostly either because of perceived environmental damage or because of possible/probable vivisection. The most interesting was one that accused PEP of involvement in the arms trade.

His last enquiry was using an on-line medical database. Here were listed all the original papers, reviews, medical leading articles and case reports, from everywhere in the world, in every language. It was updated weekly.

He searched for Millicent Sweet, found four papers, one published in quite a prestigious journal; the last of them had been three years ago and related to work she had done for her BSc. Then he searched for Robin Turner. Forty-three papers came up, some of them in the top-rated journals. One of them had been published only four months before.

He looked up from the screen, out to the cobbled mews outside. He could hear the distant sound of the traffic, found that he enjoyed the contrast between that and the quiet around the private lane where he lived. Sweet and Turner were not linked, at least academically. Were they linked by their deaths?

He disconnected from the internet, then found a pad of paper on which he wrote a series of questions.

Was Millicent Sweet's death natural?

If not was it related to her time at PEP?

Is Turner's death a coincidence?

What is Proteus? Just a code-name? Just the gibbering of a dying girl? Does it have relevance?

Lots of questions, no answers. It was early days, but for the first time he began to wonder just what they might be facing.

Eisenmenger didn't know Patricia Bowman except by reputation, and that reputation was not of the best. She had long been condemned in the small world of pathology to the grey lands of *mediocrity*, a place far more damning than anywhere that Beelzebub ruled. Neither silence nor gossip was a refuge from this drizzle of mild contempt (*Of course, she's never really published anything major*) but presumably the advantages that came with a chair – the title, the headship of the department, the increased salary – were sufficient in her view to outweigh the snide comments and the silences. Perhaps, Eisenmenger mused, she dismissed the lack of respect as driven by envies and jealousies.

"I don't really understand," she said to him as he sat before her impressively professorial desk in the office that was, as it should be, large and cluttered. "You're a pathologist, aren't you?"

But she did understand, her tone suggested; he was in the wrong role. Even if she didn't know who he was (and that, too, carried an implication that he was nothing of much import if she didn't know him) he was at least above being an investigator, a *snoop*.

"That's right."

"Then why are you interested in the Sweet incident?" Her small, greying head with its unattractive face and thin, almost gossamer hair that no amount of hair products would ever assist, bobbed in incredulity. Eisenmenger caught the phrase, *Sweet incident*, and played with it. One man's tragedy was another professor's incident; it sagged beneath the overtones of irrelevance and unregard.

"Because her father's solicitor is a friend of mine. She asked me to look into it."

Bowman leaned back in her chair. She was just a little too petite to make this an imposing gesture. Behind her a portrait of some famous pathologist or other stared into the room. "It was fully investigated at the time. The funeral directors didn't check the labels. They had somehow become transposed with those of another body; they should have checked but they didn't."

Eisenmenger might once have felt intimidated by the title, the office and the tone, but not now. Now he was too replete with tired melancholy to allow any room for fulmination. "I didn't think that they ever admitted liability," he said. Bowman ducked this with an airy, "Nevertheless, the Medical School and the Coroner are satisfied that that is what happened."

"And how often do labels become transposed like that? One I can understand, but for both the wrist and the ankle labels. . ."

She leaned abruptly forward as if a spasm in her back had brought her sudden pain. "The mortuary staff were reprimanded."

Eisenmenger felt detached from Bowman's clear determination to put a stop to this nonsense. In the two weeks since Helena's note had arrived he had stopped sleeping and begun waking in dreams. He was tired, both of not sleeping and of pathetic, self-important nonentities like Bowman.

"All the same, if I could see the report of the enquiry," he persisted. "It would be a lot easier than doing it through more. . . legal channels, and Miss Sweet's father is surely morally entitled to see it. . ." Bowman breathed in as if going to argue, then seemed to collapse. Bereft of words she waggled her head slightly as if to say, "Well, maybe."

"And then there's the matter of the post-mortem," he pointed out.

Another frown. Frowning, he mused, did her no favours. Her already contracted features became pinched into near non-existence; goblinesque, he decided. From this mask came the words. "What about it?"

He reflected that it was like taking a poor student through last year's forgotten course work. "Just a few points. For instance, I don't really understand the final diagnosis. According to the report she died of non-Hodgkin's lymphoma; Burkitt's to be precise. Yet even for Burkitt's lymphoma it was rapid and aggressive – don't forget she was apparently fit and well a week before she died. I think it's reasonable for the diagnosis to be reviewed." He paused, smiled and then went on, "And of course there may be genetic implications of this diagnosis which are of grave concern to her family. It may prove necessary for further investigations to be undertaken."

This last argument had impressed the Coroner sufficiently for his permission to be granted to Eisenmenger. Not that there were any known familial factors in Burkitt's lymphoma but Eisenmenger was glad to see that Bowman wasn't entirely sure about this. Certainly she didn't argue the point.

"It's most irregular."

He had no desire, no need and no compunction to reply; the statement might or might not be true but it didn't alter the fact that he was fully entitled to do as he requested. In any case, he had learned over the past few months not to be afraid of silence. It was Bowman who surrendered first; with a sigh she stood up and said, "Very well, then." Her tone was one of irritated acceptance.

She led him out and Eisenmenger had to admit to being impressed that such a small, such an unattractive and unprepossessing figure could radiate such aggravation; it felt like being scolded by a slightly eccentric primary-school teacher. Through the secretary's office and thence into the dingy brown corridor she led him. He looked up and down the subterranean, sublit expanse and reflected that all departments of pathology were like this; most were considerably older but all were soulless, all were uninviting of humanizing influence.

"Where would you like to start? I'll have to get a copy of the enquiry report from the Bursar's Office, but in the meantime perhaps you should meet Dr Hartmann."

He nodded assent. He had a shrewd idea what Hartmann would be like, how he would resent the intrusion and its implied incompetence or perhaps negligence, but Eisenmenger was aware that it had to be done; not to do it would only be another source of ammunition for Bowman. And the same would be true when he came to visit the mortuary. Eisenmenger knew that talking to the mortuary staff was no more than a formality – they would insist that nothing had been done wrong, that they were innocent, no matter what the truth – but he also knew that not to do it would be seen as a dereliction of proper procedure. In a way he was questioning people merely as a cover, for if something untoward had happened by design, then he doubted that his interrogation of any of the participants would expose it. It was the autopsy result that interested him.

"Professor Turner's dead, too, isn't he?"

Perhaps asking her if she had haemorrhoids or did it doggy fashion might have brought her up more quickly but Eisenmenger reckoned it unlikely. "What in heaven has that got to do with anything?"

Her tone suggested she feared he was going to start questioning her entire practice. Insecurity seemed to be all that kept her functioning, and perhaps it was the only glue that was adhesive enough to hold such disparate parts together. "Nothing. Just a bit of a coincidence – after all, they worked together and then within a few weeks they're both dead of cancer."

"He died of falling off a building."

The wittiness of the reply surprised Eisenmenger. He had assumed that she would be incapable of more than the mundane, prosaic thinking that was ubiquitous in medicine and science. "Of course. I meant. . ."

"Yes, he did have cancer," she interrupted and he saw for the first time a more typical professorial, condescending style. "In fact I think he had familial polyposis."

She turned and was walking before he could say anything more. As he caught up with her they turned a corner into an identical corridor; the effect was disorientating as if time had flicked back and they had made no progress. A door opened to their right and ahead to allow out a young man and woman in whispered conversation punctured by occasional muffles of laughter. Eisenmenger saw a scowl on Bowman's face as she stared at their backs; perhaps joviality was not a departmental policy. It wasn't until he saw the woman's profile that Eisenmenger realized who she was.

"Belinda!"

She looked up and she might have grinned a large grin had she not then caught sight of Bowman. "Oh, hello." Her companion, clearly regarding valour and discretion as indivisible before God, nodded recognition of his departmental head and hurried off.

"You know each other," surmised Bowman, her tone one of disapproval. When Belinda said nothing, Eisenmenger explained, "We worked together once."

Bowman frowned, then understood. "Of course, St Benjamin's."

To Belinda, Eisenmenger said, "I'll see you later. How about a drink?"

Belinda smiled and nodded. Before she went into the room her eyes smeared off Bowman like they might have done off spittle. That left Eisenmenger with Bowman looking at him as if he had just confessed to membership of a badger-baiting society. "Belinda's an excellent pathologist," he ventured, to which Bowman merely said, "Really?" and carried on towards the mortuary.

They found Hartmann in his office. Bowman hardly knocked and perhaps this was unfortunate because the door opened to find their quarry at his elbows on the desk, his face enveloping his hands. He looked as if he were overcome by something, perhaps grief, perhaps mere exhaustion.

Eisenmenger knew nothing of Hartmann. He had looked him up in the Medical Directory and found nothing that distinguished him from the herd – no honours, no prizes, no research degrees, no prestigious former appointments. It didn't mean that he wasn't a competent, possibly excellent pathologist, but it had made him wonder. When he had phoned colleagues with questions, they had been similarly ignorant of Hartmann and his achievements. No one had anything bad to say, but it was as if Hartmann were transparent, a hole; you knew he was there because he occupied a position, but there was nothing more to be said about him, no further description could be made.

Eisenmenger smiled and held out his hand with a murmured, "Hello," when Bowman introduced him. Hartmann too smiled but it was not a creature of grace; it skitted, like a new-born faun and, in similar fashion, fell down completely before another second had died. His handshake was wet, warm and weak; Eisenmenger felt it would be presumptuous to judge anyone from their handshake, felt too that it would foolish not to. Hartmann dropped his hand and he now stood behind his desk, both arms hanging, looking for all the world as if he were awaiting the noose around his neck.

"I've said that we will give Dr Eisenmenger all the cooperation he requires." Bowman's tone suggested she considered this an act beyond Christian duty. "These things are very tedious, but we have nothing to fear."

Well, maybe she didn't but Hartmann's reaction to the phrase was interesting. He briefly closed his eyes – for a moment it looked as if he was about to faint – then opened them to look out from a face of grey pallor.

"Oh, no," he whispered, but Eisenmenger had the idea that this was not agreement but despair.

Helena had booked the day off, for which she was extremely grateful. She didn't feel that she could work, not feeling the way that she did. The problem was that she couldn't decide how she felt. Different, certainly, but the acknowledgement that she had experienced a change did not assist her in defining what that change was. Also, she recognized that this was something *new*; of that she was certain. The third parameter she could assess was that this appeared to be good.

She wrestled with this peculiarity for much of the day while she worked on some papers at her father's old, oak desk in the study. Eventually, though, she sighed and sat back, chin down, a frown on her forehead. She had fought against the inevitable all day, but enough was enough. Helena was too intelligent to refute the undeniable; there was only one conclusion.

She was falling in love.

For years since her parents' murder and the subsequent suicide of her brother she had avoided emotional entanglement, This had not been a deliberate decision, merely a side effect of the trauma she had suffered. For a long time after the terrible days of her bereavement she had been in an unstable equilibrium of mental health, and part of that balancing had involved the severance of all outside contacts that could in any way affect her emotionally. She had withdrawn all her roots that tapped into other's lives, clamping down so that she presented to the world the smallest possible profile, and within that profile she had suppressed everything that was not intellectual. Only in this way had she survived, but there had been a cost.

She knew that some of her colleagues had used less than complimentary epithets about her. "Frigid" and "dyke" were the favourites. It followed a standard course – the attempted seduction, the rebuttal, the hurt pride, then insults, usually behind her back – and it had happened several times. The first time, she had been devastated by the virulence of the reaction, and time and repetition had failed to reduce the shock. She still found herself incredulous that human beings could be so unpleasant, especially so unpleasant in such an underhand way. Why couldn't they see that she was still normal, even if she didn't want to form a "relationship", that she wasn't interested in "relationships"?

So she had lived an abstemious life and been quite happy. Not everyone, she told herself repeatedly, needed sex. The men that she met never quite seemed to fulfil what she needed, and what was wrong with that?

John Eisenmenger had come close, she had to admit. She had felt something with him that she had not experienced before with other men. It had bothered her at first, this attraction, and she had spent many hours trying to analyse it. She had decided that part of it was his diffidence; so few men seemed able to accept that not all women wanted to be taken by full frontal assault, and John had somehow managed to convey interest combined with an acceptance that she might not want to reciprocate. This, combined with his obvious intelligence and an air of frailty and injury, had proved a potent mix.

Unfortunately it had been a potent mix of circumstances that had conspired to disrupt the tentative, fragile bonds that they had formed. The death of Marie before his eyes, especially in such a horrifying way, had induced in John a breakdown that had been complete, sudden and severe. There had also been an inevitable breakdown in their friendship; Helena had tried to keep in contact, to behave effectively as someone loving and loved, but she had known all the time that this was not a role she could make hers, not at such an early stage in their relationship. Eisenmenger's silence following Marie's death had only increased the sense that it was over. In such a cold climate, all tendrils of contact had withered.

She smiled and within her she felt a chill laugh. What a pair of emotional cripples!

And now along had come Alasdair. Ironic, really, given that she and John had only just got back in contact, and that she had felt again the old affection for him.

Alasdair whom she had known for barely three hours and in that brief time had managed something beyond belief. He had made her want him.

Just a small feeling – infinitesimal almost – but she knew it was there, and the knowledge perplexed her. How had this happened?

Certainly he had the same courtesy that in John, at his best, had secretly delighted her and made her willing to consider lowering her shield for a better look. And if Alasdair had taken that and pushed it gently one step further, then it was only a minute increment.

He was handsome, certainly, but not strikingly more so than John.

He was clearly very bright, but she had seen John work his way through a murder, seeing things that other, equally experienced pathologists had missed, and she knew that he, too, was exceptionally clever.

As far as she could tell Alasdair and John were equally respectful of her, equally well read and equally easy-going.

On an objective level, they were almost clones; which left only the subjective.

If Alasdair had an advantage, it was one that sprang purely from the non-intellectual, non-logical part of her mind. It was a part of her that she had hardly used for many years, part that she had considered almost atrophied to uselessness.

She wasn't sure if she liked its re-emergence as a force within her, but it was clear to her that it could no longer be ignored.

"What do you think of Hartmann?"

Eisenmenger had taken Belinda to small pub about a quarter of a mile from the hospital. It was her second suggestion after he had vetoed the Medical School bar as too public. Not that he would have chosen this place for either its decor, its landlord or its customers.

Belinda hesitated, which alone was eloquent.

"This won't go any further, Belinda, "he reassured her. "Do you know why I'm here?"

She was almost embarrassed. "The juniors haven't been told officially, but the rumour is that there's been a complaint against him."

Which might explain her reluctance to speak. Life as a pathologist, as any kind of medical practitioner, was punctuated by being complained about and having to investigate others who were being complained about. It was such a tight circle

Eisenmenger wondered why there weren't all giddy. "Not quite," he said.

He was drinking a pint of bitter – at least someone had had the honesty not to dub it with the sobriquet of "best" – and she an orange juice. The pub was filling up and with the people came noise and warmth and smoke. "It's a question of a single case. Not a complaint, just a query or two."

She seemed relieved. "Which one?"

"A PM. The Sweet case. I think there was a hospital enquiry."

Immediately her look of anxiety came back. "Oh," was all she said.

"You know about it, of course."

She nodded.

The first thing he had done after his meeting with Hartmann was to ask for the slides and the tissue blocks from the Sweet case. Then he had sat down and checked that each block and slide was correctly numbered with the number of the Sweet autopsy. Only then had he looked at each slide under the microscope.

All were of a tumour that had the morphological characteristics of Burkitt's lymphoma. Unsure of whether he was relieved or even more confused, he had leaned back in his chair and stared at the ceiling. How had Burkitt's come to present like that? So rapidly and with the skin involvement? Skin involvement was unique.

After perhaps fifteen minutes he had returned to the slides. This time he wrote a report on each individual slide, this time he noticed what was wrong. Not the one thing that was wrong but the cumulative burden of small incongruities.

Hartmann had taken samples of skin and had reported on them as being involved by the tumour, but in none of these slides was there evidence of epidermis or dermis, the constituent structures of skin. The same was true of the brain, the lung and the heart; all the slides and blocks labelled as showing these organs contained tumour but they could not definitely be said to be the organs themselves. Of course, he argued because he was a cautious and reasonable man, they could not definitely be said not to be the organs, for mostly these blocks showed nothing but tumour.

And then there was the lack of further investigations, nothing to confirm the conclusion that this was Burkitt's lymphoma.

Caution again guided Eisenmenger. If it had not been an autopsy case, if this had been a biopsy and the patient still alive, the lack of confirmatory tests would have been criminally negligent because the therapy for Burkitt's lymphoma was far stronger and more dangerous than that of other tumour types. But this was not a living patient; not to do more work was poor practice, but not completely inexplicable.

Again he stopped and sighed, again he stared for a long time at the ceiling.

Then he began again to examine the slides.

And this time, for the first time, he noticed that there was something actually and completely *wrong*. The slide labelled "lung" had a thin band of muscle, degenerate and almost completely obscured by tumour cells, running along one side.

Which meant that it wasn't lung because lung didn't have bands of muscle in it, although small intestine did, which was the classical site for Burkitt's lymphoma.

Suddenly Eisenmenger felt very elated, very intrigued and very sorry. Once more he went through the slides and, now that he knew what he was looking for, he found three other slides that were almost certainly small intestine, although they had been labelled differently.

He turned slowly to the blocks, his head full of wonder. He picked each one up and examined it minutely. They each bore a unique identifying number corresponding with the Sweet autopsy. On one – only one – he saw that another number had been previously erased. It was a section of lymph node.

The case had been faked.

All he had to do was find out why, which was the reason he sat now with Belinda and tried to find out a little more about Mark Hartmann and, knowing what he knew, why he found Belinda's reluctance to speak intriguing. "So, what do you think of Hartmann?"

"He's. . . okay."

"Okay as what? A pathologist, a human being or both?"

"As a human being he's fine. He's probably the most approachable consultant we've got."

"But as a pathologist he's not going to ignite the world."

She shrugged. Words, it seemed, were too powerful a magic to be used at this point.

He tapped the table with a beer mat, thinking. "He's not a lymphoma pathologist, is he?"

Perhaps feeling on safer ground she said with more confidence, "Up 'till now he's just been breast, but he's recently taken on lymphoreticular." This strange construction and phrasing, so wide open to misinterpretation that it could have accommodated a pantechnicon, made perfect sense to Eisenmenger. "And would you say he's a good pathologist?"

But again she was unwilling to say, which was sad but clear testimony on the point. He admired her loyalty.

"And yet he made the diagnosis of Burkitt's lymphoma. Not an easy one to make. Certainly not with that presentation." He looked up. "Did he show it around? Send it away for an expert opinion?"

"I don't think so."

He waited a moment, idly looking at a ruddy-faced, emaciated man who was sitting alone at the bar drinking steadily from a glass of Guinness. Eisenmenger suspected he would be there at closing time, just as he had been there at closing time for a thousand or more nights before.

Then he turned to Belinda. "I had a look at the case today."

He paused and looked at her but she didn't react. She doesn't know, he decided; her reluctance was not borne of guilt.

"He's fabricated it," he said simply.

Again he found reassurance in her response. She was astounded. Her eyes widened and her face became almost slack with the shock of his words. "What do you mean?"

"What I say. He's concocted the set of blocks from other cases of Burkitt's. I expect if you searched on the computer database for Burkitt's over the past ten years and looked for the blocks, I bet you'd find some of them missing."

"But why? Why would he do that?"

The obvious answer would be because he didn't know what the real diagnosis was, but Eisenmenger was always wary of the obvious. It explained so little more, like why didn't he just show the case around if he didn't know what the tumour was? And why did Eisenmenger so profoundly suspect that the convenient disappearance of Millicent Sweet's body was closely related to all this?

"I don't know, Belinda, but it's why I need to know what Hartmann is really like."

And then she told him. Told him of his mediocrity and his lack of confidence, told him of what she had seen at the autopsy on Millicent Sweet's body.

"More than one tumour?"

"More than twenty, from what I saw. Dr Hartmann seemed to think that there were multiple tumours as well. He was wondering about a cancer syndrome."

Not unreasonable, so why suddenly concoct a story?

"Have you read his report?"

She didn't like the question; Eisenmenger saw that in her eyes as they dropped their gaze to the table and her hands as they fidgeted. "Have you?" he asked again.

She nodded; a quick, jerked action, perhaps to get it past the radar.

"And?"

Slowly, she admitted, "It wasn't quite the way I remember it."

Somehow he had suspected as much.

"When did he change his mind?" His drink was finished but as the beer had been flavourless, lifeless and almost beerless he wasn't inclined to repeat the experience. Belinda's orange juice was still two thirds there.

"The following week. He said that we'd been mistaken. He said that he'd looked at the tissue samples and they showed Burkitt's. He showed them to me."

"Can you remember the day of the week?"

She pursed her lips. "Tuesday, I think."

The post-mortem had been carried out on Friday. Between then and the following Tuesday, something had happened to make Hartmann falsify a Coroner's post-mortem and thus endanger his career. The very fact of this made Eisenmenger intensely curious, without even considering why it should have happened.

He drew a long breath; he had a feeling she wasn't going to like what he had now to say. "Belinda, I need a favour."

As if she had guessed, her eyes held suspicion and anxiety. "What is it?"

"I want you write down what you remember from that post-mortem. Everything. Especially what you saw in the body."

She began to protest, shaking her head and twice saying, "No."

He cut through her refusal. "It's important, Belinda. It won't go any further, I promise, but I must have some idea of what the true autopsy findings were."

She didn't look convinced but she wasn't protesting any more either. Into this stretched veil of uncertainty he said only; "Please?"

At last she nodded and he smiled his gratitude.

Then, as they were leaving, he asked, "He didn't take any other samples, did he? For frozen section or suchlike?" It was asked out of weak hope and for completeness, but it made Belinda stop suddenly, just inside the pub door, where someone had carved the words "Grentz is a git" down the frame.

"He made me destroy the samples!" She said almost with wonder and he didn't know what she was talking about. She had to explain. "I persuaded him to take samples for molecular biology; samples from all the different tumours. I had put them into digest to extract the genetic material but he made me destroy them."

It certainly seemed to be more evidence of Hartmann's culpability but apart from that. . .

"He said that now we knew the cause of death, the Coroner wouldn't allow any further investigation."

Quite correct. The rules were strict. Unless it was to determine the cause of death, no tissue could be retained for analysis; if Hartmann had been interested in doing further research, he would have required written permission from the next of kin.

Eisenmenger said, "It's a pity, but it can't be helped. Those samples might have been very interesting to look at. . ."

"But you don't understand," she insisted, "The samples in digest were destroyed, but they were only half of each tissue piece that I took. Those are still there, in the deep freeze. . ."

Hartmann found that he couldn't work that afternoon. Two registrars had come to his office with work for him to check, but he had sent them away claiming that he was too busy, despite his melancholic presence behind an empty desk. By his microscope the EQA slides were still piled, the top ones gathering a light coating of dust, whilst on the other side there was a tall pile of his reports from two days before, still awaiting correction and approval. He knew that he had to prepare a lecture to be given in two days, and there were six letters still awaiting his reply. Yet despite the pressure of this accumulation of un-done tasks he did nothing. His mind was tethered by his crimes and the dread that they were gradually, inevitably, being uncovered, tethered by a leash that was not only short and unbreakable, but becoming shorter and sharper with each day, so that now it was cutting into his neck, strangling his ability to function.

He was becoming nothing but guilt, every moment's thoughts directed solely to explanation and justification of why he had done those things, why he carried no blame or responsibility; and yet every moment's thoughts were also small pebbles of further guilt adding to the weight and adding to the self-loathing. He had passed the stage of attempting to act normally, even with Annette, and was now submerged into what was almost a fugue, where the external world impinged only in a woolly and muffled way, and where the internal world had assumed nightmarish, surreal characteristics; where silence and taciturnity were both his sanctuary and his torment. He only talked with the children at any great length, and then his conversations were soaked so thoroughly in self-pity and self-disgust that even they must have wondered what was wrong with him.

Eisenmenger's arrival in the department had seemed to him like the start of the end, the event that heralded his eventual immolation, but only after a long, slow process of pain and misery, public humiliation and private hatred; a time in which the anger and bitter enmity felt towards him by Annette and her family would only be superseded by that which he felt for himself. Twice he had walked to the door of the room where Eisenmenger was working, ready he thought to talk, to confess as if Eisenmenger were not only a judge and therefore an executioner but also a redeemer. Yet he had gone away both times because he had still harboured a hope that his subterfuge might work, that he might have obliterated the traces of his crime; and the act of his going away, of turning away from confession and thereby redemption had only added to his sense of desolation. He was beyond hope and beyond goodness.

He left the department at five and was home by six-thirty, no longer caring how much time he spent with Annette and the children. He was just closing the garage door when from behind him came a soft, cheerful, chilling voice.

"My dear chap. How good to see you."

Hartmann turned to find Rosenthal. There was a smile on his lips that Hartmann found far more frightening than any scowl would ever be. Hartmann said nothing, feeling the fear liquefy his soul. Perhaps Rosenthal failed to notice Hartmann's pallor, the way his lips trembled, for he asked, "How are things? I was worried. Thought it best to pop over and see you."

He looked up at the large residence behind Hartmann. "Lovely place."

Hartmann at last found a voice, although it was not his normal one. "What do you want?"

Rosenthal expressed surprise. His reaction suggested shock, even affront. *What a suggestion! Why would I want something?* He said, "Why, nothing at all. I merely called to make certain of your happiness. Ensure that you – and your lovely wife and children – have no reason to. . .fret. "

The sentence was full of nuance and inflection, its meaning warped away from the words.

For a moment Hartmann wondered what to do. Tell him about Eisenmenger and risk perhaps anger with all its consequences? Or keep silent, risking then that Rosenthal was already well aware of the situation, that this was a test of his loyalty? The dilemma lasted perhaps two beats of his heart, beats that passed in time like aeons, then one fear overcame the other and, "There's been someone in the department. He's been asking more questions."

"But I thought the matter settled. The internal enquiry. . ."

"This is different. He's a pathologist. Employed by the father's solicitor, I think."

Rosenthal lost the smile, but none of the menace. He was, thought Hartmann, forever threatening of extreme violence, as if this fulmination was his skeleton on which the flesh and the sentiency hung.

"A pathologist?"

Hartmann nodded, thinking that he should have kept quiet, that clearly this was unwelcome news. Rosenthal said, "I trust that there is no chance that he will uncover your little. . . subterfuge?"

And the question could only be answered in the negative, for any other answer, Hartmann knew at once, would prove disastrous. He nodded, trying to construct confidence out of nothing.

For a short while Rosenthal stared at him from eyes that had lost everything except a dark coldness; then suddenly he smiled. "Well then, old chap. What is there to worry about?" He put his hand on Hartmann's back; it was a gentle hand presumably meant to comfort, but Hartmann felt only the touch of a killer.

"When will it end?" asked Hartmann. He addressed the question as much to God as to Rosenthal, but only Rosenthal replied.

"Don't worry," he said, the smile returning. "I'll take care of things."

He turned and walked away and Hartmann heard him whistling cheerfully. It took Hartmann five minutes to stop his heart speeding and his fingers trembling. When he finally walked through the front door, Annette came from the sitting room and asked curiously, "Who was that man you were talking to?"

Hartmann opened his mouth but he was so flustered nothing dropped from it for what seemed like a day. "He just wanted directions," he lied. "To the police station."

He dropped his head and walked quickly upstairs, aware that the lie behind him lay ugly and unwanted before Annette. He didn't see how her face contorted as she tried to stop screaming at his back, screaming out all the anger and fear. And when no sound came because her upbringing denied her such directness, she squeezed back tears and turned away, whispering again and again, "What's wrong, Mark? What's going on?"

Eisenmenger didn't feel that he wanted to wait. He had questions and Hartmann was the one with the answers. He called into his office early the next morning; Hartmann, though, was late and Eisenmenger found the office empty. He decided to remain and spent the time looking around Hartmann's office. He didn't exactly snoop, but there was enough disorganization with papers, slides, journals and personal effects all scattered around on various surfaces, for him to feel that he was just idly flicking through things that were clearly not private.

Which was how he found the bank receipt. Thirty thousand pounds paid in two weeks before.

"What the bloody hell. . ?"

Eisenmenger's first impression was that Hartmann looked tired, but then he realized that wasn't the half of it. Hartmann looked moribund, completely emptied of life. He looked as if he had spent the night awake, as if something terrible were stalking him from the darkness of his closing eyes, as if hell beckoned him from a future that was already decided.

"What are you doing in my office?"

"Waiting for you." Eisenmenger didn't want to believe Hartmann had knowingly changed the post-mortem findings, but the chance discovery of the paying-in receipt removed the only major question – why.

Eisenmenger viewed pathologists as the long stops, forming the last line of defence against negligence, malpractice and even murder. They were the ones who told the clinicians if they got it wrong, where they got it wrong and possibly how not to get it wrong again. They helped to spot the trends in death and disease, so that the nursing home down the road, where just a few too many grannies were ending up with broken hips or badly bruised arms, was looked at by the authorities with increased interest. They set off the alarm when the man found dead in his flat turned out on closer examination to have an unexplained skull fracture.

If Hartmann had deliberately covered something up about Millicent Sweet's death, Eisenmenger knew that the ramifications would be deep and wide. He wasn't inclined to allow Hartmann to indulge in spurious indignation.

"Have you been snooping around my office?"

He had considered having a nice friendly chat with Hartmann, letting him explain the findings – if he could – one by one. Hartmann's tone, though, decided matters differently.

"You falsified the findings of Millicent Sweet's autopsy," he said simply.

Hartmann opened his mouth but it was his eyes that spoke. They widened slightly and Eisenmenger saw that they were slightly bloodshot, and very, very frightened. A brief but eloquent pause, then, "No, I didn't. Rubbish."

One denial would have been enough; the second merely diluted the first.

"The slides and blocks that you claim are from Millicent Sweet's autopsy have been taken from another post-mortem."

"I don't know what you're talking about." Hartmann had taken to shaking his head. He had come into the heart of the room and taken a defensive position behind his desk, his briefcase in front of him, a look of indignation plastering his face like a mudpack.

"She didn't die of Burkitt's lymphoma. She died of multiple cancers."

"Prove it." It occurred to Eisenmenger that with that remark Hartmann might just as well have confessed all. He stood up. Debating whether to bring up the thirty thousand pounds, he said, "What I can't figure out is why you did it. Why cover up the cause of death?" He frowned and his voice dropped, as if he had forgotten Hartmann and he was ruminating alone. "It's not as if she died an unnatural death. Multiple cancers are unusual, but they're not a reason to bury the truth. Exactly the opposite, really. . ."

He looked up as Hartmann, who was still trying to look furious, tried again. "This is preposterous. She died of Burkitt's. . ."

He was like a man constantly repeating his order at the bar, constantly ignored. Eisenmenger suddenly seemed to come back to what Hartmann was saying. He said in what was almost a bored tone, "It's perfectly obvious she didn't. The blocks have been tampered with. And then there's Belinda. She saw the autopsy, don't forget."

"But she's only a registrar!" protested Hartmann. "What does she know?"

Eisenmenger sighed. "She's a better pathologist now than you'll ever be," he pointed out succinctly.

For perhaps half a second, perhaps only a quarter of that, Hartmann looked as if he were going to detonate. His face flinched into a sort of spasm that was gone from view at once, like a summer night's shooting star seen from the corner of the eye. He breathed out, his frame almost collapsing and, instead of conflagration, there came only repetition. "Prove it," he repeated weakly.

Eisenmenger shrugged. "Very well," he said. He was turning, perhaps slightly more slowly than he needed, when Hartmann asked, "What do you mean?" The panic was unmissable.

Still moving away from Hartmann, Eisenmenger said over his shoulder, "I'll prove it. I'll do DNA analysis on the blocks from the Burkitt's lymphoma and on the fresh tissue taken at post-mortem. I'll compare them and show that they're not the same."

He was at the door by the time Hartmann said, "But those samples were destroyed!"

At last Eisenmenger turned. His eyebrows were raised as, with a small, negating shake of his head, he said quietly, "Not all of them, Mark."

They stared at each other for a short time that could have been forever. Then, quite abruptly, Hartmann began to sob.

The next time that Helena met Alasdair he gave her a bracelet. It was exceedingly fine and clearly very expensive, and Helena loved it at once. She went through the ritual of attempting to refuse it but they both knew that she was going to accept it and they both knew that its acceptance was the first step in a process. The offer and the acknowledgement of gratitude were signs as clearly signalled as the courtship displays of the lower animals.

And yet. . .

It was going fast and Helena didn't like to be hurried. The loss of control scared her, the possible consequences made her mind dart from anxiety to fear. She sat there and found a degree of captivation that she had barely known before, that she suspected she yearned for, but still it raised faint spectres of concern. How was this happening?

Like a member of the audience at a magic show she saw the trick and she was enthralled, but she looked at the same time for the clue as to how the illusion was created. Alasdair was relaxed, charming, never seeming to push her, yet she felt a force impel her, felt a desire to deepen the relationship, while knowing that it would be for the best to take things slowly.

Was this really love?

Even asking the question in her mind embarrassed her. It was ridiculous that she should not know, that she ask the question at all, especially at such an early stage, so soon after their first, fortuitous meeting.

"So, is the law as boring as I think it is?" he asked over the dinner. His eyes were slightly creased at the corners, the voice betraying a teasing tone.

"Mostly," she admitted.

They were in a small, exclusive dining room that she had before only ever heard about. It was the type of place that defined the customers as inferior because they had to pay to eat there.

"All probate and divorce? Lawyers congregating around the disasters in life?"

When he ate, he chewed his food more methodically and with more elegance than any other man she had ever seen. Perhaps his mother had taught him to chew twenty times before swallowing; certainly she seemed to have taught him the most impeccable table manners, for Helena had noticed that he never put his elbows on the table, never drank or spoke with food in his mouth, and never started a course until she did.

"Mostly."

"So why do you do it? It would bore me rigid. Can't you find something more interesting to do with a law degree?"

She shrugged. "It's not all wills and arguments over custody of the Afghan hound."

They were drinking an expensive Rioja Gran Reserva and the bottle was already nearly empty. Alasdair put down his knife and fork, one on either side of the plate, perfectly symmetrical in their placement. "What would you say if I were to suggest another possibility?"

Helena raised her eyebrows warily. "Such as?"

"Our legal department is always on the look out for new blood. I'm sure that any application you made would be greeted with great interest."

Especially as he was Head of Human Resources.

"I'm not up on contract law."

He smiled and took her hand. "It wouldn't take you long to get back into it."

It would be more interesting than the usual high street fare, but Helena found again her normal reluctance to commit, several reasons coalescing at once in her eagerness. "Maybe," she replied. He smiled, as if he knew that she was snared, and continued eating.

The conversation meandered as the second bottle of wine decanted.

"What exactly does your company do?" she asked over handmade mints. She had heard of Cronkhite-Canada, but the name had never become associated in her mind with anything specific.

"We diversify, if you have to put a single word to it. Construction, electronics, information systems, biotechnology, pharmaceuticals, defence. Anything and everything."

"Defence?"

"Nothing heavy," he reassured her. "Mostly things like passive detection systems, encryption, stuff like that."

"And would Cronkhite-Canada really have a need for someone like me?"

He smiled. "Of course they would. Anyone with legal training and a proven track record is of interest."

She considered. "How about something to finish off with?" he asked. "They have some superb Armagnac here."

When it had been poured he said, "Why don't I make a few preliminary enquiries? Smooth the way."

She shook her head. "I won't say I'm not tempted," she admitted. "But it's too soon. Anyway there's something on at the moment that I've got to finish before I could consider anything like changing jobs."

"Fair enough." Then, "Something interesting, is it?"

She smiled as she replied, "Well, it's a little more interesting than conveyancing."

He laughed. "So there is excitement in the life of a high street solicitor!" he exclaimed in a tone of mock astonishment. Helena found herself relaxing even more. Perhaps, she began to wonder, there really was nothing to worry about with Alasdair.

Hartmann had finished telling his tale, but if the confession had relieved his soul of a burden, it did not tell on his face, nor in his whole demeanour. He looked pale, almost ready to weep again, and his hands were shaking.

Eisenmenger sat and stared at the table between them, almost as if ignoring Hartmann. There was a look of deep contemplation on his face. He held between his hands a teaspoon, which he occasionally would turn about its long axis, and occasionally would use to strike one of the knuckles on his left hand.

They sat in the outpatients' teashop, surrounded by health promotion posters and advertisements for various fund-raising activities organized by the League of Friends. Because today was the Diabetes Clinic, those around them were pretty well all obese, elderly and walking badly.

"Why?" demanded Eisenmenger. His question was abrupt, as was the action of his head coming up to stare at Hartmann. "Why go to all that trouble for a natural death?"

Hartmann's reply was almost drowned in anguish. "I don't know. Don't you think I've asked that question? Rosenthal wouldn't say."

"And both he and the girl worked for Wiskott-Aldrich?"

"That's right."

"I've never heard of them. Have you?"

Hartmann shook his head. Eisenmenger took out a small notebook and wrote down the name.

"And Belinda was right? There were multiple tumour types?"

"It was unreal. I counted seventeen in the end. There might have been more."

Eisenmenger was silent after that. His hands were around the teacup but he didn't attempt to pick it up, just stared at the trembling reflection of the lights on its surface.

"What will you do?" Hartmann's voice was small and very, very fearful, but Eisenmenger wasn't in a position to be too reassuring; Hartmann's confession had basically left no alternative course of action. Not only were there the ethical implications of falsifying the medical record, but there was also the illegality of making a false report to the Coroner, added to which there was the immorality of what he had done to his marriage.

"Try to find out what's going on. That's what I was brought in to do."

On the other side of the counter the doughty members of the Women's Royal Voluntary Service pulled the levers of their machines and thereby made loud sibilant noises as they dispensed weak tea and lump-laden cocoa.

"But what about me?"

Eisenmenger wondered what Hartmann was expecting – exoneration because of confession? Good enough for God but not, he suspected, mortal man. He didn't feel that he could offer either support or comfort.

"I don't know, Mark."

"But does my name have to be included? Can't it be left out?"

Eisenmenger found that he couldn't look at him as he shook his head and said, "I doubt it, Mark." When at last he did glance at Hartmann, he saw a look of total, horrified despair there.

Behind Hartmann an elderly, rather dishevelled man in a woolly hat and scarf sneezed very loudly over the buttered currant buns. "Please?" Hartmann's tone was desperate – or pathetic, depending on the listener, and it found Eisenmenger saddened but not moved.

He sighed. "I'm sorry."

Hartmann leaned back in his chair and perhaps it was the light in the cafe but he looked suddenly spectral. He shut his eyes as if he were now feeling faint and whispered, "Shit!"

It was only when he opened his eyes that Eisenmenger saw that he was again weeping.

Eisenmenger had the growing realization that he couldn't just walk away, that he had to give the poor bastard some way out. Feeling that he might at some point regret it, he said, "Look, Mark. Do you still have the original tissue blocks?" Hartmann nodded but didn't say anything. "Then all I can suggest is that you replace them in the block file, and write to the Coroner claiming that you've made a mistake. If you do that, I don't see why we can't proceed as if it never happened."

But this advice, though well meant, was not well received.

"But I can't! If I do that, Rosenthal will find out!"

Eisenmenger shrugged. "Not necessarily. Unless he's got contacts in the Coroner's Office, there's no reason why he should, is there?"

For a few moments Hartmann continued to look hellbound, but then, gradually, Eisenmenger saw his face change as dawning interest brought some faint hue into it.

Behind him another sneeze added a further layer of glazing to the comestibles.

Hartmann returned home late but he wasn't worried about that. If Annette were cross with him, the significance of her anger would be laughable when compared with what might soon come. He was drunk, past the stage of relaxed enjoyment, deeply mired in the slow, depressive phase, but still coordinated enough to get the key in the lock first time. In the dark of the entrance hall he took off his coat wondering where his wife was, knowing that the children would be in bed. Although there was no sound of talking he saw light coming from under the sitting-room doors some way up the hall, and it was to this that he made his way.

Annette and her father were sitting there. They were talking, weren't even looking at each other. It was like a badly created tableau in a department store window. The sense of unreality was heightened when, like synchronized automata, they both turned silently to stare at him.

For a second he stared back at them then, perhaps stung by the open hostility, something switched over his brain. Synaptic potentials realigned and Hartmann became unaccountably belligerent. "Father-in-law! What a pleasant surprise!"

He advanced into the room – into *his* room – and sat down next to Annette. He smiled at his wife and her father; a broad and engaging smile that stretched orbicularis oris into unaccustomed tension.

And still they said nothing.

"You haven't got a drink," he decided, gesturing towards the judge. "Here let me get you one." He began to get up. "Your usual, father-in-law?"

Annette said suddenly, "Where have you been, Mark?" Her question was made of something sprung with tension, it was sharp enough to penetrate the ethanolic sheen and make him pause in the act of rising. He glanced across at Brown-Sequard, catching a look of smugness that he didn't much like. Didn't like at all, actually.

"Drinking," he replied, deciding that he was fed up with his father-in-law looking at him in much the same way as his housemaster had used to look him just prior to administering some corporal punishment. "Why?"

He addressed the question to Annette but the answer came from the judiciary on his left. "You haven't been in the betting shop, have you?"

The use of the words *betting shop* was a considerable shock but he handled it quite well, saying without hesitation, "No." He didn't try outrage, merely denial, and it was all the better for it.

Then it was Annette's turn. "Where did you get the money to pay off your gambling debts?"

Hartmann found the changed direction of attack difficult to

follow. This time he paused before saying, "I do earn my own living, you know."

The sound that emerged from Mr Justice Brown-Sequard's nasal cavity was so much more in meaning and less in sound than a common snort. It conveyed enough contempt to drown his son-in-law. "Sixteen thousand pounds?"

Which Hartmann did find a little difficult to counter with much gusto. In fact he was reduced to a pathetic, "How do you.. . ?" Silence followed abruptly as he realized he had made a significant tactical error. Annette suddenly sighed as if she hadn't been able to believe it until that moment. "Oh, Mark."

There was a swiftly rising dread in his stomach. Did they know? Had Rosenthal sent the tape, despite his promises? He tried to use the fear as fuel for anger.

"Have you been snooping on me? "he demanded of Annette. "How dare you!"

But he might just as well have been using a penknife to kill a dinosaur.

"We dare," explained his wife, "because we have to. Because the family of a member of the judiciary has to be completely without flaw or suspicion of a flaw, and that includes his son-in-law."

"Are you saying I've done something wrong?"

It was her father who replied. "No. We're asking a question."

He had always felt afraid of their debating skills, of their abilities to trip up, to twist, to imply and infer. What was better? To deny, to lie or to refuse to answer? He didn't have long to decide and, inevitably he chose the wrong option. "I won a big bet." It sounded good to Hartmann. After all, they now knew that he gambled.

Brown-Sequard took this with a look of realization and comprehension. *I see!* he seemed to be saying. *Of course!* He smiled across Hartmann at his daughter who said nothing. Then he repeated, "A large bet."

The intonation was perfect. Disbelief and sadness, topped off with pity. Hartmann had been looking at the carpet, trying not to think too much about the depth of faeces beneath his paddling feet. "Yes . . .it was a treble." He kept his eyes on the judge this time. Unfortunately, it was still the wrong place to be looking.

"A treble?" asked Annette. "That must have been amazing!" He jerked his head round to see her smiling widely. "You can prove it, of course. Where the meeting was and when, the race, the winners. That kind of thing."

And that was the end of Hartmann's defence. He found himself looking from one to the other, his mouth open, his eyes slightly widened. It wasn't long before Annette got up, no longer looking at him and left the room. Hartmann watched her leave without moving. From his chair Brown-Sequard murmured, "Perhaps you should sit down, Mark."

It was as much the tone as the words that Hartmann responded to. He felt tired, tired of everything.

Brown-Sequard asked, "Where did you get it?"

Hartmann leaned back, his chin on his chest, his eyes closed. He couldn't answer, but knew he had to say something. "Why don't you just fuck off and leave me alone?"

"No!"

Eisenmenger had expected no less, although he was surprised by the sudden eruption of intense anger.

"Look, Helena, I understand your objection. . ."

"Then you won't persist in the suggestion."

Helena's flat was warm, but her whole demeanour had turned suddenly unseasonably cold, as inhospitable as the night outside. *If you are a monkey made of brass, be prepared to shed them now.* He had called on her without prior warning and had found her getting ready to go out. It had clearly been a less than optimal time to discuss any proposition, let alone this one. She was in her dressing gown when she let him in and he had then waited for twenty minutes while she made noises in the bathroom. Her eventual appearance had left him temporarily without words as he was forcibly reminded just how gorgeous he thought she was.

"How else do you suggest we proceed? I've no other contacts in the police, and neither have you now that Johnson's retired. Beverley Wharton is the logical person to go to."

"Not her. Not that bitch."

Beverley Wharton had been one of the investigating officers of the murders of Helena's mother and father. It was she, Helena believed, who had fabricated a case against her brother, leading to his suicide.

"Who else then?" He noted her hesitation.

"Get a private detective."

She looked, he thought, beautiful; like a debutante, almost. Her perfume was strong and soft, her short pale cream dress a delight to the eye. He would have liked to have known where she was going, and was desperate to know with whom.

"Who's going to pay?" he asked, he thought not unreasonably.

Which brought about another hesitation, into which he said, "You see, Helena?

"No," she declared and it was not said in a way that suggested the possibility of future negotiation. She had adopted a stance of intransigence as if they were married and this were a well-rehearsed argument. As she stood in front of him, he had the impression that she was as much defending a physical position as a polemical one. She had folded her arms and was standing with her legs slightly apart, so that her hips were accentuated. The look of determination on her face only added to her beauty, he thought.

Flickers of sadness sparkled in his eyes, yet simultaneously he began to feel annoyance. After all, she was letting her feelings get in the way. "Look, Helena. Hartmann's admitted that he falsified the autopsy report, that she died from multiple tumours. The mode of death in itself was bizarre; nobody dies from that many cancers, and certainly not when they're young and apparently well just a week or two before. If you add to that the fact that somebody wanted it kept quiet, and that same somebody was willing to pay a huge sum of money, then you've got something that not only stinks, it's crawling with maggots."

"Nobody's denying that there's something odd going on. If you remember, John, that was why I approached you in the first place."

"Well done. There is. Trouble is, if we're going to get any further, we need to involve someone who knows what they're doing when it comes to finding out details. I can't think of anyone else other than Beverley Wharton."

"She's corrupt, she's devious and she's no friend of ours – either yours or mine – remember?"

He sighed. Yes, he did remember. The strange and horrible death of Nikki Exner had not covered Beverley Wharton in glory, thanks mainly to the two of them. "A private detective costs a lot of money – hundreds, perhaps even thousands, of pounds. Can Raymond Sweet afford that?"

She ignored the question. "Why do we have to get anyone else involved at all? Why can't we do it ourselves?"

Ye gods.

"There is only one lead. Hartmann was blackmailed by a man calling himself Alan Rosenthal, apparently from a pharmaceutical company called Wiskott-Aldrich. Find out who he is and why Wiskott-Aldrich are interested in Millicent Sweet, and we have a chance of discovering what's going on."

Without moving from her station but with a glance at the clock on the mantelshelf Helena said, "They're bound to be pseudonyms."

At last.

"Precisely. Which is why we can't do it ourselves, why we need a professional. And since we can't afford a private enquiry agency, we'll have to use what we can."

"No!" This time it was actually, amazingly, sibilant. She leaned forward. "That *prostitute* is going to have nothing to do with this. Do you understand?"

She moved at last, as if falling back, a strategic withdrawal after this parry. Stung, he found himself beginning to find her irritating; a peculiarly wonderful irritation that was streaked with recollections. "No, I don't, Helena. You're letting emotion. . ."

"What the hell do you know about my emotions?" she demanded, picking up a scarf from the back of a dining chair with a whipping motion. "What the hell do you know about emotions, full stop?"

He felt furious at such hypocrisy, but it was a strangely wonderful fury, as if he were enjoying the release. "Me? Me?" he demanded. He even found himself waving his arms around, something that, once he noticed, was instantly embarrassing. "You call me emotionless? That's a good one."

Helena had wrapped the scarf about her neck and she was in the act of picking up her coat when he said this. The effect was immediate. She jerked round to face him, the coat forgotten. She opened her beautifully reddened mouth to reply, her face showing sudden outrage, but before she could say anything, the doorbell rang.

Eisenmenger was interested to see that the sound had a curious effect upon her. It caused her to hesitate, swallow the ire, then hurry to the door, offering him only a single glare. It seemed clear that whoever was expected was significant.

"Helena! Are you ready? You look ravishing!"

From Eisenmenger's viewpoint, there was certainly an affectionate clench, perhaps even something more than a peck. Helena admitted the visitor and Eisenmenger saw a man of nearly two metres, fair-haired, grey eyed and (the bastard) good looking. He was in his early forties and Eisenmenger saw fitness smoothed into him. He looked up from Helena's face, over her shoulder at Eisenmenger. His broad smile became tinged with curiosity. Catching the change in his attitude Helena looked briefly over her shoulder. "This is John Eisenmenger, an acquaintance of mine. He called in to discuss a case."

The man advanced towards Eisenmenger, confidence, friendliness and charm exuding into the space between them. He proffered a hand. "Good to meet you. Alasdair Riley-Day."

The hand was neither too firm nor too soft, too dry nor too wet; Eisenmenger felt as if he'd shaken hands with Abraham Lincoln.

"I'd best be off," he said to Helena. He nodded to Riley-Day. "Good to meet you." It didn't sound as if he meant it, at least to his ears, which didn't come as a huge shock.

He picked up his coat from the back of the sofa and moved to the door, feeling distinctly like an ambulant and green soft fruit. "We'll talk about this some time tomorrow."

Helena only nodded in a small, decisive manner, which found him strangely sad.

When the door closed behind him Riley-Day turned to Helena. "Did I interrupt something?"

She laughed. "Nothing for you to worry about," she said.

"You're angry."

"Only furious,"

"May I ask why?"

She smiled, picked up a clutch bag, put her coat under arm and held out her hand towards him. "Let's eat."

Behind her, Alasdair Riley-Day smiled.

"Daddy?"

Jake was in bed, the nightlight casting ill-defined, diffuse shadows that were ghostly comforts, memories of childhoods past and present. Annette was out, spreading her intellect over an outing of legal types, a dinner in the Strand; Hartmann was of the opinion that Annette's life was lived in a twilight, Wodehousian world.

"What is it, Jay?"

He had been about to leave the room, having read the obligatory Paddington story, on his way to Jocasta who was shouting and screaming and, almost certainly, using her bed as a trampoline. He sat back down next to his son, smiling and trying not to let fatigue make his temper brittle. His son was almost completely immersed in the bedclothes, the duvet meeting the pillow and allowing only a small pocket into which Jake could thrust his face, as if for air.

"What's a divorce?"

The question was asked with innocence and was therefore brutal to Hartmann, as if this small, skinny boy had stabbed a knife into his stomach. Hartmann was suddenly immersed in the memory of Scotland, feeling the shame rush over him.

"What?" he asked incredulously, although he had heard quite plainly. "What was that, Jay?" Jake always had a serious expression on his face, his brow lowered and pinched over dark blue eyes, his mouth slightly pursed. "What's a divorce?" he repeated.

"A divorce? Where did you hear that word, Jay?" He hoped that the answer would be the television or something, but his hopes were futile.

"I heard Mummy talking about it. On the phone today."

Hartmann was suddenly swamped again by his remembrance of what he had done. He smelt again the scent of Claire's perfume, tasted once more the slight cinnamon tang of her tongue and teeth, felt anew the softness of the flesh between her thighs and the moistness of her excitement. This time, however, there was no desire, only abhorrence, and no tumescence, only deflation. He suddenly felt tears as if they were some sort of emotional extinguisher. He swallowed and smiled at the same time; perhaps, he at once realized, a mistake.

"What did she say, Jay? Exactly, I mean."

The small face descended into deep contemplation, its seriousness far too adult to be borne by such fine, immature features. The corners of his mouth turned down and his eyebrows conjoined. Beside him Teddy also bore an expression of profound consideration but since this was a perpetual, unchanging look it conveyed not great intellect but great imbecility.

"She said that getting a divorce was the only thing to do."

A million questions, perhaps a million and one, ran through his mind. Most of them began with "How," a few began with "Why." Suddenly the concept of an end to his marriage – a terror in the dark, a phantom worse than death – was stepping into the light.

And then, "She said that they had no other choice."

Hartmann seized on the potential reprieve. "Who? Who's 'they?'"

"Auntie Charlotte and Uncle Jack."

Hartmann's relief paralyzed him. It surged into his abdomen and made him feel nauseous. It compressed his chest; restricted his breathing. The tears returned and would not be held back but then laughter followed and he was a curious mix of feelings.

Hartmann had always found his children annoying, no matter how hard he tried to appreciate them. Annette had wanted them – but only two and definitely one of each (her grasp of biology did not compare favourably with her knowledge of company law) – and he had consented, but without enthusiasm. He often wondered if this were the root of his feelings but, very occasionally, something would happen and he would have an epiphany in which he connected with a different reality; one in which he was no longer a man who happened to have children, but really and absolutely a *father*.

He hugged Jake, feeling for once that he was hugging his son, not just a child. His tears blurred the words as he whispered into his son's small shoulder, "Oh, God."

Carlos Arias-Stella looked again at the toilet bowl, now bespattered by vomit. It was a familiar sight – too familiar, if he was forced to confront some truth for a change – and it accompanied a familiar feeling of myalgia, grogginess and thudding headache. Then there was the stench.

It came again, the waxing nausea, the anticipation of coordinated, painful muscle spasm, the loss of control. Much against the advice of his higher mental functions, he plunged his head closer to the water surface, deeper into the miasmic detritus that had so recently snuggled itself in his gastrum.

He retched, involuntary noises echoing from the porcelain. There was little more than bile-stained chyme left to come and he wondered what was worse – the pain of vomiting nothing or the burning taste of semi-digested food.

The door behind him vibrated with a fusillade of thumps. "Carl? Carl?"

The handle rattled. He groaned quietly. "Fuck off, Nerys." This was addressed in an undertone to the bowl.

"Are you all right?"

He continued his monologue to his so-recently-evicted meal. "Everything's brilliant, Nerys. Just fucking brilliant. Nowhere else I'd rather be."

"Can you hear me?"

He got slowly and painfully to unsteady feet, the cistern proving to be one of his few remaining friends. The transfer to the basin successfully completed, he ran cold water, first to drink, then to sluice over his greasy skin. All the while, the accompaniment from Nerys continued, varying from percussion to increasingly panicked vocalization.

Eventually he opened the door.

Nerys wasn't unattractive. Since he had moved into her flat – seven quarrel-laden months before – his dependence on her had grown. At the start, there had just been the sex – great sex – and he had planned then merely to continue the relationship based on regular cunnilingus and explosive orgasms, but he had reckoned without the capriciousness of the heart. Affection had sprung up where it had not been wanted, and they had passed from the pleasures of biology to the pleasure of companionship.

"'Bout time, you drunken sod." She pushed past him. She was wearing her short, pink dressing gown, the one that showed her backside so nicely, but in his condition he wasn't interested in the curves of her buttocks.

"You're getting fatter," he pronounced. It wasn't altogether a lie, and it was therefore all the more effective. Nerys was obsessed by her weight. She didn't turn round but above the noise of water of water pouring into the basin she said to his reflection behind her, "It smells like a doss house in here, you pig." Her nasal Welsh twang was constructed for scorn. "You're a complete mess, you are. You're nothing but a drunken waste of space."

He came up behind her as her attention returned to her reflection, grabbing her breasts and nuzzling her neck. She passed rapidly from shock to enjoyment to mock exasperation.

"Get off, you silly sod!"

He released her, smacked her arse and went into the bedroom. He lay back down on the bed, hoping that closed eyes and steady breathing would alleviate the returning malaise. It didn't. The smell of cigarette smoke suffused directly into his stomach lining and into his strobing brain.

Nerys came in. "How much did you have to drink last night?"

He failed to find the need to reply.

"I saw you down five pints, and that was before I left the pub, so God knows how much you ended up pouring down your throat."

He found that he had to fight the nausea and fight also the irritation he felt when forced to confront his drinking habits. She continued her exhortation remorselessly. "You're going to be late for work . . . *again*."

He wasn't, actually. Nerys had never become comfortable with the life of a research assistant. To her, proper jobs were nine to five, and his habit of turning in for work at ten-thirty was foreign.

He kept his eyes shut. It made no difference, not to anything. "You're going to have to cut down, you know, Carl. It's not good for you."

Perhaps it wasn't the best time to remain silent. "It was the kebab."

It had the desired effect, for she stopped and then asked, "You what?"

He reflected how ladylike she wasn't. "The kebab," he repeated. "I had a kebab after I left the pub."

She had sat down at the cheap white self-assembly dressing table, combing her hair with a small red plastic brush. Nerys and plastic had an affinity. Depending on his mood and libido, he found it either arousing or derisory. She said sweetly, "You're a fucking liar, Carl." It was said much as God had pronounced light on the world.

He returned to his hangover.

Nerys said nothing more for a while. She stripped off the dressing gown and through near-closed eyes he watched her and thought pleasant, if pornographic, thoughts.

She said no more while she put on a blouse and short, green skirt, followed by make-up that covered more than her clothing. When she had finished she came back to him. "Seriously, though. You shouldn't drink so much." "Maybe you're right, baby. Maybe, I'll try to cut it down." He smiled.

Then she left the room with a final and affectionate, "Lazy bastard," for her beloved.

She continued to move through the flat in a practised choreography of movement – orange juice taken from the refrigerator, poured and drunk was one element, coat and shoes out of the hall cupboard then simultaneously donned was another – before leaving, the performance terminated with the crash of the front door.

He opened his eyes, twisted his head to look at the alarm clock and then relaxed. His head was still pounding to the beat of the engines of God, but the sickness was receding. At half-eight he could afford another forty-five minutes in bed.

He closed his eyes.

Pel-Ebstein Pharmaceuticals had a United Kingdom head office that dominated a broad expanse of midland moor. It beamed its imposing presence of glass curves, steel struts and rising turrets fully fifteen miles in all directions. The architecture had won awards, the local landowners had won colossal windfalls as their acres were acquired, and the local economy had won total dependence on its newest, biggest and brashest inhabitant.

As they drove towards it. Eisenmenger saw it early and hated it early; the closer they came, the greater the hatred. He could see the beauty of the architecture, could see that it was not physically out of place, but saw with startling clarity that it was as spiritually suited to its environs as a Mother Superior would have been to a mutual fisting competition. It spoke of dominance and superiority; it bullied the observer into accepting that it was far more important than all around it.

Eisenmenger was driving, with Helena beside him. Trying not to look at her legs was a full-time occupation. The journey had

143

lasted two hours, enlivened only sporadically by episodes of chat, as if neither of them could find subjects of mutual interest, or perhaps as if the subjects of mutual interest were also of mutual discomfort.

They were stopped by guards at gates that were tall and set into a chainlink fence that stretched away to either side, enclosing an area of bleak moorland that must have been several thousand hectares in extent. They were stopped again fifty metres on, having passed several black dogs roaming free. At each checkpoint they were asked for identity, the car was searched and their reason for visiting was verified by radio.

"Impressive security," Helena remarked as they drove on. On either side of them small complexes of low buildings could be reached by spurs from the road. Outside them were notices such as "Protein Modelling and Synthetics," "Biomimetics," "Artificial Memory Group," and "Neural Network Development."

"That's presumably why," said Eisenmenger. "There's a lot of high-powered research going on here. A lot to protect."

But it made him feel uncomfortable and he could sense Helena felt likewise. It felt as if they were entering a giant's maw.

In front of the main building there was a huge car park surrounding a lake from which five tall fountains rose. Swans ignored them regally as they drove past towards the car parking area. This alone was the size of a small, provincial airport, although visitors were privileged by having a small, exclusive compound relatively close to the main building.

"Quite a walk if you're late in to work," remarked Helena as she got out of the car and looked around.

"A bitch if it's raining."

The entrance foyer was suitably awesome, with an atrium that rose like a cathedral and enough marble to have brought Kubla Khan to climax. It was bright and light and airy, stretching off in various directions from a central, circular reception desk but Eisenmenger could already feel awe-fatigue beginning to take effect.

Evidently Helena felt it too for she murmured, "Are they yelling something, or just shouting it?"

And still the show had not finished for, by some means miraculous, the undoubtedly attractive but rather hypothermic blonde behind the reception desk knew not only who they were but that their escort was, as they spoke, on his way to convey them to their destination.

Thus they found themselves in the office of Benjamin Starling. It was large and plush, but by now it could have been hung with the jewel-encrusted entrails of a unicorn and it would barely have raised their interest. Starling was also big; tall but he had worked hard enough as a trencherman to ensure that it made no difference. He was obese and impressively so, clearly having to shift twenty stone every time he felt the urge to scratch his backside.

"Miss Flemming! Good of you to come." He spoke with an accent that was difficult to place; to British ears it sounded American, but she suspected that there would have been an entirely opposite impression on the other side of the Atlantic. He raised himself – apparently without effort, although Eisenmenger found himself speculating on what was happening to his arterial blood pressure and venous return – and proffered five podgy fingers. When she took them they enfolded her hand and squeezed just enough to hurt her. The flesh, she noted, was surprisingly firm and dry. He turned to Eisenmenger. "And this is?"

"John Eisenmenger. He is advising me on this case."

The same hand was proffered and this time, although Eisenmenger did not know it, the pressure applied was a little bit greater. His demeanour remained open, friendly and charming. He offered them coffee, which they declined. "You're here about Millicent Sweet."

"I represent her late father."

He had no paper on his desk, Helena noticed. To his left was a large flat screen monitor, at least sixty centimetres across, over a keyboard. He punched a few keys, presumably calling up the correct file. He turned back to them. "May I ask why?"

"Miss Sweet died some weeks ago. The circumstances were . . . unusual. I am investigating them on behalf of her father."

Somehow the adiposity of Benjamin Starling didn't hang down; his face was covered in the stuff but it defied the gravitational force that it must have felt, clinging rigidly to his facial skeleton. Thus when his expression changed, as it did now, it was not hidden, it was transparent, and the affability of the host was replaced by the more hardened expression of a potential antagonist. "I think you owe us more than that, Miss Flemming. Am I to assume that there is the potential for litigation against Pel-Ebstein?"

Somehow the concept seemed ludicrous; a belligerent gnat fighting a blue whale.

Helena said, "I think you can answer that better than me, Dr Starling. All I want to know is what Millicent Sweet did while she worked for you."

He leaned back in the dark blue leather of his chair. It creaked, but held and Eisenmenger found himself breathing again. "But you must see things from my perspective, Miss Flemming. Much of PEP's research is highly confidential. We are involved in numerous areas of pharmacobiological research, many of which cannot be discussed with unauthorized personnel, for reasons of both industrial and, I should add, national security. I cannot go into any great detail about Miss Sweet's work."

Helena was, as ever, making notes while Eisenmenger was leaning back in his rather comfortable chair and just looking at Starling. She finished, frowned down at what she had just written as if seeing it for the first time, then returned her gaze to Starling. "Am I to take it that Millicent was working on something to do with defence?"

It was disguised by an innocence of tone that fooled no one. Starling stared at her for a moment, and Eisenmenger had the feeling that Starling's gallstones (he must have had gallstones because he was so obese) were suddenly tweaking him a tad. Then Starling turned back to the screen. "She worked in the Models Development Division."

"Sounds like fun. Balsa wood and glue, or snap-together plastic?" Eisenmenger's voice was lazily amused.

The gallstones kicked a bit harder and now Starling seemed hostile. "Models Development is among our most innovative and forward-thinking divisions. We only ask the best and the brightest to work there."

"And what does it do?"

Starling's response was itself a model – one of vagueness. "Its remit is to develop potentially useful biological, biomechanical and biogenetic systems that might be exploited in the future. Miss Sweet was working in the biogenetic subdivision."

"Doing what?"

Starling had walked the road far enough. He shook his head. "I'm sorry."

Eisenmenger glanced at Helena. She asked, "She was working in a very remote laboratory Dr Starling. Why was that?"

"We have facilities all over the world. There is no significance in where she worked."

Helena saw nothing in his expression that suggested he was lying, although she knew he was. "Really? It must be very expensive to maintain a laboratory on a remote Scottish island."

Starling sighed. "Our facility on Rouna is one of our oldest. It is true that its remoteness assists in maintaining industrial confidentiality, but it is no more secure than any of our labs on this site."

"Except it no longer exists."

Eisenmenger's interjection appeared unwelcome. Grudgingly, Starling conceded the fact.

"There was a fire, wasn't there? Was that related to the work going on there?" Eisenmenger tried to sound as neutral as possible.

"No."

It was said with finality and therefore as a form of non sequitur. As such, it left them slightly at a loss until Helena asked, "Then why did you terminate the project after the fire."

For just a moment Starling was perhaps discomforted. "What makes you think we terminated the project?"

"Because Millicent had to find another job."

It was either this or the gallstones that made a fleeting glance of uncertainty flow through the fat. "That was nothing to do directly with the fire. The project was coming to an end. The laboratory was old and we think that the fire was most probably a result of an electrical fault. It had nothing whatsoever to do with the actual nature of the research – that, at least, was the opinion of the insurers. You can have a copy of their report, if you wish."

Helena opened her mouth but Eisenmenger got there first. "I don't think that will be necessary. So you can't give us any more precise information on what Millicent was working on?"

He shook his large head. "I'm sorry."

They continued for a few more desultory minutes but they had no more questions that caused Starling trouble. As they

voiced their queries his demeanour gradually resumed confidence and they all knew that they had lost the initiative.
Eventually they rose and the interview was ended.

"I'm sorry I can't be more use, Miss Flemming, but you know
how it is," Starling said, shaking Helen's hand.

She nodded, not because she did know but because these were
formalities and she was a polite woman. He turned to Eisenmenger
with a smile and a nod of dismissal. "Dr Eisenmenger."

They left, the wonders of their environment completely
powerless to impress.

They waited until they were past the final gate and free of
Pel-Ebstein's imposure before they said anything. This was not
due to prior agreement, more to a feeling of apprehension, as if
they had just been witness to something large and sleeping and
possibly dangerous.

"Well?" asked Helena.

It was then that Eisenmenger simultaneously felt alarm and
excitement explode.

"I wonder." He said this quite calmly and the fact that he
stopped the car seemed almost unconnected with the utterance.

"What's wrong?"

"I need to check something."

He got out and, to Helena's surprise he dropped onto his
knees despite the mud. For a few seconds she lost sight of him,
and then he abruptly reappeared at the front of the car. A further
disappearance was followed by his face, now grinning, rearing
up outside her driver's side window. This pantomime left
Helena pulled between mystification and irritation which she
voiced when he got back in the car, caked in equal amounts of
mud and satisfaction. "What the hell are you playing at?"

He held out his hand. On it was a small, circular device,
perhaps two centimetres in diameter and half a centimetre thick.

"What's that?"

He put the device to the gearstick and with a click it stuck.
"I'm not an expert, but I would say that it's a listening device."

Starling stared at the bare surface of his desk for a long time after
Helena and Eisenmenger had left. It was fully ten minutes before
the door opened. Starling looked up. "Well?"

Rosenthal shrugged. "They know a lot."

"But do they know too much?"

Rosenthal sat down in Eisenmenger's chair. He crossed his legs and clasped his hands. He had on his face a large smile. "Well, that's difficult to judge, but I think we can rest assured that they know nothing about Proteus. The question is has Hartmann talked? That is not clear."

"And if he has?"

"He will be taken care of." Rosenthal shut his eyes and said dreamily, "From the point of view of our security, the answer to your question is that they know something. Ergo, they know too much."

Starling, until now passive, even subdued, raised his forearms and brought them down on the oak desk with a crash. A small paperweight, made of titanium, jumped and performed the smallest of dances. Rosenthal chose not to react.

"When this started, you told me it could be contained."

"This whole situation should not have been allowed to originate. If my advice had been taken in the first place, there would be nothing to contain."

"The decision was not yours, or mine, to take."

Rosenthal shrugged. "Nor was the information on the. . . aggressiveness. . .of Proteus accurate. The assumptions we were told to plan on were out by a factor of ten. Under those circumstances, the job I have done has been exemplary."

Starling's face wasn't quite a sneer, but it was a close call. He asked, not without some sarcasm, "And now?"

Rosenthal's smile lasted no more than a quarter of a second. "Now we do what we should have done in the first place. We sterilize the project."

"Does that include those two – Flemming and Eisenmenger?"

For the first time Rosenthal seemed less than certain. "I don't know," he admitted. "We have to be careful about further 'incidents' that can be so closely interconnected." He paused, then said, "I think I need more data before a decision is made."

"And how will you obtain it?"

"I hope that problem has just been taken care of."

There was a knock on the door and a small, stern-looking woman came in with a piece of paper that she handed to

Rosenthal. As he read it a frown of annoyance appeared before he sighed and handed it to Starling.

"Not stupid, certainly. I had hoped they would take longer to find our little device."

Starling was more animated. "Don't you realize what this means? They know that we've got something to hide!"

"They knew that already. There's a world of difference between knowledge and proof."

"Well? What now?"

Rosenthal smiled. "All is not lost. I'm sure it won't be long before Helena takes her new friend, Alasdair, into her confidence. Depending on how close they're getting to the truth, we decide our next moves." He looked directly at Starling, into his eyes. "I may need to act quickly. . . and irrevocably."

Starling returned the stare but his eyes held nervousness. Then he looked down at his nice, polished desk. "Do what you have to," he said in a small voice.

For fear that there were more listening devices, they said nothing until they had stopped at a roadside restaurant. They discussed what they had learned over coffee drunk from thick porcelain mugs.

"Something and nothing, I think," sighed Helena. "It's quite clear that they're hiding something, but quite what is still not obvious, and whether it's relevant to Millicent's death is anyone's guess."

Eisenmenger was fiddling with a sachet of brown sugar, a sign, Helena knew, of concentration. He pulled it and pushed it, then bent it first one way, then the other. A two-year-old would not have been surprised when the paper tore and demerara sugar spilled on to the table.

Eisenmenger was.

He said, "I think it has. In fact, I'm certain of it."

"Why?"

"He knew who I was; knew that I was a doctor, although you didn't give me a title. He didn't even know I was coming, so that means he's had his people nosing about, looking into you. He may even have bugged your office or apartment, but I doubt it."

Surprised at the notion, Helena asked, "Why not?"

"Because he bugged the car. Why bother if he can already hear every word you say?"

"How did you know it was there?"

He made a face. "It occurred to me that it was worth excluding. PEP's big and, if they did have something to hide, it's the kind of trick they might pull. The fact that I was right implies they did have something to do with her death."

"Not necessarily. PEP could easily be worried about all sorts of issues connected with what happened in the laboratory accident, but that doesn't mean that they were responsible for her death. Especially when the two incidents are so far separated in time."

"So what have we learned?"

She looked through her notes. "We have a location for the laboratory – Rouna. Apart from that, I would have to say little of value."

"I wonder what the biogenetic subdepartment of the Models Development Division did, or does? It's such a delightfully vague designation; I wonder if that's deliberate?"

"Judging by the way PEP cloaks itself in shadow, I'd say almost certainly."

"So it's Rouna, or nothing. Will you take care of that? Find out whatever you can?"

She nodded. "Such a shame we don't have the names of anyone else working on the project."

"Except Carlos", he pointed out. "Whoever he is." He finished his coffee, picked up another packet of sugar. He was about to begin playing with it when Helena reached out and gently took it from him. "Don't do that, John. It makes such a mess."

He was momentarily taken aback before an abrupt grin flowered. Her hand was soft, her face registering mock sternness. He felt glad to be with her.

Another day done, another trip to the pub. This time, though, he vowed that it would be short, perhaps home in time to eat with Nerys. He felt guilty about the way he was treating her. True, she nagged him incessantly and in a uniquely Welsh way, but he knew that he could do far, far worse for a partner.

"Usual, Carl?"

Carlos noticed that the bartender felt no need to greet him.

Once, fifteen or so years ago, he remembered being told that it was a bad sign if the barman knew your name; what, then, was the prognosis if he knew you so well he didn't even bother to say, "Hello", if he just lined them up and listened to your opinions?

"How was work?"

Carlos shrugged. Work was work was work.

"I see there was something about your place in the paper this morning."

The Leishman was always announcing things – a new gene here, a big grant there – it was all part of the academic whirligig. Gone were the days when scientific researchers ran from publicity lest it taint the purity of their fairy grotto. Now, the more you shouted, the more money you got.

"Anything to do with you?"

Unable to raise the enthusiasm for anything more than a brief denial, he took his pint and sat alone at a table by the window. The guy behind the bar was all right but he was like the huge majority of people that Carlos met – in his mind, science was a potent and dangerous emulsion of wondrous possibilities and hideous realities. He was as ignorant of what Carlos did as he was of life on the bottom of the sea; Carlos could have sat and described the work of the Leishman for six straight hours and the poor baboon would have been not one millimetre closer to comprehension. The frightening thing was that Carlos was just a research technician – for which, (those of a more brutal, less euphemistic mind might say) read lab assistant. He didn't even do the clever stuff. He just made small contributions in the seminars and small group discussions, then went to the bench and did what he was told.

It might have been so different had the luck gone his way. . .

Bollocks!

The thought cut savagely through his self-pity and he had no defence against it. It was right; he'd had bad luck, no one would deny, but he'd also squandered the good, like the six-figure pay-out that PEP had given him not so long ago, now a memory, squandered on holidays and the so-called "good life".

That little episode had only been the last hiccough in the conspiracy between himself and fate to cock up his chances.

Once he had tried for the key to the Magic Kingdom, the PhD, but at thirty-four he was now beyond that particular aspiration. Things had happened, the thesis had never been started, the work left incomplete. He had an MPhil, of course, the consolation prize for failures in the Doctoral Thesis Handicap Stakes, but only the completely sad mentioned things like an MPhil on their CV. It ranked with the Ten Metre Swimming Certificate, the Cycling Proficiency Badge and Grade One Piano.

Once, though.

Now, he was stuck in a groove, every revolution of his life wearing it deeper, the walls being rendered higher and steeper, completely eliminating all chance of escape. Research assistants of his age either remained on a research assistant's undernourished salary for life, or they got out, started another career. If he were going to get out, though, time was nearly up.

Easy, except that it wasn't. Not only was he too old, his CV was too pathetic. School, BSc, research jobs. It was bog standard in a career where bog standard was barely better than slime-mould. If he were to move, it would only be to another variation on the theme with no chance of promotion. That was what he had done in the past, jumping from one shitpile to another, the only ever difference was the type of shit he was required to shift. His failure to achieve the meal-ticket meant everything; nothing else that he had achieved would mask that.

If things had only been different, if fate had not taken him and screwed him to the lab bench. First there had been his father's death two years into his PhD. Talk about timing! The old man had always been a difficult bastard, but he excelled himself by choosing to develop acute haemorrhagic pancreatitis at that precise moment. Exit one father, exit one PhD.

The second time, though, had been the real blow, the one that told him that Carlos Arias-Stella would not have his name on the Eternal Roll-Call of Honour. The job at Pel-Ebstein had come completely unexpectedly. He'd seen the advertisement in *Nature* just at the time he was considering moving on from a stupendously tedious job at St Jerome's that had at least produced a few publications. He had applied expecting the usual rejection by silence, but to his surprise an invitation for interview had followed They hadn't even minded the PhD-shaped hole in his CV.

And, when he had been successful and been given a contract, it had transpired that the project had been potentially huge. It had been clear from the start that PEP considered this to be high priority; various heads of various departments had talked to him, emphasizing the priority they gave to Proteus. Fucking hell, they even gave it a bloody code name.

It was perhaps the first time in his life that he had felt truly important. This was high-powered research, the most advanced biopharmaceutical research (so they told him) that PEP was involved with. A small team of six under the guidance of Professor Stein. They even made him sign confidentiality agreements. He hadn't read them in detail, although now he knew that this had been a mistake. All of this engendered within him a sense of importance, a feeling of anticipation that he found intoxicating.

The feeling had lasted, too. Even when the six of them had landed on Rouna, the colostomy of the world, it hadn't seemed too bad. The isolation had added to the air of something important, something significant. He hadn't been the only one, either. All six of them had felt then that they had PEP behind them, that the huge pharmaceutical company believed that they were embarking on something special.

A year it had lasted. In fact, it had more than lasted. In those twelve months they had had astounding success. Models Development (shit name) had nearly crapped their pants over some of the initial results. Stein had turned out to belie the initial impression of doddering unworldliness, actually proving to be both astute and receptive to input. Turner, the second in command, had gradually evolved from his initial nervous self-importance into fully grown, totally fledged arrogance; none of them had minded then, because a certain amount of pride had seemed justified. Proteus was going to be a success, and Turner had had much to do with it.

Turner, of course, had proved to be the problem; his downfall. It could all have been so different. He might even, at that stage, have had a second opportunity at the legendary PhD, had things turned out otherwise.

"Are you fucking drinking that, or just nursing it until it hatches?"

The voice rang out from the bar. "A drinking friend," as Nerys called them in a tone of the purest Welsh contempt. Carlos smiled broadly, acknowledged the shout and obligingly drank some beer, then returned to his thoughts.

Then the fire had happened, and life was no longer the same again.

He considered that thought and decided, *No. It wasn't quite like that.*

Things had started to go terribly wrong before the fire; in a way, the fire had been a relief. The event that had once again crucified him had been some months earlier, when the covers on Proteus had been removed, when the five of them had discovered that they weren't benefiting humanity but possibly bringing its end considerably closer, and all for the career of Robin Turner and the profit line of PEP.

That and the mess he had made of his personal relationships.

He drank some more beer, finishing it and replacing it almost before he had noticed. More banter was exchanged, none of it managing to stretch over his brainstem and trouble his consciousness. He sat back in his place, still lost in Rouna.

They should have known, he supposed. Rouna was beautiful – when it wasn't cold, wet, foggy or any permutation of these – but it was so lonely. Just the journey there made him feel like an explorer, awakening idiot fears that they were nearing the edge of the world. The locals weren't too friendly, either, even those who were being paid not unhandsomely to lodge them. Jean-Jacques had likened them to a lost South American tribe.

And the laboratory. Christ, what a dump! Some sort of second world war station, used for God only knew what, then picked up by PEP on lease. PEP said they were there to ensure industrial secrecy, because Proteus was so potentially valuable, they could afford no leak. Hence the location, hence the signing of confidentiality clauses. Hence, too, the man who accompanied them on the trips there and back; the one with cold eyes that did little more than reflect your own uncertainties.

No wonder he began to drink heavily. In the evenings there was little to do, other than go to the local drinking house and sit at a table in the corner, feeling watched and at the same time unregarded by the islanders, being served by the unwelcoming, one-eyed Marble.

No wonder, too, relationships began to form between the six of them. The oddest had been the one between Stein and himself. The old man, it transpired, had a son just about his age, but he had gone bad in some way (Stein had never wanted to talk about the details). Carlos and Stein had grown close, what with Carlos's own father being dead. Eventually they had been about as close as blood kin.

But it had been the sex that had caused the problem. Isolation played tricks. At the start he wouldn't have looked more than once at either Millie or Justine (certainly wouldn't have thought about impregnating them, unless it was with a six-foot dick whilst they wore a bag over the head), yet with time they began to look strangely attractive. Millie, for instance. Not a stunner, but then when the choice was between her and a scraggy sheep in a field, well, what's a man to do?

Only trouble was Turner was having similar thoughts. Seemed to think he had *noblesse oblige*. Took exception to one of the underlings taking an interest in his property. Arrogant bastard. Should have brought things to a conclusion a lot earlier – things would have been different if he had – but at the time he was afraid for his job. In fact, at the time, he had thought he had chosen the best way. Let Turner have his "victory," all cock-of-the-walk, while he and Millie engaged in games with rod and balls behind his back. Stupid cunt was so blind he didn't actually realize for a long time. . .

Gary walked into the pub. Good old, life of the party, drinking mate extraordinaire, know how to have a good time Gary. He spotted Carlos at once and shouted, "Carl! Wotcha drinking, lad?"

Carlos, it transpired, was drinking beer.

The department was in mourning. As soon as Eisenmenger entered it, he could feel the heaviness, the loss of that which leavens, that which enervates. There was nothing objective that he could discern – there was no loss of light or temperature, no sound of weeping – but it was there and real, nonetheless.

The Department of Cancer Genetics had suffered death.

Professor Turner's secretary wasn't obviously upset. She had on her face a look of determined anger. *This is exceedingly inconvenient*, she seemed to be saying. *It's getting in the way of my work.* Eisenmenger could see her point. She was on the telephone when he went into her office and it rang three times in the few minutes he was with her. All of the calls were for Turner, all were answered with the same litany. Eventually he discovered from her where Susan Warthin was located and he made his way there.

It was like all laboratories. The corridors were crowded with large freezers, liquid nitrogen stores, boxes, filing cabinets and discarded chairs. The rooms he passed contained benches cluttered with glassware, pipette racks, boxes of pipette tips and occasional pieces of undoubtedly expensive equipment, as well as equally cluttered racks of shelving, the odd centrifuge and, every now and then, a space where someone could sit and write, or perhaps just think.

Susan Warthin was housed in such a room and she was seated at such a space, but she wasn't writing and she wasn't thinking. At first Eisenmenger thought that she was asleep but then, after standing and looking at her quarter profile from the doorway, he realized that she was just staring at a photograph on the wall in front of her. The photograph was of Millicent Sweet.

He knocked on the doorframe and it brought her head round to face him. "Oh," she said softly, surprised. "I'm sorry."

"Susan Warthin?"

She nodded. Coming into the room, he introduced himself, then nodded at the photograph. "I was hoping we could have a chat about Millicent."

At the mention of the name she seemed to collapse slightly, as if something painful had just passed through her. On her face there formed a look of caution and puzzlement. He explained, "I've been asked to look into her death, and into the mix-up over her body."

It was plain she didn't want to be reminded about any of it, but it was even plainer that she wanted – she needed – to talk. Once she started, she wasn't in the mood to let him stop her. Even when he asked questions it seemed merely to divert the flow, not interrupt it. Sitting together in the quiet of the laboratory, their voices low, he felt as if he were taking confession.

"It was horrible. To die like that. She said once that it was her greatest fear."

"How long had you known her?"

"Not long. Only about a year, but we became close quite quickly. She wasn't very outgoing – people tended to see that as stand-offish, but it wasn't. She was shy, and she'd been through a lot."

157

Eisenmenger hardly ever took notes. He was afraid that writing and listening were mutually incompatible. As a student, while his compatriots scribbled he merely sat and tried to let the lecturer's words flow into him. It had worked then, it generally worked now. "A lot?" The phrase intrigued him and found his interest quickening. "What do you mean?"

But she clamped down at once, as if she had been indiscreet. "Oh, you know. There was something about a love affair."

Perhaps there was, but he could feel she was trying to misdirect him. "She used to work for a pharmaceutical company, didn't she? Pel-Ebstein?"

Susan nodded.

"There was some sort of laboratory accident, I think. . ."

She said, "Millicent wouldn't talk about it much."

"Really? Why not, I wonder."

This was safer ground. Susan Warthin didn't mind this subject. "It was hush-hush. Millicent was bound by some sort of confidentiality clause. Actually, from what she said, I got the impression that she was almost ashamed of what she'd been doing for them. . ."

A conspiratorial style had descended, one that Eisenmenger wasn't inclined to tamper with. "Ashamed?" he said, his eyebrows raised. "But why?"

Susan shook her head. "She wouldn't say, at least not directly, but I did have my suspicions."

Her suspicions, it transpired, were that Millicent had been engaged in defence work. There was no solid evidence for this, and it left Eisenmenger unsure of the value to place upon the datum. "That final phone call," he said gently, knowing it would be painful for her, "She mentioned the word, 'Proteus.' Did that mean anything to you?"

Her face was at once pained, and her answer came through the emotion of the recollection. "I remember she'd mentioned it once before. It was something to do with her work at PEP."

"But no details?"

Another shake of the head. When he asked where the laboratory had been, she shook her head. "I'd never heard of it, but apparently it was an island off the north-west coast of Scotland. She began working there about three, three and a half years ago. She was doing her doctoral thesis; something to do with targeted mutagenesis but, as I say, she wouldn't go into details."

Eisenmenger knew little about targeted mutagenesis, except that it was very high-powered cell biology.

"She wasn't even halfway through when the accident happened and the lab closed. It was a terrific blow, to have her work destroyed like that. Most of her notes were lost, along with a couple of draft papers she was preparing for publication."

"Did she talk about the accident? It was a fire, wasn't it? Did she say what caused it?"

At once he sensed they were again getting close to something she considered a confidence, but now she was more at ease, now perhaps she was willing to tread this ground. Yet it still required something more, for she hesitated, and he had to say gently, "I think it might be important, Susan. I think it might be connected with how and why she died like that."

In truth he wasn't sure of it, wasn't sure of anything yet, but he knew it wasn't a lie.

After a moment she took the chance, still clearly afraid that she was perhaps betraying her friend. "She told me once, but asked me not to tell anyone else."

He smiled, trying to emanate reassurance. Someone walked past in the corridor and for the time that the footsteps approached they were both in apprehension, a kind of stasis in which they dared not continue. Then the intruder passed by and with it went the tension.

"She said there was a fight. She didn't know all the details, but she thought that the fire started then."

"It was deliberate? Someone started it out of revenge?"

But she was quite adamant. "No. She said that something got knocked over in the laboratory during the fight. That's what started it."

"What was the fight about?"

She paused but he quickly saw that it was embarrassment, not secrecy. "She said it was over her."

Eisenmenger glanced at the photograph of Millicent Sweet. It showed the same girl as the photograph provided by her father. Perhaps neither of them represented the true nature and appearance of the subject, but Eisenmenger had seen nothing in them that suggested she might inflame two men to assault each other over her. It was certainly an intriguing thought.

He asked, "Who? Who fought over her?"

More reluctance and for a few seconds he feared that she would not tell him, but after looking again at the photograph as if looking for guidance she said, "She said that one of them was the Professor."

"Professor? Professor who?"

She sighed. "Robin Turner."

Once, when he had first started in Forensic Pathology, he had been asked to do a post-mortem on a body found in a river. He had arrived at the scene, feeling nervous, feeling inexperienced and feeling slightly nauseous, then changed into protective clothing before joining the group that had assembled inside the temporary compound on the river bank. It had been raining, he recalled, although not particularly cold. As he entered, the uniformed police, the detectives, the police surgeon all turned to look at him and he had suddenly felt elation. He was the star, he was the single most important person there. He was at once charged with confidence.

And then he had stepped forward and the crowd had parted and there, bloated, white and sodden, had been his best childhood friend.

He felt like that now.

"Turner?" he asked incredulously. "The Turner who just died?"

"That's right."

He tried to make it as clear as he could. "Turner also worked for PEP? In the same laboratory?"

She nodded. "I think they were having an affair. When the fire happened and the project was wound up, he took her with him to this job."

Turner who had died from falling off a building but who had coincidentally also had cancer.

Eisenmenger was trying to stop his mind working too far ahead and in too many directions at once. Ideas and links were suddenly making and breaking like chemical bonds in a furnace.

"And who was Turner fighting with? Did she tell you that?"

"She told me once. She only mentioned his first name, though."

Before she actually articulated the name, he knew what it would be.

"Carlos."

Frank Cowper informed the Coroner of the startling change in Hartmann's report on Millicent Sweet before he told Beverley Wharton, but only by about a quarter of an hour. She put the phone down and pondered. First Helena Flemming, now this. And when Cowper dropped the name Eisenmenger, she felt suddenly, strangely elated.

Her interest was growing.

She had eighteen ongoing investigations, a team of sub-ordinates most of whom had an IQ below that of a stapler, and a boss whose whole life seemed to turn on making sure that she was doomed, but. . .

Beverley was a gambler. Not with money, but with success. She calculated probabilities with every bit as much objectivity as a card player, and sometimes she lost, more often she had won.

She did not think that she would lose on this occasion, not now that the talismanic name of Eisenmenger had been mentioned. Anyone else and she might have dismissed it as a waste of her time. Eisenmenger she had great respect for, recognizing that he had the knack of finding trouble and then dealing with it. If he suspected something important, she was certainly prepared to spend a few hours looking into it.

Making sure that Lambert was not around, she left the station and drove quickly to the Medical School where she found Hartmann in his office. Not doing anything, she noted, just in there, as if run to earth. She also thought that he looked close to collapse. He was shivering, as if the influenza epidemic had reached him with its ague, and he was pale with large, blue-black bags beneath bloodshot eyes. Beverley smiled at him, and perhaps he interpreted that as sympathetic but was in reality because she could see that he would be easy to break.

She began the interview pleasantly, as she usually did. Her side of the discussion was predicated on knowing that something was going on, but not knowing how significant it might be, how and where it might lead. Despite this ignorance, she smelled something important. Just a ripple on the surface but she was enough of a copper to know that what had made it wasn't small, wasn't in any way unworthy of her notice.

"Now tell me, Dr Hartmann. Why did you falsify your initial report on Millicent Sweet's autopsy?"

At the question Hartmann, whose shock when Beverley had appeared in his office had now transmuted into near-total overload of his autonomic nervous system, felt himself lose consciousness for a moment. Then the world came back, unchanged and unappeased.

This isn't fair! Eisenmenger said. . .

But Eisenmenger, he knew, had said nothing of consequence. No such promise had been aired, however he might have wished it otherwise. Eisenmenger had merely promised him what would happen if he didn't try to make good. There was nothing left to Hartmann other than acceptance that it was all over for him.

He opened his mouth, suddenly and crushingly aware that he was almost certainly about to destroy his life. Only a miracle could be of any use now.

She didn't get to call on Raymond Sweet until late in the day, due mainly to Lambert, due mainly to the fact that day by day he was working his way steadily through the *Big Bastard's Manual,* and didn't want to lose the page. So here she was, tired but the scent that came to her on the wind was strong enough to carry her. She now knew that someone had been worried enough by the death of Millicent Sweet to spend a lot of time and effort falsifying it. She knew also that the person who had done it was trained in various covert techniques, a data item she recognized not only as significant, but also consequently as possibly dangerous.

She explained to Sweet who she was and had no compunction in stating quite openly that it was an official police investigation. As she suspected, her witness was delighted that his claims were at last being taken seriously. He was more than happy to repeat everything he had told Helena and Eisenmenger; indeed, now that he had, as it were, been rehearsed, he was far more lucid.

Beverley noted it all down. Again the subject of "Carlos" arose.

"I haven't been able to find anything," he confessed. There was a sheepish, almost deceitful lilt in the statement that Beverley noticed at once. She smiled gently. "It must be so difficult for you, Mr Sweet."

He looked up at once, saw in her eyes an understanding, sympathetic young woman, and responded. "Yes."

She asked after the smallest of pauses, "Would you like me to look through her things?"

His rush to accept could, she noted, be described variously as moving or pathetic; she opted for the pragmatic response and hid the emotion she actually felt. He took her upstairs and stood in the doorway to Millie's room while she suppressed her desire and her training to ransack it, and sorted gently through the sediment of a life. She looked around as she worked, reflecting that, as soon as Millicent Sweet had breathed for the final time, all of it had turned from beloved possessions to garbage.

She found her treasure in some diaries – hideously twee and overly feminine – tucked into a drawer of the built-in cupboards. Folded at the back were some letters. They were mostly from girlfriends, but three of them were, to Beverley's gaze, of purest ray serene. One was from the mysterious Carlos; there was no home address, but amongst the nauseating lovidoviness it mentioned that he was thinking of leaving his employment at the Leishman Centre in Newcastle. He didn't mention any other details, but at least she had the end of a thread, and that would have to be enough.

The other two were unexpected and therefore even more exciting. They were from Robin Turner and they were, effectively, love letters.

Beverley didn't know how Millicent's affair with her boss fitted in to the puzzle, but she recognized jewels among dung when she saw them.

"Helena?"

It was early in the morning and he guessed he would be waking her up, but it was important. He had tried three times the night before without success, leaving each time a message on her answer phone, leaving himself each time with a sense of severe frustration.

And while most of the frustration was because he felt – he *knew* – that the pace was quickening, that something hideous was happening around them, there was a still, small voice that told him she was out and she was almost certainly out with her new friend.

Jealousy?

He didn't want to use the word to himself, but that was only because he could not allow himself to analyse his emotions.

"Helena?" he repeated before she could answer. He guessed he had woken her.

"Hello?" She sounded disorientated.

"Helena, it's John."

"Oh." Her voice was breathy, the early morning weariness layering her voice with a husky lowness of tone that was almost arousing.

"I'm sorry to wake you so early. . ."

"It's all right."

". . .but I think I've made a breakthrough of sorts."

It took her a moment to grasp what he was saying and then he heard her sit up, the sheets rustling. "What?"

"Turner worked on the same project for PEP as Millie did."

"Turner?"

"They're linked, Helena. Both in life and death."

"What does it mean?" Sleep was forgotten now.

"We ought to meet, Helena. I'll tell you then." He paused. "Oh, and get back onto Raymond Sweet. Find out if he's found anything more out about Carlos."

"Carlos?"

"He might be the key to this, Helena."

"Key to what?"

"Something very odd, I think. Have you managed to get anything on PEP yet?"

"I've asked one of the partners to look into it for me; he's an expert on company law. I hope he'll have something to say to me today."

"Good. When can we meet?"

She tried to remember her diary. "Not 'till this evening, I think. Say, six?"

Six, it would have to be.

Helena lay back in bed and beside her Alasdair, apparently disturbed by the movement opened his eyes. "Business?" he asked.

Helena said only, "Yes," then reached for her dressing gown. She slipped it on, stood, tied it and then went to the bathroom. Looking into the mirror she tried to work out why she felt as she did.

164

A virgin despoiled

It was stupid and illogical – by no stretch was the term biologically applicable – but it was how she felt. The last two nights had seen such an intensification in her relationship with Alasdair that by the time he had driven her home late last night, she had been eager to take him to bed. Within six minutes of her opening the front door they had been kissing, kissing with a passion that she found joyously, wondrously empowering. She had led him to the bedroom, past the answerphone with its waiting messages, shortly afterwards.

And yet now. . .

Now she thought that perhaps she had lost something. She felt like a drunk who had binged after a decade of abstention, like a slimmer who had been sick on cream cakes. Years of discipline dissolved.

Angrily she shook her head, sharply twisting the tap to let water run. For God's sake. She hadn't taken a vow of chastity! She was entitled to human pleasures.

Yet. . .

Yet she wondered if she had done the right thing.

Then Eisenmenger somehow found his irritating way into her culpabilities. In a near-Shakespearean manner, he appeared in her mind, bringing with him yet more reproach. What the hell did it have to do with him?

She attempted to drown her demand, made silently of no one, with the water in the sink. Like a dead fly, it would not sink away.

In the bedroom, his eyes closed, his face clouded, Alasdair Riley-Day lay and considered. He considered the night that had just passed, what he had just heard, and what he would have to do now.

Helena had been an interesting fuck. Inexperienced and somewhat conservative. He had considered it wisest not to push her into the areas that he would have preferred, not on a first session anyway, and so had allowed her to dictate the pattern of play. Still, it had had its compensations. She had an attractive body and this, together with a strangely adolescent eagerness had served to keep him fairly satisfied. He had thought that perhaps in future a few lessons might enhance the experience, but suddenly it looked as if that would not be the case, not if his deductions from what he had just heard were correct.

Things were slipping. The use of the name, "Carlos," had been so surprising he had almost given himself away. That was one matter that could not wait.

From the bathroom he heard water pouring into the basin. She would be in there at least five minutes – plenty of time.

When Helena came back into the bedroom, she was alone, with not even a note to explain her new lover's disappearance. She called out, then searched each room of the flat, but she was indisputably alone. She returned to the bedroom. What the hell was going on?

Beverley's decision to drive all the way to Scotland, a drive of over five hours, was not taken lightly. She had half-concocted a story about following up on a lead on a suspect in an organized car-stealing case, but she had still to be careful. Lambert, should he decide she was moonlighting, would at once have the ammunition he needed to put a fucking great bullet in her grey stuff. She decided it was safest not to let him know. Even though the Chief Superintendent's desire for the feel and taste of her pudenda had proved a useful defence in the past, it was not an untrumpable hand; too much trouble and even a fat, toad-like Chief Superintendent could find pleasures in other vulvas.

Thus when she began her investigations at the hotel at which Mark Hartmann had so spectacularly achieved a climax of betrayal, she was distinctly nervous. From the banqueting manager she obtained lists of delegates and company representatives who had attended the meeting, noting with interest that although Alan Rosenthal's name was listed, Claire Verner's was absent. She then spoke with various staff members, hoping (but not expecting) that they might have some recollection of Rosenthal and Claire Verner; they did not. She made an inspection of the rooms that had been occupied by Hartmann and Rosenthal and found nothing. It was all as she had expected and might have been completely unsuccessful if good fortune had not struck. The woman who showed her the rooms was the Head of Housekeeping within the hotel and, just as they were leaving the room that Rosenthal had occupied, she said, "What about the watch?"

Guests left things in their rooms all the time. Many of them, Beverley suspected, then found their way into the safety of the maid's pocket, but in this case honesty had found expression and it had been given to the hotel management for safekeeping.

In the manager's office, the watch was produced. It was in a sealed envelope carefully labelled with the room number, the date of discovery and the name of the guest staying there at the time.

"We tried to contact Mr Rosenthal, but there was a problem. The telephone number and the address he gave were apparently false." The manager sounded aggrieved, as if a nasty trick had been played on him and it had clearly been Beverley's fault. He was about to open the envelope when Beverley stopped him.

"Don't!"

Startled he froze, his face wearing a wide-eyed expression, perhaps fearing a bomb.

"Fingerprints," she explained, holding out her hand, into which he dropped the envelope as if it were suddenly radio-active. "Who else handled it?"

The manager, a tall, saturnine man who gave the strong impression that managing hotels (or at least the Pretender Hotel) was not for him, did not know; the housekeeper was also ignorant. It would make life harder but it least it would not make it impossible.

She had disposable gloves in her bag, which she now put on. Inside the envelope there was an expensive, gold-plated watch. It was big and heavy and it made a statement about its owner. It was not the kind of watch that you lost in a hotel room and then didn't bother about. When she turned it over, she saw that it was engraved – *A. R.* – and Beverley Wharton decided that God was a nice old bugger after all.

She dropped the watch into Forensics as soon as she returned, but did not get the chance to begin making computer searches until the next day. Lambert had gone home, she had finished her shift and the station was relatively quiet. She had already decided that she wasn't going to do this alone; even the advantages brought by computers didn't mean that it wasn't a tedious, boring, largely unrewarding job. She had done more than her fair share of such unthinking automation to know that she would not do it now.

"Lyme?"

Lyme was possibly the most repulsive human being she had ever met, and that included those she had arrested. He exuded a sort of unsavoury odour that poisoned the air and made all around him feel faintly nauseous. He was short and squat, almost of Dickensian proportions and habits, with table manners that were legendarily deficient, and abilities as a policeman that were similarly absent. He was kept out of sight for much of the time, only brought out when strength and sadism were required in abundance.

He looked up from his present task, that of compiling the traffic offence statistics for the past month, and cast a porcine glance in her direction. As usual there was a good percentage of leer in his expression.

No chance, Fatso. I'd rather be fucked by a gangrenous leper.

"I've got a job for you."

He looked unhappy but he couldn't argue. He looked even more unhappy when she told him what he had to do, "See these names?" she asked, presenting him with the list of hotel guests and delegates. "I want each and every one of them checked for convictions. This one especially." She pointed out Rosenthal.

"What, all of 'em?" he asked, incredulous.

"Every single one of them."

"It'll take me ages." He had a whine in his voice that was constantly being exercised.

"Then you'd better start straightaway, hadn't you?"

He didn't look happy but then, she decided, that wouldn't have helped. Somehow Lyme's very existence suggested that nose picking and arse scratching had an hereditary basis.

She decided to take some light refreshment. When she returned an hour later, he had just finished and was reading a comic.

"Anything?"

"Nope." His tone suggested that he could have told her that at the start.

"What about Rosenthal?"

He smiled the smile that an enemy smiles. "Nothing."

She was used to this. Had it not been the answer she was expecting, she would have been angered by his attitude. As it was, she merely smiled back and said, "If I'd thought it was going to produce anything of worth, I wouldn't have asked a piece of useless pigshit like you to do it."

Which, pending the watch, left her with the company to investigate. She picked up the phone, dialled and then waited for a few moments. "Lucas Hammon, please."

Lucas was an old friend. An old, old friend.

"Yes?"

"Lucas? It's Beverley."

She hadn't seen or spoken to him for a long time. The sound of his voice was deliciously nostalgic.

"Beverley! How are you?"

His voice had always had a deep, rhythmic lilt, as if with every word he was trying to caress and seduce her, and it brought back wonderful memories, wonderful feelings. She knew that he would have heard of her recent misfortunes, but she also knew that he would have been one of the few who had felt genuine sorrow. Lucas was the nearest she had ever come to love.

"Not too bad, Luke. Considering."

He said at once, his voice steeped in sympathy, "Yeah, I heard. I'm sorry about all the shit, Beverley."

"And you, Luke?" she asked , not wanting to dwell on the subject.

"Fine, fine."

"Still in Fraud?" She wondered if he was still married, if he still loved his beautiful baby daughter as much, if he still liked to raid the fridge after making love.

"Nowhere else to go." He sounded content.

"Can you do me a favour?"

The question elicited the first touch of caution in his voice. "Such as?"

"I've come across a company – Wiskott-Aldrich – I was wondering if you could poke around for me. Find out who, what and where."

The voice was still lazy and easy-going as he asked, "This official?"

"Not exactly."

He hesitated, the first tangible sign that he was aware of how radioactive she had become. "It'll take a day or two, but I don't see why not."

"Good," she said, relieved. "I'm really grateful, Luke."

He laughed quietly into the phone. "Really? Like, how much?"

An image of his firm, smooth, ebony flesh whipped through her head and she smiled. "How much would you like?"

Helena came away from the firm's business meeting more than usually bored and depressed. The agenda of such meetings was invariable in construction and invariable in its execution – monotony, pedancy and orthodoxy in equal proportions, spiced with a few drops of spite – and it therefore left her invariably low, but today the emotion was magnified. She sat in her office, with the papers on a charge of embezzlement brought against Cedric Godfrey Codman spread before her, crying mutely but ineffectually for her attention. She felt a physical malaise, almost nausea, that was persistently trying to force tears from her. Tears that she hadn't until now thought were within her.

Alasdair had gone. Gone suddenly and gone, she knew, irrevocably. No note, no call of departure, just absence. Its peculiarity of manner and complete unexpectedness leaving her stunned. She felt herself falling back into the time following her parents' death, back when Jeremy, her stepbrother, had been her only hope, and when that hope had been extinguished by Beverley Wharton.

What had happened?

She looked through the events of the previous night, trying to find something that might indicate why she should have returned from the bathroom to find him vanished, only the warmth of the bed and murmur of his cologne remaining. Yet there was nothing, she was sure. She had not upset him, nor had she heard or seen anything that could have suggested this was coming. He had been happy, of that she was convinced.

So why had he gone?

It was the first opportunity she had had to phone him and she was dreading it. Ignorance was bad, but perhaps it would prove better than the acquisition of knowledge. She hesitated, eyeing the matt black plastic of the phone almost as an enemy, then breathed out fiercely as she picked up the receiver and dialled.

"Could I speak to Alasdair, please? Alasdair Riley-Day?"

But there was, it seemed, a problem. The Personnel Department of Cronkhite-Canada had never heard of Alasdair Riley-Day. "What do you mean?" she demanded. "He's your departmental director! Of course you've heard of him!"

The gentleman was apologetic but stupidly intransigent. Unbelievably he insisted that there was no such person working there, certainly not as his superior.

Helena didn't know which emotion to allow. Incredulity? Panic? Fear? Sorrow?

"Who is the Director of Personnel?"

Samantha Carpus.

"Could I please speak to her, please?"

She got to speak to her secretary, but it didn't matter. The refrain was the same. There was no one in the Personnel Department at Cronkhite-Canada – no one in the whole of Cronkhite-Canada – by the name of Alasdair Riley-Day.

There never had been.

Belinda's phonecall had been full of excitement as well as full of perplexity. She had some results from her analysis of Millicent Sweet's tissues to show Eisenmenger.

"And?" he asked.

"Well, they're a bit complicated," she began, then continued after a brief pause, "In fact, they're really odd. . ."

He felt interest prick him; a slight and pleasurable pain.

"Can I meet you? You could explain what you've found."

"It'll have to be tomorrow lunchtime. I've got so much to do . . ."

They arranged to meet in the Hospital Restaurant.

Justine Nielsen had worked hard on her thesis all night and felt that, tired as she was, the world was good. She shut down the laptop, just as the eastern sky above the New York skyline was starting to turn into a hazy salmon pink. The sounds of irate traffic were growing louder, changing from occasional horns and squeals into a more generalized rumble of sound. From her cramped space in the laboratory on the seventeenth floor of Columbia University she felt above it all. Columbia wasn't in the best part of the city, but it was still imbued with the sense of place, and Justine, relatively newly arrived, was thoroughly enjoying herself.

171

She picked up her bag, hefted the laptop carrying-case over her shoulder and made her way to the lifts. Few people were around and most of those she met were not keen to engage in meaningless chatter, a disinclination that she cherished. She had got into the habit of working at night – especially when she was writing up – some years ago when she had been an under-graduate, and she found that it suited her. Counter-intuitively, she found that it didn't interfere with her social life, since now she would go home, sleep, meet Rico for a drink and meal that evening, then return to the University for another go at her thesis.

Another advantage was that the subway was relatively deserted whenever she travelled, certainly in the direction she was going, and there was always the luxury of a seat. On odd occasions she had found that this had the disadvantage of finding herself alone with people that she found less than attractive, but she was learning that most of the danger was in her own fears; she had not yet found herself threatened.

On this day, the journey was again uneventful and she emerged onto the sidewalk near her apartment in northern Brooklyn unscathed. She had only a short walk across the street and up a single flight of stairs to her front door.

She had three locks on the door, the last being a Yale. She turned this, pushed and entered her apartment.

The explosion killed five people, including a five-year-old boy in the apartment above. The body of Justine Nielsen was never found.

"Inspector?"

The voice rang down the corridor, slicing through the smells of polish, sweat and disinfectant, the echoes racing off on every side to make a reinforcing chorus. Beverley recognized it immediately. Lambert. There were three constables and a female clerk between the two of them; she saw a range of looks on their faces, from sly amusement through to sympathy. Everyone knew that they weren't the finest of friends.

"Sir?"

"I'd like a word with you. Now."

Even for Lambert he sounded, she thought angry. Then she reconsidered; actually, incandescent could have been an underestimate. She had been about to set out on a tour of the local public houses, not with the idea of inebriation but because it was part of an ongoing enquiry into contraband cigarettes. It was Lambert himself who had told her to go, but she was by now used to such capriciousness. She turned and walked back past the onlookers, ignoring their attention. She had a shrewd idea what this was about.

In his office, Lambert sat in his chair, the action one of violence rather than gentility. The chair, an aged thing of tatters and tarnishes, squeaked feebly. She followed him in, shutting the door very deliberately, preparing herself for the onslaught.

"What's going on?" He sounded, she judged, like a man who thought he knew exactly what was going on, but she risked prevarication.

"Sir?"

"Don't, Inspector," he warned, his voice seeming to come from somewhere dark and dangerous. Indicating two folders in front of him he said, "Unauthorized computer searches. Unauthorized forensic tests. Those I know about; what else is there?"

Lyme. She couldn't prove it, but then she couldn't prove that two and two were four, and that had never bothered her. She took three deep breaths and cross her fingers behind her back. "It's the Macleod case, sir."

He frowned. "What about the Macleod case?" Cars stolen to order, shipped abroad within twenty-four hours. Macleod was making tens of thousands a month out of it.

"I had information that Macleod spent a night in Glasgow, at the Pretender Hotel. I thought it worth checking out."

He didn't believe her but she didn't care about that; all that mattered was whether he could disprove it. "Why the secrecy? Where's your report?" He knew better than to ask her where the information had come from.

"It was a long shot. I didn't think it worth making a fuss about unless it panned out."

He stared at her. She wondered why he hated her quite so much, what lay behind his enmity. Then he said, "What about the watch?"

Smooth as a lover's sigh she replied at once. "It was found in Macleod's room. I thought we might pick up who he saw while he was there. Same reason I did a search on the guest list, sir."

Again the stare, then he picked up one of the folders and thrust it at her. "Maybe you struck lucky, Inspector." He sounded not so much congratulatory as in discomfort. "One of the four partials on the watch was on the file. Follow it up."

She took the folder, feeling both elated and anxious. The last thing she needed was Lambert pestering her about this particular line of enquiry. There would have to be some creative report writing. Still, hey-ho, nothing she couldn't manage.

He dismissed her with nothing more than a slight but curt movement of his head.

Outside she opened the folder. The partial fingerprint had belonged to Adam Rytand, which was fine, but then she turned to his record and things became very interesting indeed. Rytand was no ordinary criminal; far from it. Rytand was ex-special services which meant he was trained for a huge variety of dirty operations, including, no doubt, blackmail; it also probably meant that he was a killer. He was on file because of a burglary offence eleven years before, nothing stolen.

The problem was that Rytand was dead, killed abroad seven and half years before.

Beverley Wharton knew then that Eisenmenger had been right, that here was something rotten just waiting to be punctured. Here, she was certain, was an opportunity and she was damned to hell if she was going to let Lambert spoil it for her. Somehow or other this would be to her advantage, and no one else's.

Smiling, she moved down the corridor clutching the file to her chest. She decided that the first thing to do would be to find Lyme.

It hadn't been a good day. The gene transfer experiments had failed again and the nude mice were still not developing signs of the expected neurological deficits that would have meant that they could be used as a model for multiple sclerosis. Dr Sommer, the post-doc for whom Carlos was working and the one behind both sets of experiments, hadn't actually accused him of incompetence, but there had been a sort of hint in the air as they discussed what might have gone wrong.

Also his morning headache would not behave and dissipate with the usual remedy of rehydration, non-steroidal anti-inflammatories and extra- strong mints. Nerys had shown her dissatisfaction that he had once again come in drunk and unable to contribute to her erotic pleasures by crashing two saucepan lids over his head as he dozed fitfully.

No, not a good day.

He had heard the news from a friend of an acquaintance. *Turner's dead.* Surprised, he had asked for details. It had happened a few weeks before, apparently. Turner had fallen from the top of a car park. Possibly suicide.

Carlos had no desire to suppress his immediate response – *serves the bastard right* – and for the first few hours quite enjoyed the thought that Turner was dead. Only later did his mind come to dwell on Millie.

He still held affection for Millie. She had become for him something of an innocent in the series of events that had ended their time on Rouna and he could not blame her for her part in the events. He had written to her, attempting to express that feeling, had even once visited her in that crappy flat she lived in.

He wondered how she was.

Just before six that evening, he rang Turner's laboratory to speak to her. He got through to Susan Warthin.

Helena stared out of the window not because the view was today more worthy of scrutiny, but because she had found herself unable to sit at that bloody desk a moment longer. For a brief but glorifying instant she had thrilled to the thought of taking Cedric Godfrey Codman, and his embezzlement of three hundred and thirty-nine pounds, sixty-seven pence, and casting them to the city's winds; but, perhaps fortunately, the moment had passed. Now she clutched her arms around her chest, locked together in rigid control, staring at sky, at something that was outside and therefore endurable.

She could feel herself shaking.

Something was terribly, terribly, wrong.

A knock on the door and then, before she could do anything more than turn, it opened and in came Stuart Carney. Eyebrows raised, he asked, "Have you got a moment, Helena?"

She was about to say that no, she didn't have a moment, when he continued, "Only I've got the info you wanted on Wiskott-Aldrich."

This stayed her refusal. Deep breath, then, "Of course. Come in. Coffee?"

He accepted, as he always did. Only after he had tried on several occasions to initiate trivial conversation designed to ingratiate himself with her, did they begin discussion of Wiskott-Aldrich.

"It was a sod of a job, actually."

Helena liked Stuart. He was slightly too tall, slightly too skinny and slightly too diffident, but all of them in a way she found appealing. This tendency towards a near-imperceptible exaggeration of qualities and physical attributes continued when she considered the width of his grin, the indelicacy of his language and the wisdom of his wardrobe. He had asked her out on numerous occasions, and on some she had accepted, but in her perception Stuart was forever a friend, no matter how much he sometimes made her laugh.

"It took me much longer than I thought it would." He didn't exactly let the sentence trail, but it was a damned close-run thing. With a mouse-sized pause, he added, "In fact I was here until nine o'clock last night. . ."

This time he definitely did let the sentence trail. His eyes held a pleading look, but Helena couldn't resist letting him suffer just a little. "Last Friday I was here until eleven," she pointed out, deadpan.

"Oh." His eyes shifted their gaze downwards in perfect synchronization with the corners of his mouth. Had she strangled a kitten Helena would have felt no less cruel.

"But I am grateful, Stuart."

The result was immediate and marvellous to behold. She felt good just to see it, felt that she had increased the sum of mankind's joy. He grinned so widely she lost sight of the ends of his mouth. He murmured, "Well it was nothing really."

"So what was so difficult?" she asked, before he could ask her out for a meal.

He had with him a box-file and this he now opened. "To put it simply Wiskott-Aldrich exists in name only."

"A dummy?"

"Pretty much. It's based in South Georgia – that's the godforsaken one in the South Atlantic, not the American or the Russian one."

"Is that a tax haven?"

"Actually, it's not any kind of a haven."

"Then why there?"

He shrugged. "It's a long way off, I suppose. I must admit, though, it's a first."

"Okay. So if it's a dummy, who's hiding behind it?"

"Ah. That's where the trouble started. The trail leads through several companies and corporations, some of which are real, some of which are just shells."

"Is there any pattern as to what these companies do?"

He scanned two sides of A4 that were covered in scrawl. After a while he said, "Not really, but then there never is in cases like this."

"What do you mean?"

The opportunity to impress brought out the most irritating and most enchanting aspects of Stuart, she reflected ruefully. He almost cleared his throat as though he were appearing as an advocate before a particularly impressionable High Court Judge. Leaning forward, his hands clasped and his forearms on the beech of her desk, he explained, "If you're trying to hide money, you don't make it easy by sifting it through obviously connected companies. You add a little diversity to the mix."

She considered this. "So, where does this trail lead?"

"Nowhere exciting, I'm afraid."

"What about Pel-Ebstein Pharmaceuticals?

Stuart's surprise was translated into a portrait of open mouth, opened eyes, reared head; she saw such innocent surprise at her question, such a naif, that she almost felt pity for him. With Stuart what you saw was not only what you got, it was all that he possessed. "Pel-Ebstein? But how. . ?"

"So they are behind it?" she asked excitedly.

Stuart's hesitation acted as something of a depressant. "It's not that simple. It's not that A leads to B which leads to C, and so on. It tends to get very complicated, very quickly. Also, it's quite boring."

"Bore me, then."

He handed over a list that he took from his box. On it Helena counted sixteen names.

"See what I mean?" he asked.

Except that she didn't, for her eyes were fixed on one of the sixteen names.

Cronkhite-Canada.

"Helena?"

She felt light-headed, as if about to faint, but she fought to retain some sort of appearance of command. Sighing, she asked, "Look, Stuart. Just tell me one thing. Is it possible to prove that Pel-Ebstein are behind all this?"

His face suggested that he found the question completely beyond his ability to comprehend. After a few seconds of facial contortion and faint, guttural squeaks he eventually said, "Well, you can prove a tentative connection, but you won't ever prove anything as direct as Pel-Ebstein using Wiskott-Aldrich for nefarious purposes. There are so many interconnections involving other businesses, it's almost a meaningless question."

He left, still hoping for more than he was going to get, still unable to find it within himself to ask. Helena sat and brooded for a long time, silence her only companion. Maybe there could never be legal proof, but there were other forms of certainty. PEP, she now felt certain, was behind what had happened to Mark Hartmann.

Jean-Jacques Renvier was enjoying a pastis in a small cafe near the Picasso Museum in Paris. He had not worked for several months and didn't much feel like working now; life was good. Daphne, his newly acquired, and exceedingly affluent girl-friend was late (late again was a more apposite and accurate description, but Jean-Jacques appreciated that money distorts time just as much as mass and energy) but he would forgive her.

He smiled, thinking of his good fortune. Yes, he had to admit, he had been lucky this time. When the fire occurred at the laboratory he had, not unnaturally, been afflicted with a feeling of uncertainty concerning the future. What would happen now? Learning that PEP were going to close down the operation had increased this alarm. He was a lowly laboratory technician – one of the paid staff rather than one of the high-flying intellectuals – and he knew companies like PEP did not consider them much above the laboratory animals he was required to clean out; it was not an aspect of his career that he had dwelt on when recounting his career to Daphne. Yet, surprisingly, they had offered him further employment and, to his surprise, it had been in his native country.

In fact, they had been surprisingly solicitous towards him. . .

In truth, that had worried him.

At first, he had wondered if Proteus. . .

But the blood tests had been negative and their concern for his future had, they had explained quite logically, been because his participation in the project meant that he possessed information that was very commercially sensitive.

Which was why he had recently left his job with PEP and was now trying to make informal contact with one of its competitors, Li-Fraumini.

Where was she? She had said that she was coming from her grandmother's, a not insignificant abode in Montmartre; she had to keep the old bag sweet because this was the source of all things pecuniary in Daphne's life. Another pastis would, he decided, be welcome. He turned to attract the waiter's attention and was therefore surprised to see a man sitting at his table when he turned back.

"M. Renvier?"

He said that he was. The other was short and slightly fat. He had friendly eyes and the kind of face that would never look clean-shaven. "I am from Li-Fraumini."

Jean-Jacques was surprised but delighted. "I didn't expect you to contact me so soon!"

A welcoming, reassuring smile. "Believe me, Monsieur, we were very interested to hear from you. Very interested indeed. Can we talk?"

Jean-Jacques hesitated. "My girlfriend's due. Could we not make an appointment to meet? Perhaps tomorrow?"

Still the expression of happy reassurance, even as the man was shaking his head. He gestured towards a car parked, illegally, just down the road. "Absolutely. My boss is in the car. You will need to make the arrangements with him."

Jean-Jacques continued his vacillation but, when a glance up and down the street saw no sign of Daphne, he said, "Well, if it will only take a few moments."

He walked to the car with the short man just as the waiter brought out the pastis.

He never drank it. One minute later, in the back of the car, he was shot through the right temple and two hours later he was buried in a specially prepared lime pit, just to the north of Orleans.

Luke had done well, an impression that was obvious both from his surroundings – his office was quiet and orderly, his colleagues not obviously drawn from Nature's earlier efforts – but also by his attitude. He had always exuded charm and confidence, but now he transmitted a sense of complete assuredness. He might not yet have arrived, but he knew that he was close to the entry.

Beverley found herself wondering at her own position, sensing within herself a hint of inferiority. It was neither a comfortable nor an accustomed thought but it did make her momentarily wonder if she were doing the right thing, if she shouldn't even now go to Lambert and lay everything before him. If he chose to ignore it, that was his mistake.

But Beverley Wharton was not moulded into that particular shape. A single setback in a career that had been otherwise relentlessly upwards, that was all she had suffered. She had now the chance to obliterate that abnormality; she would take it.

Luke made her welcome, giving her coffee from real china, seating her in a chair that was padded. He wanted to make small talk, but she was in a hurry. "Tell me about Wiskott-Aldrich, Luke."

He hesitated and at once she sensed something wrong. "Problem?"

He bobbed his head, his mouth grimacing. "Maybe, maybe not."

When he said nothing more, she put her hand on his and said quietly, "Please? For old times' sake?"

He smiled and then, from a drawer, he produced a file that he pushed towards her. "Wiskott-Aldrich is an interesting company. Somebody's laid a lot of camouflage on it, just so that people like me can't quite work out who actually owns it, and who actually uses it."

"Who does own it?"

"Pel-Ebstein Pharmaceuticals."

She had a feeling he would say that. She had no feeling whatsoever that he would then say, "There's a suggestion in the files that ghosts have been using it."

She stared at him, then at the orange file she was holding. Ghosts – national security. Was he joking?

"Just a suggestion, of course. Nothing concrete."

There never was, not with ghosts. These were ghosts, though, who could hurt. It changed matters, raised the stakes, but it didn't make her any less intrigued. Far from it. She said, "There was a fire at a laboratory owned by Pel-Ebstein. It was on some island somewhere off Scotland. I need to know more about it."

He sighed. There was a veneer of insouciance but she knew him well enough to see worry beneath. She took his hand having first glanced around to ensure that there was privacy. "I've missed you."

He looked down at the hand. When his face came up, there was a huge lazy grin on it. "You're one saucy bitch, Bev. One saucy bitch."

He laughed, loud and booming. She smiled, enjoying his happiness, and was taken by surprise when it abruptly ended and he leaned forward close to her ear and whispered, "You – and me – we need to be careful of this. Very, very careful."

"My god! What are you doing here?"

Nerys had a voice that could slice cheese. He grinned. "I live here, don't I?"

She laughed. "Ha! You puke, shit and snore here, but I'm not sure you live here."

He fought the immediate reaction of annoyance. She was, after all, entitled to be slightly mad at him. "Look, Nerys, I know I haven't been much company lately. . ."

"You don't say! Not much company!' That has got to be the understatement of the decade!" There was so much sarcasm in her voice he found himself fearing to drown in it.

"But I'm trying to put things right between us."

She looked sceptical. "Oh, yes? And how are you doing that?"

He shrugged. "Look, I'm sorry, Nerys. I've been a shit, but I promise I'll behave. I thought we could have a takeaway. Nice night in, a bottle or two of wine." He put his hand under her chin and smiled the smile that he knew she liked.

She snorted, but something told him he was winning. "Isn't that just typical! He manages to choose the one night of the week when I go out."

He tried to work out which day it was, decided that it was Thursday, then remembered her pottery lessons. "Oh, God. Night class. I'm sorry, Nerys. . ."

The irritation resurfaced. "How could you forget, Carl? Every fucking Thursday I go out."

"But I did, really. Do you have to go? Can't you leave it for once?" He almost won her round. Her expression had softened and she was clearly no longer incandescent, but she was a dedicated potter.

"I must," she said.

Left alone he sorted a can of lager from the fridge, sat down and drank from it thirstily. Without company he was forced to think and his only thoughts were centred on his former colleagues.

First Turner, then Millie. It was incredible.

And the way she had died. . .

He told himself that it was coincidence. All six of them had tested negative after the fire. . . they had seen the results. Therefore, it had nothing to do with Proteus. Simple.

He dug in the breast pocket of his jacket, pulling out his address book. It would do no harm to ensure that Jean-Jacques and Justine were all alive and well.

By the end of the evening, he was a very frightened man indeed. He knew that he had to leave, that quite probably his life depended on it.

But where could he go?

His mother was still alive, but he had never got on well with her, hadn't even talked to her for four years; anyway, if someone were going to look for him, it was an obvious place to go. There were various people he knew in Newcastle, some of whom would probably be willing to put him up for a day or two, providing he didn't tell them that he thought somebody was out to kill him, but they were too close; he needed distance. Various ex-girlfriends suggested themselves, then excused themselves as he recalled how he tended to exit relationships rather abruptly.

Suddenly it came to him that he didn't have many friends left.

In fact, he had only one person to whom he could now turn. Perhaps the one person who might be able to explain just what was going on.

"I hope this is going to help you." Belinda was more nervous than Eisenmenger had ever seen her before. She fidgeted, playing with the folder that she had brought with her into the hospital dining room. Eisenmenger played with the food, wondering simultaneously why she was so jumpy and whether the folder would provide better provender if he sunk his molars into the cardboard rather than the *Chicken à la King* on his plate. At the very least it would be a Stewards' Enquiry on the decision. He noticed that Belinda had declined to take nourishment, presumably because, since she worked there, she knew what to expect; probably still had the heartburn. Helena, perhaps exhibiting some primeval and previously untapped instinct for survival, had intuitively opted for bottled water.

"Let's see, shall we?" he said.

He laid down his fork, thankful for a distraction. Like every hospital restaurant he had ever known, it was decrepit; did they make them that way? It was well past the lunchtime rush so that they were part of only a small crowd in the large, gloomy rectangle with its regular rows of plastic-topped tables and their more haphazard foot soldiers, the chairs. A sprinkling of porters, a drizzle of junior doctors, the odd, flurried shower of nurses were all that remained, like detritus left when the flood had ebbed. Their jaws trudged their way through the fare with grim tenacity, only their eyes telling of the distress that their taste buds were feeling.

"What I did was to extract both the DNA and the RNA. . ."

Aware that Helena probably wouldn't have the necessary scientific background, he interrupted. "Helena's not medical. You'd better keep it simple." He glanced across at the lawyer, who nodded her gratitude. Belinda started again.

"What I did was to digest the tissue samples so that I could extract the genetic material. DNA is the stuff that genes are made of – if I analyse that I can tell whether there are any structural abnormalities in them. RNA is the stuff that acts as a messenger between the genes and the rest of the cell; if I analyse that I can tell which genes are being switched on. Cancers can form because of structural abnormalities in the genes, or because genes are being switched on or off when they shouldn't be."

Helena managed a nod that implied comprehension and probably, Eisenmenger reflected, she did understand.

"The problem with RNA is that's very, very fragile. It was never designed to last long, so in order to preserve it, you make a DNA copy of it, called cDNA.

"You can then analyse the DNA using things called *Restriction Enzymes*. Basically they cut DNA at specific points in the sequence. If the structure has changed, the points at which they cut are changed. The fragments they produce are therefore of different sizes to normal. If you use fluorescent markers and run the fragments through a special machine, you can see which pieces have altered in position and therefore deduce what abnormalities there are."

"Fluorescence scanning?" asked Helena and Eisenmenger laughed at his own presumptuousness. She smiled a smile at Eisenmenger that telegraphed her triumph.

Eisenmenger bowed his head. "My apologies if I was patronizing" he said. "I just assumed. . ."

"Oh, don't worry, I don't really know much about it, but I'm a lawyer. I spend most of my life trying to understand other people – their jobs, their hobbies, their psychologies. A year or so ago I had a case involving DNA evidence. I picked up a few terms but never really managed to grasp many of the principles."

Belinda looked at Eisenmenger. "Carry on," he suggested.

"You get a printout that looks a little confusing at first. . ." She produced a roll of paper on which was a graph extended on the x-axis; a line formed peaks and valleys of varying magnitude while along the axes were numbers. Eisenmenger moved his plate on to an adjacent table and she spread it out on the table, so that they could see it. Helena moved her chair closer.

"And?" he prompted.

Belinda opened her mouth as if ready to impart a coherent, reasoned account, then shrugged, smiled and said merely, "It's chaos."

"Meaning?"

"Each tumour sample I analysed has at least sixteen genetic structural abnormalities. Many of them have dozens more."

Helena asked, "And normally? What would the results be like in most cases of cancer?"

"Just a few abnormalities. Maybe as few as one, maybe as many as ten, twelve."

"So these cancers are aggressive? Is that what you're saying?"

Belinda nodded. Helena commented, "That tells us nothing we didn't already know."

"There's more," Belinda interrupted. They looked at her.

"Many cancers have their own characteristic abnormalities, but here they've all got the same basic set."

"The sixteen you mentioned?"

She nodded. Then, as they digested this, she went on, "The analysis of the cDNA confirmed expression of a constant subset of genes in all tumour types. Most of them have got a whole lot more besides, but these are always there. Even in tumours where normally you wouldn't expect to see them."

Helena asked, "Chaos? Genetic chaos? Is that what you're saying?"

Belinda hesitantly replied, "Yes and no. You see, cancer is a step-by-step sequence of genetic events, each contributing to the development of the tumorous cell. Along the way, though, other things go wrong with the genes that probably don't directly add to the process of carcinogenesis. Those are termed 'secondary events.' Here there are huge numbers of such events and the overall picture is one of chaos, but underneath it all, in every tumour, there are always these sixteen genetic changes."

Eisenmenger said, "Are those sixteen changes characteristically seen in any kind of cancer?"

Belinda shook a worried head. "I asked around, just to make sure. No one I spoke to knew of any tumour that you would expect to see all sixteen in."

They looked down at the printouts, each with their thoughts.

"It also shows something else." She said this hesitantly, almost apologetically. Another roll of paper was produced and flattened for their perusal. "This," she said, pointing at a huge peak, far to the right of the graph.

"What's that?" asked Eisenmenger.

"I didn't know at first. It shouldn't be there, though. Also, it's in every sample"

Surprisingly quickly, Helena asked, "You mean that it's contamination?"

Belinda admitted, "That was certainly the first possibility I considered. I used PCR – Polymerase Chain Reaction – to analyse the cDNA. It's notoriously prone to contamination like this."

Helena seemed to take this as negation of everything, but Eisenmenger said, "But you're not sure? Can you sequence it? Find out what it is exactly?"

"I did that. I got someone in the virology lab to help me because I haven't done much sequencing."

"And?" Helena noticed that Eisenmenger was by now impatient, excited. "What is it?"

She produced more paper, a lot of it. A much, much longer graph with four lines undulating up and down in green, red, blue and black, seemingly going on for metres. Above each peak was a letter – A, C, U or G – endlessly repeating in a random pattern.

"All of the samples gave the same sequence. When we ran it through the databases looking for areas of similarity with known genes we got a peculiar result."

Eisenmenger was staring at the letter sequence as if he could read it directly. Helena asked, "What do you mean?"

Belinda was looking genuinely bewildered by now. "It contains all sixteen genes, interspersed with sequences that I'm having a tough time interpreting. Also the introns are missing."

That one missed Helena by a long way. "What does that mean?"

Eisenmenger was still staring at the sheet as he said, "Genes aren't easy things. God, whoever, made them in bits called, 'exons' – 'exons are separated by long stretches of DNA that are apparently useless, at least as far as constructing genes is concerned – they're the 'introns'. When a gene is expressed and translated into RNA, only the exons are actually used; the introns are excised and discarded. Some people have speculated that the introns aren't useless, we just don't know what they're for yet."

"So why is this significant?"

"Because it's difficult to think of a reason why all sixteen genes should turn up strung together in a line and without their introns." Suddenly he smiled but it wasn't a joke that he had to tell. "At least, not a natural one," he said.

Eisenmenger gave Helena a lift to her flat. There had been a time when he would have expected to come up with her if only for coffee and talk, but he thought it wiser not to presume too much. As he pulled up outside he noticed that it was in almost the same place as the time when Marie had suddenly appeared, nearly knocking Helena down, spitting jealous delusion like acid. When he commented on this, Helena barely heard him.

"Look, Helena. What's wrong?" he said at last, infuriation overcoming delicacy. "You've been behaving as if you're in another universe all evening."

She had been about to get out, her body language suggesting she just wanted to be out of his presence. His question appeared momentarily to act as a spur to this for she was almost out and gone before she stopped, one foot on the road surface, and turned back to him. She wore a resigned, almost deflated expression as she said, "You'd better come up. I think something terrible has happened."

Beverley had returned to the station. She wasn't about to trust pondlife like Lyme with any more work. Anyway, things were starting to look interesting, although she didn't yet know precisely what it was that was interesting. Not yet. Several hours' work, though, might just make the shape of things clearer.

She began by running checks on Millicent Sweet and Robin Turner, finding nothing of fantastic interest. She discovered that Turner had been recently married and noted down his address for future reference. Then, aware that it was getting late, she tracked down the number of the Leishman Centre, Newcastle, dialled it and was put through to the Personnel Department. A problem soon showed itself, for she found that the phone was answered by a young woman who appeared to function despite having shit for brains.

"I can't give out the information."

She was entirely right, and Beverley knew it, but that wasn't the point. She had to find out who and where Carlos was, and she had neither the time nor the inclination to involve the local force in an unofficial enquiry.

"Look, I told you. I am Inspector Wharton. I am a member of the police. I must have that information."

"How do I know you're not lying?"

Sweet holy fucking Jesus!

Beverley hated the Geordie accent, finding it almost contrived. "My dear, I'm not asking for the combination number of the company vaults. Nor am I interested in discovering whether the Chief Executive wears women's clothing and sticks cucumbers up his arse as a party trick. All I want to know is have you ever had an employee by the name of Carlos somebody or other and, if so, his full name and where he lives."

"There's no need to be dirty."

"This is important, love. Don't fuck me around."

"Well, really!"

Give me the strength to cope with this. "What's your name, love? I need it because I'm going to charge you with obstructing the police. This is a murder investigation, I'm on. I haven't got time for fucking jobsworths like you."

At last she made an impact. There was a pause, then, "Murder?"

"That's right. Murder. So be quick and tell me what I need to know, there's a sweetie."

It took a further ten minutes and referral to her line manager, but eventually the girl came back. There had only ever been one employee at the Leishman Centre for Neurological Diseases with the forename of Carlos – Carlos Arias-Stella. However, he had not reported in for work that day. No message, no reason given.

"You must have a home address for him."

It was a flat in the city centre. They even had a phone number for it, but when Beverley called it, she met a problem. Carlos Arias-Stella had left. The woman didn't know where he had gone and, judging from her tone, wasn't in a fit state to help her find out.

For the moment frustrated, she turned her attention to Robin Turner's widow.

Rosenthal called at the anonymous block of flats just as the rush hour was dying and the harsh, neon-lit contrasts of light and dark, something and nothing, presence and absence, began to bite into his eyes. His face was hardened into an expression that by losing its humanity, gained in a sort of beauty. The eyes, in shedding softness, donned clarity and lines that Leonardo might have massaged into stone; the mouth thinned the lips and accentuated the jawline, the cheekbones more noticeable. Rosenthal was never more handsome than when he was going to kill.

The journey had been long and somewhat rushed, but he had wanted this task himself while the others, located as they had been across the world, had been left to local organizations. It was a matter of pride as well as professional confidence that he do this one himself; this one, and then the final one. Still, he had always had a liking for Newcastle. Some of the best men he had ever known had come from the city or its surroundings; some of the best men who were now part of a dead past that would not let him be.

He sniffed the air, finding the sweet, cloying aroma of malt, presumably from a brewery. He hated beer, hated it as much the people who drank it. He wondered if Carlos Arias-Stella drank it; presumably he did, considering the name.

The front door was solid; wood that had recently been repainted for perhaps the twentieth time and a small panel of frosted, toughened glass. Beside it was a panel of six buttons and six small grilles, illuminated by the circular light above that was strung about by dirt-encrusted cobwebs. There was a smell of urine.

All except number four had names beside them, the letters scrawled in different shades of biro on tatty pieces of card, and then slid into tiny metal holders. Rosenthal pressed the button beside number four, having first checked that no one was in the street.

A burst of static and, behind it, a noise that might have been human, just as easily might have been Neptunian.

"I'm here to see Carlos. Carlos Arias-Stella."

More static, this time longer. Length did not lead to comprehension, though. He repeated his little speech and was again rewarded by white noise and indistinct harmonics.

"I'm sorry. I don't understand you."

Even more of the same, although it seemed to be getting angrier. "Is Carlos there?" he enquired when it finished.

As if in answer, there was a load buzz from the door in which he heard a faint click. He pushed it open, then moved quickly inside, past the two bicycles and the post that had been piled on a small table. He guessed, correctly, that flat four was on the middle of the three floors. He saw no one as he climbed the steps.

The door to flat four was open and a short, early middle-aged woman was standing in it. She was slightly overweight and she looked upset, two qualities that caused Rosenthal some amusement; fat, angry women always seemed to think themselves an irresistible force.

"That bloody speaker phone! Never worked properly, and will they do anything about it? I'm the only one who complains, of course. Everyone else seems happy to put up with it. . ."

While she ranted, Rosenthal was figuring options. Her presence was a complication, but not an insurmountable obstacle. The question was how much she would need to be involved. If Carlos could be persuaded out of here without her, then she would not need to be killed. If not. . .

"I'm here to see Carlos."

She made a face. "Not again! He's not here. He's disappeared. When I came back this evening, the little shit had packed his bags and buggered off."

Even as Rosenthal was moving forward, and pushing her out of the way he was thinking that he believed her, but that didn't matter. He had to make sure.

"What the hell are you doing?" she demanded as she stumbled inside the living room of her flat. "Listen, you'd better get out of here, mister. I'm giving you ten seconds. . ."

He had stopped and was assessing the flat, but now he turned, his face unchanged. With one hand that was gloved in tight, pale yellow latex he grabbed her chin in a grip that she felt move her lip. "Shut up," he advised. He didn't shout, didn't whisper.

Her eyes widened as his grip stayed, then tightened momentarily before he released her. He shut the door gently, still looking directly into her fear-brightened eyes. Without touching her again he gestured that she should go and sit in a large, leather armchair that faced the television. She complied, not daring to break eye contact.

It took him two minutes to search the flat, a further four to search through the correspondence on the kitchen table and in the letter rack by the toaster. She was telling the truth, it seemed, for neither was Carlos physically there, nor was there evidence to suggest that he still abided there.

Then he came back to her, standing in front of the television while she looked up at him as if he were a god and she the supplicant.

"Do you know where he went?"

She shook her head quickly. He had no means of checking this,

190

unless things were going to get messy. "Are you positive?" This was asked in a silky tone that under some circumstances might have been intimate, under these was menacing.

She caught the implication. "Yes! Oh, God, yes!"

He decided she wasn't lying.

He would have gone then, but something she had said came back to him. "What did you mean, 'Not again'?"

She was only too eager to please now. Gone was the belligerent flat-owner with a weight problem. "The police telephoned. They wanted him as well."

"When?"

"Earlier this evening."

"You're sure it was the police?"

"Oh, yes. Wharton, she said her name was. Inspector Wharton."

He considered the possibilities. The likeliest was that it was Flemming posing as a police officer, but it was just conceivable that it really was the constabulary. In which case, it might be coincidence.

He wasn't trained to be optimistic. In the company he had always known, optimism had usually proved a fatal flaw. He bent down over her, his face so close to hers that he could see the hairs on her top lip. "If you tell anyone about this, I'll come back. Understand?"

She nodded.

Without looking at her again, he walked quickly from the flat, aware that her eyes were following him all the while.

Helena had hoped that by confession she might achieve some improvement in her mental and physical state. Ever since her discovery that Alasdair didn't exist, that Cronkhite-Canada was connected to Pel-Ebstein, she had been feeling a dreadful malaise manifest by dark depression, enervation and nausea.

Part of this had come from anger and embarrassment that she had been fooled, and fooled, it appeared, so easily. Within the space of a few days this man had penetrated defences that had hitherto proved impregnable. How had this happened? What technique had he used so effectively?

The questions were repeated endlessly throughout the day, the answers remained silent.

Another part of it – and she was forced to concede this quietly, when no one was listening – was because she was going to have to tell John Eisenmenger nearly all that had happened. It was a prospect that did not please – far from it – but at least she had hoped, as she finally accepted the inevitable and invited him up to her flat, that admission of the events would palliate the symptoms.

It didn't seem to work.

Eisenmenger listened to everything she said, ignoring the faltering of her words, the facial grimaces she had involuntarily allowed. When she finished, he had merely sat there and looked thoughtful. She felt like a stripper who had been upstaged by a televised football match; naked and for nothing.

For a while he said nothing and she, equally silent, was forced to endure it. Then, "Of course, you realize what this means?"

It meant many things to Helena but she had the feeling that few of them had impinged on John Eisenmenger. "What?" she asked tiredly.

"There's a clear link between this 'Alasdair' and Pel-Ebstein. That can only mean that this is even bigger than we thought. First the bug on the car, now this."

Big deal.

She felt so exhausted she was ready to drop. She asked, "You keep saying this is big, but do you have any idea of what, precisely, is going on?"

He raised his eyebrows, looking at her with half a smile, half an apology. "I think I know what killed Millie Sweet. What I don't know is why she died when she did. Or, for that matter, why she got what killed her." He took a breath after that, then went on, "Although I have some theories."

Eisenmenger was a simple soul, so what came next was a very small piece of a very large surprise.

"In the name of all that's holy!" Helena screamed rather than spoke. "When will you stop speaking in bloody riddles? What's the matter with you? Do you enjoy driving people round the bloody bend with your superior bloody knowledge?"

Eisenmenger, until now immersed in possibilities, was abruptly brought out to face realities. The transition, much as had probably occurred when sea creatures had first flopped upon the land, took some adjustment. Indeed, for a while he was actually fighting for breath.

Helena found herself also exhausted by the outburst. She closed her eyes upon Eisenmenger's look of complete bewilderment.

Eventually, almost as if a very small and very lost little boy were calling for big sister, she heard him say, "Helena?"

She opened her eyes to find him looking with a frightened expression at her, leaning forward, hands clasped and stretched out. "I'm sorry, Helena. I. . . I didn't realize."

She snorted.

He hesitantly got up and then came and sat next to her on the sofa, allowing a small gap between them. "I knew that what you were saying was hard for you. I guess I thought that by ignoring how you felt it would help you."

She sighed. "When are you going to learn, John?"

"Learn what?"

"That emotions are just as much a means of communication as talking is. If you ignore them, you're blind. In fact, you're worse off than the blind, because emotions don't just convey information, they *heave*. They move and they shift, shaking the ground of those who experience them and those who are near, so that if you don't recognize that they're there, you're going to fall down, and you're going to keep falling down."

He considered this. "Pathologists do terrible things, things that most people would find impossible, but we tell ourselves that we're doing them for the best of motives. But I'm not sure that's enough to excuse to ourselves what we do. So the next trick is to ignore the emotions. Become 'clinical,' in the jargon, so that the autopsy is just an intellectual exercise, the body no longer a human being, just a puzzle."

"So all pathologists have lost their emotions?"

"I wouldn't go that far. I think most of us can switch them on and off, when appropriate."

"And you?" she asked, her voice softer now.

"I got stuck in the 'off' position. First Tamsin, then Marie. The world seemed safer that way."

She put out her hand, touching his. "I know how you feel."

They exchanged uncertain smiles, the moment subsiding.

"What now?" asked Helena.

"Tomorrow, I take these sequences that Belinda's produced and see if I can find someone at the Medical School who can make sense of them. If I can do that, I'll be a lot nearer some sort of answer."

She nodded. "Let me know if you have any luck." She paused and suddenly seemed embarrassed. He thought that perhaps he ought to leave, but as he rose her hand shot out and held his wrist. When he followed her arm to her shoulder and thence her face, her eyes were large and bright.

Rosenthal's instincts were shouting at him to speed down the motorway but he knew that to be caught and documented by the police would be disastrous. His whole life depended on being transparent, there but hard to see, so he kept to the speed limit, never exciting curiosity.

He was angry. The surveillance operation on Arias-Stella had gone wrong, for which disciplinary action would have to be taken. The cover on all the Proteus subjects had not been total, but it had been designed to detect two things – sudden illness or a change of address. That it had failed was his ultimate responsibility but he would see to it that the retribution was shared appropriately.

Still, there were other questions to be answered more immediately. Where had Arias-Stella gone? Was this Inspector Wharton genuine and, if so, why were the police now interested in Carlos?

The implications were disturbing. Perhaps Hartmann had gone to the police as well as the lawyer. Perhaps the lawyer had amassed enough evidence to go to the police herself.

But neither of these seemed to explain matters satisfactorily. If someone knew enough to locate Arias-Stella, presumably they knew a whole lot more, and that implied that someone knew almost everything about Proteus and the work that had produced it. Yet if that were true, the whole house would be falling in on him. Him and PEP.

And also, he thought it odd that this police inspector had phoned. Surely a personal call would be normal procedure?

Despite the urgency to return, he stopped at the next service station to make some calls, not daring to use his mobile while driving. He initiated some enquiries into Inspector Wharton and he also ordered twenty-four-hour surveillance on Helena Flemming and John Eisenmenger. Most importantly, he started the search for Carlos Arias-Stella.

Siobhan Turner was still in mourning, but had plastered over it phlegm and stoicism and resolve. Unfortunately, so thick and uneven was this layer of normality, this facade, it was little better than a mask. When Beverley Wharton called on her that evening she found the sight almost painful.

"I'd hardly got to know him." This wasn't quite her opening sentence as they sat down in the large conservatory at the back of the large house, but it was fairly early on in their relationship. It didn't require Sherlock Holmes to deduce that the glue holding her together wasn't yet dry. There was a pungent odour of lilac around them.

"How long were you married?"

"Only a year."

Beverley had the inkling that discovering the truth of Robin Turner's relationship with Millicent Sweet was going to be a delicate business.

"Not long, then."

She laughed. She was smoking her second cigarette of the interview and had insisted that Beverley join her in a gin and tonic. There had been a kind of desperation in her invitations, her tone, her whole demeanour. Beverley hadn't had the cruelty to refuse her.

"You're an attractive woman, Inspector." This was as between two attractive women and, in truth, Beverley had to admit that, despite being closer to her last breath than her first tooth, Siobhan Turner was not a plug-ugly female of the species. "Are you married?" When Beverley shook her head, the Professor's widow said, "Would that be because you've also found men to be bastards?"

"Most men. I'm waiting for one of the few who isn't either a bastard or already chained."

Mrs Turner laughed at that. "I was luckier. Oh, yes, the first time I caught one of your bastards with my chain. He was not only a philanderer, he was a crook. Caught by Customs and Excise for VAT evasion, then topped himself on the day before the trial. The second time I got it right."

Beverley had been in the force long enough to know that there was never going to be a right time to dip into the bag filled with awkward questions. "Does the name Millicent Sweet mean anything to you?"

She frowned whilst breathing in smoke. "She worked with Robin, didn't she?" There was a pause and the furrows of her frown deepened. "Didn't she die? Just before Robin did."

"That's right. Did he ever talk about her?"

For the first time she showed something less than total openness. "What's this about?"

Beverley had anticipated this and hadn't come up with an entirely satisfactory response. "I just want to make sure that it was nothing more than a coincidence," she began, but suddenly things were getting rocky. At once Siobhan Turner was asking, "Why shouldn't it be?"

"We have to check, Mrs Turner." This anodyne had no effect at all.

"I don't understand. Why are the police interested in Robin's death? It was an accident, wasn't it?"

"Of course." Beverley layered on reassurance like antiseptic cream on a spot. "Of course. Millicent Sweet's death was natural. With the inquest on your husband's death coming up, I'm just making absolutely certain that there was nothing we've missed. The Coroner's office is fairly certain that it was accidental, I just need to make that one hundred per cent."

It was a fairly good story. It was plausible and Frank Cowper had agreed to back her up should Mrs Turner have a suspicious mind, albeit at a price yet to be negotiated.

"I was told he was drunk. That wasn't like him. And what was he doing in that car park at that time of night?" She finished her cigarette by sucking out its life as if it were giving her more than early death, or perhaps because it *was* giving her early death.

Beverley also had wondered these things, but she wanted answers, not more questions. She glided over Siobhan Turner's suspicions. "As far as you know, he had no enemies, did he?"

She suddenly took a downturn. "Everyone loved Robin." She sipped her drink.

Taking this impossibility with inscrutable fortitude, Beverley asked, "Where did he meet Millicent Sweet?"

"It was before I knew him. They both worked in the same laboratory. He worked for Pel-Ebstein then."

Pel-Ebstein again.

"So your husband was there when the accident happened? The fire?"

She nodded.

"Did he talk about it?"

She was lighting another cigarette as she tried to remember. A glance at her watch told Beverley that her time was limited.

"There was a fire, I think. I don't known what caused it – he didn't seem to know. Anyway, once it started, it couldn't be put out. Not surprising, judging by what Robin said."

"Which was?"

"The lab was old. Almost a ruin already. There were inadequate fire prevention precautions and the lab was so isolated once the fire started, there was no one to put it out."

"Isolated?"

"Oh, yes. Somewhere off the Scottish coast, I think. He used to joke that the only thing to do was shag the sheep."

Or each other.

Siobhan Turner continued, "You know, I always thought it was odd. Such a big company like Pel-Ebstein, and they have a laboratory like that."

Aware that at any moment Mrs Turner might realize that none of this could be of any relevance to her husband's fall, Beverley could only press on and hope. "What work was he doing?"

A shake of her head. "He would never say." A nostalgic smile. "Said once that it was something to do with national security. I ask you! He was only a virologist!"

Only? As if such people were failed roadsweepers. But it was clearly meant affectionately.

"Then why wouldn't he tell you what he did for Pel-Ebstein?"

"I don't know! He was usually quite happy to chat about his work. Some nights he used to bore me rigid. I couldn't understand half of what he was doing."

Beverley noticed tears in her eyes as she imbibed a large measure of gin. She had lit another cigarette and was giving it a good going over.

"Did he tell you who else was working with him when the fire happened?"

For the first time Mrs Turner seemed to think that this line of questioning was odd. A fleeting frown, though, was the only signal. "Not many people, I think."

"Did he have any records from that time? Research papers, that kind of thing?"

This time she reacted. "What's this got to do with how he died?"

"You mentioned that he had been involved in some sort of work that might have had a security rating. I think it would be as well to check on the details."

197

"Why? What's going on?"

Seeing suspicion solidifying like wall between them, Beverley risked a morsel of precious truth. "Millicent died of cancer. When your husband died, he was also found to have early cancer. I want to exclude the fire as a cause of those tumours."

She stared at Beverley for a moment, then shrugged. "His papers are still in his office. I haven't touched them."

"May I see?"

The office was on the ground floor, surprisingly small and tidy. "He kept the old stuff in those files." She indicated a shelf high up above the desk.

"May I take them?"

"Why not?"

There were six of them, all old and yellowed, the cardboard dusty and torn. Outside, in the hall, Beverley said, "Thank you."

For perhaps the first time something she said, something innocuous and produced merely out of politeness, pierced the armour against grief. Robin Turner's widow forgot to be composed, looked as she really was – lonely, desolate and without hope once more.

"Oh, my God," she whispered. Her cigarette, which had never left her fingers, became another corpse and, as she hurried Beverley from the house, she could say only, "Please, I'm feeling rather tired."

As the door closed behind her, Beverley saw the last of a lonely woman and saw also that the glue holding her together was water-soluble. She shifted the weight of the files, wondering if this was going to lead anywhere other than a long, sleepless night.

Hartmann didn't know how he was feeling and hadn't known for a few days. He tried to tell himself that things were looking brighter, that possibly the dread was lightening and that, for the first since Alan Rosenthal had first made his unbidden appearance in his life, he could see a future. Having done what Eisenmenger had suggested – returned the blocks to their original condition and written to the coroner offering profuse apologies over his "mistake" – such optimism did not seem undue. It was true that Patricia Bowman had taken it upon herself to conduct a long and rather confrontational interview with him when she learned what had happened, and the telephone call from the Coroner had also caused a distinct rise in his anal sphincter tone, but he thought that he was over the worst. The important thing was to avoid any more being said in public and the Coroner's decision not to hold an inquest (Hartmann had assured him that the death was still natural, just slightly more peculiar than previously disclosed) would help.

But this was insufficient to make him an undeniably happy soul.

What if Rosenthal finds out?

He had a deep, well-rooted fear that Rosenthal had ways and means of finding things out. It would take just a careless phrase, or perhaps it would be another bribe, another act of blackmail.

That he would act on such information, and act in exactly the way that he described, was not a source of uncertainty for Hartmann.

And even if Rosenthal did not immediately learn of what had happened, there was still Eisenmenger. Clearly he believed the death extremely odd, and he was being employed to find out more. If he discovered that it had in fact been unnatural, then nothing in the whole of God's stinking creation would stop that becoming public.

In some ways he felt more than ever like an ant scurrying for cover under the trampling laughter of a murderous child.

"Hello, Mark."

He had been completely absorbed by his endlessly reiterated terrors and grievances so that the smooth, almost chummy voice that he knew so well and feared so much made him visibly recoil.

"Bit jumpy, aren't you?" The question was smeared out of unruffled concern, as if Rosenthal really did care about his state of mind. "Something wrong?"

Hartmann rushed, hurried, to reassure him.

They were standing just outside the Medical School entrance, its featureless red-brick walls climbing above them. The evening air was cooling rapidly from cold dampness to icy frost.

"I thought I'd make sure you were still happy, "continued Rosenthal. He had on a black, woollen overcoat and his breath was easily visible in the lamplight around them, but Hartmann thought he didn't actually look cold. The impression was almost one of a bad actor who didn't know how to play the part of being chilled despite all the special effects. "As far as you know, there are no problems, are there?"

Hartmann looked nervously at Rosenthal, trying to hear suspiciousness or see hidden knowledge, but there was nothing. "None at all," he said and to his delight the tone sounded genuine. Rosenthal at once smiled and straightened, his whole body language changing. "Good! Good!" Then, "You had me rather anxious."

It was Hartmann's turn to smile. He risked some addition to his positive reports. "Everything's going fine. No comebacks at all."

"Excellent!"

Then Rosenthal hesitated and the smile went. For two seconds – two seconds in which Hartmann felt hysterical certainty that Rosenthal knew – he stared at the pathologist from eyes that were pale and blue and death-soaked. The gaze brought with it stasis for Hartmann; isolation from the external, passing world. He saw his doom. . .

The moment broke as shockingly as glass. Rosenthal put the smile back in place, the world re-intruded and Hartmann breathed again. "I think it's over," opined Rosenthal. "I really do."

Rushing to catch up, still confused and not completely sure, Hartmann said quickly, "Yes, yes."

"In which case, I have something for you." From the left-hand pocket of his overcoat, Rosenthal produced a package, wrapped in brown paper and sealed with parcel tape. He held it out.

Hartmann took the gift, staring at it in the kind of wonder that the front row at the Sermon on the Mount had probably felt. "Is this it?" he asked. Then, just in case it was a joke, "Is this the tape?"

Still smiling and staring and looking at him from glacial eyes, Rosenthal nodded and confirmed.

"But. . . but why?" Hartmann was clutching it tightly. Disbelief and still-nagging suspicion made him wary.

"Oh, let's just say that I have no further use for it."

He almost felt like crying. He brought the package to his chest, then remembered something. "But you said there were copies. What about those?"

Rosenthal shook his head and, putting his hand on Hartmann's arm, said, "I've disposed of those. I thought you might like to receive just the one copy. A gesture, if you like."

Rosenthal dropped his hand and began to turn away.

Hartmann asked, "And you don't want me to do anything more?"

Without turning back, Rosenthal said, "Everything's taken care of. Everything."

They went to bed, but did not make love, a decision that was made silently and with total consent from them both. Just holding Helena, feeling her soft, firm warmth beside him was enough for Eisenmenger.

She said into the darkness, "What really hurt was the fact that I thought I was always in control and Alasdair, whoever he was, proved how wrong I was. In the space of a few days he showed me up for what I am."

Eisenmenger muttered something.

"What?"

"'Human'. I said, 'Human'. That's all it showed you up to be."

She thought about that. "A fool would be nearer the mark."

He laughed. "Same thing." And he was pleased to hear her laugh with him.

"John?" she asked after what seemed like a lifetime, as if they were drifting together not into sleep but into old age.

"Yes?"

"What's going on?"

"Ah."

"Do you know, or don't you?"

"I'll tell you tomorrow when we have the sequence on Belinda's little oddity."

"So it's not an artefact?"

"I fear," he said with what almost amounted to sadness, "it is very far from being an artefact.

She didn't like the tone of his voice. "What is it then?"

He paused a long time before saying, "I think it might be our killer."

They had arranged that Eisenmenger should come round to her flat at six and the hours until then were filled with the mundanities of a parole violation and Mr Codman's embezzlement. She felt – she *knew* – that she wasn't giving of her best, not with Eisenmenger's final, enigmatic and frightening remark replaying itself as a sort of soundtrack to her work, but she tried as hard as she could. Eisenmenger's attitude also recurred ceaselessly. She had seen that shift into deep contemplation before; it was contemplation laced with epiphany. In such a mood he knew already where he was going, he was merely finding the right stages to get there, the right flecks of evidence to add to the picture that he was painting. A portrait of the truth.

She decided to cook, although she wasn't particularly hungry; it seemed more of an anthropological gesture than a need to ingest sustenance. She hadn't long started before Eisenmenger arrived, bearing wine. His attitude was one of exhausted satisfaction, but she saw also something else, something that she could not define.

"Well?" she demanded, to which he at first he didn't reply. Then he smiled and said, "Some wine, I think."

While she thought, *Jesus Christ! Why does he have to be so bloody irritating?* she said, "Have you made any progress?"

"Oh, yes. Things are clearer now." He paused as if suddenly considering what he had just said. "Clearer. Definitely clearer."

It was then that she realized what was wrong with him.

He was afraid. She had never seen fear in him before and it was unsettling for her. Before she could say anything he suddenly perked up. "Are you cooking? Good."

He moved past her into the kitchen and she was left with nothing other than to follow him. "John?" Her hand was on his arm and he turned as she asked, "What's wrong?"

About to deny, he opened his mouth, paused, then said, "I'm hungry. You cook and I'll tell you." He kissed her lightly on the cheek.

She resumed her preparation of the meal and Eisenmenger poured wine while watching her. For some reason he was surprised that she was expert; why, he wondered, should that be unexpected? She had never married, had always lived on her own, so of course she had acquired expertise in the preparation of food. He, in contrast, was a relative ingénu when it came to solitary existence. First married then, after the divorce, living with Marie, he had always had someone else to take at least a share of culinary duties and consequently he had tended to specialize in those dishes that were easy, quick and high in flavour.

The wine was good, and he could find himself wanting to drink a lot of it, but he was acutely aware that time was short, that up to that moment they had meandered in this investigation, but that now things were changing. It was almost an effort to concentrate on the problem; part of him was aware that he was prevaricating, that he didn't want to face what he suspected.

"Okay," he began. "To return to the beginning. We have a young girl who died from multiple cancers. She died apparently within a week, maybe much more quickly."

Helena was measuring spices into the bowl of a food processor. "You say that that's impossible."

"Well, they say that nothing's impossible in medicine, but this is equivalent to predicting the winning lottery numbers every week for a year."

"So the questions that follow are firstly – from a biological point of view, how can this have happened? – and secondly – is this connected to her time at PEP? Specifically with the accident in the Laboratory."

"The first answers the second," he remarked as he wrote down notes. It came across almost as a spoken thought.

"What does that mean?"

He finished writing and then looked up, his face unreadable. Helena had taken some pork fillet from the refrigerator but she just put it down on the chopping board, looking across at Eisenmenger.

"For most of today Belinda and I have been showing the sequences in the 'artefact' that she hadn't been able to identify to various people in the Medical School. It took a bit of work, but eventually, with a lot of luck and guesswork, I think we can now say what they are."

"And?"

"Do you know what a retrovirus is?"

She shook her head.

"Viruses are relatively small lengths of nucleic acid – genetic material – within protein packets. Like us all, they're interested in only one thing – reproduction. Because they haven't got many genes, they use our genes to do it. They get into our cells and subvert our intracellular machinery to make copies of themselves. The genes they carry within them are merely the tools with which they achieve this.

"In most viruses the genes, like ours, are made of DNA, but retroviruses have opted for RNA, which means that they have to convert their nucleic acid into DNA, using something called 'reverse transcriptase,' before they get to work in the cell.

"What Belinda discovered was the DNA version of the genomic material from a retrovirus."

The food was for the moment forgotten. "So it was natural? Is that what you're saying?"

He uttered a single, harsh laugh. "If ever God makes a virus like that one, then we'll know that He's run out of patience. No, Millicent Sweet's death was no more natural than if she'd had a gun barrel put in her mouth and the trigger pulled.

"This is a manufactured virus. This, I think, is Proteus."

"Oh, Christ, Luke. . ."

"Like it, Bev? Or would you prefer me to do this. . ?"

He shifted his hips slightly, at the same time bringing his large, warm hands up from her vulva, along the contours of he abdomen, to rest on her breasts, nipples held gently under his palms. She was kneeling on the bed, arched back, her hands on his hips behind her. He was kissing her neck, but then without saying any more he pushed her forward and down in a position of bestial subservience. This time his back was arched while she was down and accepting each of his thrusts, eyes closed, mouth open. When he leaned forward and took her breasts in his hands while still inside her, she began to feel herself falling into the delicious abandonment of orgasm.

It didn't take him long to finish, although he stayed there for teasing minutes afterwards, slowly moving, slowly exciting. When he came free there was a genuine sense of loss inside her and she would have liked to have continued, but there was business to be done. She moved forward, twisting so that she could look at him over her shoulder. She sighed, then asked, "Food?" Luke's grin was broad as he slapped her buttock. "You bet."

And so they sat at her small kitchen table, the room lit only by the fluorescent strips under the cupboards, and he ate a huge cheese and tomato sandwich while she sipped a bottled beer. Every time she moved she could see that he watched her breasts under the silk of her gown. She enjoyed the attention, always had; the time to start worrying was when it stopped. Men were always looking at women's breasts and she figured that she'd rather they were hers than some other bitch's.

"Did you do what I asked?"

His mouth was full, his chewing, as ever, methodical and slow. When Luke ate she always felt that she was witnessing geological rather than biological processes. The mastication slowed but didn't stop while his eyes looked at her out of an expression that was curious. The swallow that eventually came was deliberate. "The fire? At the PEP laboratory?" he asked. On her nod he pursed his lips but didn't immediately say anything. He fetched a bottled beer for himself, opening it with a twist of the cap. Only after he had drained it to halfway, the fluid sinking down past a regularly oscillating Adam's apple, did he say anything more.

"Why do you need to know about that?"

Beverley knew Luke well, but here was an aspect that was strange to her. Abruptly he seemed to have become slightly distant, almost faintly hostile. It was part of the job to ask colleagues to do things, often things that were unofficial. This culture of self-help underpinned the more conventional methods, made it more efficient, so what was his problem? He had asked her for help often enough, and this certainly wasn't the first time she had wanted his assistance.

"Is there a problem?"

His denial was convincing, failing only because it didn't convince her. "Not at all."

She smiled, leaned forward, gave him a different view. "Fucking liar."

He laughed lazily and for the first time she noticed that they were whispering. She wondered why. Was it so deep, dark and secret, this thing that they were languidly dancing around? He said, "You're tainted, Bev."

She admitted to surprise and not a little hurt. She had thought better of Luke. "Do you think I don't know that? I've got a boss who looks as if he'd like to puke every time I walk in the room; I've got people working for me who are barely able to shit and blink at the same time, yet they look on me as if I'm no better than used toilet paper. Everyone treats me the same, no matter who they are and no matter how well I do. I don't need you to tell me I'm tainted, Luke."

He put his large, comforting hand out to touch her cheek. Despite herself there were tears in her eyes while in her mind there was the refrain, *I will not let them break me down.* "I'm on your side, Bev," he murmured softly. "You were unlucky, I know that. There but for the grace of God, and all that."

She had clasped his hand against her cheek, enjoying, just for once, the comfort of a touch with no subsequent cost to pay. She had clamped her eyes closed, damned if she was going to weep openly. She hadn't realized how much all this had been getting her down.

"I just meant that there may be a problem," he explained.

She thought, *Oh, fine. Another problem.* Eyes still clamped shut she asked, "What kind of a problem?"

He dropped his hand, found another beer and sat back down.

"The fire was in a small laboratory facility owned by Pel-Ebstein Pharmaceuticals on Rouna. Rouna is a small island off the north-west coast of Scotland. It has just a few hundred inhabitants, mostly fishing and sheep-farming."

"You say the laboratory was small – how small?"

He flicked a small smile across his face. "Very, very small. It employed all of six people."

Beverley was astonished. "Six? In total."

"Yeah. And this place is *remote*. We're not talking about rural; we're talking lost. It's a three-hour boat journey – if you've got access to a boat – from Ullapool. Ullapool is so far north there isn't much left of the good old UK once you go past it."

She was trying to fit this into what she knew. "Private, then," she murmured. He nodded. "Oh, yeah. Play the music as loud as you want on Rouna."

"Must have been lonely."

"I gather they roomed with locals near the laboratory. I don't suppose the natives were too inviting."

"And what were they researching?"

"Ahh," he said gravely. "That was interesting. The local police report – there's no one stationed on the island, so someone has to come in from the mainland – mentions virological research, but the insurance report talks about something called, "Biological Model Development".

"Whatever that is."

"Yeah." He gave her a long, serious look that she returned. "But virology, that would be viruses, wouldn't it?"

"I guess." He was covering something, saying nothing but communicating as much as he could at the same time.

"The common cold, that kind of thing?"

He said nothing and she was left unsure what that meant. "And how did the fire start?"

He was finishing off his sandwich now. "Another slight discrepancy. The insurance report talked about an electrical fault – this laboratory was *old* – but the witness statements that the police took fairly consistently talk about a fight."

"A fight?"

"Between Turner, and a laboratory technician, Carlos Arias-Stella."

Familiar names.

"Cabin fever?"

He shrugged. "Maybe. There were four males and two females in the group. Perhaps the maths was wrong."

"Have you got their names? The people in the research group?"

He didn't respond at once. He picked up his plate and put it in the sink, the domesticated species of male. From there he said, "You know someone tried to censor the witness statements?"

She was astounded by this news. "What do you mean?"

"What I say. Names were struck through. Words like virology, also."

"But how did you find out?"

He smiled. "I went to source. Ullapool has one police house and one policeman – Sergeant MacCallum, who's God's gift to bureaucracy. He makes copies of everything, probably even of his nose pickings. They forgot to censor his versions."

If this were so, then the conclusion had to be that Robin Turner hadn't lied to his wife in hinting at national security.

"There's some bad news, I'm afraid." His voice was sad, almost one of melancholy.

"What?"

"These files must have been marked. Alarms rang somewhere."

The pulling of records was not done without an audit trail in place. It was possible to find out who asked for what and when. Normally the system was dormant, except for files that were considered "sensitive," or when someone was the subject of an internal investigation.

"Oh."

"I got a visit. They were keen to know why I was interested in the laboratory fire on Rouna."

"You didn't tell them. . ?" She was sure of Luke, but she couldn't help wondering. He shook his head and she tried to convince herself that he wasn't lying. "I didn't need to, Bev. Your name came up quite early in the conversation."

Shit. Whether he was lying – it was not inconceivable that he had dropped her in the dung to save his own career – or not was irrelevant. She was no longer working unseen. Doubtless Lambert would soon know all about it; just the excuse he needed.

She had reached the pivot on the seesaw; time to decide. She could drop it at once, opt for damage limitation (after all, her only crime thus far had been unauthorized use of resources), or she could continue. This was huge, but she still didn't have evidence of anything, merely an instinct that she was poking a stick into something very nasty. Effectively she was relying on her experience as a police officer and on the intuition of John Eisenmenger. If he were wrong, or if she failed, there would be no hope of survival for her. Say goodbye to the pension, hello to the murky, crappy world of the "security business".

She asked, "But you've got the names?"

He sighed, as if she were a persistent child who wouldn't stop pestering. He left the room, went to the bedroom where his jacket lay in a disorganized heap on the floor. What he gave Beverley was just a scrap of paper on which were six names:

Robin Turner
Millicent Sweet
Maurice Stein
Jean-Jacques Renvier
Carlos Arias-Stella
Justine Nielsen

"Thanks."

He pulled two more beers from the refrigerator. "I wouldn't be too hopeful about getting anywhere with that list."

"Why not?"

"I checked them out. Turner and Sweet you know about, but Nielsen's also dead. Her flat in New York exploded a few days ago, while she was in it." While Beverley was digesting this, he went on, "Also, Renvier's gone missing from his home in Paris, a few days ago."

She was so stunned by this news, she was temporarily dumb and, into this absence, Luke said, "Stein's missing too, but he has been for a long time. Vanished just after the fire and the winding up of the Research project."

She knew then that she wasn't going to stop just yet.

By mutual, unspoken consent, they waited until the food was prepared and they were sitting at the rounded dark wood of the dining table. Eisenmenger had sunk into his habitual mood of deep contemplation. Helena served the food and sat opposite him, pouring more wine for both of them. He began to eat but if he enjoyed it, the evidence eluded her. She had the premonition that here, essentially, was life with John Eisenmenger in miniature.

After perhaps five minutes, he began talking quite spontaneously. "To understand what they did, you've got to understand cancer." She was left to assume that "They" were Turner and Millicent Sweet. "Every cell in your body, bar a few, has thirty thousand genes. Each gene codes for a protein; some of the proteins are structural, making the shape and "skeleton" of the cell, but most are enzymes. People think of enzymes as things in washing powders that dissolve dirt, but actually they're catalysts. They make chemical reactions work that won't ordinarily work. Enzymes drive the biochemistry that makes life.

"Enzymes work in complex networks and hierarchies. One switches on a reaction that in turn switches on eight more that not only switch on another fifteen but also switch off six of the original eight and another eleven besides. We haven't got anywhere near discovering one per cent of the network of interactions yet. But it's clear that there are some enzymes that are fundamental – they're the master controls. They initiate and control major things like cell division, cell death, and so on. If they go wrong, then you have a problem with that cell, because it won't be doing what it's supposed to do. It becomes a rogue cell. You are a multicelled organism – that means that, although you feel like a single entity, you are in fact a composite, billions of cells working together, and for that to work, each and every cell talks to its neighbours. Every cell gives orders and, most importantly, obeys orders.

"In cancer, one of the important genes – 'oncogenes' – goes wrong in one cell. It might be caused by a cosmic ray, too much booze, smoking, not enough tomatoes, it doesn't matter. If that malfunction results in a growth advantage for the cell, if it starts to divide when it shouldn't, or doesn't die when it should, then all the daughters will have the same mistake. You get a growing subpopulation of cells with that error.

"Now, cells are at their most vulnerable to mistakes when they're dividing. The consequence of that is that this little subpopulation becomes more likely to acquire yet more genetic abnormalities. If mistakes contribute to the growth advantage, they will persist. This creates a positive feedback cycle of error that results in a cancer."

He had stopped eating and she waved her fork at him to remind him. He stuffed in some more, then continued, "The sixteen genes in that virus are sixteen of the most fundamental, and therefore the most dangerous, oncogenes."

"So they created a cancer-causing virus? Put the sixteen genes into a cell and sit back and wait for a cancer."

"They did more than that. I don't understand half of it – I suspect we never will – but they overcame several major problems with the process. For a start off, if you put sixteen oncogenes into a cell – even if you put them directly into the genetic material of the cell, as a retrovirus can do – their expression will be low and erratic. Somehow they made the process fantastically more efficient. I guess, but I don't know, that a lot of the unknown sequences are redesigned promoters and enhancers – they're things that seem to accelerate gene expression.

"Then they had the problem of what to do about anti-oncogenes."

"What are they?"

"Cancer is not just a process of things going wrong. There are also mechanisms that act in the cell to put things right. Thus there are genes that code for proteins that repair other, damaged genes. There are also genes that act as 'cellular policemen.' If a cell goes badly wrong, they force the cell to commit suicide.

"But think about it. If for some reason those genes don't do their job, that will tend to lead to cancer as well. Those genes are the anti-oncogenes because their absence or lack of function also tends to lead to cancer.

"Ideally, if you're designing a cancer-causing virus, you want some way to get rid of the anti-oncogenes."

210

"You think they managed it?"

"They had a tutor from nature. Human Papilloma Viruses – HPVs – cause lots of trouble for humans, from warts to cancer. The ones that cause cancer do so by mopping up anti-oncogenes with their own protein 'sponge'. I suspect that Proteus virus has a similar mechanism."

She thought the food palatable but the more he spoke, the less flavour she noticed. Even the wine was losing its bouquet. "Why?" she asked. "Why do it?"

"I don't know. I can guess but unless we can find someone else from the laboratory, it will remain guesswork."

She knew his guesswork. "Tell me, anyway."

He put his knife and fork down. "Models Development' is an odd title but a model, in the medical sense, is a system that mimics a disease process. Thus you might take a mouse egg, knock out both copies of, say, the retinoblastoma gene, let the mouse develop and you have an organism that you know will get a malignant tumour of the eye. That's your model; you can use it to examine the disease, examine possible therapies, and so on.

"I wonder if the aim of the work was the development of a cancer model. Perhaps transfecting cell lines to make new variants. Apparently Millicent Sweet was working on targeted mutagenesis; I wonder if it was her job to fine-tune the thing. Make it do exactly what it was supposed to do."

"You'll have to explain targeted mutagenesis."

"A not-unclever technique whereby you alter the coding sequence of the DNA in exactly the way you want. Using computer modelling you can predict what changes you need to make to produce the effect you desire. Theoretically, you can design your own genes, thus design your own proteins. I suspect that's why a lot of the sequences aren't recognizable from the database; poor Millie put the finishing polish on the means of her own execution."

"So it got out, during the fire, and what? What exactly do you think happened?"

He had resumed eating, still unheeding of anything other than the thoughts in his head. "It was a virus. As I said, viruses get into cells. Actually it's very difficult to get DNA into cells by other means. So they used a virus, just adding to and subtly altering its genetic information. Sixteen genes that were guaranteed to turn a cell to cancer. When it escaped – presumably because a vial broke, or a containment hood was breached – it would have been as an aerosol, ready to be breathed in."

"And Millie Sweet breathed it in."

"Millie Sweet, and maybe Robin Turner. When he died, he was just developing cancer too, don't forget."

"But they breathed it in two years ago. I don't understand why they didn't get cancer earlier. "

"I wondered that. The answer, I think, lies in a short DNA sequence that Belinda found. A trigger. A switch, if you like, that turns on the oncogenes. Until the switch is flicked, the virus is inert, just sitting there, in every cell of the body."

"And the switch? What activates it?"

"A temperature of forty Celsius."

"What's the point of that?"

"It's a common trick. It enables you to control exactly the start of the experiment. In this case, though, it was a trigger being squeezed. Millie got the flu, and a week later she was dead, turned, if you like, into the perfect biological model of cancer. Ironic, really."

"So this whole business has been to cover up the accident?"

He nodded, then finished eating and seemed surprised that there was no more food. Certainly the tone of his voice when he said, "That was really rather good," suggested a man who had not been paying attention.

Luke's "late shift" was over and he was gone, back to his family. Beverley hated these times, moments when the advantages of the single life were exhausted, when there was only her, and the shame and dread. In the darkness of the post-coital night, there were too many memories, too few hopes; a time when wishes were worthless while regrets abounded. Insomnia caught her heart with its cold hands and didn't even need to squeeze, for the chill was enough, the languor of the blackness.

They were getting worse, these bouts of depression. Worse since the fiasco of Nikki Exner, when her ascendancy had been abruptly terminated. Not surprising, she reckoned, for without achievement she was nothing. Her whole existence was predicated on processing life – hers, her colleagues, her enemies – and converting it into the substrate of her success. No success, no life. A simple equation, like e=mc², but just as powerful, just as profound, just as inescapable.

She sat up in bed, feeling sore where Luke had played a little roughly with her. Still, he was a good boy; responded well to a warning squeeze of the balls. She put on the light by the bed, staring at herself in the mirror on the wall opposite. *What are you going to do with your life now?*

It wasn't a question she wanted to answer, certainly not at three in the morning, but whoever was doing the asking wasn't interested in the time of day. Time was running away from her. When she had been assigned to Lambert's team, she had understood that it was a penance; a punishment for past misdemeanours, maybe a chance to start again.

The problem was that Lambert had made it clear that he had a different view of the matter. He hadn't wanted her, had decided that she was irredeemably bad, and wasn't about to expend any effort trying to improve her. Probably any effort he did choose to expend in her direction would be purely to stick the proverbial into her crotch.

Beverley was not naive. She had come across people like Lambert on several occasions in her career, but usually there had been more equality of weapons. She had possessed not only ability but also the reputation for ability. Once those had gone, she was severely wounded.

And of course, there had always been the possibility of being "amenable". . .

Now not only was she without repute, she was without the opportunities to shine, and nobody was asking for any "amenability".

Crap! She rejected the word at once. *Say what you mean, girl.* Willingness to have sex.

There was a time when she would not have felt the need to use such a euphemism, when she would not have felt a seep of sadness at the more accurate expression. Afraid that she was going to cry, she grabbed a tissue and blew her nose as if the act would destroy the tears. She got up, put on a gown and went to find some whisky. When she had found it – and with it lost her self-pity – she sat in the living room and thought through what to do.

Lambert was looking to kill her off and her only chance was to go to the extreme; find out what was going on with

213

Pel-Ebstein. Three, maybe four, deaths in a month were too many for chance, even if this news had come from a vacuum. And such deaths! Beverley had seen many exits from the world, seen the cruelty, the inventiveness, the peculiarity and the ever-present stupidity of the myriad ways that people died, and there was something about these that seemed to her to be far from ordinary. The details that Luke had recovered concerning the others who had worked in that ill-fated laboratory were scanty but they intrigued; no doubt about that – they intrigued.

No bodies, for a start. One case in which the poor girl had been blown to pieces by a gas explosion, another in which a young man had just vanished from a Parisian cafe, leaving his girlfriend wondering where he was. In this last case the French gendarmerie, too, had concluded that he was dead, the witness statements suggesting some form of kidnap attempt.

And then there were the dates. Separated by a few days, as if someone had been moving from one to the other. And Carlos Arias-Stella had vanished, his girlfriend believing him to have left her, but Beverley wondered about more sinister possibilities.

What, then, about Stein? Disappeared some two years ago – nothing heard or seen from him since. Was that significant? Was he dead? Was he very much alive and connected with all this?

The recent incidents had happened in different countries and taken individually there was no reason to suspect some form of conspiracy; only if you knew to look for a pattern did you see it. Her experience and training told her that the next steps were to investigate these deaths from the point of view of a potential organized assassination list, at the same time initiating a search for Carlos and Stein. Without Lambert, though, she didn't have the resources to do the former; with Lambert she wouldn't be allowed to do the latter. Lambert would do one of two things – either he would take what she knew and use it, excising her completely from the investigation and any subsequent praise, or he would simply take what she gave him, forget it and use her misdemeanours to make sure that she was permanently excluded from promotion.

And if she neglected to mention anything to him?

Continue.

That was easy. One word, three syllables, eight letters. Like a Home Office directive it said what to do, but not how, precisely, to do it. Strategy without tactics was like asking a deaf man to review the Proms.

It was a huge gamble.

Her name was already being mentioned. Lambert would soon learn something of what was going on, either unofficially or officially, and when he did her time would run out. If she proceeded without him then at the end she would have to have something beyond dispute, something that would justify her insubordination, her decision to cut out her superior.

She could, of course, proceed to locate Arias-Stella, hoping that he was both alive and able to provide all the answers, but could she risk it? She still didn't have the faintest idea what was happening around her, except that people were dying. Some of them were dying in odd (but apparently natural) ways, some of them were dying in obviously unnatural ways. She did not know how it was all connected, but connected it was.

She looked at herself in the mirror, relieved to see a look of determination back on her face, surprised as she witnessed a smile evolve, almost as if she were watching a stranger, as if she were a voyeur.

The idea seemed to come to her after she saw herself smile, a moment of dislocating strangeness, an eerily significant and pivotal event.

In such a moment as this, she now realized, she needed allies.

"Have you heard from Raymond Sweet?"

They were still up, still awake, although the pulse of the night was at its slowest and weakest. They half lay, half sat on the sofa together, his head on her shoulder, her eyes closed in sleepiness, his eyes still open, still bright. He couldn't stop thinking, stop wondering. He was missing something, he knew.

"No. I'll ring him in the morning," she replied dozily.

He sipped some more wine. "Why," he asked suddenly. "Why are they so scared?"

"Who?"

"PEP."

She still had eyes that were locked away behind closed lids. "Because they don't want anyone to find out. Maybe the others involved in the accident may also be contaminated, in which case their liability is potentially enormous."

He considered this. "No," he decided. "It doesn't work. Surely they have no liability if it really was an accident."

"Not necessarily."

"So. . ." He lapsed into contemplation.

"We really need to talk to Carlos, whoever he is," Helena said.

"Or the others who were there."

"But we don't know who they are. We have no way of finding out, either, now that both Millie and Turner are dead."

"Yes," he agreed but his voice carried something else.

"I know that tone," remarked Helena. "What is it?"

"Turner died. Turner had early stage cancer, too, presumably the virus – Proteus – being switched on. Turner, though, fell to his death from the top of a multi-storey car park."

"And. . ?"

"Convenient, really. If you didn't want things to get out about Proteus."

Helena was very awake now. "My God," she whispered. Until that moment this had been about a multinational company using dirty tricks to hide an accident, avoid possible litigation. Eisenmenger's remark cast altogether longer, darker shadows. "They killed him? To stop him talking?"

"Maybe."

"But what about the others? What about Carlos?"

"Yes. What about them? PEP seem to be quite efficient. Perhaps they're already dead."

He let this float between them. He said nothing more for a while. He knew what they would have to do, the problem was to persuade Helena. She said, "I can't believe this. You're asking me to accept that PEP are going about killing people to cover up a laboratory accident? That's a dangerous game, if ever there was one."

He leaned forward to pick up the wine bottle, holding it up for Helena. She declined and he emptied it into his own glass. "They tried to bug the car."

"Yes, and they blackmailed Hartmann, but what you're proposing is a different order of magnitude."

"Maybe I'm wrong. Until we find the mysterious Carlos, we won't know anything more for certain."

More of the silence, more of the night's slow pulse.

"What must it have been like? Knowing you had that thing in

your body, just waiting to explode, never sure when, if ever, it would begin to kill you?"

"It would be awful," he murmured. "If you knew."

It took her a moment to appreciate what he said. "She didn't know? You think that somehow she didn't realize?"

"It would explain why they had to kill Turner. He was close to Millie and so would have known how she died. Perhaps he drew a few conclusions that they didn't like."

"But I still don't see why they should be doing this if it was just a laboratory accident. If what you say is correct, then either PEP feel that there is incontrovertible evidence of their direct liability for what happened to Millie and the others, or. . ."

He waited for her. She continued slowly, as perspectives shifted in her mind, ". . .Or they did it deliberately. They infected them with Proteus to see what would happen."

Her voice was soft with horror.

Rosenthal spent the night with an old friend, revisiting places and memories with her, always the gentleman, always the considerate one. Through all the quietness of their conversation and the warmth of their embraces, his mind was never gone from the problems that he now faced.

It was too early to know whether the police were officially involved in the search for Carlos Arias-Stella but he was inclined at this moment to suppose not. He had managed to acquire a brief curriculum vitae of Beverley Wharton and it was clear to him that she was a maverick. Her methods of investigation supported the contention that on this occasion, as before in the past, she was pursuing her own interests. Rosenthal was well aware, however, that this did not mean that she wasn't a threat, merely that she was a containable threat.

It seemed likely, too, that Arias-Stella had somehow come to learn something of what was going on. This was possible, since although the subjects had been fairly well separated in terms of geography in order to minimize contact, in a world of easily accessible interpersonal communication, it had proved impossible to eradicate it. Turner's original insistence that the Sweet girl should accompany him when the Proteus team had been relocated had been one of the factors working against him, one that should not have been allowed. It had, though, and there was no more to be said. Rosenthal worried about what was, not about what should have been.

Yet Rosenthal doubted that Arias-Stella knew anything much, just enough to worry him, make him run for cover. It was imperative to find him, though; find him and deal with him.

But how? Two strategies were immediately obvious. The first, the safer, was to use the resources of PEP to locate him. PEP had a well-established and efficient security and investigation section (indeed, Rosenthal was a covert part of it), who could draw on manpower and money to track Arias-Stella down, probably only taking a few days, and they were already at work. The second was to piggyback Wharton. Allow Wharton to find the quarry, then cut in. This might require rather more "cleaning up" than the first option, but he doubted it; if Wharton knew enough to want to talk to Arias-Stella, she knew enough to merit his attention anyway.

And clearly the lawyer and her friend would have to go, too.

So he might as well use both strategies in parallel, waiting to see which one was the first to succeed.

Content in his planning, he once again turned his attention to the girl beside him. She was sleeping, but not for much longer.

Eisenmenger woke early but found he was alone. He rose, pulling on some clothes, wondering where Helena was. The sounds of crockery took him to the kitchen where he found her emptying the dishwasher. She was dressed, bright and washed, but there was something in her attitude that Eisenmenger noticed at once; something he could not at first define.

"You're up early."

"We've got a lot to do. I've got appointments until eleven, but then I should be able to get away. I'll take a few days' leave."

He began to help her, aware that he was probably going to put everything away in exactly the wrong places. "For what reason?"

She took a large dish from him just as he was about to put it in a low cupboard; apparently it went in an eye-level cupboard on the opposite wall. "We've got to find Carlos as soon as possible. He's our only hope of sorting this thing out."

It was true, of course, something that he had realized some while ago, but her determination still left him depressed. He tried again with the cutlery, and was again ushered away. "Sit down," she suggested, the tone containing more than a hint of the imperative. He obeyed.

"Well, the first thing to do is to contact Raymond Sweet," he said.

Her back was to him while she sorted the knives, forks and spoons. "I've done that. He rises early."

Eisenmenger perked up. "And?"

"Unfortunately, he still has no further information. He was delighted to tell me, though, that the police were taking an interest in his claims."

Eisenmenger's surprise wiped everything else from his head. "What?"

Helena turned. That Eisenmenger found the look on her face odd would be untrue; he found it worrying. She looked as if she had appendicitis.

"The police called. Very sympathetic, taking many notes. Then, because he had been unable to bring himself to look through Millie's things, the police officer did it for him. He said she was very respectable. He said she found something, too. A letter from Carlos. She's taken it away with her."

Eisenmenger, guessing the answer, asked tentatively, "She?"

Helena smiled but it seemed to hurt. "Beverley Wharton."

"Bloody hell," he murmured. At once, Eisenmenger found himself trying to work out what this meant. How could she have found out? Was this official? What did it mean for them? While these questions flowed into him, he dropped his eyes to the surface before him.

"John?"

It took a moment before he responded. "Mmm?"

"You didn't tell her, did you?"

He found the question so surprising that there was another delay before it found the right connections in his brain. "No." He said this quietly but firmly and, hopefully, convincingly. An involuntary recollection of his last encounter with Beverley Wharton almost blinded him. Helena stared for a second or two, then nodded. "Well, she knows something. More than we do, apparently."

Eisenmenger was moving on to the ramifications of the news. It made it all the harder for them, especially if they were going to work on their own. . .

219

He missed Helena's next remark.

Would it, he wondered, be possible to contact Turner's wife? Perhaps she knew something. . .

"What?" he said, his auditory cortex suddenly getting the attention it deserved.

"I said, you'll have to contact her."

He eyed her cautiously, not wanting to misinterpret her words. "Who?"

"Beverley Wharton." Through a face that appeared to have been vacuum-packed to her facial skeleton she went on, "I may be ill-disposed to her, but I'm a realist, John. As you said, she's the only one we know who has the resources and expertise. Now she has the one piece of information we could have used to get further in this matter, especially now that we may be dealing with murder, we have to make contact with her, see what she knows, let the police take over."

"Are you sure?"

She sat down opposite him.

"I'd rather work the docks as a prostitute than have contact with that cow, but I'd never forgive myself if people died because of my opinions about someone. Yes, I'm sure."

He nodded, relieved and at the same time aware that this was not a happy moment for her. She said, "You'll have to make the first contact, though, John. I couldn't bring myself to do that."

He took her clasped hands. "Okay. I'll arrange a meeting."

Eisenmenger wasn't even sure if she still lived at the same address. If she'd moved, he wouldn't have known what to do.

Even if she were still there, would she help?

She had no reason to like Eisenmenger, plenty to wish him ill. And he knew that she didn't do things for charity, just for Beverley Wharton. Which meant that the only way he was going to get her on side was to make it worth her while.

He rang the bell to her flat and waited. It was nine in the evening and he began to think that she wasn't in. He had first called the police station where she now worked, had been told that she was off duty, but that didn't mean she was at home.

There was a peephole in the door, making him feel observed and uncomfortable. The air smelled of furniture polish and, quite strongly, money.

He was just about to go, having decided that she was either not in or at least not in to John Eisenmenger, when he heard the sounds of locks turning and a chain being pulled back.

She had clearly been asleep for her hair, somewhat longer than he recalled, was a mess and her eyes were slightly puffy. She wore a black silk dressing gown and a look on her face that was part hatred, part amusement and part curiosity.

"John Eisenmenger," she said flatly, as if telling him to leave two pints of semi-skimmed.

He smiled. "Apologies. I didn't realize you'd be in bed."

Without saying anything she stood aside so that he could enter, but she stayed where she was as he walked into the room, only closing the door when he was standing in the middle of the large lounge area. He said, "I'd forgotten how nice this place is." She lived on the top floor of a converted warehouse, complete with beautiful view of the city from a corner of the lounge that was completely glazed.

"Perhaps you've forgotten a few other things, too."

She was stunning. Nothing wrong with his memory on that one. "I expect you're surprised to see me."

She laughed, though it would have killed a comedian to hear it. "You could say that," she said. She walked slowly towards him. "I should kill you. At the very least gouge your eyes out."

"I don't know what you mean."

"At least try to make it sound convincing."

"Beverley. . ."

By now she was standing in front of him. In her eyes there was no sign of emotion. "They carpeted me," she said. "They took me apart. I'm lucky still to be on the force."

"You tried to screw me," he reminded her. "All I did was find the truth that you tried to hide."

For a moment she was still angered, then she was bemused, then she said, "And I thought you were trying to screw me." There was a sly humour in her voice. She laughed and this time it sounded happy. Which made the slap when it came all the more unexpected and all the more painful. It rang in his ears and made the mast cells in his skin explode with unpleasant substances.

"Don't ever stab me in the back again," she suggested, her eyes suddenly bright, hard and bright, bright blue. She turned away and sat down.

"To what do I owe the pleasure?" she asked. If there hadn't been a host of inflammatory chemicals spreading throughout his left cheek, he might have been fooled into thinking that nothing had happened.

He indicated the seat opposite her and sat when she nodded.

"I think you can help me."

"Of course, John, dear. And you can help me by finding something toxic and swallowing it."

"Look, I appreciate you might not think that anything I've got to say is worth listening to, but this is important."

"To whom? You or me?"

"Both of us. Possibly, I think, everyone."

She raised a fine and languid eyebrow. He found himself once again entering a type of enchantment. Abruptly she leaned forward and it was not obviously a sexual gesture but it found him admiring her figure under the dressing gown. "Okay. Tell me."

Eisenmenger had finished but Beverley Wharton had not changed her attitude. She had listened to what he said whilst lying back on the sofa, her head forward and her eyes fixed upon him intently. Her legs were stretched out in front of her, crossed at delicious ankles. He felt that she was studying him, which he didn't mind, except that she hadn't offered him any hospitality and he felt thirsty. He had not told her everything, merely what he judged she might already know with enough embroidery to intrigue her. He hinted at PEP's involvement, but he gave few details even when she asked for them.

At last she said, "A pretty tale, well told." Her voice had a skeleton's bones of indifference. "But what of it to me?"

"You went to see Raymond Sweet."

Her eyes widened slightly, the only expression of surprise he detected. "Ah," she murmured. "I see."

"Was that an official visit?"

She weighed her answer before admitting, "Not entirely."

"So what's your interest?"

With a grave smile she said, "I also heard that Millie Sweet's death might have been. . . complicated."

"So where do we go from here?"

She gave the appearance of considering all the options. "We should perhaps take this to my superiors; let them handle it." He

222

could tell from her tone that she wasn't going to do that. She didn't disappoint. "But there isn't enough here; all we have is speculation and innuendo backed up with scientific mumbo-jumbo."

He forgave her the blasphemy. "So. . ?"

She stared hard at him and he had a feeling that he was entering a period of haggling. To pre-empt her, he said, "We need some help to trace Carlos. He's obviously the key to all this. You might be able to help."

Beverley smiled, shining condescension as if it were the light of benevolence. "Maybe, and maybe not. That's not the question, though, is it? What do I need of you?"

He had expected this, had come fully stocked with patience. "I think that what we know and what you know are different. I think that together, we might just be able to crack this. Separately, I think that you're as lost as we are."

She smiled, but said nothing. He hadn't made a joke and so assumed the smile was a request for more humility.

"I know you've got nothing to thank me for, Beverley. . ."

She laughed. Had he made a joke he would have been fooled into believing that she was greatly amused.

"Do you know how shitty my life has been of late?" she demanded.

Of course he didn't know. "I don't think you can blame me, Beverley," he pointed out as mildly and reasonably as he could. "You tried to screw me, but in the end you were screwed yourself. That's life."

She said nothing for a long time, her face expressionless and therefore full of apparent fury. Then she sighed and relaxed into a smile. "Fair enough," she conceded. "However, it changes nothing. There is nothing here for me, other than possible trouble."

"This is big, Beverley, I can feel it. It has to be. Hartmann's bribe alone tells us that, without taking into account the organization required to steal the body and get it cremated."

If she was persuaded, it failed to shift the look of doubt. He continued, "What harm is it going to do you if you just make a few discreet enquiries? Either you'll get nowhere – in which case all you've done is waste a couple of hours – or you'll strike lucky and we'll have a way into this."

"But what do you think is going on? You haven't said."

"I'm not sure, Beverley," he admitted. "All I have is theories and suspicions. I think that Millie died because she had been infected with a man-made virus. I think that maybe Turner died because he knew all about it."

Suddenly she stood up. It was clearly a sign that he should leave and he, too, got to his feet. She went to the door, still giving no sign of what she intended to do. He followed her and they stood for a moment, her hand on the door lock.

When it came, the slap loosened his left second molar and smacked his jaws together so that he bit his tongue. He managed a brief, "Christ!" before he put his hand to his jaw and jerked his head back, too late and too little as the return slap came from the other side. While various noises rang around his cochleas and he reflected that she could have slapped for England, he heard Beverley say, "Don't ever fuck with me again, John, understand?"

He was still trying to recover equilibrium when he looked up, smiled and said, "But I don't understand, Beverley. You're supposed to be such a good fuck."

And she laughed, as if this were the greatest compliment she could have received. He asked, "Will you help us?"

The kiss that she gave him then almost made up for the violence, almost made him want to return to the time when he had come so close to lying with her, when she had somehow intoxicated him. . . "Maybe," she said, and abruptly he was back in the present, as she shut the door. He didn't see a broad smile spread over her face.

The atmosphere was not so much tense as rigid, as if time were stuttering lines, as if the three of them were picking their way carefully along a path, whilst eyeing each other warily. If he had been caught between an angry tigress deprived of its cub and an erupting volcano he couldn't have been more nervous. It had been agreed, in a manner rather reminiscent of the great international peace negotiations of old, that they should meet in a wine bar; Eisenmenger had even thought it wise to pick one roughly equidistant between the police station and Helena's office.

It was a lunchtime in a lifetime.

The darkness of the wine bar – Eisenmenger, despite the hostility that oozed around him, was side-tracked into wondering why all wine bars were dimly lit – gave them a spurious privacy in the playing out of their animosities.

Things started badly.

"I do so enjoy a pleasant drink with friends," was Beverley's opening remark. She was clad in a white dress that was spotless and creaseless and shameless; Eisenmenger neither noticed nor ignored.

Helena, herself wearing a short royal blue dress that Eisenmenger was pleased to notice appeared disinclined to cover her legs, had arrived last, her eyes sliding across Beverley Wharton much as they might have smeared across road-kill. Such light as there was glowed crimson, giving her hair a deep, cuprous shimmer. Eisenmenger had already bought white wine for all of them, mainly because he thought it unwise to leave the two of them together without a chaperone.

"Are we the best you can manage for 'friends'?"

If Helena had sounded any colder there would have been frost on her larynx.

Beverley smiled. "Don't put yourself down, Hel. May I call you Hel?"

Helena hated the diminutive but ignored the question. Instead she said, "Hope we're not keeping you, Bev. There must be some murderers you're trying to catch."

As she said this she put on her face a smile that quite plainly said, *Remember Nikki Exner? Remember how you fouled up?*

Eisenmenger could feel the atmosphere beginning to reek with noxious gases. "Perhaps we should get down to business."

Beverley flicked her eyes off Helena and on to Eisenmenger, but only after a second had silently screamed to its death. "Yes. Perhaps we should." She sipped some wine.

"You went to see Raymond Sweet. May we ask why?"

But it wasn't to be that easy. "I'm here because you asked me to be here. I thought you needed help; I don't see why I should answer any questions."

"But we need to share what we know."

Beverley Wharton raised an attractive, well-shaped eyebrow. "Do we? From my point of view, I have something you want. What do you have that I need?"

Eisenmenger sensed that Helena was about to unleash something. He said quickly, "We have context. I suspect that

you know enough to appreciate that finding Carlos is important, but I doubt that you have much idea of what's behind it
all." The guess was reasonable, and he followed it up with a
pertinent question. "If you don't need us, why are you here?"
He watched her reaction, was unsure if his words had been
wasted.

Ignoring this, Beverley made a great show of not hiding her
smile. "Carlos? You don't even know the second name, do you?"

Helena's voice when she spoke was not far from feral. It
reminded Eisenmenger of a cat faced by a fox. "You don't realize
the nature of what you're dealing with. You don't know the
importance of finding him, whatever his name may be."

The policewoman stared at her. Eisenmenger for the first time
was able to read her face, seeing the uncertainty he had guessed
was inside her. Helena, however, hadn't finished. "If you don't
feel you can cooperate with us, we can always go to Chief
Inspector Lambert."

Eisenmenger was lost but he saw whatever was happening
was not to Beverley Wharton's liking. He looked anew at Helena,
who wore a look he had never before really recognized on her
face. She continued, "The funny thing is, I contacted your station,
and they seemed to think that you were ill."

The wine bar smelled of damp. It wasn't an unpleasant
odour, and it heightened the sense of being in a cellar, but
suddenly Beverley Wharton seemed to think that she could
detect a certain tang of rot. Her face hardened while around her
eyes there was a darkening that emphasized the dangerous
brightness of her eyes. She and Helena regarded each other for
long moments that seemed to Eisenmenger to meld into a
single heart's beat.

Then she nodded and Eisenmenger had the feeling that it was a
sign of acknowledgement. She put the glass to her lips, skimmed
the surface, put it down and murmured, "Congratulations."

Helena's voice sounded almost tired as she said, "So, can we
cut the crap? I don't want to be here any more than you do, but
John's persuaded me that we need you and it seems obvious that
you need us."

Eisenmenger asked, "Just how official is your interest?"

"Not at all." She sighed. "Not at all. This is my baby; mine and
mine alone, for the time being."

"May I ask why?"

A shrug. "Something's going on – Hartmann told me what happened to him – and I'm being told that Pel-Ebstein are in it up to their proverbial, but beyond that, you're quite right. I don't know any details and I don't have any evidence. Without evidence, I'm going to be laughed out of the force."

He glanced at Helena who was clearly unconvinced by this, and he, too, had the feeling that she had calculated how much to tell, how much to leave lying. Her story wasn't without contradiction, but he let it go.

"And you think that we can supply the details? But what do we get in return?"

"You get my help."

"You haven't found Carlos yet?"

She smiled knowingly. "Not yet. Nor Stein, if you were going to ask." Here was a new name to them and Beverley didn't miss their looks of perplexity. "You don't know that much, then." Cutting in before Helena could react, Eisenmenger said, "I suspect that you know some things, we know others. As I told you, we need each other."

For a moment, Beverley looked as if she might argue, then decided against it. Eisenmenger looked at Helena and he raised his eyebrows. She shrugged. *I suppose we must.*

Beverley took an age but eventually she said, through a down-turned mouth, "I guess that's fair. Okay. I think we have a deal."

They didn't shake hands.

The enormity of what they were dealing with overwhelmed them. When Beverley's information was combined with what they either knew or suspected, the canvas grew and stretched and the picture on it became far deeper, far darker than they had hitherto suspected. The wine bar became a sanctum, the world outside dangerous

Helena found herself fighting feelings not just of shock but also of actual nausea as she learned of the death of Justine Nielsen and the disappearances of Maurice Stein and Jean-Jacques Renvier. Eisenmenger, as ever working his way through ramifications, possibilities, improbabilities and outcomes, found himself almost overwhelmed by what they now knew. It was as if they had previously possessed only a sketch, and now they had a three-dimensional sculpture; as if their beliefs were now solid and coming to hunt them down. Beverley found feelings of excitement wrestling with unfamiliar suspicions of uncertainty. Her instincts had been proven right – this was huge – but it was clear that the forces they were intending to oppose were consequently huge. Perhaps too big, perhaps literally overwhelming.

When Beverley had informed them that two of the survivors from the laboratory fire had died within a few days of each other, there was shocked silence until Eisenmenger said quietly, "Mr Rosenthal is very efficient."

"Rosenthal, Rytand, whatever his name is, trained in the Special Forces. Died in them, too, if the official record is to be believed."

"Not a bad cover, being dead."

"But why? I still don't see why all these people had to die." Helena sounded almost pained.

Beverley said, "At the moment, that's not what concerns me most. I think the thing we have to worry about is our own exposure. Rosenthal has apparently dispatched, or ordered the dispatch of, two and perhaps three people; he'll have no problem with dealing with two amateurs and a rogue police officer."

Eisenmenger said only, "Thanks," while he thought, *she's absolutely right.*

He was unsure if Helena appreciated that. She said, "We don't have enough to go to the police officially. We have to find Carlos Arias-Stella; he's the only witness left."

Beverley smiled, superciliousness in two soft red lips. "Well, thanks, Helena."

And suddenly they were there again, caught on a thermal of rising tension. Eisenmenger asked, "How long will it take to find him?"

The difference in her attitude when she addressed him was painfully apparent. "Difficult to say. It may only take a few hours, it may take days, even a week or more. Sometimes we never find people we're looking for."

"Great." Helena made one syllable carry an essay's worth of sarcasm.

Beverley turned to her. "I'll find him. And I'll find him alive."

Nerys had spent the next day at home, calling in sick. Although she failed to appreciate it, she was in fact in shock, her mind still dwelling on what had happened during those ten minutes late last night, an involuntary retelling of the tale, bringing with it each time more of the churning fear she had at that time experienced.

Yet the more she relived it, the less she could appreciate what had happened, what it had meant.

My God, Carlos must have got himself into really big shit this time.

Yet Carlos had never struck her as villainous. Lazy, drunken, good-for-nothing – pick your adjective – but not *bad*. Irritating, irredeemable, inexplicable – the adjectives were unceasing – and she loved him. More importantly, she had seen within him love for her – a sight she had so rarely glimpsed.

That scary bastard who had been after him, though, had been evil, that had been obvious. Whatever Carlos had done, she knew that she could forgive him. She might have been getting pissed off with him, but not enough to shop him to someone like that, even if she had known where he was. No wonder he had disappeared, being chased by a psycho like that.

She sighed. "Why didn't you take me?" she asked sorrowfully.

Thirty hours passed before they met again, this time in Beverley's flat. They had been hours in which Helena had fretted, Eisenmenger had brooded. It had been a miracle that they hadn't erupted into a conflagration of irritability.

When Helena and Eisenmenger parked, Helena looked up at the converted warehouse and said, "She lives here?"

"Top floor."

She shook her head. "Why do I smell an odour?"

"Surely not corruption?"

"Either that or the drains are blocked."

They were admitted when they pressed the button by Beverley's name. No words were exchanged, but then the closed – circuit camera rendered communication unnecessary. They made their way through the entrance foyer, subdued lighting and pastel shades, while the scent of polish on the warm wood surfaces stole up on them, enticing them into a conspiracy of opulence.

When Beverley opened the door to them she nodded at Helena, her face stony, while for Eisenmenger she managed a brief, weak stretch of the lips. She looked tired.

She didn't offer them a drink.

As she sat, Helena looked around. "Nice," she remarked, although the tone was noticeably lacking in appreciation and anyway Beverley ignored it.

"Any news?" asked Eisenmenger.

"There's been nothing to locate either Stein or Arias-Stella. Stein seems to have just dropped out of the world right after the fire. There's been nothing since – no sightings, nothing. He hasn't even used a bank account, it seems. I'd say he was dead, but it's hard to die without some sort of official trace being left."

"Unless someone murdered him," remarked Helena. Beverley looked at her.

"Yes, well. . ."

Eisenmenger murmured, "And now, perhaps, the same has befallen Arias-Stella."

"His family home has been contacted; they have heard nothing," Beverley said. "After that, I came unstuck; unless you have a criminal record, there's very little information that the police have access to, through normal channels." She paused. "However, I've still got some friends left. I've managed to compile some further information on Arias-Stella which might help us."

She indicated an open file on the low table that separated them. Eiserimenger leaned forward and picked it up. He held it so that Helena could see, going through its contents. Birth certificate, school records, university records, tax details, social security details, even medical records. A life – or at least the bureaucratic definition thereof. There was even a photograph.

Helena asked, "Where did you get this?"

Beverley misunderstood what she meant. "I told you, I've still got friends. We've spent the last twelve hours working to compile this." She didn't mention Luke by name, although he had done most of this with her.

"No, you don't understand. There is no way that you should have access to three quarters of this stuff."

Beverley's reaction was as if she had been transfused with blood enriched with patronizing contempt. "Isn't there? How quaint." She moved on, as if an irritating child had been dealt with, saying, "I'd rather you didn't take this away, but you're free to peruse it now." This was addressed to Eisenmenger, and Eisenmenger alone.

"Hang on a minute."

Beverley turned cold attention upon the irritating child again. She raised silent eyebrows.

"You have no legal right to this information."

The sigh coated the room with a kind of joyous derision. "Oh, come on, Hel. This is the real world. This is the place where bastards fly planes into buildings, and where the nice chap who lives next door and who drinks in the pub every Sunday lunchtime just happens to be sending out little parcels of anthrax spores to politicians and media companies."

"We aren't searching for a terrorist, just a witness."

"And how else do you suggest we proceed? He's vanished. Not a trace of him to be found anywhere."

"He'll turn up eventually."

Beverley laughed. "Oh, yes? The only difference between us, Hel, is that in my job, you can't afford to sit on your backside while the legal bill mounts up. In case you've forgotten what this is about, let me remind you. He is our only witness to what happened in that lab and to what PEP were up to. Without him, we have nothing; certainly not enough to go to my superiors with. That means PEP wins. Do you want that?"

"Of course not, but. . ."

"Not cricket'? Is that your problem? I don't notice Mr Rosenthal playing by any sort of rules."

Helena shook her head. "So, the end justifies the means? Why is it that I catch a whiff of fascism when I hear someone say that?"

A disgusted sound came from the back of Beverley's throat. She turned to Eisenmenger. "Can you try and persuade Snow White?"

Eisenmenger, suddenly the object of their scrutiny and wishing he wasn't, said cautiously, "In an ideal world, we should treat this like high-level nuclear waste. But. . ."

Beverley couldn't resist a triumphant smile; Helena snorted. Eisenmenger, looking not at them but at the dossier, added, "There are two further factors to consider." He looked at Helena now. "We have to find him before Rosenthal does. Also, we have to find him before Proteus is activated within him. If either of those happens, we've failed."

Before Beverley could say anything he went on, "Ordinarily, I'd agree with you, and, yes, you're quite right that the ability to

231

collect this sort of stuff on an innocent person is alarming, but just at this moment, I'm rather glad it can be done."

Helena said nothing, looked disgusted. Beverley murmured, "Well, I'm glad someone sees sense."

He looked at Helena. He wondered for a few seconds if she would walk out. She asked him, "Is there no other way?"

"At the moment, Carlos Arias-Stella is just a name. If we're to find him, he's got to become a person; a person who makes decisions. If we know the person, we may be able to predict how and what he decides. This," he indicated the file, "should help to turn him into a person."

Helena considered this, then nodded, although her body language suggested that she was far from happy with this compromise of her beliefs. Beverley, thankfully, said nothing. Eisenmenger took the file and began to read, handing the sheets on to Helena who made notes. Beverley, at last perhaps taking pity on them, got up to make coffee just as Eisenmenger asked, "What about the photograph? How did you get hold of that?"

"He has a passport," she replied simply.

An hour later and they had been through all of the documents. They had a life sketched out. Born thirty-four years ago to a Spanish doctor and his wife, Carlos had had a middling academic record that had precluded any thoughts of following his father's career, despite an aptitude for science. He had gone to Norwich University reading biochemistry, then gone on to a PhD, but the unexpected death of his father from a ruptured aneurysm halfway through had spoiled that. The remarriage of his mother had not been a happy circumstance for Carlos. There was a list of casualty admissions for minor injuries, all of which mentioned inebriation, together with two cautions for drunkenness.

Three jobs in quick succession, all of them as research assistants, had followed; from these one publication graced with the name of Carlos Arias-Stella had emerged; there was even a copy of it and, as far as Eisenmenger could tell, it wasn't an unworthy effort, but that didn't matter. The groves of Academe had changed since Plato's day; quantity was all, quality was secondary.

The job at St Jerome's must have looked unpromising – plant genetics hardly causes priapism even amongst the aficionados – but the work had unexpectedly shed light on the cell kinetics of cancer. Three papers in highly rated scientific publications had followed; suddenly the CV looked a lot better. Then had come the post at PEP.

It was quite noticeable that from this point on, information became sketchier. The bank accounts began to look a lot healthier; the numbers suggested that not only was his salary markedly increased, but at the same time the number of withdrawals plummeted. It was only when, after twenty-two months, the fire had happened that life had returned to the Arias-Stella accounts. The reports on the fire were very interesting to them; the initial police reports that Luke had found for Beverley contrasting so markedly with the insurance investigators' conclusions.

And then the pattern had returned. Three more casualty admissions, all involving ethanol, one more run-in with the local constabulary. The job at the Leishman Institute – not one of the world's great academic institutions – had saved him from probable ruin.

Beverley sat opposite them while they went through the fat dossier, saying nothing. When they had finished, she asked, "Well?"

Helena said only, "Remarkable."

Beverley smiled warmly. "Thank you."

Eisenmenger was wordless for a while. Then, "Somehow, he's found out that something's wrong."

"Presumably."

"There's nothing here about his personal life," said Eisenmenger, after a pause.

Helena murmured, "Not even Big Sister has total control." Beverley forbore to comment. Eisenmenger leaned back, eyes closed, seeming almost to be asleep. Helena took up the line. "Probably he's found out about Millie."

"So he'd contact one of the others, " Beverley went on. "Then he's gone from one to the other, finding out that that they've just met their ends."

"And suddenly he realizes that of the six on Rouna, he's probably the last left alive," said Helena.

They glanced quickly at each other, as if shocked that they could actually cooperate in a universe such as this. Eisenmenger said, "So he runs. But where? Do we actually have enough information to guess?"

Helena asked of Beverley, "So what surveillance are you using? I assume that you have some sort of access to covert operations?"

Showing no reaction, Beverley said, "The two standard ones. Any credit or debit transaction using cards registered to Carlos Arias-Stella, as well as any use of a telephone number registered to him, will be notified."

"Not when he farts?"

Even Eisenmenger opened his eyes at that one.

Beverley said nothing, while Eisenmenger asked, "What's the delay in notification?"

"Twenty-four hours."

Eisenmenger remained silent, but looked unhappy, as if this were not the ideal.

"In twenty-four hours Rosenthal could have found him and killed him." Helena seemed to find some delight in locating a potential drawback.

Eisenmenger sucked in air, then abruptly stood up. "It's not a bad backstop, but I think we've got to work out where he's gone without relying on looking for any ripples on the surface that he might make."

He held out his hand to help Helena up. Beverley stayed sitting. She asked, "So what happens now?"

Eisenmenger didn't seem to hear; he was already heading for the door. Behind him, Helena said, "We'll let you know."

Hartmann's mood as he returned home was still unfamiliar to him. Elation. Even the syllables of the word were foreign in his mind, their coincidence producing a strange, but not unpleasant noise. For two days now he had been happy, had constantly repeated this single, simple collision of sounds.

Elation.

He knew that it was one of those few moments in life when happiness was all there was, all that there needed to be, when no outside force or event could spoil his world. He even felt good about Annette, about the children, about his life as a whole.

But he was wrong. . .

The police car parked in the road outside was of interest, but not sinister. Even the presence of his father-in-law's rather stately car did not trouble him, so happy was he. He guessed that they might be related.

As soon as the door closed behind him, a small face appeared from the relative gloom of the first-floor landing. "Daddy?"

He perhaps should have known something was wrong then, but the unaccustomed inebriation of elation dulled his perception. "What is it, Jay? Why aren't you in bed?"

Jay had been crying. He came down the stairs holding on with a hand held high to touch the banister rail. As he came nearer and into brighter light, Hartmann saw that not only had he been crying, but he was also terrified. Something changed in Hartmann's world then.

"What's wrong, Jay? Has something happened? Is it your sister? Or Mummy?"

The little boy looked at him and said, "Mummy's been upset. She's been crying."

"Why? What's happened?"

If Jay knew, he didn't have the chance to answer, for it was then that the doors to the sitting room opened and Piers Brown-Sequard stood looking out at him. His gaze fell first upon Hartmann, then flicked down to Jay. Hartmann saw in that single instant such loathing, such anger, and yet such triumph, that he knew at once. The truth of what had happened, of his situation and of his future where all there in that single glance. He was paralyzed by the realization, the transition from what he had thought to what he now knew.

"Go back to bed, Jake." Brown-Sequard smiled at the boy who looked in turn at Hartmann, but Hartmann was no longer interested in anything his son might have to give or need.

"Go on, Jake," urged his grandfather. "I'll be up in a moment."

He was reluctantly obeyed. Once the small boy had gone from sight, another glance fell across Hartmann, then Brown-Sequard turned and went back into the sitting room.

It was some minutes before Hartmann joined him. His footsteps felt plumbic.

Brown-Sequard was standing before the fireplace. In his hand was a glass of brandy; on the coffee table was a videotape. Hartmann felt that he was close to fainting. His respirations were as noisy as a scuba diver's, his heart no longer beating but striking his chest wall, slapping it with vicious intent. He said nothing, just standing there, a little away from the tape.

235

Brown-Sequard again cast a malevolent gaze upon him. "You know what that is?" It was even there in his words, this loathing, as if there so much bile inside him it slipped out whenever it could, grasping any opportunity to escape.

Hartmann looked again at the tape. He said nothing, though. Words seemed now to be treacherous.

"It came late this afternoon. *Special Delivery.*" Brown-Sequard snarled the last two words, as if this were the final, crowning insult. "One to me, one to Annette."

Hartmann continued to stare at the black, plastic video cassette. Brown-Sequard was finding eloquence as he went on, the sentences following one another in a rather less staccato manner. "I played it fairly quickly. Thought it was odd, but obviously had to play it. I played it and. . ." He paused for some hyperventilation, then, "I rang Annette at once, but I was too late. She had already played it. . ."

Suddenly Brown-Sequard seemed to experience a form of brief seizure, for his words were interrupted and he twitched. Then he took four steps around the coffee table, came up to Hartmann (still addressing the tape with a fixed gaze) and brought his fist up in a poor, ill co-ordinated right hook. He was quite a small man, and not a boxer. The blow hurt Hartmann, but it did little more than cause his head to move slightly, then to look blankly at his father-in-law.

Brown-Sequard was off on a different course now. Gone was explanation, replaced by condemnation. "You unspeakable little shit! You disgusting, perverted piece of excrement! How dare you? How dare you do those things? How dare you betray Annette and her children?"

He was loading up some more ammunition – more un-answerable questions and pithy adjectives – when at last Hartmann found voice. "Where is she? Where is Annette?" His voice was plaintive.

Brown-Sequard's reply was poison-tipped with contempt. "That is nothing to do with you. You are never going to see her again. You are never going to see the children again. You will leave this house – her house – tonight, and you will not return."

Hartmann said, "I'd like to see her. Try to explain. . ."

Brown-Sequard was already shaking his head, a smile on his

face that was far more menacing than a frown would have been. "No. You will leave now."

Hartmann awoke. "You can't do that. . ."

"Yes. I can. The police car outside is here at my request. They will escort you out if you refuse to go voluntarily."

"But that's not legal. . ."

"By tomorrow lunchtime there will be a court order forbidding you from approaching my daughter or her children. Divorce on the grounds of adultery will also have been commenced."

Hartmann was sinking now into despair. The words, the demeanour, the tape, all combined to crush him. The shame, the horror, the fear, all these formed a luminous mass of rampaging fear in his head. Questions, too, came to plague him. Who else had received copies of the tape? His parents? The Medical School? The Royal College?

He tried once more. "Please?" It might not be too bad if he could at least salvage his marriage, if he could at least be given something to stop him drowning.

Brown-Sequard said only, "No. Get out, and don't come back."

Hartmann stood still for some seconds, his thoughts disconnected, both from each other and from action. He kept thinking that it might not be as bad as it appeared, that he might still rescue something of worth, something on which to base the rest of his life.

Then Brown-Sequard said, "I have written to the General Medical Council and I will be passing the tape to the police."

And then he saw his future, bright and clear.

They went to Eisenmenger's house. It was the first time that Helena had been there. Her first thought was that it was a considerable improvement on his last domicile, her second (her last on the subject) was that she could see no proof that he had actually taken up residence. The only sign that anyone had even been present were some papers on the dining table by the small bay window. She peeked into the kitchen but again the surfaces were bare and opening the refrigerator only yielded light. At least the perfume of damp was absent.

Eisenmenger was distracted to the point of invisibility. When she offered to make him coffee she had to be satisfied with no answer for assent. When she brought it out, he was sitting at the dining table, looking at the papers, scribbling on others. She sat opposite him, peering down at the words, phrases and fragments he had written. *Where would he go? Does he suspect infection? Girlfriends. Random? Is he dead?*

Helena waited, sipping her coffee.

Eventually, a sigh signalling his return, Eisenmenger stopped staring at the white paper and looked up. He was genuinely surprised to see the coffee. "Oh. Thanks."

"Has inspiration struck?"

He frowned and shook his head. "No. Not this time." He swallowed half of the coffee. "Have you got your notes from Beverley's file?"

Helena produced them from her briefcase. "I appreciate the practicalities of the situation, but aren't you in the least disturbed by the existence of such a file? That she could amass such a document, and in only one day?"

He really wanted just to think about the case, but he could see that this was important to her. "Does it disturb me? Yes. Does it surprise me? No. The state's ability to acquire knowledge on its citizens has never been greater, but will undoubtedly become greater still."

"I'm not naive, John. I'm aware of what the security services can and do get up to in the name of 'national security,' but this is an ordinary police inspector we're talking about. She shouldn't be able to access information like that."

He couldn't stop a small smile as he asked, "Are you entirely sure that your concerns are about civil liberties in general?"

Helena was suddenly defensive. "Meaning?"

Realizing that the smile had been a mistake, Eisenmenger tried to sound conciliatory. "Perhaps the fact that the 'ordinary police inspector' is Beverley Wharton makes the situation slightly more difficult for you."

If he had thought that their recent closeness meant that he had seen the last of Helena's temper, he was now corrected. "Why shouldn't it?" she demanded. "You might have persuaded me to ally myself with that bitch for the sake of Raymond Sweet and the truth, but that doesn't mean I've forgiven her. She destroyed my step-brother, and she ruined my life at the same time. I've still to make retribution for that."

"Of course. I didn't mean. . ."

"You meant that I wasn't being objective. That's always your opinion. Why do you think that I can't stop my emotions from interfering with my judgement?"

"I don't. . ."

"Is it perhaps because I'm a woman?"

Eisenmenger felt as if he were fighting fire with paraffin. "Not at all. I just. . ."

"Or is it because you see me as damaged in some way? Is that it? So scarred that my whole perspective is skewed?"

Helena was working up a fair velocity as she flew down the avenue of his attitudes, real and misconceived. He tried again. "I don't think that at. . ."

"Don't you?" she demanded and Eisenmenger found that he had had enough. "No, I bloody don't! Now, will you stop interrupting me and listen for a change?"

It silenced her, but it did nothing for international relations. She wore a face of rapidly respiring ire. As calmly as he could he said, "I appreciate how you feel about Beverley Wharton; really, I do. One day, I will take great pleasure in helping you prove your stepbrother's innocence and her complicity, but not now. Now we have to fight Pel-Ebstein Pharmaceuticals. They are big – huge – we are small. We are infinitesimal. Without help, we don't stand a chance."

She said, "That doesn't mean I have to like it."

"I don't ask you to like it. I merely ask you to endure it, preferably in silence."

She opened her mouth but said nothing. One deep breath later she said through a grimace, "You ask a lot."

He stretched out his hand to take hers. "We have to find Carlos before Rosenthal does."

She nodded.

Rosenthal picked her up in a nightclub. She told him her name was Bobby and she claimed to be nineteen, but a brief perusal of her handbag when she went to the restroom just before they left told him that she was in fact seventeen. She was impressed with his car, clearly congratulating herself on a wise choice; he wondered what she would say in a few hours' time.

The flat he took her to was one of several he had access to. Its luxury found approval in Bobby. Rosenthal found some champagne in the refrigerator, poured two glasses, and settled back. Bobby, he guessed, would know what to do.

She did not disappoint.

She downed her glass of champagne (he forgave her the cavalier treatment of a fine vintage), stood up and slipped her short red dress off. It fell away as if it had rehearsed this routine a thousand times and her underwear followed obediently. Rosenthal looked her up and down, nodded, then stood. He turned and walked away from her, into the bedroom. She followed without a word.

They spent the rest of the evening trying to set in their minds the sequence of events. Helena said, "The Proteus project was to develop a virus that was loaded with genes that cause cancer."

They were sitting together on a small blue leather sofa. They had eaten a takeout pizza and were now drinking red wine. Eisenmenger could have been asleep.

Helena continued, "Tell me again why they might want something like Proteus."

There was a silence in the room, allowing the distant grumble of the traffic in the city to intrude. "What they were trying to do was to investigate the mechanisms involved in carcinogenesis – the development of cancer," Eisenmenger said quietly. "One of the techniques is to use a virus to introduce genes into cells to see what effect they will have. As I said, viruses are the perfect vehicle because hundreds of millions of years of evolution mean they have perfected the difficult task of injecting foreign genes into cells."

"So Proteus was. . .what? Something the rest of PEP could use for cancer research?"

"Presumably."

Somebody walked down the narrow mews whistling the melody of a hymn.

"Okay. A fire occurs. There's disagreement about its cause, but that doesn't matter."

"Doesn't it?"

"Well, I can't see that we need to worry about the cause."

He remained silent for a moment. Then, quite suddenly, he leaned forward. "Jesus!"

Helena, the glass to her lips, looked at him.

Eisenmenger remained crouched forward. On his face there was revelation. "I'm an idiot!"

She waited.

"Beverley was right."

Helena, looking as if she had swallowed a slug, asked, "What about?"

"National security."

"So?"

He was thinking. "Maybe we've believed the cover story."

"What cover story?"

"Models Development."

She sighed. She was used to being here. "What are you talking about?"

"Perhaps they could have used it as a model for cancer, but they didn't need to hide it away to that extent. It was innovative and it was probably sensitive, but it wasn't going to make PEP a billion dollars, at least not for a long time. Why did they go to all that trouble to site them on a small island off Scotland?"

"If not for commercial reasons, then why?"

He didn't answer directly. "The temperature-sensitive trigger . . ." It was a murmur, nothing more.

Helena took sustenance from the wine. She could have asked what he was talking about, but she knew that Eisenmenger was just enunciating thoughts as they came to him, that he would tell her when he knew himself.

"The trigger's not just a safeguard, it's actually the beauty of the whole thing."

He drained his wine, pouring more for himself but forgetting Helena; she took the bottle from him while he looked somewhere she could not see.

"Proteus is a weapon," he said at last.

Beverley sighed deeply. Luke massaged her shoulders, his strong, broad hands working her muscles, releasing the tension, allowing her to forget her troubles. He sat astride her, as naked as she, enjoying both the feel of her flesh and the reflection in the large mirror behind the head of her bed. Enjoying it very much.

She opened her eyes, saw him looking and propped herself up on her elbows, giving him an added bonus in the view. "Why is it that men like to spectate when they make love?"

He laughed, a beautifully rich, deep sound, made for relaxed reassurance. "Only if there's something worth looking at."

"And I was told women were vain."

He took her shoulders, caressed them, then brought his hands down her back. He shifted himself backwards so that he could track down to her buttocks. She made a deep throat noise, shifting as the tips of his fingers came together, then delved a little more deeply. She shifted, eyes closed, legs slightly wider.

He sighed, "My, my."

She felt him pry inside her and she gasped.

"Proteus would perhaps work as a generic system for cancer – transfect a cell culture or laboratory animal, wait for the tumours to develop (and we know that it's extremely effective), then you can test whatever therapy you like – and maybe that was the cover story, but it wasn't the real reason for developing Proteus."

He was pacing the small room, a feverishness sheening him, suffusing the space. Helena watched him, her eyes fixed, as if afraid that he was sickening.

"The temperature-sensitive trigger is an old trick in cell transfection systems. It enables you to control the start of the experiment, but think of it, Helena. You have a virus that infects an individual – no symptoms, no sign that they have in every cell of their body a minute grenade, primed and waiting. You could do it years in advance. Fifty years, fifty hours; absolute control is yours, because you have the ability to pull the trigger.

"Then, when the time is right, you introduce a second virus. This one is pyrogenic – its sole purpose is to induce a fever. The virus infects, propagates, the body temperature begins to rise, degree by degree, thirty-seven, thirty-eight, thirty-nine, thirty-nine point nine. Nothing happens, but the individual feels awful because of the fever. Then forty degrees Celsius and, in every cell, Proteus awakes and begins its work. Within perhaps two days, cancer consumes the victim, devours them, as effectively as the worms eat our corpses, only this time the corpses are alive while the feeding occurs."

"A biological weapon."

"Exactly. But a beautiful one. If you were mad enough, you could spread this one around the entire world. You could infect all the billions that grub out their lives on the husk of Mother

Earth, then just wait. There would be no way to eradicate it once it was released. You just wait until you feel you have to use it. That Middle Eastern state proving a bit of a nuisance? A nasty little influenza epidemic ought to see to that. Nobody could point a finger. There would be no need for the usual sabre waving, the tedious emptiness of diplomatic anger.

"But there's even more. The scale is your choice. The control is yours. You can kill one or you can kill ten million; if you can adjust the second agent, limit it or spread it as you wish, you can have your godhead over as much of the world as you want."

Helena couldn't help it. She felt sick at the thought, but it was so monstrous, she found herself unable to believe it.

"But this is hypothesis, right?"

Eisenmenger stopped suddenly in his pacing. He turned his head to Helena. "Three people have either died or disappeared and are presumed dead. Turner fell to his death, ostensibly an accident until you happen to know the context. Hartmann, unlucky enough to perform the post-mortem examination on a victim of Proteus, is blackmailed into falsifying his findings." He shook his head. "I can't help feeling that this is all a bit over the top for an unfortunate laboratory accident."

She picked her way through the implications of what he was saying. "PEP wouldn't do this on their initiative. They would have a backer."

"More than just a backer. . ."

They looked at each other. "A national agency of some kind," she said quietly.

He nodded. "Of some kind. Maybe ours, maybe not." He looked up as a car horn sounded quite close by in the street. "A state is the only institution that takes for itself the right to deprive an individual of their life", he whispered.

Helena felt very small indeed.

She was whimpering, might have been begging him to stop had the gag not been in place, but this only aroused Rosenthal further. He had tied her down, blindfolded her and was, as he liked to think, "using her". He knew that she liked it really. The whimpering was all part of the game, playing a role, just as he was playing a role. He caressed her, enjoying her moistness; it was further proof that she was as pleased by this as he was.

True, there were a few bruises, and he had accidentally made her bleed when he had bitten her nipple too hard; made her squeal at that one.

He whispered into her ear, "Let me in again, Bobby."

More whimpering. She was good.

"Come on, Bobby. Let me in, like a good girl."

She struggled against the bonds. Her legs remained closed. He sighed. "Oh, dear."

Bobby smoked, probably thought it was a clever thing to do. Perhaps in future, he thought as he lit one and held it over her right groin, she'll think better of it.

Luke had timing; God, he had timing. For minutes that seemed like hours they stayed together, he inside her, she crouched, enjoying the feeling of completeness. He leaned forward, hands around her breasts, the movement adding to the pleasure. She opened her eyes, saw him smiling back at her.

"Enjoying yourself?"

"Kind of."

He straightened up, hands on her hips, beginning to work in earnest. She decided that this was better than any massage.

In the middle of the night, Eisenmenger woke Helena. At one o'clock she had gone to lie down in the bedroom, leaving him still pacing, still working things through in his head. He was sitting beside her on the duvet, gently shaking her and calling softly. She looked groggily at the clock; *four-thirty.*

"What is it?"

"We've got to go. I think I know where Carlos might be."

She sat up. "Where?"

"Rouna."

Rosenthal had to impress on Bobby that she was rather ungrateful, but he was remarkably effective at such tasks and she quickly appreciated his point. She remained unhappy – tearful, snivelling and sullen – and he had to get her something for the burns, but at least she had stopped screaming abuse.

He poured her more champagne, watching her from the armchair by the bed. She gulped it again, he was sorry to note. She would need a lot of training to appreciate the good things in life.

"Do you want to spend the night here?" he asked. "Or shall I get you a taxi?"

She sniffed. Even with red eyes and tear-stained make-up he found her attractive. If she wasn't careful, she wouldn't get the choice.

"I'd better go."

He nodded, rose and phoned for the taxi. As she left, he gave her two hundred. She opened her mouth to object, saw his eyes give a warning, said nothing more.

Alone, he returned to the bed and lay there in the darkness, waiting. Waiting was something he was good at. He'd waited a long time over the years; it was what soldiering was all about. Those who couldn't cope with the waiting didn't last long, for it was in the periods of quiet, of anticipation, that the preparation was done, that deeds were planned but more importantly that the body and mind were perfected.

Be patient, keep silent. That's what they'd taught him were the most important skills for a soldier. Shooting straight, learning how to kill (but never learning to like it, merely to appreciate its place in things), survival in extreme environments – all these were necessary, but all of them were as nothing without the ability to wait and the ability to be silent when silence was required.

The room took him to its soul, absorbed him, blanketed him with its void, and there was thus nothing, not even breathing.

His father had died early, but not early enough. In only six years of life Rosenthal had seen and now remembered enough of his father to prevent mourning. His father had had a liking for cruelty and that Rosenthal could not forgive; it was necessary but should never be enjoyed for its own sake, a method, not a goal.

He didn't think that he had been an exceptional child. Perhaps more reserved than usual, perhaps more intense, but not delinquent, not violent. Academically above the norm, athletically the best, entry into the armed forces, thence into Special Services had been swift, easy and rewarding.

His death, five years later, murdered in the Middle East by mercenaries had been only the briefest of inconveniences; very soon it had become a positive boon. It wasn't that life in the army had been bad, but the advantages of non-existence came as a pleasant surprise, allowing him freedom unknown to others. A career in "cleansing" – a euphemism if ever there was one –

followed and as his reputation for efficiency spread, so too did his rates of remuneration. Even Her Majesty's Government found that someone who was dead had their uses. He became the ultimate freelance.

The decontamination task for PEP had followed a less direct involvement in the Proteus Project as Security Consultant. As usual, though, when things went shit-shaped, his was the first name bawled over the tannoy.

And it would have been a lot easier if the information upon which the whole operation had been founded had not been flawed. Bloody scientists. On a number of occasions during his career, it had been the scientists who had cocked up, requiring him to put things right, clean up their catastrophe. He had lost good comrades because of such incidents; good men who shouldn't have been sacrificed because of others' incompetence. Still, he reflected, eyes open, listening and alert but totally quiet, things were nearing an end. Just a few small matters to clear up, then all would be done.

The key was waiting. If necessary, waiting for days, weeks, months. Years, perhaps. He began to sleep.

The phone in his pocket vibrated and he had answered it with the one word, "Yes?" before it could do so again.

Movement. F and E. Travelling north.

"Report hourly."

He ended the call. So here it was. He knew that this was significant.

He reasoned that he could afford an hour of sleep before taking personal command on the ground. He closed his eyes.

A thought, unbidden and unwelcome, brought him to wakefulness. The date. What was the date? He had lost track, but it didn't take him long to work out that it was the twenty-first. The alarm clock by his head – the only illumination in the entire house – told him that it was two forty-five.

It was an absurd time to phone, but he knew that there would be no problem. If he didn't phone now, he would probably not get the chance again and that would be unforgivable.

He rose, left the apartment without being seen, then found a call box. From it he made his annual call to wish his mother a happy birthday and let her know that she was not yet alone.

In the morning, Beverley was woken from a dream of company

and light by the phone. She was alone, of course; her whole life was coloured by that bitter, recurrent observation. Company in the evening, solitude in the morning.

"Yes?"

"Beverley? It's John Eisenmenger. We're in Carlisle, on our way to Scotland. I thought you'd better know."

She looked at the time. Seven-twenty. God, they must have started early. "Why? Is it Carlos?"

"I think he's gone to ground on Rouna, where the lab was."

"Why there?"

But he didn't answer. "If I'm wrong, it'll be up to you. We'll be out of it."

Don't be wrong, then.

"Is it wise?"

"Look, I can't explain why, I just think it might be the place he'd go to."

She had respect for John Eisenmenger's sometimes-unearthly reasoning. She didn't argue.

"If I hear anything, I'll let you know," she said.

"Likewise."

It proved to be a long and tedious journey. Even though they had made relatively good time to Carlisle, thereafter the roads became narrower and they were caught by the rush-hour traffic through and around Glasgow. Thereafter, although there were fewer cars, the roads became steadily more twisting and dual carriageways a thing of a delightful, distant memory. It wasn't summer but the highlands seemed to attract caravanners as much as it did midges. The weather, too, decided that the illusion of vacation should be difficult. First it became overcast, then it began to drizzle steadily and then, as they bypassed Fort William, Gaia gave full vent to her malevolence.

They reached Ullapool at eight in the evening. Helena had had the foresight to find the number of the only local hotel that was open, and book a room. They didn't bother with an evening meal.

Rosenthal guessed where they were going when the report came in that they were north of Glasgow. His own contacts had failed to find any trace of Arias-Stella; he had nothing to lose by following their line, plenty to gain by getting there first. He wasn't interested in whether they were right or not. If they were wrong, he had wasted nothing.

He rang three numbers, arranging a helicopter, but the arrangements would take several hours and the weather forecast was bad. He didn't bother allowing anger into his thoughts. Time was not the limiting factor, not once they had found their way onto a remote island off north-western Scotland, where there was no easy way to escape.

He smiled.

They would wait, perhaps feeling safe. Once they were on Rouna, whether or not Arias-Stella was there, he could solve at least some of his problems.

Apart perhaps from the Grim Reaper, Lambert was the last person Beverley wanted to hear from.

"You're unwell, I understand."

"That's right, sir. Flu. There's a lot of it about."

Over the phone he sounded of an even more distantly related species. "Flu."

How did he do it? How did he turn one monosyllable into a complete diatribe of disbelief?

"That's right."

A pause, but one that intimated more menace, more scepticism. He didn't actually pronounce the phrase, *Oh, yes?* but it rang through the space in their dialogue like a distant but discordant parakeet. "Are you recovering?"

The more she thought about it, the more she liked the allusion.

"Yes, I think so, sir."

"And you'll be back, when?"

She was wondering that herself. The departure of John and the Snow Queen had found her feeling slightly spare, whether or not they were right. She might just as well wait for news at work, under the foetid dragon's breath of Lambert, as at home.

"Probably tomorrow, sir."

If he tossed his hat into the air, he did so without a sound that she could hear over the admittedly less than perfect phone-line.

"Good," he announced, the word ending with a dying fall.

Their communication was terminated.

"Well, fuck you," she said tersely. Which was odd, because he was one of the few people she knew that fell neither into the category of those she wanted to fuck, nor into the one of those she felt it would be useful to fuck. She stood, anger making her shake rather more than she would have liked to admit. *Bastard! Bastard! Bastard!*

She was aware of how inarticulate she was in such profane repetition, but aware too that she had nothing else. Lambert had presented no weakness to her that she could use; no sign that he desired her, no hint that he possessed those traits that were so useful once discovered. Her one chance was that she could somehow uncover – and prove (never forget the need for proof) – what PEP had been up to.

The phone rang again. Surely it wasn't Lambert back to taunt her?

"Yes?"

It was Frank Cowper. In a voice totally devoid of everything but puzzlement he told her that he had just learned that Mark Hartmann had hanged himself. He had thought that Beverley ought to know. She thanked him, slightly distracted in tone, then she sat back and wondered. To do with her? Was she in some way to blame?

Suddenly she felt dirty. It was just after noon, but she had yet to dress. She decided she needed a shower, aware that the desire for ablution – perhaps absolution? – was becoming habitual following intercourse. Washing away sin? She doubted that it was that straightforward because she knew from experience that nothing, without exception, was straightforward.

Under the water, as hot as she could stand (the pain, perhaps, another sign of guilt-punishment cycling) she washed, relaxed and enjoyed feeling the stigmata of Lambert dissolve away from her. She just stood under the water, hands on the tiled wall, mouth open, breathing steadily.

Her thoughts turned to Eisenmenger.

Was he right? He had the habit of being right, she knew; it had cost her dear once. But Rouna? Why in God's name did he think that Carlos would go back there to hide? Surely he would stand out on such a place, easily spotted if PEP had decided to station spies.

Yet, why should they? What was there for anyone to return to? It wasn't as if the laboratory still functioned, or even existed as anything more than a burnt ruin.

Still, whether right or wrong, she couldn't lose this time. If they were right, the agreement was that she would be their sole police contact; Carlos would make his statement to her and her alone. If they were wrong, there was still a good chance that the ears and eyes that Luke had deployed for her would find Carlos; she wouldn't need Eisenmenger and his little tartlet at all.

Even if the worst case happened – Carlos dead whether because of Proteus or because of Rosenthal's attentions – she hadn't actually done anything that could be traced back to her.

At least she hoped not.

She turned off the shower, banishing such negativity, stepping out and drying herself with a pale pink bath sheet, enjoying the feeling of the material on her skin. She admired herself in the mirror. Not bad, not bad at all. In fact, fucking good.

A small voice, mocking and spiteful, whispered, *Good fucking, too.*

The telephone rang again.

"Bev?" It was Luke.

"Yes?"

"We've got a bite."

Part Five

The man who owned the fishing smack was enjoying himself. Eisenmenger wasn't. Far from it. His stomach muscles were telling him to stop vomiting, his throat was wondering why all the traffic was suddenly going the wrong way, and his brain had decided that hell was a concoction of ozone, diesel oil, darkness, water and fish. He stood huddled at the back of the small, paint-flaking cabin, trying to ignore the lack of attention so assiduously applied by Helena and their captain.

Helena, whose only inconvenience was unsteadiness of her feet in the rolling sea, looked back, caught his eye, and came to join him. The cabin was poorly lit, and perhaps that was why she didn't try to hide her grin, but Eisenmenger had the suspicion there was more to it than that.

"Are you feeling better?"

He tried to give her a confident smile but somewhere between his cerebral cortex and his facial musculature, the nerve impulses went astray. Any movement of his skin seemed stiff, while any movement of his head produced vertigo. In the end, he satisfied himself with a necessarily curt, "What do you think?"

The grin didn't diminish, despite the fact that the boat hit a particularly solid wave, causing her to stagger slightly. Behind her their captain was peering into spray-filled night.

"Who'd have thought it?" she asked of no one and everyone. "That you should suffer from seasickness."

"Amazing," he agreed.

They had arrived at Ullapool only four hours before. Their plan had been to spend the night at the hotel, then cross to Morrister, the only town on Rouna, the following day. There was a regular ferry service, but it was more likely that they would have to find private passage. As soon as they had arrived it became clear that they could not afford to wait, however. The low pressure that had been with them over the second half of their journey had abated slightly, but a storm was coming. If they did not cross that night, the forecast suggested that they would not reach Rouna for at least two days.

Market economics had come into play. After following the advice of the hotel staff, they had gone to one of the local bars, thence directed to what was termed a restaurant, was in reality more of a cafe. In this place of grimy wooden panelling, dimness and dilapidation they found their man; their man if they paid him three hundred, one-way. More than slightly shocked by this demand, made without shame or even guile, Helena and Eisenmenger had hesitated but, as was pointed out to them, nobody else would go out that night, not for any money. It was only the fact that Helena had thought to visit a cash dispenser in Carlisle that meant they were in any position to take advantage of this generous offer. Thus they employed one Frankie Munro, owner and operator of the *Ocean Beauty* – a description that might once have been accurate but which was now merely wishful – and thus they found themselves in the middle of heaving blackness, cold and wet, and, in Eisenmenger's case, ill.

Helena tried conversation. "It's odd. I'd never realized I wasn't seasick."

Eisenmenger had decided that pressing his head back against the wood of the cabin wall, almost trying to meld with it, might alleviate the malaise. He also decided that not speaking would help.

"He says it won't be too much longer."

In Eisenmenger's universe, where by some strange relativistic effect each second stretched and curled lazily into days, this did not elicit much acclaim. He managed a groaned, "Good," more out of politeness than joy. Munro glanced back and even if Eisenmenger had not seen the smile the very movement was contemptuous.

Helena gave Eisenmenger a sympathetic smile and moved back carefully to the front of the cabin, next to Munro. She asked, "Do you make the trip to Rouna often?"

Munro was only slightly taller than Helena, but his physique was compact, his forearms appearing muscular beneath the tatty green sweater he was wearing. He had a slight squint around which there had formed a deep scowl. He said nothing for a while then, in an accent that was peculiarly soft, "Why would I want to go there?"

Which was a question that was probably not impossible to answer, but proved beyond Helena.

"But there must be times, like this, when someone needs to get there quickly."

He might have been considering this, but he might also have been calculating pi to a thousand places. Finally, "Sometimes."

"Recently?"

He looked at her at last, long and hard. "No."

"Not a man, travelling on his own? A day or so ago?"

He had turned back to the view through the glass. The lights of the boat formed a soft, ill-defined cocoon in which they seemed only to move endlessly up and down; there was no impression of forward progress at all.

"I told you. No."

Well, it was worth a try.

She turned away, and he said, "He caught the ferry."

Startled by this concession to civility and helpfulness, she asked, "Really?"

He gave her a look as if such small talk were for imbeciles, then resumed his perusal of the sea. Helena glanced back at Eisenmenger who despite occupying the pits of despair, had a look of quiet satisfaction on his face.

Rosenthal's rendezvous was in a field on the Wiltshire-Hampshire border at midnight. He was dropped from the car in a deserted lay-by of the A303 at eleven-fifty, not even looking back as the driver took it away, accelerating to sixty miles an hour, taking care not to exceed the speed limit. Within three seconds he had vanished from the roadside, climbed over a stock fence and was running to the meeting point.

He arrived just as the helicopter touched down, so that he didn't even have to break stride or accelerate. It was on the ground less than five seconds. Inside was a pilot and, behind him, was Bochdalek.

Rosenthal had not had the chance to choose his companion, time had been too short, and the presence of Bochdalek would have to be endured, but he was far from the perfect choice.

Technically proficient but, in Rosenthal's opinion, flawed, for Bochdalek enjoyed killing. Blood was to Bochdalek a sign of success, a thing to be savoured. Rosenthal's position was not one of ethics but of practicality; while Bochdalek was indulging in some psychopathic revelry he was vulnerable, which made his comrades vulnerable.

None of this showed as he nodded at Bochdalek, strapped himself in, put on the headset and tried not to show that he hated flying.

Bochdalek asked, "What's this about?" His east European accent and slightly high, whining tone gave Rosenthal memories of conflicts he'd rather bury. He shook his head, indicating the pilot in front of them. Bochdalek made a face but said no more.

Stirling. Arias-Stella had withdrawn one hundred and forty pounds – destroying his bank balance – from a cash dispenser in Stirling on Tuesday. You didn't need a degree in geography to work out where he had been heading.

Eisenmenger had been right. Arias-Stella had gone back to Rouna.

Beverley went to the bedroom and began to pack a bag.

Lambert would have to wait for her return; she felt a relapse coming on.

Eisenmenger had hoped that returning to dry land would bring an immediate end to his torment but he was desperately disappointed in this optimism. As he stood on the quayside of Morrister in the darkness, his head continued to tell him that he was still being tossed erratically around and this sensation was actually worse than the real thing.

Munro had radioed ahead for the harbour master to help them, clearly being of the opinion that neither Eisenmenger nor Helena was going to be of much use. Even though the harbour was protected from the worst of the swell, Helena had been impressed by the considerable seamanship that Munro had shown in coming alongside safely and without damaging the boat, but this was short-lived because he turned to her at once and said, "Journey's over. I want you off. Now."

She opened her mouth to reply but Eisenmenger, who had risked disengaging himself from the woodwork and come to stand behind her, said in her ear, "He's worried about the weather. He's got to get back."

She swallowed her words and they took their meagre luggage out into the rain and wind. The harbour master helped them ashore and the *Ocean Beauty* cast off without further acknowledgement from Munro. The rain increased, the wind likewise, and they had then the first sense of what they had done, where they had come.

It wasn't a particularly happy feeling.

The harbour master looked at them, his attitude suggesting that he, too, was wondering what on earth he had before him. He was wearing a long, thick, waterproof jacket, the hood pulled tightly around his bearded face, whereas Helena was bare-headed (but at least in something reasonably waterproof) and Eisenmenger's wardrobe had yielded only a scruffy wax jacket.

"Is there somewhere to stay?"

The harbour master closed his eyes, perhaps against the water dripping into them, perhaps because he could not quite believe that they had come all this way, in this weather, at this time of night, with nowhere arranged to sleep.

"There's a tavern. Marble's place."

He pointed behind them, then began to walk in that direction, leaving them to pick up their bags and follow.

Carlos dug his fork into the can of tinned fruit. Grapefruit. He hated grapefruit; had done since childhood, when his father, insisting on the medicinal properties of citrus fruits, had made each member of his family eat a whole one every morning. He shivered at the flavour, the sharpness and acid turning his mucous membrane to cloth. Jesus, he was hungry, had to have been to eat the muck, but tins of grapefruit were his only resource; the freezer and cool box had been empty.

He finished the tin and threw it inaccurately at the waste bin; it bounced off the top and clattered to the flagstones. With night coming, the temperature was dropping, a fact that his fingers and toes were increasingly vociferous in proclaiming. Soon he would begin shivering, his nose would run and he would feel wetness run down numbing lips, a salty dessert to the meal. Now that the oil had run out, life was not going to be good. He looked through the window at the dusk. The wind was blowing hard and increasing; soon it would be gale force. He remembered only too well that on Rouna there was never calm, that the locals, when they had talked to them at all, took great delight in warning them how it sometimes drove incomers mad. Rain smacked the windowpanes. Rain on Rouna tended to coruscate rather than caress.

He considered his options again. This exercise he performed approximately every twenty minutes, as if repetition would increase both their quantity and their quality, but he had only two and neither was top-notch. Stay here or carry on trying to find Stein's house. Staying here had the advantage of not inviting attention but the irksome disadvantage of no decent food and no heating. Moving on meant that he would find Stein more quickly (and the more he thought about it, the more desperate he was to locate the old man), but the weather looked as if it were as hungry as he. It might find him a tasty offering. He went into the sitting room, unsure of what to do. He perched himself on the sofa. Had it been necessary to run? Wasn't he just panicking?

In truth he didn't know, but he thought he had been wise not to wait for certainty. *Certainty in this life is one of the few luxuries we will never have.* One of his father's aphorisms. When the old boy had been alive, he had come out with them all the time, and it had been a sort of family joke. Annoying, too, especially when school friends or girlfriends were there. Yet now they came to him more and more often and, although his father's face was no longer perfectly drawn in his memory, the voice and these quanta of reason were completely realized to him.

After the fire, after the arguments and recriminations, and after they had come to realize the monstrous trick that had been played on them, he and the others had drawn a pact of sorts. Nothing dramatic – no cut thumbs and signatures in blood, no oaths in the name of the elder daemons – but an understanding. That they would keep loose contact with each other, an awareness of where they all were and what they were doing, just in case PEP lost faith in its confidentiality agreements and decided that there was too much to lose if they should talk.

It hadn't worked, though. PEP had come like some sort of silent avenger, taking them all, one by one. No chance to warn anyone.

Except for Millie.

Millie had died of cancer.

What, he wondered, were the chances of one in six dying of cancer at the age of twenty-two? Fairly small, he knew. And she had apparently died quickly; an unexpected death.

Could it have been Proteus?

But she had tested negative. They had seen the results – all of them were clear of contamination following the accident.

So. . .

So the results were wrong.

And if the results were wrong for Millie, perhaps they were also wrong for him.

He was shivering, but not just with cold. In fact, suddenly the cold didn't seem so bad after all.

The wind began to moan about the house, as if it were a lover, moaning in a deathly cold passion.

He decided to wait in the house until morning.

The tavern didn't have a name. Nor did it have much paint on the woodwork, a carpet on the floor or a welcoming atmosphere. When they walked into the single public room, silence didn't quite fall but there was a definite diminuendo, and they had the feeling that more than a few pairs of eyes fell upon them. It was cloudy with smoke, and old brown stains adorned every flat surface including the floor. There were perhaps twenty people in there, all men, of all ages. Behind the bar was a shortish man, completely hairless, rather shabby in appearance, and wearing an eyepatch. Around his neck was a silver chain, from which hung a curious, shrivelled and yellow object that proximity showed to be a finger.

Eisenmenger felt it incumbent upon him to take the lead.

"Mr. . . Marble?"

The man behind the bar nodded but didn't actually articulate. Eisenmenger found himself wondering what was wrong with these people. Why did they never use their God-given gift of language?

"Could you put us up for a few nights?"

He eyed them. He was cleaning a glass and Helena noticed that his left forefinger ended rather abruptly. There followed a period of silence between them in which their host presumably considered the prudence of taking in people such as they. Then, another nod. He put down the glass, gestured with his head to a door to their left in the corner of the room, and turned away from them.

"Sam!"

The unexpectedness of this bellow colluded with its loudness to startle them both. From a doorway at the back of the bar a young girl of perhaps twenty came into the bar. "Look after the bar."

She nodded meekly and Marble allowed them through to the back of the tavern. He led them up a flight of stairs that creaked noisily, thence onto a small landing above which a single lightbulb, weak and feeble, cast shadows far deeper than the dark.

Their room was off this landing, and contained a high double bed. A wardrobe whose doors didn't quite close, two wooden chairs and a dressing table.

"Bathroom's next door, on the left." Having concluded the sales pitch he said, "Twenty a night, in advance."

"Breakfast?"

"Fiver extra. Each."

It was Eisenmenger's turn to pay. He gave Marble fifty pounds, notes that were received with relish. As if this bestowed on them some legitimacy, he seemed to relax slightly, even volunteering the information that, "You can 'ave tea in the morning, if you like."

The possibility that the delightful Mr Marble might appear before their bed in the morning, even if he were bearing a tray of tea things, was alarming for both of them. They declined.

He left them and as the door closed behind him they stood staring at each other before bursting into stifled laughter. They held each other, exhausted, glad and not glad to be there. Too tired to wash, they undressed, checked the bed for unwanted occupants, and climbed in.

"What have we done?" asked Helena.

"Probably nothing useful, but we've got to try."

"Did you see his finger?"

Eisenmenger sighed. "The psychology must be fascinating. I wonder where he keeps the eyeball."

The room was cold and draughty and outside the storm was increasing. They held each other tight for warmth and for comfort. Eisenmenger fell asleep with Helena's perfume softly touching him.

Beverley drove through the night, wondering why she had a feeling of sick dread settling in her stomach.

Eisenmenger came slowly out of sleep, bathed in a feeling of happy tranquillity. It was as if he were back in a perfect childhood that he had never known – that no one had ever known – a world where negative emotion was gone, where there was bright illumination over all things physical and spiritual.

Contentment.

And gradually this dreamlike state came to encompass the fact that Helena was beside him, warm, smooth, asleep. She was positioned on her side facing towards him, her right arm stretched towards him, the hand resting on his shoulder. Her mouth was slightly open, the regular whiteness of her teeth slightly exposed. He felt an intense feeling of love that bordered on incapacitating.

And then reality precipitated around him, its sharp angles puncturing what he now saw as a reverie, a place where actuality was a disguise worn by hopes and desires.

They were on Rouna, a place where Carlos had run, where he suspected Stein was hiding.

He moved his hand to look at the time, in the process causing Helena to open her eyes. He saw incomprehension yield to memory as she realized where she was, why she was there.

"Come on," he said. "Time to get up."

She took a deep breath, then lay back on the pillow. "What time is it?"

"Seven."

She looked pained but said nothing. He put back the covers and swung round to sit on the edge of the bed. They were both naked and, in truth, he found some embarrassment in this, not because they had made love, but because they hadn't. He pulled on some clothes, then risked a glance back at her.

"I'm first for the bathroom," he said.

"Fine." She stretched lazily exposing her breasts and he had to force himself to look away. It was too much like a love tryst, not enough like a desperately serious search to find answers. He found his washing things and left for the bathroom.

When he returned, Helena was dressed enough for decency and she took her turn in the bathroom. By half past seven they were on their way downstairs.

Marble had retreated to his taciturnity, leaving their breakfast to be served by his daughter. It wasn't too bad either; not brilliant, but not inedible. Kippers, eggs and bacon, coffee and toast, served in the bar room. In the light of morning the room seemed somehow barren of soul, the impression not helped by the stacks of glasses on the wooden top of bar, and the odour of smoke that persisted despite the open windows and breeze flowing through. They sat in the corner of the room, on old, cracked leather seats, at a table that wobbled just enough to mean that their coffee was never still, indeed often leaped from cup to saucer. It was while they were wrestling with the problem of retaining any liquid in the cups while sawing through a particularly obstinate piece of bacon that Sam returned and Helena, tiring of the labour, asked, "Do you get many visitors?"

She had already guessed the answer to this but it was at least a way into the business at hand.

"Not really. The odd one now and again. Usually bird-spotters." She pronounced the last word with an inflexion that was less than complimentary.

"And now? Are we the only ones visiting?"

"Just about." It was an answer that was no answer at all.

Eisenmenger put his knife and fork together on the plate, trying not to make the action a judgement on the cuisine. "Delicious," he said politely. "Did someone come across a day or so ago? On the ferry?"

She looked at him from a face that was impassive but clearly fronting someone who wondered what the hell it had to do with him. Helena added, "We think he might be visiting Professor Stein." Still nothing. "He does live here, doesn't he?"

Sam began collecting the plates. She had almost finished before she replied. "There's a man called Stein lives in the north. Don't know that he's a professor, though."

Rosenthal and Bochdalek had been dropped on the eastern part of Rouna, the emptiest part of a sparsely populated island, just before dawn. The helicopter had not even touched soil and had been gone from their hearing before they had been there a minute. They had moved at once inland, covering the ground, despite the gusting, sometimes glacial, wind and the slicing rain. By dawn they were about two kilometres from Stein's house and it was here, in a small hollow ringed by gorse bushes, that they stopped for a breakfast of dried fruit and water. For the first time Bochdalek was told what was required of him. Nothing special, just the murder of four people.

They moved off to find a spot from which they could see Stein's house and all the ground around.

Nothing special at all.

The old man was writing when the sound of the knock on the door came to his ears. It echoed slightly, a harsh sound that was unwelcome, almost alien. It had been so long since he had heard it, there was more than surprise in him; the feeling was more akin to panic. He looked up from his words, unsure of what to do. No one called, so what did this mean?

He guessed.

Not details, not prescience, but an overview, a conclusion.

His retreat was over.

He knew better than to try to hide, or run, or fight. He was too old to do other than acquiesce in what was to come and, accordingly, he rose from the table and went to the door. The hall was accurately named for it was bare, large, cold and harsh; merely a space. He hardly knew it, so infrequently had he been in there. He shivered, as if crossing a cold continent.

The locks on the door were not used to manipulation. His weak, aged fingers slipped off the cold metal repeatedly, not helped by the condensation. The chain proved recalcitrant; he wasn't sure quite how it worked.

Eventually he managed to open the door, at last allowing daylight into the hallway; its delight was no less when finally it fell on Tutankamun's life insurance. He peered out into the wind and water. "Yes?"

Carlos was wet. He was also cold and he was hungry, but the damp won out. "Professor?"

It took a few moments but at last he was recognized. "Carlos?"

"Can I come in? It's very cold out here."

Another consideration, as if this were the suburbs, then the face withdrew and there was more rattling of door furniture. The door opened and from halfway behind it Carlos was proffered a smile. "Of course, my boy."

It took Eisenmenger and Helena an hour to cross the island, although they were lucky that there was a relative lull in the weather. Only as they approached the end of the journey did the rain and wind pick up again. They came to the top of a small hill and there, two hundred metres distant, was the rear of a house. They knew that it was Stein's because Marble's daughter had described it quite accurately, especially the long narrow conservatory running along the back of the house.

They positioned themselves behind a blue stone cairn, moss and lichen clinging gamely to its weather-scarred crevices, wondering what to do. Watch and wait, or go down and make themselves known? It was difficult to concentrate on what was happening before them, for the wind took their hearing, the cold and wet took their concentration, and the drizzle took their hope.

A rhinoceros could have sneaked up behind them, but didn't; Rosenthal and Bochdalek did. They didn't hear a thing until Bochdalek pulled the bolt on his machine pistol; then they both jerked around to find two gun barrels pointing directly at their heads. Both Bochdalek and Rosenthal were wrapped up against the weather far more effectively than either Helena or Eisenmenger, but she knew at once who was standing over her.

"Alasdair." She sounded disappointed, as if she had been hoping that it might not be true. He said nothing, but his companion asked of him, "Alasdair? What kind of a cover name is that?" He laughed but Eisenmenger noticed that his eyes never left the spot on Eisenmenger's forehead that the gun barrel was also interested in. Rosenthal ignored him, said only, "Hello, Helena."

Eisenmenger heard complete uninterest in his voice and it was this that made him truly afraid, truly appreciative that this man was intent on killing him. He found his mouth suddenly thick with mucus. He glanced across at Helena, seeing fear there but also anger. She asked, "What now? Execution?" This was in a voice of sarcasm that almost completely smothered the sound of her fear.

Bochdalek grinned even more, then nodded enthusiastically. "You betcha." He pushed the barrel right against Eisenmenger's forehead, laughing; Eisenmenger knew then that he was only a few more heartbeats from his death, that this man wanted to see his flesh, bone and brain emulsified. He looked into the eyes and saw nothing but excitement. He held his breath, wondering why he was bothering to try to hide his terror. He felt a tremor in his breathing, a dampness on his skin as he waited.

Rosenthal said quietly, "Not yet." It was a command, much as he might have given to a retriever. Bochdalek looked disappointed but obeyed. To Eisenmenger and Helena Rosenthal said, "Come on. Let's get dry."

He beckoned them to stand by waving his machine pistol at them. As they complied, Eisenmenger glanced cross at Helena; she looked worried but was apparently coping far better than him.

Carlos had wondered what he would say when he spoke again to Professor Jacob Stein, but in the end it was easy. His fear found eloquence, his anger overcame any awkwardness that he might have felt in having to confront the man who had been his superior.

He sat down in one of two armchairs either side of the empty fireplace, Stein in the other. He looked at the old man, noticing how he had aged, how he looked thin and worn. The house was icy and draught-filled.

"You've come a long way to see me, Carlos."

"I think you can guess why, Professor."

Stein looked at him, mouth slightly open, tongue lurking just inside the darkness of his mouth. It was a typical attitude of the man. Even with the sound of the weather leaking into the room and finding nowhere soft to hide, the noise of his breathing was loud. Then he nodded slowly. "Proteus."

"We're the only ones left, Professor. Do you realize that? The others have either disappeared or died."

Stein's shock made him speechless for a second. Then, "Died? Disappeared? What do you mean?"

"Millie was the first. She died of cancer."

Stein's face showed genuine shock, his voice betrayed complete bewilderment. "The first? What do you mean?"

"Justine was blown to pieces, and then within a day or two

263

Jean-Jacques disappeared. Turner had his accident just a few days before that."

Carlos saw confusion immersing, drowning, Stein. It answered one of the many questions he had brought to Rouna, and he was relieved that Stein was innocent of one crime at least.

"We're being killed, Professor," he explained gently. "We who worked on the Proteus project."

But Stein could not grasp what he was being told. His face was contracted into an unbelieving frown. He leaned back in the chair and Carlos saw tears in his eyes. Carlos tried to be gentle as he said, "I think we're on the list as well."

There was a distant crash from somewhere at the back of the house, a sound of a glass shattering. Both of them looked up at it.

"What was that?" It was the question of a frightened old man. Carlos shrugged, but his face showed almost as much fear as Stein's. He rose and went to the door that led out on to the hallway. Before he got there, this opened and in came first Helena, then Eisenmenger. Bochdalek, covered by Rosenthal, followed them. Their entry into the room caused Carlos to sigh a soft, *Shit*, and briefly close his eyes.

Rosenthal ordered Carlos back to the armchair, making Helena and Eisenmenger sit on two dining chairs that Bochdalek brought from the table. It made quite a cosy tableau, perhaps in preparation for a group photograph, one that they could each keep as a memento; *this is when we all died.*

Stein was strident in his understandable indignation, an emotion cultured from his years of academic standing and his ignorance of what was happening around him. As soon as they had come into the room he had asked of Rosenthal and Bochdalek, "How dare you? Who are you? How dare you break into my home?"

Then he had recognized Rosenthal. His face had transmuted instantaneously, the speed almost one of comical proportions. He had collapsed back into the chair, saying only, "Oh, you."

Rosenthal failed to acknowledge this tribute. Bochdalek, who had perched himself on the sofa, his pistol pointed in their direction, laughed at the questions. "You're the Professor?" he asked. "You're the smart one?"

Stein looked at him. "Will someone tell me what's going on?" Then, to Carlos, "Do you know?"

But Carlos was as confused as he was. It was Eisenmenger who said, "Perhaps we should make some introductions, Professor. My name's John Eisenmenger, this is my colleague, Helena Flemming. These two," and here he gestured at Bochdalek on the sofa and Rosenthal, who was pacing in front of the window, "are of uncertain designation. This one goes by various names, most commonly Rosenthal. His companion, I'm afraid, is as unknown to me, as he is to you."

Bochdalek bowed his head in greeting but declined to provide any form of nomen.

Stein looked no more informed. "They have come here finally to terminate the Proteus project," Eisenmenger added helpfully.

Carlos whispered, "Double shit."

At last Stein began to comprehend the situation. To Rosenthal he said, "You've come here to kill us?"

Rosenthal was checking the windows. To the glass he said, "The Proteus experiment has ended. The results are in."

When Stein looked confused, Eisenmenger explained helpfully, "The utility of Proteus has been proved, Professor. You did a good job."

The old man took the compliment much as he might have taken the discovery of a cat's furball on the carpet. "You keep an eye on them; I'll check the rest of the house," Rosenthal said to Bochdalek, from the window.

His companion nodded and Rosenthal left, moving quietly on the bare floor.

Helena asked of Carlos, "What happened in the fire? How did it start?"

Carlos glanced at Stein then said, "We thought Proteus was just a high-tech cancer tool. Something to induce cancers in cell systems for future pharmaceutical research. Then we found out that there was more to it."

Stein raised rheumy eyes to Eisenmenger and Helena. "It wasn't my fault. We thought that we were doing something noble. Helping to combat cancer. It is what I had dedicated my life to. Then we found out that we were doing exactly the opposite. We found that someone had taken the project and, with a neat twist, had made it a weapon, a killer.

"Proteus. A biological weapon like no other."

Bochdalek seemed to find this fascinating. His face betrayed absorption. He said in a tone of wonder, "Really?"

Stein turned to Helena. "You must believe me. When I gained the funding from PEP, the project was exactly as Carlos and the others thought it was – a generic system for use in the development of novel anti-cancer therapies. The project was hijacked, but not by me."

Helena asked, "If not you, then who?"

Looking at Carlos, Stein said, "Robin Turner."

Rosenthal went from room to room, checking cupboards, behind doors and the view from the windows. All were empty, as he had expected. All were cold, dusty and lonely, except for a large room on the top floor occupying most of the back half of the house. Its windows gave a panoramic view of the northern part of Rouna, with the single track that led to the house at its centre, stretching for a long way to the horizon. Satisfied that no one was going to disturb them – why should anyone want to call on a lonely old man, kilometres from the nearest neighbours? – he turned back to the room. This was part study and part laboratory. Rosenthal wasn't experienced in science and scientific equipment, but he was surprised by how sophisticated and new some of the equipment seemed to be. A lot of it too. He poked idly into some of it, discovering centrifuges, fridges and freezers, amongst other pieces that were completely foreign to him.

Then he looked at some of the many files and papers that were both piled on the desk and stacked on the shelves in the far corner of the room. He understood little of it, but he did come across a name he recognized – *Proteus*.

Carlos hadn't reacted. Stein went on, "Turner's a clever man; a good scientist but also an unprincipled one, although I didn't know it then. Right from the start he must have seen the weapons potential of Proteus and persuaded PEP that there was more to be gained than just a few hypothetical anti-cancer drugs."

"Turner's been murdered," Eisenmenger pointed out softly.

Shocked, Stein stared at him for a moment. "Murdered? But who?"

Eisenmenger nodded towards Bochdalek. "His friend, I think." As Stein looked across at him, Bochdalek gave this mocking acknowledgement by dipping his head, and the old Professor turned away from him in disgust. To Eisenmenger, he said, "Whatever he did, he was a good scientist."

Rosenthal returned, carrying a file. He waved it at Stein. "Doing some further work on Proteus, were we, Professor?"

Stein looked up at the file. "Someone had to try to find a way to combat what we had done."

"Have you succeeded?" Carlos asked.

The shake of Stein's head was almost one of shame.

Rosenthal said, "Never mind. Better brains than yours have failed. Still, I'm glad that I found these. If any of these had been found, it might have proved embarrassing." He put the file in a large carry-bag, then to Bochdalek he said, "We wait until dark." To the rest of them, he said, "Now we have quite a while to wait before we can leave. If you're good, we'll make do without restraints, but just give us one sign that you're not the kind, cooperative people I think you are, and I'm afraid we'll have to tie you all up, and that will prove very uncomfortable. Understand?"

"We can all have a nice time," Bochdalek added. "We can listen to a story for entertainment." He smiled contentedly.

Rosenthal sat at the table in the window. Eisenmenger asked of Stein, "So PEP shipped you out to Rouna. Didn't you wonder why they sent you all the way out here?"

The old man shook his head. "I was naive. Starling told me that they considered this project to be of the highest priority, that several other companies were interested in the idea. I was told that Rouna was the safest place for us. I believed that."

Carlos came out of a reverie. "I still don't understand how we failed to spot what was going on."

Stein said, in a low voice, "Because Proteus was preciously close to a biological weapon already. And every modification that Turner suggested could be interpreted as an improvement to my original idea. Even the temperature-sensitive trigger seemed to be a logical, reasonable improvement to the system."

Helena asked, "What about the accident? How did that occur?"

It was Carlos who answered. "On Rouna there was precious

little to do, what with the weather, the lack of contact with the islanders, and the intensity of the work. It was inevitable that we would form relationships, begin to see each other differently. Hell, after months and months of that life, I would have fucked a hole in the wall.

"Anyway, I fell for Millie. She fell for me, I think, but only in a small way. Turner was also interested. Justine and Jean-Jacques had pretty much become a unit, so there wasn't anywhere else to turn." He paused, perhaps out of misty-eyed memory, perhaps out of something darker. "I think she felt sorry for us." He smiled. "Anyway, that's what I like to think." A deep sigh. "She tried to juggle Turner and me, but it was never going to work."

Bochdalek was grinning broadly and Helena saw him run his tongue along first his top, then his bottom, lip.

"I had to put up with it. Millie was happy and I was in love with her. Turner was a better bet for her; after all, where was she going to go with a lab tech?" It was like hearing confession. His voice was filled with years of memory, purified by remorseless, relentless remodelling, so that now his love was one of the foundations of his self-respect, and the whole of it had been petrified by her death.

"I could have coped, I think, had Turner not decided that he wanted her for himself. He came to see me, full of piss and importance. Claimed some sort of *noblesse oblige* because I was only a research assistant."

"What happened?"

"I told him to piss off. Telling me to wash up the test tubes was one thing, ordering me not to spend time with someone I fancied was something else."

"And did he piss off?"

Carlos laughed. "Yeah. He wasn't a great man of action."

"And what did you do?"

"First I had a drink or two. Then I fell asleep, I think. Went to see Millie, to tell her what Turner had said." Before he could be asked, he went on, "She'd gone to the lab, though, so I followed her there, which was unfortunate, because Turner had had the same idea.

"Turner was talking to Millie in the laboratory. He had his back to me and she spotted me over his shoulder. I must have looked pretty pissed off, because she came to me at once and tried to stop me from approaching Turner, but I just pushed past her."

Stein was shaking his head in sorrow as he listened.

"I didn't know what I was going to do and didn't care at that moment. He was standing in front of a fume cabinet, but the significance of that was lost on me. I wanted him to know that I wasn't going to let him get away with treating Millie like that. We had an argument. It wasn't particularly romantic; nothing Hollywood about it. We just started to scuffle, swearing at each other, then got down to pushing and shoving, kicking and scratching.

"The others came in, of course. Jean-Jacques thought it was great fun, a superb entertainment, but the others were trying to stop us."

Stein said, "I had no idea what was going on. I was. . ." He shrugged and smiled, "Blind to everything but the work."

"That was when it started to get vicious – I mean vicious, like I'd decided I really didn't think he deserved Millie, didn't even deserve to live, and he was getting down to racism and obscenity. And Jean-Jacques was egging me on; he had no love of Turner either, thought he was an arrogant bastard. Anyway, the emotional temperature went sky high and that's when it happened. I mean, I just wanted the cunt dead; we were on different sides of the room and he was practically reverting to the savage. He began to come at me, so I picked up the heaviest thing I could find and threw it at his head. It was a water bath, half-full. If it had hit his head, life would be a lot different now, but it didn't. He dodged and I think for a minute he thought he was going to get to analyse my internal organs at close quarters with a scalpel, but then the water bath landed, and things changed.

"The crash that it made was unbelievable. It went through the glass front of the fume cupboard, smashing all the glassware inside, water splashing everywhere. At the same time, some of the water got into the electrical points. There was a lot of sparking and hissing, steam or smoke began to fill up the cupboard, and then there was a gentle 'pop.' That's when the fire started.

"He looked around and I saw him freeze – but only for a second, as if the signal from reality central was momentarily interrupted – and then he screamed. He didn't scream anything coherent, he just made a noise. When he looked back at me, I saw something I'd never seen before, not on anyone's face. It was someone drowning in total fear."

He stopped. Stein took up the story. "The fire spread incredibly rapidly. Because of the fabric of the building; it was nearly falling down before. There were fire extinguishers, but most of them didn't work, and those that did had no noticeable effect. We were forced to evacuate almost at once."

He sighed. "It was the next day when Turner told me. He was, as Carlos has said, terrified. I didn't really understand why. True, we were all depressed, but he was scared." He looked across at Carlos. "Do you remember?"

The young man was nodding slowly, a look of vague recollection frowning on his face. "He was, wasn't he?"

Stein said to Helena and Eisenmenger, "He had been working on a parallel project. He had taken Proteus and subverted it beautifully. . ."

"Beautifully?" Carlos was incensed.

Bochdalek spoke, much as a film buff might enquire about a particularly tricky point in the plot. "What is this Proteus?"

Suddenly Rosenthal wanted to join in as well. "Careful. You may not want to know." At which Bochdalek raised his eyebrows, "Really?" he asked.

"No more than you need to know. Remember?"

Bochdalek grinned broadly, waving the gun around carelessly. "I think the fact that I know that four people die here tonight is perhaps already too much for my safety."

Rosenthal said nothing more. *Your decision.* Bochdalek turned to Stein and whispered loudly, "He loves me."

Helena asked, "And you really had no idea?"

"No. The tasks were split. I was concentrating on the culture system, leaving Turner to perfect Proteus itself. The results he reported were clearly. . . fabricated."

Carlos said irritably, "Whatever. What he had to tell us was that Proteus was more than just a little model for cancer and he told us it was likely that, because of the fire, we were all carrying Proteus, and that Proteus was a very, very efficient killing machine."

Bochdalek found this snippet fascinating. He was becoming more and more engrossed in what was being said. Helena, who was nearest to him, began to wonder.

Stein said, "He showed me his notes, his sequence data. It was incredible. . ." he paused to eye Carlos, then went on, "He'd done an amazing job. He'd packed in an amazing number of oncogenes, promoters and recessive gene blockers; he'd used all three reading frames. It was a work of art." He cast his eyes downward, perhaps ashamed at his enthusiasm. "It was the perfect weapon."

Carlos took up the story. He sounded tired, cynical. "So suddenly, not only had we all been working on the biological equivalent of the nuclear bomb, but we discovered there was a high probability that we'd been infected with it."

Bochdalek whistled quietly. Talk of weapons excited him.

Stein sounded tired. "I had called Starling as soon as it happened. He responded quickly." He looked up at Rosenthal who was still surveying the window's view. Rosenthal said lazily, "The start of my romance with Proteus."

Eisenmenger suggested, "Let me guess what happens next." Bochdalek nodded enthusiastically. "Yes, yes," he implored, apparently unheeding of Rosenthal's previous advice, so taken up in the drama of the situation was he.

"Mr Rosenthal arrives complete with one or two colleagues to find out what happened, together with one or two people to take blood tests on you all."

Bochdalek looked across at his colleague, then said to Stein. "Is that right?"

Stein's nod brought forth admiration for Eisenmenger. "Go on," Bochdalek urged.

"I guess the police were fairly interested, too, and they began to ask awkward questions, but Rosenthal took command. The story of some sort of electrical fire was concocted – not too far from the truth, so credible – and any mention of the nature of the research was suppressed." Of Carlos, he asked, "Was there some sort of bribe?"

"Relocation to wherever we wanted, within reason, plus a lump sum of a hundred thousand each, tax free, provided we stayed absolutely quiet about the research. We were also reminded that we had signed strict confidentiality clauses that, should we break them, would have had fairly heavy consequences."

Eisenmenger smiled at Rosenthal. "The carrot and stick

approach? You're quite practised in that, aren't you?" Rosenthal acknowledged this by cocking his head slightly, expression unchanged. To Stein, Eisenmenger said, "And what about you?"

"I was outraged. I felt betrayed, both by PEP and by Turner. I was going to go public, but then. . ." He paused before, in a slightly lower voice, "The confidentiality clause was brought to my attention, and. . ."

He stopped, clearly ashamed. Surprisingly, it was Rosenthal who explained. "The good Professor has a son who has a fondness for heroin. We were able to help."

He didn't explain what form the help had taken and Stein obviously wasn't inclined to elaborate, saying only, "When my wife died, we drifted apart. He was lost. It was my fault."

Eisenmenger turned back to Rosenthal. "But what about Turner? You stopped work on Proteus – wasn't he upset?"

Rosenthal shrugged. "He was more concerned about whether or not he was infected. I think the possibility that he might die from his own little bug rather put him off that line of research."

Bochdalek's eyes were flicking from speaker to speaker and Helena saw that his gun was no longer horizontal. She began to wonder if she might get the chance to grab it, or at least kick it. But what about Rosenthal?

"So the project was terminated, and everyone was taken off Rouna. Except you, Professor," Eisenmenger said.

"I elected to stay."

"Why?"

He took a deep breath. "I was by far the eldest of the group, and I had no one to return to. I decided to retire here. Also, I thought to try to rectify some of the wrong I had unwittingly done."

Eisenmenger looked at him for rather longer than necessary before continuing, "And they waited for the blood test results to come back." Turning back to Rosenthal he added, "Which you faked."

Bochdalek cheered under his breath, as if pleased by this particular example of perfidy, but the reaction of Carlos and Stein was very, very different. Carlos went grey, his face slack, his head bowing to his chest. He said softly, "So it's true."

Stein looked at Rosenthal, the movement sudden. He clearly

had trouble accepting what he had heard, its significance. He turned to Eisenmenger, who nodded sadly. "I'm afraid it's true. Proteus did get out in the accident, and you were all infected. Presumably the fire sterilized the area afterwards, but by then it was too late for you."

Stein continued to stare, then dropped his gaze. "I sometimes wondered. I suppose I was too scared to check."

Rosenthal continued as if nothing had been said. "When all the tests came out positive, we knew we had a problem. There is no cure for Proteus, so they were effectively dead; the problem became how to handle the situation to the best advantage for Pel-Ebstein."

Helena said quite distinctly, "You bastard."

He bowed, a mocking acknowledgement. "Whatever you think, I had been given a job to do. Really there was no choice, if you look at things in purely pragmatic terms. If we had told the subjects of the true results, the prediction was that security would be breached extremely quickly – after all, they would have nothing to lose by running to the papers, and plenty to blame us for.

"So we decided to turn the situation to our advantage. Turner had been close to the endpoint, and it seemed logical to see how effective Proteus really was. We told everyone that they were negative, then watched and waited. Sooner or later one of them would get ill with a fever of sufficient severity to trigger Proteus – what happened then would give us a huge amount of data on Proteus."

"Was no one suspicious?" asked Helena. "Did they all just take what you said at face value?"

"Turner asked to see the actual read-outs. Then he even demanded that he be allowed to repeat the tests himself, but we had predicted such a possibility. The samples were switched by sleight of hand when the blood was taken. He analysed my blood."

Carlos said, "When Turner said that he was happy, we all took the results as accurate. I think we all decided that we might as well take their offer and forget about it. After all, Proteus was over, or so we thought."

Eisenmenger found himself wondering about that, and he searched Rosenthal's face for a clue as to the accuracy of that assumption. He saw nothing. He said, "And then, eventually, Millicent Sweet died. She died so rapidly, you didn't have a chance to control matters."

"She died rapidly and she died of a huge number and variety of tumours. Proteus proved how effective it was – too effective, as far as keeping things quiet went. It was obviously an unnatural death, and we couldn't afford that conclusion to be drawn, so we had to manipulate matters."

"Mark Hartmann."

"Yes. Dr Hartmann. His participation proved to be one of the easier matters to arrange."

Helena's eyes flicked over Bochdalek's gun. His finger was near the trigger, but not actually touching it.

Rosenthal yawned. "Anyway, fascinating as this is, night is coming, and I think that we should get on with matters."

Outside the wind and rain were picking up again. Although still day, the light was so gloomy as to be all but without purpose.

Stein asked, "What are you going to do?" It probably wasn't the most perceptive question he had ever asked and it received little consideration from Rosenthal as he replied briefly, "Kill you."

Bochdalek rushed to elaborate. "Phosphor bombs. Very hot, burning without residue. Perfect for disposing of bodies."

Carlos asked, "Is that how you got rid of Jean-Jacques?"

Rosenthal said only, "I'm afraid I don't have the precise details with regard to M. Renvier's demise. Needless to say, it was achieved so that no useful earthly remains survived."

Suddenly there was a loud knock on the door. It seemed to crack along the hallway and rumble into the room. At once Rosenthal was at the window, carefully peering from behind a curtain. He backed away. To Bochdalek, he said, "Police."

Bochdalek said, "I thought you'd been watching." This possessed more than a suggestion of mockery.

"There was nothing on the track for miles."

The knock came again.

Rosenthal said to Stein, "Come on. Answer it."

The old man hesitated, but eventually stood up. Bochdalek's finger returned to the trigger and the gun straightened up. Rosenthal took Stein by the upper arm and walked him out to the hallway. Bochdalek said through a smile, "Suggest you all keep nice and quiet, like sleeping babies."

Rosenthal whispered to Stein. "You put the chain on, you open it and you make sure that whoever it is goes away happy. Understand?"

"But. . ."

"Understand?" This time Rosenthal dug the barrel into his ribs and he nodded. The chain went up and he opened the door, letting in coldness and damp.

"Professor Stein?"

Through the crack in the door, the old man nodded.

"My name's Sergeant MacCallum, from the mainland. I think we met a couple of years ago, following the fire."

The old man nodded, but didn't seem inclined to reminisce. In fact, MacCallum thought that he looked under great strain. He thought it odd, too, that the old man should have his door on a chain – after all, this was Rouna, not Glasgow.

"Could I come in and have a word?"

At once the old man was shaking his head. "No. No, you can't."

MacCallum was wet and he was cold. It was gloomy with night, this far north, soon to be upon them and he didn't want to be there. He felt it unreasonable not to be allowed to move two metres into the relative warmth and dryness. Stein was an incomer, but that didn't mean he had the right to be inhospitable.

He glanced to his right, where Beverley, shivering with so much cold and rain she hardly had bladder control, was crouched down. She nodded for him to continue.

"Are you sure, sir? It really is most uncomfortable out here."

"No! It's not convenient. I'm . . .I'm not well. You might catch something. You can say what you've got to say from there."

In the front sitting room they could feel the draught coming from under the door and hear Stein's replies to silent queries from outside. Bochdalek, in particular, was most intrigued by this play for voices and, although he kept his eyes turned towards his prisoners, his attention was clearly outside.

Helena caught Eisenmenger's eye, gesturing with the slightest movement of her head towards Bochdalek.

Oh, God! She must be joking!

But she wasn't, as she clarified by repeating the movement, then adding a nod in his direction and the merest hint of a kick at Bochdalek's gun.

Is she suicidal? He's a killer, for God's sake! This isn't a Hollywood blockbuster.

He tried frantically to tell her not to commit this lunacy, that it would fail, that it would end in catastrophe, that they would all die, but his slight staccato shaking of his head and his deep frowns were either misinterpreted or ignored. Helena just nodded firmly.

Eisenmenger, accepting that he might as well halt the spin of the earth, began feverishly to work out a way to help her. The one thing on their side was that they weren't tied up.

Feeling that what he was about to do was both futile and foolish, but aware that his mind was afflicted by a strange cerebratory paralysis, he said suddenly to Bochdalek, "He'll have to kill you now. You know too much."

Bochdalek brought his eyes and his attention to Eisenmenger. "You reckon?" he scoffed.

"Rosenthal is exterminating everyone who knows about Proteus. He thinks we're the last. That must include you."

Bochdalek shook his head confidently. "He won't kill me. We're comrades. We've killed together before." This last was clearly a source of pride.

Eisenmenger saw that Helena was preparing her move. Bochdalek was occasionally glancing at her and at Carlos, but it was superficial. Eisenmenger asked with a sneer, "Ever killed anyone who deserved it? Or were they all innocents? Babies, perhaps? Cripples, the blind, the mentally handicapped?"

Bochdalek was blank for a moment and Eisenmenger was momentarily afraid that he had gone too far, that this man would hurt him, but then a wide grin split his face and he began to laugh.

It was then that Helena kicked out at the gun. Eisenmenger started forward but Bochdalek wasn't playing by their rules. When the kick connected, the gun didn't fly towards Eisenmenger as it was supposed to do but remained stubbornly in his hand. It didn't even move much, remaining pointed at Eisenmenger's chest. Bochdalek was grinning even more broadly.

"Tut, tut," he said. "Black marks for you two. . ."

He was about to continue, but this time he was genuinely off guard and when Carlos picked up the fire poker by the side of his chair and flung it at his head, it hit with a soft but very satisfactory thud.

This time the gun was dropped and Helena was on to it while Bochdalek, clutching a gash on his forehead from which blood was running down the side of his nose, stood up and cried a tight, hissed, "Ow!"

She came up, holding it as if it were a ray gun from the twenty-eighth century. By now Carlos was standing, as was Eisenmenger. They were watching Bochdalek take his hands from his face, shake his head and regain composure; they saw Helena finally manage to get a grip on the gun, point it in Bochdalek's direction, then try to stop it shaking. She didn't succeed.

Bochdalek saw the gun, saw Helena and began to grin again. Eisenmenger edged towards Helena, hoping and not hoping that she would give him the gun. He had a strong, and completely unfounded, sense that his ignorance of firearms was somehow superior to hers.

Bochdalek took a step towards her. He was only about a metre away. Eisenmenger wanted her to take a step back, but there was nowhere to go and anyway, she didn't look as if she wanted to. "Don't make me," she warned.

Bochdalek laughed. He turned to Eisenmenger. "She ain't going to shoot me, is she?"

Eisenmenger felt he knew her better, but even he wasn't entirely sure. The look on her face was determined, the look in her eyes less so. Bochdalek was looking still at Eisenmenger but at that moment he turned suddenly to Helena, jerking forward, as if to grab the gun. He stopped short but Helena jumped visibly and there was even a little squeak.

"See?" said Bochdalek, again to Eisenmenger.

"Don't do that again," warned Helena.

A face of comical fear, made again not at Helena. Then he smiled and in less than a second, he whipped around, snatched forward and grabbed for the gun. Helena, though, was faster. She jerked the gun down under his grasp and it was then that she must have pulled back slightly on the trigger.

The bullets sprayed out of the gun in a stunningly loud burst, the recoil flicking the muzzle upwards slightly. It lasted less than a second but perhaps thirty rounds were fired. Helena's face showed as much surprise as fear.

Most of the rounds missed, splintering into the floorboards in a short line behind Bochdalek. Only four of them hit him, an untidy line of black holes across his groin, slicing across the top of his penis and scrotum. He looked surprised, then staggered, then, as he gazed down at the blood that was pumping out and around his groin, as the pain made its lazy but devastating, agony-laden way to his brain, he began to scream, and scream and scream.

"We've had information that you may be in danger."

Stein's face was difficult to see and MacCallum couldn't be sure but he thought that perhaps the old man nodded slightly. His words, however, were of a different timbre. "Danger? That's ridiculous. What are you talking about, man?"

"We think that an old colleague of yours may be looking for you, and that he may pose a danger to you. Carlos Arias-Stella."

The rheumy eyes were momentarily obscured by a slow blink then, a quaver adding a curious vibrato to the words, "That's rubbish! Poppycock!" It was almost hysterical. It could have been petulance but MacCallum thought that there was something more.

He looked again at Beverley. *He's here already.* They both understood. He turned back to Stein and it was at this point that the sound of something heavy falling on the sitting room floor came to Rosenthal and the old man. Distracted, Stein hesitated; Rosenthal was listening, his gun still stuck into the ratchety ribs of the Professor. He heard faint talking. *What the fuck are you doing, Bochdalek?*

Stein began again to speak. "There's nothing to worry about. Carlos won't hurt me, honestly. Even if. . ."

The shots interrupted him.

Beverley heard them quite clearly, as did MacCallum. Another look was exchanged, then Beverley began to rise from her crouched position.

Rosenthal also heard the shots, calculating as best he could what had happened, what he had to do now. He made his decision, tightening his grip on Stein's arm, then pulling him backwards so that he fell awkwardly on the bare, polished floorboards. Then the screaming started.

MacCallum put his face to the gap, now vacated by Stein. "Professor? Professor? Can you let us in? Can you. . ."

He didn't complete the repetition. Rosenthal's gun came around the edge of the door, angled upwards and in the space of a long, loud second, thirteen bullets exploded behind his eyes, a spray of flesh forming a fine vapour above his erupted skull, at once whipped away by the wind.

Helena was staring at Bochdalek, the gun still pointing at the line of holes in the floor. Eisenmenger was moving to take it from her when the gunshots from the hall sounded. He stopped, acutely afraid that things were exponentially decaying. Bochdalek was now grovelling on the floor, covered and surrounded in his blood, clutching his groin and keening. For a space between seconds they seemed to Eisenmenger to be clotted into inaction.

It was Carlos who pulled them out of their stasis. He came forward and took the gun from Helena, breathing rapidly and clearly almost panicking. "We've got to get out of here, before he comes back." He looked at Eisenmenger, saw shock and insisted, "Come on!"

Eisenmenger found reality again with difficulty. Bochdalek was pumping out blood by the litre and would soon be dead, regardless of what attempts were made to try to save him. On Helena's face was a look almost of apology, but her immobility told of deeper effects than that. Eisenmenger took her hand gently and said, "Come on."

They turned away, then Rosenthal returned.

Beverley smothered a small yelp of shock as MacCallum, now crested by an untidy crown of blood, bone and hair, fell backwards on to the crazy paving, eyes open and blind. She put her knuckles into her mouth, trying to fight through the incredulity and unreality, trying to begin operating on basic, professional principles. She didn't need to bother to check whether MacCallum was alive or dead.

This can't be Carlos Arias-Stella, can it? Has he flipped? Then where did he get the gun? It sounded like a machine pistol, but where would

279

someone like Carlos Arias-Stella get such a thing? If not him, then who? And where were Eisenmenger and Flemming?

The door was still on the chain and there seemed to be no reason to believe that her presence was known to the gunman; she had to remain undetected, which meant finding another way in. She began to move away from the door, towards the windows of the sitting room, crouching low.

It was getting dark and she was amazed to find that it was actually possible to feel yet colder and wetter than hitherto. It made moving slow, stiff and sore.

The old man was on the floor, moaning. Rosenthal, assessing him as irrelevant, stepped over him, but he was surprised when Stein's hand reached out and grasped his ankle. The grip was amazingly strong. He staggered, swivelled and, despite being off balance, neatly kicked Stein hard in the right hip. The old man released him at once, crying out sharply. Rosenthal ignored him and walked to the sitting room door to listen. He heard moaning and whispered talking. The door was pulled to, but not closed. He stood to the right of it, gun raised, half behind the wall. Then he kicked it open.

Beverley heard the crash just as she was about to risk peering over the windowsill into the room's interior. She crouched even lower and waited.

Rosenthal looked down at Bochdalek, up at the three retreating figures, fixing on Carlos. He raised his pistol and fired a half-second burst into his abdomen and chest.

What the hell was happening in there? Beverley felt as if some surreal psychosis had settled around her. Much as she feared the consequences, she had to find out what was going on in there. She tentatively raised her eyes above the wood of the window ledge.

Two bodies on the floor, both blood-bathed and clearly dead or dying. Helena and Eisenmenger standing, facing a man she didn't know who was holding a gun on them. Surely too old for Carlos. . ?

Inspiration struck. *Rosenthal.*

She lowered her head and continued to make her way across

the front of the house in the hope of finding a way in. What she would do then was a plan waiting to be formed.

Rosenthal made them pick up the body of the dead policeman from outside the door, keeping his gun on them at all times. Eisenmenger took the head end but, even so, Helena looked uncertain whether to vomit or faint or both. Having added the corpse to the body count in the sitting room, they returned for Stein, taking him into the sitting room. The old man was in great pain and could neither stand nor sit, so they laid him on the floor with a cushion for a pillow. Any movement of the left leg caused him to whimper. "I think you've broken your hip," said Eisenmenger.

Stein was shaking, ageing with every breath. Eisenmenger said to Rosenthal, "He needs painkillers."

His reply was a shrug. "He'll be dead soon, anyway. You all will."

Helena said, "You're not human. You just don't care, do you?"

"My dear Helena. I kill for a living. Killers who care don't exist." He indicated with his gun that they should sit in the dining chairs.

"Did you have to murder Carlos?"

He sighed as if explanations were tedious and should have been unnecessary. "He had the gun, he had already shot my companion. He was a threat, so I removed the threat. Anyway, he had Proteus; he was a walking dead man."

Helena laughed, a savage sound. "You're wrong. I killed him. I killed your precious friend."

Rosenthal was surprised, then smiled. "Well done," he said gravely. "Welcome to the most exclusive club that there is."

Stein was losing consciousness. Rosenthal looked out at the darkening sky and said, "Time for me to go." He went to his bag and produced a skein of plastic washing line that he threw to Eisenmenger. "Tie up the gorgeous Helena. And do it properly – hands behind the back, each foot to a leg of the chair. Tight."

Unravelling the line, Eisenmenger asked, "What are you going to do?"

Rosenthal considered. "Well, the plan was that you should all die in an explosion and blaze. I don't see why that should change."

"Won't it look odd? All these bodies, including a policeman? And the authorities are going to think an explosion odd, given that this is a domestic house."

Rosenthal's smile was appreciative. "There speaks a pathologist. You're quite right. It's going to look bloody odd, but I don't particularly care. The lack of naturalism in the situation, whilst it offends my artistic sensibilities, has to be accepted. The important thing is to ensure that there is no connection between what happens here and PEP. It's all going to be a big mystery."

Eisenmenger felt that he was running out of arguments, that anyway the arguments were fairly pusillanimous. "But my presence, as well that of Helena and Carlos, all that will be proof of a link." He had tied Helena's ankles and was now starting on her wrists. Rosenthal watched him all the time.

"That would be true, if there were going to be any recognizable remains." Eisenmenger had now finished. He returned to his chair. Rosenthal grabbed his right wrist from behind; the grip was excruciatingly hard. Within twenty seconds his hands were bound. Rosenthal tied each ankle to a leg of the chair, again from behind so that Eisenmenger could not kick at him. Then he stood, walked over to Helena and checked the bindings.

From his bag he now produced a dark grey disk, approximately thirty centimetres in diameter and six high. He showed it to them. "This is going to kill you. It explodes, producing a temperature of approximately five thousand Celsius, at the same time distributing burning phosphorus to a distance of twenty metres. It has been adapted from an anti-tank mine, and it has an anti-tamper device. One movement and it explodes."

"Something you picked up at the corner store?" asked Helena.

He smiled, but didn't answer. Instead he said, "Whatever remains of you will be beyond even the skills of one such as Dr Eisenmenger." He looked at his watch. "In fifteen minutes, I shall be gone. At the same time, this will detonate."

Beverley stood in the hall listening to everything that was being said. She had crept all of the way around to the back of the house, gingerly trying every window, eventually finding the back doorway where Bochdalek and Rosenthal had gained forcible entrance. This led through the kitchen and past a large, walk-in pantry where she had come across not only a double-barrelled shotgun but also a box of cartridges. It wasn't exactly a high calibre rifle, but it was better than just having a knitting needle and sadly misplaced over-confidence. Thanking a God that she had hitherto considered at best a nuisance, at worst non-existent, she had examined the weapon. It wasn't in the best condition but it would fire. She slipped two cartridges into it then, as gently as she could, she snapped the gun back together, hoping that the action was good, that it wouldn't require too much force and too much noise to lock.

Her luck continued. She put as many of the cartridges into the pockets of her jeans as she could carry, then ventured out of the pantry, trying to recall at least something of the basic firearms course she had attended too long ago.

Now she stood and listened to the conversation, wondering what to do.

She had to find out the topography of the room, particularly where Rosenthal was. After Rosenthal had kicked it open, it had swung back and was now about twenty centimetres ajar, the light spilling forth away from her. She moved to the doorframe, still well out of the light. She would have to risk looking into the room, hoping that Rosenthal was turned away. Taking a deep breath and praying to her newly attentive God, she moved forward as slowly as she could.

Her supplication worked. Rosenthal was facing away from the door, standing in front of Eisenmenger, although Helena was still visible, tied to a chair, on his right. Stein was apparently unconscious on a sofa, further to the right and, on the floor in front of the doorway, there was a body rising out of a pond of blood, kneeling as if it too had found God, only with less success than her. It looked like Beelzebub had had a go at installation art.

Her problem was that she could not intervene, not with a shotgun in her hand, for Rosenthal was too close to the others; the chance of hitting them was close to certain. She watched as Rosenthal indicated a large device on the floor in front of the fireplace, a dark grey cylindrical object, presumably the explosive device that he had been talking about.

Helena enquired, "Is that thing another of PEP's humanitarian products? Another example of the good they're doing in the world?"

Rosenthal squatted down over the bomb, doing something to it that she couldn't see. His face was hidden, but his tone when he spoke again was a composite of amusement and admiration. "You know, Helena, you really are a special woman." After a pause, he said to Eisenmenger, "She's not a bad fuck, either. In case you wondered." His tone was ostentatiously confidential, two mates in the pub.

Eisenmenger looked at him, his face unmoving. "I'm sure she's delighted to be rated so highly by such a connoisseur."

Helena contented herself with a murmured, "Bastard."

Rosenthal stood up, his back still to Beverley. Another glance at the watch. "Time to love you and leave you."

He turned away from them to face the door and it was then that Eisenmenger's eyes met Beverley's. He spoke loudly to Rosenthal, but it was too late. Rosenthal had already seen her.

Rosenthal's neocortex didn't actually register the partial face-shape by the door frame; it didn't need to. The machine pistol, previously pointing to the floor, began to come up before he even knew that there was anyone there.

Beverley saw him turn, was pulling back even, but there was the briefest moment of eye contact. She glimpsed the gun starting to rise.

The barrel of the machine pistol became horizontal, the trigger was pulled and the ammunition began to demolish the wood and plasterwork.

Beverley dropped as low as she could, moving away from the door, back along the corridor. She was expecting the gunfire, but its deafening volume coupled with frighteningly rapid splintering of the wood and plaster just above her head almost made her momentarily catatonic.

Then it stopped and there was nothing.

Helena heard Eisenmenger's call to Rosenthal but didn't know why he was bothering. When Rosenthal raised the gun and started firing she was completely surprised at this unexpected twist of madness. Wondering if the man had flipped, if he was just going to dissect them both with gunfire before he left, she could only watch his back and wonder.

The gun was empty. Rosenthal was already reaching for another ammunition clip.

Either he's having to reload, or it's a trick, hoping to lure me into the doorway.

If it's a trick I'm dead.

If it's not a trick and I wait too long, I'm dead anyway.

She came to a crouch, brought the shotgun round into a useable position, took one deep breath and darted forward into the doorway.

Rosenthal had the clip in and was already bringing the pistol back up when Beverley appeared before him. There was no break in the motion of the gun.

Beverley saw the gun rising, saw that he was effectively shielding Helena but that Eisenmenger was fully exposed, only some five metres away. She had no choice but to fire. She tried to aim to the right side of Rosenthal but she dared not deviate too much, lest she miss altogether. She pulled both triggers at once.

The twin explosions boomed into the room. Suddenly Rosenthal's chest was stripped of clothing, skin and flesh, leaving only an irregular, edge-singed, blood crater. His face was turned suddenly into red, ripped meat, oozing blood from everywhere before the smoke had dissipated and the echoes in their ears died. The arm holding the pistol was reduced to a bloodied limb, no more, the pistol still gripped.

He collapsed at once, already dead.

Eisenmenger watched as Beverley appeared in the doorway. She was in a crouched position, a shotgun held with its stock pressed against her right hip. He could see, too, Rosenthal's arm coming up, the clip being pressed into position by his left hand as he did so. He didn't have time to think anything about what this might mean.

He saw the flame-flecked blasts from the shotgun barrels, heard nothing, then felt agony all over his upper body and face.

He lost consciousness at once, unaware that Helena had screamed, "John!"

Beverley remained crouched for a second after the blasts. Then moved back behind the door, straightening as she did so. She was immediately aware of a pain in her right hip, where the recoil had gouged into her. Ignoring this, she broke the gun, fished two cartridges from her pocket, reloaded and snapped it back together. Only then, the gun held again ready to use, did she advance carefully into the room.

Although Rosenthal was obviously dead, she held the shotgun pointed down at his body, pushed him over and pulled the gun from the remains of his hands. Only then did she look over at Helena and Eisenmenger.

"Shit."

Helena was staring at her, her expression partly malevolence, partly dread. "You've killed him," she whispered. "You've killed him, you idiot."

Beverley rushed forward, dropping the shotgun and lifting the head from the chest. The face wasn't pretty. She felt for a pulse.

It took a moment, but she found one. "He's alive."

Then she turned to Helena, untying her bonds. "I take it there were only two of them."

"Yes. He's got some sort of rendezvous arranged, though."

Beverley indicated the bomb. "Did I hear him say that it's got some sort of movement sensor?"

"That's right."

Beverley looked at her watch. It was difficult to be certain but she estimated that they had a maximum of twelve minutes. She finished untying Helena. "Can you walk?"

She nodded.

"Right. First we take John, then Stein. Then we come back for the bodies, starting with Sergeant MacCallum. If we don't have time for the other two, so be it."

This wasn't a suggestion and Helena accepted that Beverley ought to command in such a situation. They untied Eisenmenger then, each putting their head under an arm. He was semi-conscious but of little help in supporting himself. They had to be careful not to disturb the innocuous grey cylinder close to his chair.

286

They basically had to drag him over the floor. By the time they reached the front door, they were already exhausted. Opening the front door brought forth complete darkness and swirling rain, silver droplets like fish caught in the light from the house. They continued dragging Eisenmenger along the path, then on to the grass.

"How far?" asked Helena, shouting breathlessly over the rain and wind. Beverley's only answer was an equally gasped, "Further."

At approximately fifty metres from the house, Beverley said, "Here," and they laid him on the wet grass in the darkness, wind and rain. It was too dark to see from their watches how much time remained, so they just started running back to the house. Once back there, Beverley estimated that they had nine minutes.

Stein ought to have been easier because he was lighter, but they were becoming tired and although he was barely conscious, the pain from his hip as they dragged him cause him to writhe and twist as they went. It seemed to take even longer to get him to a safe distance.

Helena was starting to feel faint but she said nothing as they ran back again. Her breath was corrosive as she gasped, her legs were like leaden lumps of ice because of the cold, the wet and the strain, and her head was one thumping mass. She glanced at Beverley, seeing similar signs of approaching collapse. In the hall, Beverley's watch showed six minutes.

MacCallum's erupted head was facing them as they entered the living room. "We'll take him by the legs. Drag him out."

They each grabbed a foot, wheeled him around and pulled the body along, trying not to look at the train of blood, hair and bone splinters that marked their passage. There was a sickening thump as they dragged MacCallum over the doorstep and onto the path. When they reached the grass, they were able to get up a little speed, for the rain eased the corpse over the ground.

They reached Stein and Eisenmenger, both ready to drop. Beverley, scarcely able to talk, said, "Forget the others."

Then she vomited, bent double, retching and wrenching in the cold, icy, every-pouring rain.

Helena sank to her knees in the grass. She felt the world coming and going, swinging like a huge building about to topple into rubble. She kept wanting to vomit but was unable to do so. She was so wet that her clothes enveloped her, clinging and abrading her skin; her chest and throat hurt more than she thought possible, with every breath slicing like razor blades into her chest. She felt sick, as if every Christmas dinner she had ever eaten was sitting there and begging to come back and visit, and for once she was desperate to see vomit, feel the acid in her mouth.

The wind was rising and becoming even more polar. They might be safe from the explosion but if they didn't get out from under the weather soon, they would all die of exposure; certainly Stein wouldn't last more than a few hours out here.

She tried to ignore the fact that her body was no longer hers, was now in the possession of the more malevolent devils in hell, and rose to find Beverley.

Eisenmenger opened his eyes to see sunlight and feel warmth. No pain, no fear, just quiet. He felt as if he had returned to the past, sunny days and beautiful, strange places where adventure was harmless and responsibility banished. He lay there and listened to his breathing.

He turned his head, feeling the grass rustle against his hair. Tamsin lay to his right.

She was unburned, her pretty face smiling at the sky, her profile showing the pale skin of youth.

Turning to his left, he saw Marie. Her eyes were closed, her complexion unspoiled. She, too, looked at peace.

Never before had Tamsin and Marie been together; he wondered what it meant.

Happiness? Contentment? A completion?

Maybe that's what it signified – maybe at last his daemons were to be angels, his nightmares to be daydreams.

He turned his head once more to Tamsin and even before he saw her he smelled the familiar stench of burnt grease, felt the cracking of charred flesh, saw the stark contrast of blood-red lines separating islands of black charcoal. Tamsin's eyes were now seared with torment.

He knew what he would see when he turned his head to Marie, but did so anyway. Marie's face and body were wreathed in flame, fire that clung and caressed, licking her bubbling flesh, entering her silently screaming mouth, raping her with its intimacy.

He squeezed dry tears back, jerked back to the sky. So it wasn't over, there was still more pain to come.

Suddenly the sky darkened, cold rain began to fall and he felt a freeze seep into him. His face and chest were a network of stinging sores of agony, but he was back in the real world and he knew why contentment was not to be his.

The Proteus project had yet to be ended.

Beverley saw Helena's stumbling form coming towards her only as a silhouette against the lights of the house. She knew why she was coming, had had the same thoughts herself. She started to get painfully to her feet.

Helena could only faintly see the various bodies alive and dead that were littered around. She made out Beverley rising to meet her, but then another movement caught her eye – Eisenmenger.

What was he doing? That he was trying to get to his feet was obvious, but the reason was less so. She went to him, ignoring Beverley.

"John? what are you doing."

In the near dark she could just make out that the rain had washed away much of the blood, leaving dilute streaks and black pockmarks over his face and neck. His lips seemed almost shredded.

He mumbled something but she couldn't decipher it. He was on his knees, trying to rise to his feet.

"What did you say?" She tried to force him gently back down but he resisted. Beverley joined them. "Is he all right?"

"He's saying something, but I can't tell what it is." To Eisenmenger she asked, "What's wrong?"

She put her ear close to his bowed head so that she could hear his rasped breath sounds.

"Proteus."

She heard him say it, at once assuming that he wasn't making sense. "It's over. We're safe, John."

But he shook his head, still resisting her arm that was resting across his back. He lifted his head and whispered through a grimace, "Stein said he was working on a cure."

"I know, but. . ."

"He must have a samples in his laboratory. The explosion will spread it. . . perhaps over the whole island."

It was quite clear and quite coherent. Appalled she looked up at Beverley, feeling suddenly the ground no longer solid.

Beverley hadn't heard. "What did he say?"

Eisenmenger felt unconsciousness pulling him down. As he sagged, Beverley knelt down to help Helena with his dead weight. "What did he say?" she repeated.

But there wasn't time to explain. Helena was already running for the house.

How long have I got? Three minutes? Two? Maybe only thirty seconds, and therefore not enough. Not nearly enough.

If she thought her throat and chest had been hurting before, within twenty metres of running through the sodden grass she knew that she had yet to understand the half of what pain was all about. She vaguely heard Beverley's voice calling after her. *Probably thinks I've gone mad. Maybe I have. Must be a kind of lunacy to go back in, to run towards a bomb that spits out burning phosphorus.*

She tried to think about what she would have to do, rather than about the pain in her body, the terrors in her head. It would presumably be in a laboratory, but what would it look like? A solid or a liquid? On the bench, in the refrigerator or in the freezer? And supposing he had deliberately hidden it, to fool any snoopers, or anyone charged with saving the lives of everyone on Rouna?

It might not even exist. John might be wrong – an unintended practical joke, the last that she would never laugh at.

She reached the hallway and enough light to see her watch. Perhaps three minutes – upper end of expectations.

It must be upstairs. Rosenthal went upstairs when he found the laboratory.

She pounded up the steps, the added exertion nearly causing her to faint away.

For God's sake! Keep conscious, you silly bitch!

There was a long, right-angled landing at the top, seeming to stretch away into dark infinity. The light switch was on her left and she pulled it down as she passed. She began opening doors, glancing in at each room then running on. Bedrooms, a bathroom, an airing cupboard, more bedrooms. In one there was a door on the far side of the room that was locked. She didn't have the time to investigate further, but she didn't see how it could be the laboratory because from the window she could see that she was at the corner of house and that the room behind the door was no more than a metre or two wide. Probably an en suite.

How much time left? Only about two minutes. Could be more, could be less.

At the end of the landing there was another flight of stairs, this one narrower, a light switch at its foot. She flipped it but no light came on.

Bloody great. She was already running up the stairs, trying to concentrate on anything other than the slowing agony she now felt in every muscle, every tendon, every bone. She was almost at the top when she slipped, missed her footing and her left shin cracked into the wooden step. She slipped down five steps, grabbing frantically at everything and anything she could reach, and then the true meaning of torment was blessed upon her as a pain so sharp, so large, so remorseless in its desire to smother her came into her head that she felt true blackness, true eternity start to descend.

No. No, please. Please don't do this. Please. Please. Please. Please. . .

She fought it off, picked herself up and tried to run up to the top of the flight, but again she stumbled, this time because weight on her left leg brought more explosions of pain.

God, it's broken. What now?

The question came and then was gone because she wouldn't contemplate giving up. She had to hop up the stairs using only her right leg, but she made it.

It was a small landing, the light from below revealing only four doors. By limping she found the pain reduced a little, but every step made her gasp and made her want to cry.

Come on, you bitch. Come on!

The first was filled with junk. The second was a shower room, dank and clearly unused for years.

It's going to be the last one. Of course it is.

She opened the third door, her left leg starting to feel as if were molten. Every time she put pressure on it, she had a sense of something grinding. She was gritting her teeth all the time, merely clenching them even harder when she leant on that leg.

She opened the third door, expecting nothing, finding gold.

Hardly able to believe her luck she limped in, leaning on the bench to her right, knocking off a large conical beaker that was near the edge. It smashed to the floor and her next few grating limps crushed glass as she went. She was aware that she was starting to yelp uncontrollably as she went

Well, here you are. Time probably run out, but you've arrived.

She looked around the room. She saw a laboratory, like a hundred television pictures, a hundred films. Benches, glassware, shelves, items of unknowable equipment.

How am I supposed to know what to look for and where to look for it?

She had no information to work on. Through the pain she tried to ignore the nihilism of the thought, finding it seditionist. She paused, ignoring the urge to do something, anything, and tried to concentrate.

Where do you put a virus?

There was something that looked like a chest freezer over on the wall between two windows. She stumbled over towards it, opened it and looked and found herself lost in rack upon rack of tubes, all filled with dark pink fluid.

Is this Proteus?

Maybe it was, in which case they were all dead. There was far too much for her to take to safety. There must have been five hundred test tubes. She picked one out. *Plasmid 324 Anti-enhancer.* She knew more about the inside of a Turkish wrestler's underpants than she did about virology, but she guessed none of this was what she wanted.

She looked around. On the benches were various mysterious items of equipment – could they be hiding Proteus? She opted first to go for the large refrigerator and upright freezer on the opposite wall. She hobbled over as quickly as she could, the pain in her leg now so intense that she had to adopt a near-stumbling gait as she moved in order to reduce the weight on it.

Why hasn't it come yet? It's going to come soon.

She reached the refrigerator, opened it and saw it at once. Stein had been methodical, the good scientist, and he had ensured that there would be no mistake. The plastic vial was labelled with a clarity that was absurd. PROTEUS – what else? She grabbed it and thrust it into her jacket pocket. Then she turned and began to force herself through the regular spearing pain that was movement. She reached the door to the lab, went out on to the small dark landing, thence to the stairs.

Where is the explosion? It should have gone off by now. Why hasn't it? Perhaps it won't, perhaps he didn't set it properly. . .

The first step demonstrated with harsh but elegant efficiency that getting down the stairways was going to be even worse than going up. The only way she could manage it was by leading with her other leg, grabbing the banister rail with her free hand, and effectively sliding in jerks and hops downwards.

She made it to the first landing, with relatively little increase in agony, glad to be in the light and closer to escape, but aware that to get out she would have to go past the bomb – if it went off at the wrong time. . .

She hobbled along the landing, cursing its length. The torment in her leg, grating with acid venom every time she moved was being joined by groaning, whining protest from all her other muscles as they were strained by what she was asking them to do. Her mouth and throat felt sandblasted, her chest a bag of burning coals. She made it to the end of the landing rail, put her hand on the newel post to help her turn to go down the last flight when the whole house shook violently, and there was an almighty, booming explosion and a rumbling, rolling cloud of searing hot flame reared up the stairwell to consume her.

Beverley had been left shouting into the wind as Helena ran off. What the hell was going on? She had started to run after her but she soon stopped. She wasn't a coward but there was no point in blindly following her into a house that was shortly going to explode. She looked back at Eisenmenger, who had come to again and once more was trying to rise. She knelt down beside him. "What's going on?"

Eisenmenger, by now on one elbow, said, "Got to get Proteus." His lips were ragged and his words were slurred.

"Proteus?"

"There must be a sample of Proteus in there. Got to get it." He painfully and slowly was trying to get on to his knees. Beverley put her hand out to him. "Don't bother. Helena's gone back in."

He looked at her, shock and fear brightening his eyes.

Beverley looked at her watch again. Already it was two minutes after the time she had estimated to detonation, still no explosion, but still no Helena. She had found the keys to the Land Rover in MacCallum's pockets and had brought it as close as she dared to the house, the engine running. If Helena appeared, she could at least get her away from the vicinity as quickly as possible.

Then the ground floor of the house turned yellow-white, the windows erupted and a sudden, deafening bang made her jump. She watched in horror as bright white droplets of burning, viscous liquid fell, hissing into the wet grass around her, like acid-filled fireflies.

Helena had turned away, pivoting on her injured leg, the scream of agony suddenly an old friend, a nodal point around which she could at least focus. The heat clamped itself to her back, tried to claw around her face, into her eyes. She dropped to the floor, but the heat on her back was getting exponentially worse.

Christ! I'm on fire!

She rolled on to her back, trying to smother the flame, like a dog in the dust. Her eyes saw small but expanding points of fire all around her on the floor, smoke becoming fat and turgid as it snaked its serpentine way around the walls and ceiling. Flakes of ash hovered everywhere around her.

At last the fire on her back was out, but the atmosphere was rapidly becoming unbreathable. Already the heat was stripping the lining of her mouth, nose and throat, while there came to her a horrible roaring rush of noise, like a great beast calling for more nourishment. Through the smoke she saw flickering lights dancing with ominous shadows on the wall of the stairwell. She rolled on to her front, then on to her knees. She edged forward to peer around the newel post, already very much aware of what she would see down the stairs.

It looked like the seventh circle of Hell.

Beverley knew that nobody was going to get out of there, even if they survived the initial explosion, but she wasn't going to turn away without at least trying. Hoping that nothing else was likely to explode, she put the Land Rover into gear and sped forward, stopping about ten metres from the fire; even inside the car the heat was intolerable. She'd never be able to get closer. She reversed a short way, turned hard left and drove fast around the side of the house, then to the back.

Here it was hot, but bearable. Through the windows she could see flame beginning to tongue its way into the rooms at the rear. She manoeuvred the Land Rover so that it was facing away from the house then, leaving the engine running and both doors open, she went to the back door and entered the house.

Helena wondered how long she had. Too long, she suspected. And would it be the smoke or the fire? God, she hoped that it would be smoke. Surely she was owed that? She sat on the floor, her back against the landing banisters, coughing almost continuously now. Waiting. She checked that she still had the vial that contained Proteus safely in her pocket.

That's what it all comes down to in the end. Waiting. As soon as we're born, we start the process of waiting for death. Our lives are merely diversions to occupy the time.

The smoke was so dense now that could hardly see the doors opposite her. The noise of the fire was getting louder, too. Louder and more menacing. . .

Abruptly she opened her eyes. She had almost lost consciousness. The heat was hideous. She began to crawl away from the heat, back along the landing, thinking to get as far away from the fire as she could.

She was aware that all she was doing was looking for a place to die.

In the kitchen Beverley found a drawer full of towels. She pulled out two, wet them thoroughly and put one around her head, covering her nose and mouth; the other she put over her shoulder.

The room was filling with smoke and there was low grumbling, flecked with sporadic crackles, coming from behind the door. She went to the door, feeling the heat, hearing the lascivious sounds of attentive flames. She decided she would really rather not open it, not unless she had to. If Helena had been downstairs when the bomb exploded, she was dead. Her only chance was to have been on one of the upper floors, but that meant that her only hope of rescue was if there was another staircase. It was a big house; it was a possibility, but not a certainty.

She looked around the kitchen. There was another door in the far left-hand corner. When she opened it, it led her through to a long narrow conservatory against the middle of the back of the house. The plants within were all long dead, left to decay to sand-coloured dust. At its far end was another door; this was locked but the wooden frame was rotten and a single kick with her heel got her through.

A dimly-lit corridor, and even here there was a pungency of acrid smoke. *The whole of the front must be ablaze. It's going to collapse soon.*

Another complication.

At the end of the corridor, having stumbled over piles of newspaper, many chewed into dust and shreds by mice, she reached another door. It didn't appear to have a lock, but there were newspapers piled high against it that she had pull down and move aside. When she looked back, there was definitely more smoke.

She opened the door.

A staircase.

She allowed herself a brief spasm of hope, then ran up the stairs, to find a minute landing . . .

. . .and another locked door.

For fuck's sake!

There was no room to kick. She put her shoulder to the door but this time there was no help from rotten wood and the door held. She did it again, but there wasn't enough room to give her a reasonable run up, and the door still wouldn't give.

Something flipped. Anger, frustration, disbelief and sheer, bloody obstinacy curdled inside her and formed a gestalt of rage. She began pounding with her shoulder into the door, again and again, as hard as she could, ignoring the increasing pain. She started to shout, to scream. The towel around her face became unravelled, allowing her words and cries to be loosed upon the smoke and smell of burning.

When the door gave, it did so suddenly, as if playing a trick, so that she was injected suddenly into the room, her fall being broken by a bed. Raising her head, her eyes met an ancient alarm clock on the bedside cabinet; it was identical to one that her mother had once owned, and somehow, incredibly, she was momentarily back in her childhood, safe and warm and unaccountably content.

She picked herself up at once, overcome by coughing, for the smoke in the room was far denser. She put the towel around her face and head again, then headed for the door, still coughing, her chest muscles feeling not only in torment but also loose, as if she were shaking herself to bits.

Surely it's not locked. Please?

This door was hot, the handle unbearably so. There was smoke framing it, liquidly stroking its edges. If it opened onto a closed space in which there was fire, she would be incinerated very quickly when she opened the door, probably no matter where she stood. Yet she hadn't come this far to leave now, not like this.

She grabbed the bedspread off the bed, wrapped it round her hand, turned the handle and pulled, wondering what it would feel like to be in the face of a giant blowtorch. . .

There was unbelievable, blasting heat and, for the smallest part of a second she thought that she was being roasted, but then she knew that she was not dead. Not yet.

It could have been the inside of a blast furnace. There was just smoke; smoke and heat, illuminated by yellow-orange fires that were smeared out by the soot and ash and dense smoke. She began coughing at once – this time, real coughing, as if her lungs were completely unable to live with what she gave them, as if they were thrashing about in torment.

She stepped in. The brightest light was ahead of her and to the right; it was from here that a noise of greedy roaring was coming. She looked around, saw that she was at the end of a long corridor, doors on both sides; a landing, she surmised. She had no choice about which way to go; unfortunately that way was towards a fiercely bright, roaring light. It looked like the heart of hell. If she went too far along the landing, she would not only fail, she would most probably die.

She dropped to her knees and began crawling through ash. At once she was questioning how long she could last, for the heat increased with every step.

A few more seconds. That's all I've got. I'll have to turn back if I don't find her in that time. I don't see that I'll be able to search anywhere else. Supposing. . .

She inched along the floor. Whenever she reached a door, she opened it, went in and hoped that her cursory search, curtailed by lack of time, would reveal Helena. She tried calling out each time, but the towel muffled her voice and the crescending, shaking noise around her all but snuffed it out.

Then, superimposed upon this cacophony, there was a much louder shaking rumble, thunderous in the claustrophobic space that the heat allowed her. A huge amount of plaster and dust fell around her and on her, and she felt the entire fabric of the house groan and roll slightly to her left.

It's starting to collapse. Must have been the front going. This bit'll be next. Time's running out. . .

She was searching by feel now, for her eyes were stinging so much, bathed in tears like a lost lover's weeping that her swollen eyelids were closing to protect them.

And then she found her.

Helena was buried under soot, plaster dust and ash, a burial mound illuminated on the far side by the consuming monstrous fire beyond her. Curled into a foetal position, head towards her, perhaps even her thumb in her mouth, so childlike and innocent was the posture. Clearly she had tried to get away from the fire.

Beverley didn't wait to see if she were conscious – she might not even have been alive – she just took hold of the cloth over her shoulders and began pulling. She had long ago lost the spare towel she had brought and didn't even think about it. She just knew that they had seconds, possibly fewer than she realized, and that she had to pull and pull and pull.

Her own towel slipped. It was now dry and clogged with soot and she had thought at the back of her mind that it must be all but useless, but at once the coughing in her chest leapt hugely and painfully, so deep and abrasive that she was sure that she was coughing blood. With one hand she thrust the material into her mouth, then carried on pulling.

She reached the door to the bedroom by which she had entered and, pulling Helena's body through, slammed the door behind her. Then she stepped over her, picked up the alarm clock on the bedside cabinet, ran to the window and smacked it at the glass. Again and again she smacked, until the window was gone, only the most obstinate shards left clinging to the ancient putty.

She thrust her head out, dropping the towel. It was densely smoky out there, but infinitely cleaner than inside. Her lungs thanked her grudgingly, still coughing, less angry.

Another rumble of thundering vibration.

She took one deep breath, then ducked inside. Again she grabbed Helena, pulling her around the bed, towards the door to the back staircase. She almost made it on one lungful, and when she did breathe, her chest fell back at once into grazing agony.

At the top of the stairs, she had a decision to make that was no decision. The nice way would have been to pick Helena up over her shoulder, transporting her in stately style as in all the best dramas about fire, but there was no room for such an easy solution, and anyway she was too weak, in too much pain, for such a neat solution.

Again she stepped over the inert form, so that she was between Helena and the top of the stairs. She went down a few steps, turned and began half-pulling, half-pushing Helena down, the body bumping on each hard wooden edge. "Sorry, Hel," she murmured.

Twice she stumbled, nearly falling to the bottom, Helena in tow like a rolling boulder, but both times she stopped herself. Once Helena's form threatened to overwhelm her with its momentum, as if in protest at such rough treatment.

She made it to earth noticing that the air was slightly clearer.

Come on, nearly there.

The third crash was so loud, so near that she fell against the wall to her left. It felt as if she were in the middle of an eruption, as if the world were being ripped apart around her. It lasted for several seconds, not ending abruptly, but going on and on, dying and rising, a thing that refused to end. When she put out her hand towards the right-hand wall, it was hot; very hot.

It must be just the other side. The fire must be nearly through to here.

Her back had decided that enough was enough. As she bent yet again to her task, it sent pain down the back of her right leg, a spear inserted cleanly and ruthlessly into her bone. She began to move backwards, inevitably slowing with the pain and with the tiredness.

How long?

She kept glancing at the wall, saw plaster cracking along its entire length.

299

Come on. Come on.

She reached the splintered door frame, pushing the swinging door with her backside, having to pull Helena over a small but snagging step.

The temperature vaulted and on her back she felt burning. She turned around. Looking into the house was a row of windows in the centre of which were French doors. Behind them was a conflagration, vividly bright, flames shooting out from cracks and crevasses in and around the windows. As she watched, glass panes were cracking, then imploding as air was consumed inside.

Fucking great.

She guessed that the kitchen at the far end would by now also be lost to the fire. Her only chance was to get out by some glass doors halfway along the conservatory. Even to reach those she would have to get past grasping flames that were already climbing up the side of the house, inside the conservatory.

She bent down again, profaned against her back, and pulled.

She went as fast as she could – small, shuffling steps but fast ones – but still the flames caught her on several occasions, making her curse and cry out and weep all at once. On one of these, her clothes caught alight and she had frantically to pat it out, dropping Helena as if she were merely a heavy bag.

At the doors, Helena was again dropped. At last, she had luck. They were locked, but the key was there; she turned it, opened the door and again grabbed Helena.

Then she pulled and shuffled, pulled and shuffled, first over paving covered in fire debris, then over wet grass.

It was still raining, rain that was the most God-given, holy and precious thing that ever she had known. She could have added her own tears to all this, she was so relieved, but still she kept pulling.

She reached the Land Rover, but any thought of getting in was gone. She was too far exhausted to do anything more than pull Helena to its far side, then collapse into the wet grass.

Her last thoughts before unconsciousness were two: *She'd better fucking well be alive*, and, *She'd better fucking well have got Proteus.*

Marble and his daughter found them. The fire could be seen from every point of the island and he was only the first of many who came, not to spectate but to help. Within minutes of his arrival, there were fifty or more. They lifted Stein, near death, into the back of an old van, its floor unswept and covered with hay and sheep droppings. Eisenmenger, unconscious, was laid next to him. The body of Carlos and the body of Sergeant MacCallum, with its crown of blood, was lifted with reverence into the back of Marble's old Morris Minor, the questions that it invoked were not voiced by anyone.

It took them longer to find Beverley and Helena and, by this time, the house was completely collapsed, although the fire would take a lot more rain and two more days to die. They put them into the back of the Land Rover and the Harbour Master drove it back to Morrister and the tavern. Then they left in a long line of vehicles. Even had they known of the presence on Rouna of Carios, Rosenthal and Bochdalek, there would have been nothing for them to do.

Eisenmenger, Beverley and Helena were flown at once back to the mainland by Air Ambulance. Stein died of exposure, acute subdural haemorrhage and a fractured hip; he was buried on Rouna. Sergeant MacCallum's body was flown back to the mainland by police helicopter.

The ruins of Stein's house were searched by police and fire authorities. A few charred bone fragments were all that was found of the two bodies; DNA testing proved ineffectual, for the small amount of genetic material that they had once contained was totally denatured by the intense heat. Only the positioning of the bone fragments gave a clue that there had been two bodies in the house.

They also found the heat-warped remains of two machine pistols, any identifying features removed either by human hand or by fire.

The opinion on the cause of the blaze was provisionally made as some form of incendiary device of unknown type.

Eisenmenger recovered first, not even needing intensive care, unlike Beverley and Helena. He visited them both daily, hating the clinical sparseness of the unit, its never-ending orchestra of bleeps and sighs, murmurs and concern. They had been put in beds opposite each other, as if their history of antagonism had been taken into consideration, but it didn't matter, for Helena's injuries meant that she took far longer to recover, and she was sedated and ventilated for the whole of Beverley's stay.

On the day of his discharge his visit to Beverley found her awake but so full of lassitude as to be near moribund. Her chest was still intensely sore, and she was liable to hacking, tormenting fits of coughing, but, despite some pallor, she looked remarkably unscathed. Opposite her, by contrast, Helena's face was brightly red, due partly to superficial burning and partly to carbon-monoxide poisoning. A ventilation tube poked impertinently from her mouth, tied by untidy, ragged bandage to her head, while blood dripped into her left arm, dextrose saline into her right, and a thicker plastic line fed into the side of her neck. Her hands were bandaged, both eyes were black, and the lurking form of a cast on her leg could be seen under the bed sheet.

Referring to his scab-flecked face, Beverley said, "Hi, hand-some." Beverley's voice was a husky whisper, leaving Eisenmenger fighting off guilty feelings of arousal. He smiled and then glanced across at Helena, almost furtively.

Beverley caught the movement. "How is she?"

"Stable."

She frowned. "Is that good?"

He shrugged. "Better than unstable, but if she stays stable and never improves, well. . ."

He broke off, and she could see how distressed he was. Her gaze rested on Helena and she murmured, "She'd bloody well better improve. I wouldn't like to think I went through all that for nothing." Despite her flippancy he saw genuine concern. He said, "Thanks."

At once her demeanour changed. "It's my job."

"Thanks, anyway."

She refused to crack the attitude. "If I went through all that, only for her to die, I'm going to be very unhappy."

"She'll be all right."

She heard fear in the certainty, but said nothing.

Helena was on the ventilator for another four days, during which time Beverley made a rapid improvement, moving quickly from the ITU ward to the general medical ward, and thence home.

She returned to her flat a week and a day after the fire. She was still weak and there were areas of a healing burn on the left side of her abdomen and on her left hip. Luckily they were only second-degree burns and therefore not going to scar; unluckily they were bloody painful.

She spent the next two days almost continuously in bed, a situation that would have lasted for at least another twenty-four hours had she not had a visitor.

Lambert.

He looked as if he had swallowed a particularly psychotic wasp.

"May I come in?" He ignored the fact that she was dressed only in a gown. She stood aside and he came in. He even sat down, although she didn't actually ask him to do so.

"You lied to me."

She had expected something like this and found no need or compulsion to respond.

"You also kept me out of the loop with regard to this case."

She sighed. He was going to suspend her – what the hell? "Only because you would have either ignored what I said, or cut me out of any investigation. Deny it if you like, but you and I both know that you have behaved like a complete shit towards me."

"That is my privilege, your problem. It does not excuse your behaviour."

She said nothing more. He asked, "What happened?"

"You've seen my statement." It was a guess.

"Poppycock about manufactured viruses, international conspiracies, murderers. Libel about Pel-Ebstein. Yes, I've seen it."

"Has anyone analysed what Helena got out from the fire?"

He hesitated. "I'm told that it does seem to be some form of freeze-dried viral material," he admitted. "Whatever that means."

"And Dr Eisenmenger's statement?"

He snorted. "Eisenmenger agrees broadly with what you say. For what that's worth."

She waited. Lambert was so rigid you could have run a flag up him, but she knew that he had one redeeming quality – he was honest, even to himself.

"We'll never prove anything, The few remains from the fire are beyond identification. There are no other witnesses."

She had already guessed as much. "So they get away with it."

He grimaced. "I accept that something happened on that island – there were two machine pistols, as you said, and the opinion of the fire people does not contradict your statement – but there is nothing – I repeat nothing – to link Pel-Ebstein Pharmaceuticals to any of this."

She wondered where the endpoint was. Congratulations or condemnations.

He lowered his voice, almost in anguish, as he said, "I'm coming under . . .pressure."

Not, she judged, a statement made to elicit sympathy. "To do what?"

"Bury it."

"And me?"

He paused. "It all depends. If your statement were to be amended. . ."

She had never seen him look so ill. She had always thought that she would enjoy to see him in such a state, yet strangely she understood. "I would like a transfer," she pointed out. "I think that we would both want me to have a transfer, wouldn't we?"

He nodded, looking at her. She enquired, "Out of interest, what would happen if I told them to fuck off?"

But they were both pragmatists, squeezed into that box by their occupation, and he knew that it was not a question that required a response. He stood up and went to the door. "I've been given what I am led to understand are all the existing copies of your original statement. They will be shredded. Someone will call to take a new one."

She had remained sitting and he let himself out. Before he closed the door he said, "There's no need to hurry back."

When Helena had first come round, his relief had been too much for him and, embarrassed, he had left at once, before she saw him. When he returned an hour or so later, she was asleep. It hadn't been until the next day that they actually spoke.

"You really are a silly bitch."

She smiled. "Thanks." Her voice, like Beverley's, was croaky and somehow enticing.

"I mean it. You shouldn't have gone back in."

"You were going to."

"I knew what I was looking for."

"You were peppered with buckshot and looked as if the acne fairy had singled you out for the special treatment. I doubt you would have made it to the front door, let alone to the laboratory."

They lapsed into uncommunicativeness.

"Well, anyway," he conceded after a while, "It could have been the end of you."

She sighed and when she responded it was in a reflective tone. "Yes, it could." More intrusion from the staccato sparseness of sounds that were an ever-present part of the Intensive Care experience. "Where is she?"

He perhaps ought to have tried guessing the subject of the question, but he didn't. "Already discharged."

She said nothing to that for a while and he thought it wiser to examine one of the strange bleeping boxes that always accompanied ITU patients, like mechanoid guardian angels.

"She went in after me." This in a tone that was almost wondrous.

"She said it was her job."

He was forced into more consideration of the wonders of modern medicine. Then Helena pointed out, "She didn't have to, did she? She could have left me to burn. There was no one to know, was there?"

And he took a deep breath and admitted that no, she needn't have done that.

Then a nurse came to do nursely things, and the subject was lost.

It was ten days later that Helena came out of hospital and was driven home by Eisenmenger. Her lungs were still badly affected by the amount of smoke she had inhaled, and there were burns on her back that had required skin grafting; she had to sit with soft cushions and even these were scant comfort. Her hands, at least, were healing well, and her leg, although still in a cast, had stopped hurting.

Her mood, though, was thunderous and, in a strange coincidence of Gaia and girl, so was the sky.

"The bitch."

It was familiar stuff, somehow comforting, he thought.

"She did save your life," he pointed out.

"I know that," she replied, snatching at the words to get past them "But that doesn't excuse what she's done."

Eisenmenger had expected his news to be taken badly. "I don't know, but I would guess that there was some form of political pressure put on her."

They were just passing into England, through the sweeping valleys of Cumbria.

"Are you making excuses for her?"

Bloody hell, she's recovering fast.

"No. I'm suggesting that she is perhaps less the idealist, more the pragmatist."

"More sensible than me?"

She was firing replies at him with enough enthusiasm to pull a muscle. He tried to remain calm. She was still far from well. "Helena, all I'm saying is, that she's the kind of person who would prefer to save herself the trouble of a hopeless battle."

She opened her mouth to argue, but Eisenmenger arrived first. "After all, we've come out of this knowing the truth but unable to prove it. Those involved have all died, and any connections between what remains and Pel-Ebstein have been destroyed."

At once she said, "So we just give up? We just accept that a multinational company thought it commercially advantageous and morally acceptable to attempt to manufacture a virus that causes uncontrollable cancer? That it used murder and blackmail and extortion to try to cover it up? That we both nearly died; that we were both nearly murdered?"

He appeared to be concentrating on his driving, but the road was straight and there were no other drivers. After a few minutes of listening to the road surface he said, "Yes, I'm afraid we do."

Raymond Sweet sat again in Helena's office, seeming as displaced as ever. He sat in the chair, neither expectant nor uninterested, appearing rocklike enough to have understudied St Peter.

He listened to what Helena said, his face unmoving, much as Buddha presumably stared at the sins of the world. When she finished, he asked, "So this thing, Proteus, killed her?"

"We think so."

"And she didn't know what she was working on?"

"Almost certainly not."

"But it was an accident?"

"Well, yes. . ."

"Are they liable for the accident? I mean, was it negligence?"

Helena looked pained. She didn't seem to be making the right connections with Mr Sweet. Eisenmenger looked on, amused but invisibly so.

"No," she admitted. "But that's not the point. Millie was duped into working on something that was highly amoral, illegal even."

He was thinking hard; thinking to Raymond Sweet was an all-consuming occupation, something to be done in isolation, while the rest of the world ceased to breathe, stood and looked on. "What about the police? What are they saying?"

Eisenmenger admired Helena then. She took the question much as a seasoned pro took uppercuts and sneaky blows below the belt.

"They see no reason to proceed. Some of the evidence is. . . conflicting, and none of it is particularly strong."

He said nothing, looking at his hands and, Eisenmenger had to admit they were remarkable things, with their rough, diffuse scarring and nails bitten to tattiness. Helena said tentatively, "We would be willing to carry on." Eisenmenger heard the plural pronoun with some surprise. Since he had not been consulted, he assumed that she was talking in an imperial, figurative sense, perhaps assuming some sort of righteous partnership with her God. He would have made comment but she continued talking. "We could see what we could uncover. I'm sure that we would have some success in establishing something. . ."

Sweet was shaking his head and it continued a slow, methodical oscillation as he looked up at her, the smile on his mouth wide, the tears in his eyes bright. "No."

He said nothing more; he didn't need to. He stood, picked up his coat and courteously shook first Helena's, then Eisenmenger's hand. Before he left he said only, "Thanks for what you did. I knew that there was more to it than they said."

Openly crying, he departed.

Helena sighed and looked across at Eisenmenger. Before she could complain, he said, "You did enough, Helena. He's able to grieve now."

But she couldn't see that. "But it's so unjust! Is no one interested in finding out the truth?"

He leaned forward, reaching for her hand. "We know the truth, remember?"

"Fat lot of good, that is."

"Maybe not. But the funny thing about the truth is that it doesn't always pay to know it. Sometimes ignorance is best."

"What does that mean?"

"Raymond Sweet had questions, we answered them. If he goes on, there's the danger of never being able to come to terms with his daughter's death. I think that there's a part of him that wants to move on. After all, as far as Millie's death was concerned, it was an accident."

She didn't look happy, but she nodded doubtfully.

"I'd better be off," he said. "I expect you've got work to do." She did, but that was the least of her concerns. As he stood she took his hand.

"I think it's about time you forgot a few of your daemons."

"Easier said than done."

She put her hand around the back of his neck to pull his face towards hers. Then she suggested, "Try harder." Her tone was stern, her lips full and red and ghosting a smile. For a few seconds he just looked at her, then he whispered, "Yes, ma'am."

They kissed, and then she let him go and he felt a peculiar emotion that only later did he place; it was happiness At the door he asked, "How about dinner tonight? Maybe go to the theatre?"

She had returned to her desk. She seemed suddenly distracted and it was nearly a minute before she replied. "Yes, lovely."

"I'll pick you up at seven."

She hesitated. "Half past." When he raised his eyebrows she explained, "I've got to see someone after work."

Helena had arranged to meet in the same wine bar, territory that neither could claim as her own. Helena was there first, Beverley arriving a few minutes late. Helena had already bought herself a glass of Merlot; Beverley neither asked nor was offered a drink, buying her own glass of Chablis as she came in.

"You had something to say?" Beverley's tone suggested that, though she had thought long, hard and deeply, she had been unable to unearth any reason why they might want to talk.

"I wanted to thank you."

Beverley smiled as a victor smiles. "For what? Saving you?"

"That's right."

Beverley toyed with the stem of the glass. "Thanks," she said.

They each drank some wine, their eyes everywhere but on each other.

Perhaps the lack of gratitude for the gratitude grated, for Helena said then, "It doesn't change anything."

Beverley's eyebrows, thin as her lips at that moment, rose and curved quite gracefully. "Really?"

Helena was staring intently at her. "You risked your life for me, I acknowledge that. . ."

"Thanks." This a murmur, barely struggling above the background noise.

". . .but that doesn't cancel what you did to me, to my family."

"Your parents were murdered. You're not blaming me for that, are you?"

Helena said flatly, "You murdered Jeremy."

"No, Helena. Your stepbrother committed suicide in prison."

"You framed him."

Beverley shook her head. "That's your invention. There is no proof of anything like that."

"There's no proof that PEP were responsible for Proteus and all the deaths that followed, but we know they did it." Helena smiled, then added after the briefest of pauses, "Don't we?"

Beverley took a moment to consider her response, as if she had a huge choice of options before her. "You know, the difference between you and me, Hel, is that I stop when I see a fucking big elephant in the road, but you carry on, shouting at the thing because it shouldn't be there."

"So Jeremy died because of. . .what?"

"Stepbrother Jeremy died because he decided to hang himself. I had a tip-off that he was involved. It turned out to be accurate. Accept it."

"You planted the evidence."

Beverley raised eyes to heaven. "Fantastic, Hel. Watch me while I weep."

"I will get you. Believe it, Beverley."

Beverley's glass was drained. As it hit the genuine oak of the table between them, she said, "Believe what you want, Hel. Believe what you want."

She was looking into her small, cream handbag, checking that everything was there, as if she had spread its contents on the table at some stage during the conversation and was concerned to retrieve it all. "In the mean time, give my regards to John."

Helena heard an implication, but it trailed into the background conversation and was therefore lost.

"What does that mean?" The question was one of those that people have to ask, knowing that the answer will slice through their eyesight, dissect their certainties.

Beverley was standing, irritatingly shapely. "John's a wonderful man. You're very lucky."

She turned away and over her shoulder came the words, "Give him my very best regards."

She left, and Helena fought with conjured daemons, dreadfully afraid of what she was thinking.

Part Six

Benjamin Starling lifted the phone, asked for a number in Norway, and then waited. When the call was answered, he said, "I think that we can reactivate Proteus now."